Y0-CAA-357

Acclaim for
A Matter of Degrees

"Mix a little Dan Brown conspiracy with a little Philip K. Dick sci-fi and what do you get? *A Matter of Degrees,* the new blockbuster mystery thriller by Alex Marcoux. Weaving a genre-bending tale of a conspiracy, cover-ups, and murder, Marcoux returns to the game with beloved characters from her earlier novels *Façades* and *Back to Salem,* bringing them together in an explosive mix of spine-tingling action. Devastated by her brother's unexplained suicide, Jessie Mercer launches a no-holds-barred investigation leading to a centuries-old conspiracy that threatens the very foundations of the world—and Jessie's life! *A Matter of Degrees* is definitely an out-of-this-world read and should not be missed."

Sherry L. Stinson (outlookpress.com)

"If you were drawn into the contemplation of ancient secrets and the societies who still guard them today by *The Da Vinci Code,* go one step further and infiltrate one of those societies, the Freemasons, in Alex Marcoux's vividly imagined *A Matter of Degrees.* For those who like suspense meted out by strong women, there are heroines here with courage to send chills up your spine—and to break year heart."

Lynn Vannucci
Author of *Coyote*
and *Revolution in the Garden*

"Fasten your seatbelt and prepare for a wild ride. In *A Matter of Degrees,* Alex Marcoux has brilliantly twisted religion, Freemasonry, reincarnation, and Egyptian mysticism into a rollercoaster ride of suspense. Think you know what will happen next? Think again!"

Lisa Gardner
New York Times bestselling author of *Gone*

"A riveting look at the Freemasons and conspiracy theories with a paranormal twist, *A Matter of Degrees,* by Alex Marcoux, is a must-read for any Dan Brown devotee. This book is for anyone who ever wondered what happened behind the closed doors of a secret, all-male society, and for anyone captivated by strong women who aren't afraid of operating outside of the box. I couldn't put it down!"

Christine Goff
Two-time Willa Literary Award Finalist;
Author of *Death Takes a Gander*

"Alex Marcoux is a rare writer. She can weave an engrossing, exciting, and romantic tale that leaves you totally satisfied and wondering when the next book will be written. This book is a compelling story and Alex is a welcome voice in the literary world."

Kris Radish
Author of *Annie Freeman's Fabulous Traveling Funeral,*
Dancing Naked at the Edge of Dawn,
and *The Elegant Gathering of White Snows*

"A multilayered story of intertwining lives and loves . . . . fast-paced and suspenseful, this novel will sweep you into an exciting world of conflict and intrigue and the ultimate conspiracy."

Robin D. Owens
PRISM and RITA award winner;
Author of *Heart Mate, Heart Thief,*
and *Guardian of Honor*

NOTES FOR PROFESSIONAL LIBRARIANS
AND LIBRARY USERS

This is an original book title published by Harrington Park Press®, an imprint of The Haworth Press, Inc. Unless otherwise noted in specific chapters with attribution, materials in this book have not been previously published elsewhere in any format or language.

CONSERVATION AND PRESERVATION NOTES

All books published by The Haworth Press, Inc., and its imprints are printed on certified pH neutral, acid-free book grade paper. This paper meets the minimum requirements of American National Standard for Information Sciences-Permanence of Paper for Printed Material, ANSI Z39.48-1984.

DIGITAL OBJECT IDENTIFIER (DOI) LINKING

The Haworth Press is participating in reference linking for elements of our original books. (For more information on reference linking initiatives, please consult the CrossRef Web site at www.crossref.org.) When citing an element of this book such as a chapter, include the element's Digital Object Identifier (DOI) as the last item of the reference. A Digital Object Identifier is a persistent, authoritative, and unique identifier that a publisher assigns to each element of a book. Because of its persistence, DOIs will enable The Haworth Press and other publishers to link to the element referenced, and the link will not break over time. This will be a great resource in scholarly research.

A Matter of Degrees

HARRINGTON PARK PRESS®
Titles of Related Interest

Elf Child by David M. Pierce

Shadows of the Night: Queer Tales of the Uncanny and Unusual edited by Greg Herren

Inside Out by Juliet Carrera

Façades by Alex Marcoux

Weeding at Dawn: A Lesbian Country Life by Hawk Madrone

Treat by Angie Vicars

Yin Fire by Alexandra Grilikhes

Egret by Helen Collins

Your Loving Arms by Gwendolyn Bikis

To the Edge by Cameron Abbott

Back to Salem by Alex Marcoux

Cat Rising by Cynn Chadwick

Maryfield Academy by Carla Tomaso

Ginger's Fire by Maureen Brady

A Taste for Blood by Diana Lee

The Meadowlark Sings by Helen Ruth Schwartz

Girls with Hammers by Cynn Chadwick

Minus One: A Twelve-Step Journey by Bridget Bufford

The Tenth Man by E. William Podojil

A Matter of Degrees by Alex Marcoux

A Matter of Degrees

Alex Marcoux

HPP

Harrington Park Press®
An Imprint of The Haworth Press, Inc.
New York • London • Oxford

For more information on this book or to order, visit
http://www.haworthpress.com/store/product.asp?sku=5721

or call 1-800-HAWORTH (800-429-6784) in the United States and Canada
or (607) 722-5857 outside the United States and Canada

or contact orders@HaworthPress.com

Published by

Harrington Park Press®, an imprint of The Haworth Press, Inc., 10 Alice Street, Binghamton, NY
13904-1580.

© 2006 by Alex Marcoux. All rights reserved. No part of this work may be reproduced or utilized in any
form or by any means, electronic or mechanical, including photocopying, microfilm, and recording, or
by any information storage and retrieval system, without permission in writing from the publisher.
Printed in the United States of America. Reprint 2007

Excerpts from *Rule by Secrecy* by Jim Marrs (2000, New York, HarperCollins). Used by permission of
author.

Egyptian ritual on page 172 from *The Sacred Tradition in Ancient Egypt: The Esoteric Wisdom
Revealed* by Rosemary Clark (2000, Woodbury, MN, Llewellyn Worldwide, Ltd.). Used by permission
of the publisher. All rights reserved.

Portions of the thirty-second degree lecture on pages 157-158, 188 are from *The Deadly Deception* by Jim
Shaw and Tom McKenney (1988, Shreveport, LA, Huntington House Publishers). Used by permission.

Portions of the master mason ritual on pages 72-74 (Chapter 12) and Jessie's meeting with Stonewall on
pages 81-84 (Chapter 11) are from www.saintsalive.com/freemasonry/blue_lodge/blue_lodge_index
.htm and www.saintsalive.com/freemasonry/blue_lodge/master.htm.

PUBLISHER'S NOTES
The development, preparation, and publication of this work has been undertaken with great care. However, the Publisher, employees, editors, and agents of The Haworth Press are not responsible for any er-
rors contained herein or for consequences that may ensue from use of materials or information
contained in this work. The Haworth Press is committed to the dissemination of ideas and information
according to the highest standards of intellectual freedom and the free exchange of ideas. Statements
made and opinions expressed in this publication do not necessarily reflect the views of the Publisher,
Directors, management, or staff of The Haworth Press, Inc., or an endorsement by them.

This is a work of fiction. Names, characters, places, and incidents either are the products of the author's
imagination or are used fictitiously, and any resemblance to actual persons, living or dead, business es-
tablishments, events, or locales is entirely coincidental.

Cover design by Kerry E. Mack.

Cover Illustration © Tyler Creative.

Library of Congress Cataloging-in-Publication Data

Marcoux, Alex.
   A matter of degrees / Alex Marcoux.
      p. cm.
   ISBN-13: 978-1-56023-611-5 (pbk. : alk. paper)
   ISBN-10: 1-56023-611-6 (pbk. : alk. paper)
   1. Women novelists—Fiction. 2. Reincarnation—Fiction. 3. Lesbians—Fiction. 4. Egypt—Fiction.
I. Title.
PS3563.A6365M38 2006
813'.6—dc22

                                                                                      2005024244

For
Mom & Dad

Author's Note and Acknowledgements

When I write, I allow life's events to inspire where my stories go and then somehow filter the information onto the pages. After reading this book I'm sure you'll wonder what events triggered me to ponder the ancient Egyptian mysteries, gardens of Sumer, Mary Magdalene, or the Knights Templar. You may even wonder what took me inside of Freemasonry's Blue Lodge and Scottish Rite. As a woman though, how could I?

For those of you who have followed my writing from *Façades* and *Back to Salem*, I thank you for continuing this journey with me, and it really has been a journey. As you have seen, my stories are a bit more complex than my earlier work. If your memory is good you will see the subtle connections between the characters of the three books. For those of you who aren't familiar with my earlier work, thank you for hopping on board! It's not too late, because we're really just getting started!

An endless list of authors' work helped percolate this story onto the pages. They include Michael Baigent, William Bramley, Manly P. Hall, Richard Leigh, Henry Lincoln, Jim Marrs, and Zecharai Stitchin. The Masonic rituals dialogue is based upon excerpts posted on "Saints Alive in Jesus" Web site (www.saintsalive.com) which is provided by the Ex-Masons for Jesus and Ephesians 5:11, Inc. (http://www.ephesians5-11.org). I found *The Deadly Deception* by Jim Shaw and Tom McKenney helpful in capturing the essence of the ceremonies, as well as providing the lecture for the thirty-second degree. Books by Rosemary Clark and John Van Auken were helpful in depicting the ancient Egyptian rituals and customs.

Sincere thanks to everyone at The Haworth Press for making this book a reality. Thanks to my copy editor, Nancy Deisroth, who has

Published by The Haworth Press, Inc., 2006. All rights reserved.
doi:10.1300/5721_a

been along for the ride since *Facades*. Over the years there have been endless drafts and enthusiastic volunteers who have read my work and provided valuable insight. Thank you Aggie, Janet, Joe, Kris, Sandra, Sharon, Sherry, and Susan. Thanks Mom, for reading it and not going off on me!

In every writer's life there is a support system, a team of people cheering you on from the sideline. My support system changed dramatically while I wrote this story. There has been one voice, though, since the story's inception. One individual has walked by my side, held my hand when I've needed it, and smiled for no reason other than he is with me. I hear his giggle in my head as I write this. I want to thank my son, Preston, for being with me since this story's maiden voyage.

This book took years to research, write, and rewrite. To say it's a work of passion is an understatement. I cannot say that the theories expressed here are my beliefs, because my own develop as my journey unfolds. My hope is that *A Matter of Degrees* opens minds to other possibilities no matter how outrageous, improbable, or impossible they may seem, because we owe it to ourselves to seek Truth. But also, I hope you enjoy this tale!

Prologue

Long before the region was called Iraq—
before the ancient empires of Egypt, Greece, or Rome.
Even before the first ancient civilization of Sumer—
there was E.DIN.

It was Enki's compassion for the slaves that altered his life, and the lives of humankind. He wanted something more for them. *Why couldn't a select few be given the knowledge of eternal life?* Enki pondered, as he verged upon his brother's sanctuary.

Apart from the sporadic swish caused by sand displaced beneath their sandals, there was silence. Pensively, Enki trekked onward with two guards on his heels. His half brother, Enlil, had summoned him. Enki suspected that his activities from the previous evening had been exposed. This, he knew, would have infuriated his younger sibling. Considering the possibility, he understood what Enlil was capable of. As the supreme ruler of E.DIN, Enlil had the power to relegate Enki's status of second-in-command.

Deep in thought, Enki pressed on toward the palace. Since he returned from AB.ZU, where he supervised the mining operation, he had been outraged by Enlil's mistreatment of the slaves. To Enki it was simple; the slaves fulfilled their purpose. They mined the council's precious ore, and here in the fertile gardens of E.DIN, they harvested their fruit. Although the slaves served the council well, they had wretched and pitiful lives, ignorant of wisdom, pleasure, or their fundamental essence. Treated like animals, they lived and died toiling for Enlil and the supreme council.

When they reached the palace chamber, he waited silently, towering over the men that had escorted him there. Enki recalled the initiation from the previous evening, and how he had shared with the

Published by The Haworth Press, Inc., 2006. All rights reserved.
doi:10.1300/5721_01

chosen slaves about elevating their consciousness and finding true light.

"Leave us!" Enlil's voice bellowed from the entry. As the two guards disappeared into the palace, Enlil emerged and stood before Enki, his powerfully built body adorned with gold trinkets.

"You have done it this time. What were you thinking?" Enlil's anger glared through his steel gray eyes. "You know that as long as the slaves remain spiritually ignorant *we* stay in control."

"Brother, there were—"

"Don't call me brother." Enlil cut him off, his voice echoing within the chamber walls. "Your harlot mother was my father's only weakness. You shouldn't have been sent here."

Enki was familiar with Enlil's acts of aggression toward him, but something was different this time. "Enlil, the workers serve their purpose. I chose a select few to teach our ways."

"Anu would never approve."

"Father isn't here to discuss this."

"Marduk would never approve."

"My son is also not here to debate the issue," Enki said calmly.

"When Marduk arrives, you will never see him."

"What are you saying?"

"You've outdone yourself, Enki." Enlil retreated to the entryway where he effortlessly grabbed a staff and, with thickset arms, clashed it against a golden disk. The clanging reverberated in the tiny room; guards quickly entered and surrounded Enki.

"What is the meaning of this?" Enki asked evenly.

"You . . . " Enlil advanced so that the brothers were eye-to-eye. With the exception of their muscular frames, there was little resemblance between the men. "You are banished from E.DIN."

A smile came to Enki's lips. "You're not serious."

"Oh, but I am. Enki, you are to be exiled! I will spread the word among the slaves that you are a mortal enemy of the supreme council. They will learn that *you* are responsible for everything bad that happens to them, and that it is *your* intention to spiritually enslave them."

"But that's not true." Enki's voice rose. The guards grabbed him and he struggled to free himself, but there were too many of them.

"People will fear you." Enlil's voice soared above the resistance. "They will know that you are evil and loathe you."

For a moment, Enki's effort ceased. "Why are you doing this?"

"You will never be a leader, Enki. My work will rise above you, and you will be called Abaddon, and from where I will put you—you'll be the keeper of the bottomless pit." The evil in Enlil's eyes flashed, and his laugh would echo in Enki's ears forever.

At first his only sense was smell. He was face down in the soggy soil, and the terrain reeked of decaying earth. Enki tasted the foul sludge that had coated his lips. He pulled his partially submerged face from the dank mud, and sat upright. His head throbbed. His sandals were nowhere to be found. The only thing he had been left with was the robe on his back.

Rather than the plentiful gardens that he had become accustomed to in E.DIN, Enki was surrounded by shallow water and tall grass of swampland. It was then that he remembered Enlil's men tossing him into a pit. He found the bump on the back of his head, the basis of his headache. A quick glance behind him confirmed the wall of earth, almost two men high, from which he had been thrown.

A hiss drew Enki's attention to the thick reeds that stirred close to him. Then he spotted the black water moccasin slithering within inches. The snake's head abruptly shot up, flashing its venomous fangs, forked tongue, and white mouth. Hissing angrily, the snake lunged toward his face. Skillfully, Enki seized it within a finger's length of his eyes. The serpent thrashed about, trying to free itself from Enki's grasp, but it was no match for the powerful arm. Enki stood. The snake succumbed, and when all resistance was gone, he dropped the snake at his feet. Slowly, it slithered into the shallow water.

Enki studied the surrounding area. On three sides the earth was high above his head, on the fourth face there was an endless marsh. He stepped forward, into the swamps.

The years passed. At first, his time had been consumed with his own survival. Then one day, movement in the swamp caught Enki's attention. Upon closer inspection, he saw a man with darker skin than his own. Here, Enki met a slave that had escaped from E.DIN. He discovered that other men and women lived there, choosing freedom in the swamps over their lives of bondage in E.DIN. These people welcomed Enki, and he embraced them.

Against Enlil's edicts, Enki taught the uninitiated ethics, justice, and how to seek true light. To the chosen ones, he explained the mysteries of life and the great secret of humankind's creation. It was here, in the snake-filled marshlands of Mesopotamia, that Enki formed the Brotherhood of the Snake.

One

It was late. If she had been more attentive, Rachel may have noticed the silence in the hallway outside her office door or the absence of sunlight from her window. Perhaps even, if she weren't so absorbed in her work, she would have become aware of the growl in her stomach from missing dinner. But it was the chime of the clock that drew her attention to the time.

"My God! It's already ten o'clock."

Rachel looked back at the cryptic notes that were spread on top of her desk, but her eyes bothered her. She removed her reading glasses then rubbed the base of her skull. As her fingers massaged the deeply rooted knots, her long dark hair fell loosely around her face. She rotated her neck, first from front to back, and then full circles to help relieve the headache that had plagued her that evening.

When her head turned, she caught sight of her reflection in the window. She paused, and then looking past her silhouette, Rachel gazed upon the glitter of the office buildings from her elevated location. She had always admired the view of Manhattan's skyscrapers from her office. She stood and stretched her arms over her head.

"I should go home," she whispered to herself. Then her vision returned to the notes sprawled across her desk, and she replaced the glasses to the bridge of her nose. Rachel sat and continued her work, as if a spell had been cast upon her.

As a field reporter for one of the more reputable television news programs, Rachel Addison had become accustomed to the late hours at the network office building. She had worked for *Over the Edge* going on five years. Presently, she was working on a controversial project connecting secret societies with various politicians. She continued massaging the knots in her neck as she studied notes concerning the

Published by The Haworth Press, Inc., 2006. All rights reserved.
doi:10.1300/5721_02

Council on Foreign Relations (CFR), the Trilateral Commission, and Freemasonry.

Whack! A sudden knock from the hallway outside her office door startled her. *Who's here this late?* she wondered, and the door opened abruptly. Instinctively, Rachel sprang to her feet as Steve Mercer barged into her office.

Rachel stared at the other field reporter, then she possessively gathered the notes that had been spread on her desk and stuffed them into a manila folder. "My God, Steve! You scared me," her voice was more hoarse than usual.

Steve closed her office door. "Good." He moved closer to Rachel. "Someone needs to put some sense into your head." It was almost a whisper.

Rachel pulled the reading glasses from her face and stepped away from her desk. "What are you talking about?"

He approached so that they were inches apart. "Drop your story on the secret societies."

"I will not. It's a good story. People have a right to know."

At six-two, Steve towered over her. "If you value your life, Rachel, you'll drop it and burn your work." He spoke calmly and softly then turned away.

"Are you threatening me?"

He turned back. "No. But I *am* warning you." His exit was as abrupt as his entrance.

Two weeks later, Rachel received an anonymous tip to meet someone in Nyack about an updated list of CFR members. The CFR is the granddaddy of modern American secret societies. Rachel arrived at the agreed-upon meeting place, The Hudson House, but her contact never showed. She finished her coffee, and headed back to the city.

Opting for a more scenic route, she chose highway 9W for her return trip, a hilly and winding road that ran along the west side of the Hudson River. To her left was a steep embankment with houses perched on the incline leading down to the river. To the right, the embankment continued its rise high above the road.

When traffic moved on this one-lane road, it was quicker than the Palisades Parkway. Today, however, she came upon a traveler that was out for a leisurely ride.

Rachel braked as she advanced toward the slower car, but the brakes didn't respond. "Shit!" She stomped the pedal, but there was no effect. Her pulse quickened as she sped toward the other vehicle.

She honked; hoping the car in front would get moving. Instead, the man braked. With no place to go, Rachel swerved to the left, becoming trapped in the approaching traffic lane. There were no advancing cars. *Thank God!* Her Saab darted around the slower vehicle. With eyes glued to the road before her, she never saw the man gesture with his finger.

Rachel had traveled this road on many occasions. She needed to manage the next turn, then the grade shifted uphill a short distance. Sixty-five. Seventy. The tires squealed as the vehicle veered around the winding curve. At seventy-five miles per hour and white knuckles clenched to the steering wheel she approached the upward incline. Steadily, the Saab slowed. Sixty . . . fifty . . . forty . . .

Rachel exhaled. With her sleeve, she wiped the perspiration from her brow. But now what? The slope would change soon. She couldn't continue on the snaky river road without brakes. She spotted the uphill driveway to a stately home on her right. At thirty miles per hour, Rachel veered up the steep grade. The back end of her vehicle fishtailed. She smashed a retaining wall, slamming her head against the door window. Coasting up the driveway, she slowed to fifteen miles per hour at its summit. Given the choice, Rachel collided with a mature tree rather than a garage. The airbag inflated.

Her heart pounded. There was blood on the airbag. Instinctively, she groped her forehead, the source of pain.

Two

During the hours that passed, Rachel's emotions had fluctuated from fear, to disbelief, to denial, but now she was just pissed off. It was dark, and she fumed as she approached the entrance to Steve Mercer's Scarsdale home. Faced with a door knocker or a fancy lit doorbell, she hammered the door unkindly. Seconds later the foyer light came on and a shadow appeared through the stained glass window beside the door.

Steve Mercer opened the door slowly. Rachel Addison stood before him. Her silk blouse was bloodstained, and she had a discolored bandage on her forehead. He was speechless.

"Tell me what the hell is going on, or I'm going to the authorities!" she said.

Steve widened the door. "Come in," he said calmly. Nonchalantly, he glanced around the upper-middle-class neighborhood. Satisfied with what he saw, he closed the door. "This way." He led her into his kitchen and pointed at a bar stool, "Take a seat."

Stubbornly, Rachel leaned against the counter.

Steve removed a facecloth and box of bandages from a nearby linen closet. He drenched the cloth at the kitchen sink, and then approached her. "What happened?"

As he attempted to remove the discolored bandage, Rachel pulled away at his touch. "I didn't come here for a Band-Aid," she complained. "What's going on?"

"Rachel," Steve's voice softened, "let me help you." He nudged the bar stool, inviting her to sit again.

"Fine," she took a seat. "But what the hell have I gotten myself into?"

With a flick of his wrist, Steve removed the bandage, revealing a long gash. "How did this happen?" He washed her forehead.

Published by The Haworth Press, Inc., 2006. All rights reserved.
doi:10.1300/5721_03

"I received an anonymous call from a man claiming to have an updated list of CFR members. He suggested that I meet him at a restaurant in Nyack." Rachel faltered.

"Go on."

"He never showed. But, while I was in the restaurant someone cut my brake lines." Steve finished applying a new bandage and Rachel grabbed his hand. "What's going on? Why did you warn me?"

His eyes met Rachel's and she released her grip. "Before I say anything, what is your investigation uncovering?"

"Are you familiar with the Freemasons?"

"Yes. It's a brotherhood that has been in existence for centuries."

"It's a secret society that has a secret society within it."

He smiled. "That's not exactly what I understand."

"Most Freemasons believe they're involved in a fellowship where they share camaraderie and participate in humanitarian concerns, like the Shriners. Even in this *visible* society, though, they take blood oaths to protect their occult secrets. But most Masons are unaware of an *invisible* society that's dedicated to protecting an ancient sacred secret."

"And what *is* this ancient sacred secret?" Steve asked.

"Well if I knew that, it wouldn't be secret, now, would it?"

"Where were you going with your story?"

"I was showing that the majority of our presidents were Freemasons, and linking members of the Trilateral Commission and CFR with Freemasonry."

"There has to be something else. Most of that has been documented before."

"Certainly in some unread conspiracy magazines and out-of-print books, but why hasn't a reputable TV newsmagazine like *Sixty Minutes* done it?"

"It's not newsworthy," Steve shrugged his shoulders.

"Don't insult my intelligence! Why did you warn me?"

"I heard that your investigation was concerning powerful individuals." Steve's eyes searched Rachel's. "I didn't want to see you lose your career over it."

"How did you hear this?" When Steve's unwavering blue eyes wouldn't leave Rachel's, she pressed him further. "I'm not asking you to reveal your source, Mercer! How'd you come by this information?"

"I'm a Freemason."

A lump stuck in Rachel's throat. "I see."

"No, you don't see." Steve sighed and ran his fingers through his thick brown hair. "I've been a Mason since right out of college. I've completed the initiations of the Blue Lodge and the Scottish Rite, and for the last two years I've been the Junior and Senior Warden, and in a couple of months I'll be the Worshipful Master of a Blue Lodge in White Plains. In my twenty-three years of being a Mason, I have *never* seen any behaviors inconsistent with ethical, fraternal, humanitarian, educational, or patriotic concerns."

"And yet, you heard something. You heard that I was becoming a threat. And look what happens—my brake lines are mysteriously cut!"

"I didn't say that," Steve said.

"You didn't have to. Could you explain the Freemason degrees? Reading about it is very confusing." When Steve didn't respond, she pushed for more. "Oh, come on, I'm not asking you to break some ridiculous blood oath. I'm just asking about the structure. Please?"

"Men start in the Blue Lodge. Here there are three degrees: an Apprentice, a Fellowcraft, and a Master Mason. Most never proceed beyond the Master Mason because it's expensive and time-consuming."

"What *is* beyond the Blue Lodge?"

"Two other lodges—the York Rite and Scottish Rite. The Scottish Rite has thirty-three degrees. The York Rite graduates to the equivalent."

"How do you get to the thirty-third degree?"

"By invitation only."

"How long have you been involved in the Scottish Rite?"

"Over fifteen years."

"And you've *never* been invited to the thirty-third degree?"

Steve shook his head. "No. And I wouldn't. You see, although I'm politically and socially involved in my Blue Lodge, I'm not very involved in the Scottish Rite. I'm also not a Degree Master."

"What's a Degree Master?"

"For each degree in the Scottish Rite, each lodge has a Degree Master to perform the ritual or teach it to candidates during an initiation."

Rachel looked deep into Steve's blue eyes. "You can change all that."

"Meaning?"

"You know the game! Play it to increase your chances of getting an invitation!"

"Now, why would I do that?"

"To satisfy that nagging feeling you have in your gut."

"You're very presumptuous."

"Are you denying it?"

Steve didn't respond. He wondered if his concerns were that obvious.

"What do I have to do? Impersonate a man and become a Freemason myself to uncover the sacred secret?"

He laughed, but when he realized that she was getting more upset, he shook his head. "I'm sorry. It just wouldn't work."

"Why? Women have impersonated men for centuries, to earn what they rightfully deserve. Take a look at Pope Joan."

"Trust me, unless you have your breasts removed, you'll never make it through the first three initiations." He changed the subject. "Drop your story, at least for now."

Rachel shook her head, clearly frustrated. "I have to get out of here," she said abruptly, and made her way to the door.

The following morning, Steve slipped into Rachel's office. He shut the door behind him and drew near her. "Are you going to drop the story?"

"No! I've come this far."

There must have been a part of him that admired her spunk as remnants of a smile emerged, only he turned his back to hide the grin. His gaze fell upon a collection of pictures on Rachel's bookshelf. He picked up a portrait of an attractive man in his mid-forties. "Who's this?" he asked.

Rachel smiled when she saw the picture. "That's my father." She reached for another picture of her family, consisting of her father, mother, and herself.

"Is this you?" he pointed to a freckle-faced ten-year-old.

She nodded. "Yes."

"Where'd the freckles go? You were so cute." Steve grinned, intensifying his smile lines. He pointed to another picture. "Is this your parents' wedding picture?"

"Yes."

"Your father ages gracefully."

"Yes, he did. Other than styles changing, you'd never think my father aged a day. It's actually spooky, but I keep hoping that I take after my father's genes."

Steve's eyes combed the picture of her parents. "You have a strong resemblance to your father; same dark hair, blue eyes, and cleft chin." He returned the portrait to its shelf. "I noticed that you spoke of your father in the past tense."

"You are observant," Rachel said. She locked her desk drawer then moved to the door. "We have a meeting in two minutes."

Steve glanced at his watch. "I'll see you there. I need to go back to my office."

Neil Samson, the executive producer of *Over the Edge,* arrived at the weekly staff meeting a couple minutes late. He was pale.

It was Rachel who noticed. "Are you okay, Neil?"

He sat in a chair. "I just got a phone call from my wife . . ."

Steve had just entered behind Neil. "What is it?" He asked.

"Albert Robbins . . ."

Rachel recognized the name of the CFR member. "What about Albert Robbins?"

"Albert was found last night . . . dead."

"How?" Steve asked.

"The strangest thing. The man was poisoned in his own bed . . . by a snake. A king cobra! His wife found him when she returned from a business trip last night."

An alarm blasted. The obnoxious noise blared throughout the offices and hallways. "What the hell is that?" Neil demanded.

"It sounds like a fire alarm," Steve said.

"A fire alarm? Oh my God!" Rachel whispered. She bolted to the door, opened it, and smoke seeped into the conference room. Once in the corridor, Rachel saw the smoke coming from her office. She dashed through the thick smoke. At the office threshold, she witnessed her desk engulfed in flames. Neil grabbed Rachel's arm, stopping her from rescuing her research on secret societies.

Seconds later, Steve brushed past them with a fire extinguisher. It took him a couple minutes to snuff out the flames. By this time, a crowd had gathered in the hallway. All eyes were on Rachel, who couldn't take her sight off the destroyed desk.

Steve emerged from the office, his clothes coated in soot. Rachel glared at him and then turned on her heels and fled. He followed silently until they were out of sight from the group. He rested his hand on her shoulder.

Abruptly, she turned and snarled. "Get your hand off me! You can tell your friends they won, and I never want to see *you* again."

Rachel thrust open a nearby restroom door. There was a small lounge with two chairs. She sat. Her mind raced. *Prick. He saw me lock my desk.* She felt like such a fool. Steve had used her. *How could I have been so stupid?* Rachel moaned. *I'm sorry, Daddy. I won't give up. I promise.* For a moment, she became lost in her past.

Rachel watched her father, Charles Addison, as he studied the chessboard and deliberated on his next move. Then he picked up his polished-stone bishop and moved it to protect his threatened king.

Rachel was eager to move her rook into place. "Check," the eleven-year-old said.

A smile came to Charles's face. "Is this my last move?"

"Yup."

The father and daughter had been playing this game going on two months. It had become customary for them to play five moves a day and Rachel had her father on the run over the past week.

Charles studied the board and moved a pawn into place to sacrifice the piece. "There. I guess our game will have to wait until I return from my trip."

Rachel didn't expect the move. "Why would you sacrifice your pawn, Daddy? You know you can just move your king to avoid my attack."

Charles smiled. "Strategy, Rachel. Pawns are dispensable. You use them to further the king's purpose."

Rachel studied the board. She was glad that was their last move, now she had some time to reconsider her own strategy before they played again. "When will you be back from your trip, Daddy?"

"In a few days."

"Where are you going?"

"DC." He studied his daughter, and smiled. "You are a very special young lady, you do realize that, don't you?"

"I know I am special to you, Daddy."

"You are special to the world, Rachel."

"I'm sure all fathers think that way about their children, right?"

"I'm sure," he smiled. "You know I love you, don't you?"

"Of course, Daddy. Why are you asking?"

Charles became serious. "Chances are I won't always be in your life, sweetheart. I just hope you'll always know I love you very much."

Rachel looked into her father's eyes. "Daddy, why are you talking this way?"

"Like I said, it's only natural that I will pass on before you, like your grandfather passed on before your mother."

"That's years away. Don't get me all depressed before you leave on your trip."

"I'm sorry, Rachel. I just never spoke about this with my parents. It's something that's haunted me, over the years, wondering if they truly loved me. Just remember, when the day comes that I pass on . . . I will always love you and always be with you." Charles kissed his daughter tenderly on her forehead.

Rachel shook her head, trying to disconnect from her past. She pulled the polished-granite pawn from her jacket pocket and studied the chess piece. Discoloration revealed where her fingers had worn the stone piece over the twenty-plus years. "I know you love me Daddy," she sobbed lightly. "Even after all this time, I feel like you're still with me."

Three

During the three months that passed Rachel continued investigating secret groups in her spare time. For the network, she worked on an assortment of stories. The most interesting was the CIA mind-control experiments of the 1960s and 1970s, when the CIA had developed techniques to bury memory, creating amnesia.

It was after work hours, and Rachel was working in her new office. Thump! The sudden knock disrupted her thoughts. She glanced at her watch; it was nine o'clock. "Who's there?" She listened but didn't hear a thing. "Hello?"

The door opened slightly. A tall silhouette stood in the hallway. Rachel strained to see who it was. "Who's there?" she demanded.

"Don't you ever go home?" Steve stepped through the doorway.

"Didn't I make myself clear—I never wanted to see you again?"

"Oh, perfectly clear!" He shut the door, and took a seat across from her.

Rachel studied his every move. Steve Mercer was a good-looking man. His thick dark hair was accented with graying sideburns. He had a nice build. It was hard to guess his age, perhaps late forties or early fifties.

"Just hear me out, and I'll leave." Steve hesitated. "I didn't set the fire. And you were right about that nagging feeling." He was careful how he phrased his words.

"What feeling?"

He reached for a message pad and tore off a sheet. "That the two of us are being considered for Henry Shafer's replacement." He moved a finger to his lips, gesturing for Rachel's silence, and scribbled on the paper.

Henry Shafer was one of the anchormen for *Over the Edge.* Earlier in the year, he had announced that he would retire the following year.

Published by The Haworth Press, Inc., 2006. All rights reserved.
doi:10.1300/5721_04

"It would be better if we maintained a civil business relationship." Steve handed the note to Rachel, pointed to it, then said, "Do you think we can do that?"

Rachel read the note: *Meet me at McNally's Pub. Ten o'clock.* "Yes. We should be civil to one another."

An hour later, Rachel parked herself across from Steve in the pub. "Do you want to tell me what the hell's going on? My office is bugged?" she whispered.

"I wouldn't put it past them. I didn't have anything to do with the fire, Rachel."

"Is that what this is all about?"

"You were right about my nagging feeling, and I just wanted to let you know that I've been playing the game. I'm a Degree Master in the Scottish Rite."

It took Rachel a moment to understand what Steve was really telling her. "Do you think you'll get an invitation?"

"I don't know. I do know that since I've played the game, I'm hearing more things and I'm getting more attention at work. My annual review wouldn't be for another four months, but last week, Neil gave me a raise."

"Is he a Mason?"

"Yes."

"Is he a member of the Thirty-Third Council?"

"I'm not sure. Freemasonry has a pyramid hierarchy. You can find out who is below you, but not above. And from what I've gathered, the thirty-third degree has its own pyramid structure."

"Then, who's top dog? Do you have an annual election? Or is it a dictatorship?"

"I don't know. The secrecy of the organization doesn't allow that information to filter down. Because of the chain-of-command, only two people know the leader's identity. Those two people have two others reporting to them, and so on." His voice softened. "I'm sorry about the fire. You clearly had them nervous. What exactly *were* you working on?"

Rachel smiled. *Do you really think I'm going to confide in you?*

As if reading her mind Steve said, "I wouldn't blame you for not answering."

She contemplated whether to tell him. When he wouldn't divert his eyes, she took a chance. "I've already told you some of this. I was connecting secret societies, specifically, the Trilateral Commission, CFR, Bilderbergers, and Freemasons. In my story, I had emphasized that members of these societies exert control over corporations and banks, which control the essentials of modern life. I had demonstrated that the objective of these groups is to bring about a one-world government."

Rachel and Steve were silent as the waitress served a beer and a glass of chardonnay. When she left, they continued.

"Who was named in your report?" He whispered.

Rachel hesitated. "The Rockefellers, Morgans, Rothschilds, the banking system, and the Federal Reserve."

"Well, that's one assortment I wouldn't want to piss off. What about the banking system and the Federal Reserve?"

"The Fed is the central bank of our country. But the government doesn't create money, the Fed does. Did you know that there hasn't been an impartial audit of the Federal Reserve, which began in 1913?"

Steve retrieved a dollar bill from his wallet. "I'm sure you know that the dollar bill itself shows Freemason involvement in the Fed. George Washington is a famous Mason." He flipped the bill, "The pyramid and the All-Seeing Eye are also Masonic symbols."

"Yes. Along with the apron, compass and square, letter G, and the Star of David. What's with the letter G anyway? Or is that one of those secrets you've taken a blood oath on?" Rachel's eyes teased.

Steve whispered. "Some believe G stands for God. Others believe it means geometry. Several speculate that the terms masonry and geometry are one-and-the-same. The modern geometric symbols are believed to be fragments of geometrical secrets of the Medieval Mason. From what I understand, though, the mysteries have been lost."

"Or perhaps only a select few know them," Rachel's eyes settled on Steve's.

"I've been thinking about the question that was bothering you the last time we spoke," Steve admitted. "You know, how come *Sixty Minutes* or even *Over the Edge* hasn't done a piece on this?"

"There's a group of conspiracy theorists that suggest that the media is a pawn of and actually controlled by secret societies," Rachel offered.

The months passed. It was Friday night, and Rachel was driving home from work when her cellular phone chimed. "Rachel Addison."

"Do you have plans tomorrow?"

Rachel recognized Steve's voice. "Why?"

"Are you familiar with Middletown?"

"Up toward the Catskills?"

"That's correct. There's a Holiday Inn at exit 122 on Route 17. Meet me in the restaurant at ten." Steve hung up.

Under different circumstances, Rachel may have been excited about their mysterious meeting. Today, however, she was angry to be beckoned by his call and her anger swelled as she searched the restaurant for Steve. "What the hell is going on?" she asked as she settled in the booth.

"Shh." He didn't want to draw attention to them. He casually sipped his coffee then turned Rachel's mug upright for the approaching waitress.

"Coffee?" the waitress asked Rachel.

"Please."

The waitress left and Steve got right to the point. "I heard that you've been continuing your investigation."

Rachel had been so careful. How did he know? She couldn't deny it.

Steve reached for Rachel's soft hand and he squeezed it. "You must stop," he whispered. "It's too dangerous." He released her hand.

"It's also important."

"What is so important that you're willing to risk your life?"

Rachel wondered if she could trust him. There was a part of her that must have, since she had agreed to meet him. "My father . . . was a Mason." Her voice was distant.

"Your father was a Freemason?" Steve's tone was caring. "What happened?"

Rachel closed her eyes for a moment. She needed to detach herself from what she was about to tell him. "When I was eleven, my father went to DC for a Freemason meeting. Something happened while he was crossing a bridge. His car ended up in the Chesapeake Bay."

"I'm sorry." Instinctively, Steve took Rachel's hand. His tenderness surprised her, and when he sensed it, he released his grip. "He died, and you believe the organization is responsible for his death?"

"Yes. I've had my suspicions. It was almost like he knew he was going to die. The month before, he increased his insurance policy and paid off the house."

"Is it possible that it was suicide?"

Rachel shook her head. "Not my father. He loved life too much."

"Could he have been doing what you're doing now, and got himself killed?"

"I don't know. I just know that since I was a child, I vowed I would learn about this group. I need to understand why my father spent so much time away from us."

"What are you working on now?"

"Assassinations," she whispered.

"Can you expand on that?"

Rachel faltered. Internally she debated whether to confide in him. *I don't have to tell him everything,* she decided. "Do you know what greenbacks are?"

"It's when the government issues debt-free money through the U.S. Treasury."

"Who would get hurt in that scenario?"

Steve appeared thoughtful. "I guess the banks."

"There have been only two times when the government issued debt-free currency—during the Abraham Lincoln and JFK administrations." She paused. "Both presidents were assassinated."

"Coincidence," Steve shrugged his shoulders.

"John W. Booth, Lincoln's assassin, was a member of the Knights of the Golden Circle. I'm not sure if Oswald was a Mason, but he claimed to be a pawn, and that he wasn't acting alone. The ballistics supported that theory, but he never had a chance to elaborate on it since he was murdered two days after he was arrested."

"So you're suggesting that the banks killed them?" Steve fought to hide his disbelief.

"I think Kennedy got himself killed because he was a mover and a shaker, which pissed off big corporations and the Fed. Did you know that Kennedy approved National Security Action Memorandum Number Two Hundred Sixty-Three, which called for disengagement in Vietnam? One month later, he was assassinated."

"Are you implying that he was killed because he was going to pull troops out of 'Nam?"

"I think he pissed off the wrong people. Disengagement from Vietnam might have been the last straw."

"Listen to what you're saying. Why would he be killed for ending a war?"

"Steve, who benefits from war? I'll tell you—the banks, big corporations like steel and oil; do I need to go on?"

Steve sighed. "What else are you looking at?"

"The Reagan assassination attempt by Hinckley in 1981."

"What about it?"

"Reagan conducted a press conference a month after his recovery, and in it he claimed that he thought he was shot by a Secret Service agent, accidentally of course. He said that he didn't feel the pain until he was in the limo and a Secret Service man was on top of him. The FBI's report claimed that one of Hinckley's bullets ricocheted on the limo's door as he was being pushed in."

"Sounds plausible," Steve said.

"The bullets were the exploding kind. How come the bullet didn't explode when it hit the metal door? Also, Hinckley himself claimed that he was part of a conspiracy. He even wrote about it while he was waiting for trial. And yet, the FBI confiscated his papers and without explanation concluded that he had acted alone.

"The judge that heard Hinckley's case ordered the witnesses and the attorneys not to disclose the content of his documents to the public. Would you believe they went to trial and neither side brought up a conspiracy?"

While Steve didn't really know what to say, Rachel couldn't stop herself from continuing. "John Hinckley Junior was the son of a wealthy Texas oilman who was a longtime personal friend and political supporter of George Bush, who at the time, was Reagan's vice president."

"Yes, I know."

"And Hinckley's brother scheduled dinner with Neil Bush the night Reagan was shot."

"Rachel, these are just unrelated facts and they don't prove a thing."

"Here's another fact, George Bush was a Trilateralist, a CFR member, and the former CIA director. Some conspiracy theorists allege that one of the CIA's primary purposes is to protect Freemasons and other secret societies." Rachel leaned closer. "Bush was also a member of the Skull and Bones."

"Have you connected the existing administration with any of this?"

To Rachel, Steve's question felt like a two-by-four to her head. She had become so caught up in discussing the information she had forgotten who she was speaking with. "Let's change the subject. Tell me something about yourself, Steve."

He sensed the change in Rachel. "I guess there's not much to tell. You know where I live and where I work. I'm not married. My parents died when I was in my twenties. I have a sister, Jessie. She lives outside of Los Angeles. Rachel . . . what do you need from me, to trust me?"

"Trust is earned by getting to know a person."

"You get to know people by spending time with them. We don't have that luxury. We shouldn't even be seen together."

"I realize that," Rachel said. "I'd like to trust you, Steve. In some ways I must, because I met you here."

"Rachel, trust me about this—back away and drop your investigation for a while."

"Okay. For a while."

"What are you doing next Saturday?" Steve asked shyly. "I was thinking that perhaps we could meet, away from the city, perhaps take a drive upstate."

"Why?"

Steve averted his eyes. "Maybe we can spend a little time together . . . an effort to earn each other's trust."

Rachel shook her head, "I'm not sure, Steve. Do you think that's smart?"

"It was just an idea. Think about it." He wrote his cell phone number down on a napkin and passed it to Rachel. "No pressure. If you're interested, call me."

Rachel debated all week whether to call Steve. In the end, she called him and they started meeting every other weekend. They always met someplace remote, away from the city, for a late Saturday afternoon lunch. After their meal they would walk, then part. Each eagerly waited for their next meeting. Their friendship grew and, as expected, so did their trust in each other.

During one lunch, Steve demonstrated that trust. "I haven't told anyone this," he said as his fork cut into his salmon. "I have a second house."

"You do? Do you have a wife and kids, too?"

"No," he said, "just a getaway house in the Catskills. I usually spend my weekends there. Nobody knows about it. Next time we get together, would you like to meet there?"

Later that week, while Steve was surfing the Internet, he stumbled upon an interesting article. He printed it, placed it in an envelope and addressed it to Rachel. "I wonder what she'll think of this."

Two weeks later, Rachel arrived at Steve's cabin near Jewett, in the Catskill Mountains. It was a simple A-frame, nestled in a densely wooded lot. The house had two bedrooms on the main level with a larger bedroom on the upper floor. One of the small bedrooms had been converted to an office. There was a small dining area with a table set beside the tiny kitchen. The scent of freshly roasted turkey filled the air, which impressed Rachel, since she was an awful cook.

After dinner, the couple ventured out on their customary walk. But it was a cold winter day, so their trek was cut short. When they returned to the cabin, Rachel made her way toward her car. Steve followed close behind her, until she reached the Saab.

Rachel opened the car door and nestled between the door and the car, shielding part of her body from the bitter wind.

Steve smiled and shyly moved closer to the door that separated the couple. "I had a good time," his eyes strayed to her lips, "as usual."

Rachel smiled. "I did too," she whispered, but the words were lost in the wind.

"Rachel, there's something that I've wanted to do for some time."

Rachel didn't have a chance to ask Steve what that was, as his lips had found hers, and they kissed. The car door between them prevented him from taking her in his arms, and when they parted, neither one could take their eyes off the other.

As Steve approached her for a second kiss, she raised her fingers to his lips. "We shouldn't do this. Not while it's this complicated."

Steve knew she was right, and retreated. "You're right. Tempting," he said, "but not smart."

Time passed. Rachel and Steve started to meet weekly. Outwardly, they acted as if their intimate moment never happened. Steve's mountain home was the perfect place to spend time. It was Rachel who realized that they had not discussed conspiracy theories or secret societies in over a month.

It was a rainy spring Saturday and Rachel was en route to the cabin. She hadn't seen Steve in two weeks as his sister, Jessie, had visited him for Easter the weekend before. She felt a wave of excitement at the thought of Steve, and in that moment she wondered if she was ever going to be honest with Steve about her feelings for him. For today, anyway, it didn't matter. What had become important to her was that she had developed a type of friendship with him that she had never shared with another man. For today, that was enough.

It was about four o'clock when she knocked on the cabin door. Steve opened the door and uncharacteristically hugged her. He must have sensed her surprise, because he backed away, grinning. "I'm sorry. I'm just so excited. I have some great news. I've been waiting since Tuesday to tell you."

"What is it Steve?"

"Let me tell you over dinner. Your timing is perfect. Appetizers are ready. Do you want to freshen up before dinner?"

As usual, when Rachel joined Steve on the couch, she found everything to be perfect. A fire was ablaze in the fireplace, candles were lit on the dining table, and appetizers were set up on the coffee table.

"So what have you been waiting to tell me?"

"I have two surprises. First . . . ." He handed Rachel an envelope. She opened it. There were two cruise tickets, one in Steve's name, and the other in Julie Harris's name.

She shrugged her shoulders. "What's this?"

"It's a weeklong cruise, for the two of us. There are two adjoining cabins," he said shyly. Then his eyes met Rachel's. "Haven't you wondered what it would be like to spend more than an afternoon together?"

"Maybe . . . but a week?"

He smiled. "Just think about it, don't say no until you've thought it through."

"Who's Julie Harris?"

"It's an alias I set up for you so that we can travel together." He handed Rachel a passport with her picture and the name Julie Harris.

"How did you do—No, forget it. I don't want to know."

"There's something else." Steve paused and his eyes met hers. "I received a special delivery at work this week." His face lit up. "I got an invitation."

She mirrored his excitement, and smiled. "An invitation for what?" Then it hit her and her smile slowly vanished. "My God, Steve, you got an invitation for the thirty-third degree?"

He nodded. "I got the letter from the Supreme Council on Tuesday."

The smile on Rachel's face was gone.

"What's wrong?" Steve asked.

Rachel sighed. "I don't know. We haven't spoken about all this conspiracy stuff in such a long time. I don't like the thought of you going there."

"Rachel, this is what I've been working toward."

Rachel shook her head. "I don't have a good feeling about this, Steve."

"Look, the cruise is two weeks after my initiation. It'll be a great way for us to digest what I learn in Washington."

"Washington? Washington, *DC*?" Rachel panicked when she realized that was where her father was going when his car plunged into the Chesapeake Bay.

"Rachel, that's where the Supreme Council is."

"Don't go," she said abruptly.

Steve was taken aback with the way Rachel was acting. "I have to go, Rachel. I already responded to the invitation. The initiation is next month."

Four

He walked the temple courtyard alone. It was dark; the sun from Ra had long set and without the moonlit rays from Thoth he would have been in complete darkness, like most Egyptians. To live in complete darkness would mean having no insight of oneness with God, or no connection to the light. He understood that Thoth's light had been cast to help the chosen ones recall the original light, the consciousness, the intuitive knowing. He had been a chosen one but today found no comfort in it.

His heart was heavy, even burdened, as he continued his trek toward the sanctuary. Tall pillars bordered the passageway, supporting the high ceiling. As he moved further into the hypostyle the ceiling shielded the moonlight, leaving him in total darkness. But he knew his way and soon saw the glow from a torch that dressed the entry of the sanctuary.

Once in the temple, torches lit the sacred area. He approached the walls, studying the colorful murals that reflected the gods and goddesses, serpents, and pharaohs. When he came upon the portrayal of humankind's creation he stopped.

He understood the symbolism of creation. The circle represented god's consciousness and how god conceived first man in his image. To show the diversity of those who worship Ra, the scarab—representing the lowest form of life—along with the first human and the goddesses Isis and Nephthys worship the solar disk.

He was sad as he glanced at the painting. He had pledged his silence to go into the Egyptian mystery schools. Here, he had mastered initiation after initiation. He learned to free the soul from his flesh and blood and found the mystery to eternal life. As a high priest, he had full knowledge of the mysteries along with mankind's creation, and this is what haunted him.

Published by The Haworth Press, Inc., 2006. All rights reserved.
doi:10.1300/5721_05

It is not right that the truth be kept from everyone, he thought. *It is wrong to suppress the spirituality of humankind. All have a right to know who we are.* His head ached. With his hands, he massaged his temples, then the base of his shaven skull.

There was a stir from behind. He turned just in time to see the curved metallic blade plunge into his lower abdomen. Stunned from the horrendous pain, he stumbled. His eyes wandered to his white linen apron, which quickly soiled as blood streamed from his body. As he fell to his knees, the blade was pulled from within him, escalating his pain. He swiftly covered the wound with his hands, trying to prevent his life force from leaving, but the blood continued to seep through his fingers. He saw his rival leave. His cowardly assailant never looked back.

The weakness deepened, and although his eyes remained open, darkness overcame him. Lifeless, his body fell on the stone floor.

"Oh, God!" Jessie gasped. Abruptly she sat up, completely disoriented. Her heart pounded wildly and instinctively she felt her stomach for blood, only to feel sweat. Beads of perspiration had also formed on her temples and beneath her long hair.

From the moonlight filtering through a window, Jessie gathered that she was in her own bed. "It was just a dream," she mumbled.

There was a stir in the bed, beside her. "Jess? Are you okay?" Taylor whispered. When Jessie didn't respond, she sat up and wrapped her arms around her. "What's wrong, Jess?" Her voice was slightly husky.

Jessie sat wide-eyed and silent as her heart recovered from the nightmare.

"Are you sick?" Taylor felt Jessie's forehead. "You're all clammy."

"It was just a bad dream," she whispered. "Sorry I woke you. Go back to sleep." Jessie threw off the comforter and started to get out of bed.

"Where're you going?"

"I won't be able to sleep now. I'm going to do a little work."

"Jessie, it's one-thirty!"

"I'm sorry I woke you." Her eyes met Taylor's familiar eyes. "You go back to sleep." Jessie leaned over and kissed her gently. "I'm fine."

Jessie slipped on her robe, and descended the circular stairwell of her contemporary home. She was almost at the bottom when—

Thump! Thump! The noise from behind her startled her. She turned to find Maxwell following her. She lifted the black cat. "You scared me," she confided. The cat purred at the attention. "You can't sleep either?"

In the kitchen, Jessie brewed coffee. She poured herself a cup, sipped, then retreated to the sunroom, where she nestled in a loveseat with an old journal. She leafed through handwritten pages until she found a blank side, and then started to write. She wasn't there but a moment when she felt eyes upon her. Movement from the sunroom entrance caused her to jump, just before she saw Taylor standing in the doorway.

"Taylor, you scared me!"

She approached and sat beside Jessie. "Are you okay?"

Jessie smiled. "Sorry, I just had a bad dream."

Taylor eyed Jessie's dream journal. "And you're trying to interpret it?"

"Just record it. I'm not sure I want to know what it means."

"What was your dream?" Taylor asked patiently.

Jessie tried to collect her thoughts. "It was just strange, but it felt so real. I was a man and I think I was in ancient Egypt. I was upset about something. I think I was a priest and somebody stabbed me in the abdomen and I died. It just seemed so real."

Taylor understood why her partner was on edge. "Do you have any idea what it could mean?"

"Blood usually means loss of energy."

"Is anything draining you right now?"

Jessie shook her head and her long brown hair fell in her face. She pulled it from her brown eyes. "No. I don't think so."

"What about your work?"

Jessie Mercer was a novelist and screenwriter. Only months earlier, she had abandoned the sequel to *Deceptions,* one of her best-selling novels that had been made into a motion picture. She had been writing its sequel when the movie was released, and she started noticing similarities between the plot of *Deceptions* and her own life. It was then that she learned that she was precognitive, able to psychically sense future events. Taylor and Jessie found themselves drawn into a web of treachery, deception, and murder. Fearful that the *Deceptions* sequel was also a glimpse into her own future, Jessie abandoned the project and had since been brainstorming new stories.

"I've been researching and outlining a couple different stories. After our Salem experience, I'm a little gun-shy about what to write."

"What are you working on?"

"I have two ideas for stories. The first is about aliens that live among us."

"Aliens?" Taylor's big blue eyes beamed in disbelief. "I didn't realize you wanted to break into sci-fi."

"I'm not sure that I do, but it's just something I'm considering."

"Is that what you're researching?"

"No. I haven't started that project, yet. I'm working on another story about the Trilateral Commission, Council on Foreign Relations, and the Bilderbergers."

"What are they?"

"They're modern-day secret societies. One of the ultimate conspiracy theories is that these groups actually rule the world. I thought it'd make an interesting story."

"My God, Jess! If that's not energy draining, what is?"

Jessie smiled. "You're probably right. The research is exhausting. Do you think that's what my dream refers to?"

"I don't know. What's your story about?"

"It's about a TV reporter who gets tangled up in a web of conspiracy with these secret groups and, of course, has to save the world from the bad guys."

Taylor smiled and she shook her head. "Where do you come up with these ideas? Have you talked with Steve about it? We just spent Easter weekend with him, did you tell him what you were working on?"

A smile came to Jessie's lips, creating a solo dimple on her left cheek. She shook her head. "I don't want Steve to think his sister has gone off the deep end. Besides, he seemed to have a lot on his mind this trip."

"So which story are you working on first?"

"I'm not sure. Maybe both. With you leaving next week, you won't be around to distract me, so I should be able to crank out two books this year."

Taylor Andrews was a successful singer and actress. She was under new management, and since she had taken too much time off the previous year, her new manager suggested a world tour. She was scheduled to be out of the country the rest of the year.

Taylor rested her head against Jessie's shoulder, and Jessie held her. She stroked Taylor's long dark hair away from her attractive face, so that their eyes could meet. She kissed her forehead softly. "Why don't you go back to bed? I'll be fine."

"I would prefer to stay here with you."

Jessie reached for the afghan that hung from the back of the loveseat and spread it over Taylor. She took Taylor in her arms, and the two snuggled together until Ra's sunrays fell upon the San Gabriel Mountains.

Five

That Friday Rachel and Steve stood awkwardly across from each other, avoiding eye contact, while waiting for a conference room. Steve's hands were plunged deep within his pants' pockets, and Rachel shuffled through the papers she carried. A strain had developed between them because of Steve's invitation to the thirty-third degree, and Rachel had refused to meet him on subsequent weekends.

Later during the meeting, Steve took a major blow to his ego when Neil Samson announced that Rachel would replace Henry Schafer the following season. After the meeting, Steve cornered Neil, preventing him from leaving the room. "I was surprised by Rachel's promotion." Steve's eyes penetrated Neil's, demanding an answer.

"Steve, the latest focus group suggests that the existing anchors are too testosterone heavy. We wouldn't solve the problem if we put you there. Don't worry, I hear the boys upstairs have something bigger and better lined up for you."

On the way home from work that day, Rachel's cell phone rang. She hesitated to answer when she recognized Steve's number on the display. "Hi," was all she could say.

"Congratulations."

She smiled. "Are you okay? I think I was just as surprised as you."

"I'm fine. Honest." Steve sounded sincere.

There was an uncomfortable pause. "Are you on your way to DC?"

"I'm driving down tomorrow. Can I call you when I get back?"

Memories of Rachel's past flooded back to her. She recalled losing her father during his trip to DC. She had developed a newfound friendship with Steve and didn't want to sound superstitious. "Can I dissuade you from going?"

Published by The Haworth Press, Inc., 2006. All rights reserved.
doi:10.1300/5721_06

"I would have to give you an 'A' for effort. The initiation and ceremonies run from Sunday through Wednesday morning. Can I call you when I head back?"

"Of course. Be careful, okay?"

"I promise. Talk with you next week."

In that moment, Rachel realized just how much she felt for Steve. Indeed, she loved him. "Good-bye, Steve."

That Saturday evening, after Steve had settled into his hotel room, he called his sister.

"Hello," Jessie answered.

"Hi, Jessie."

"Steve? How are you?"

"I'm fine. Did I catch you and Taylor at a bad time?"

"No! Taylor left Wednesday for her world tour. I was just working on a new project, and your call is a welcome distraction."

"What are you working on, now?"

"Actually . . . two projects. But neither one seems to be working. They just don't *feel* right."

"What are they about?"

"One of them I call *Among Us,* and it's my first shot at science fiction. It's about aliens walking *among us.* The second is *The Ultimate Conspiracy,* and that's a suspense thriller about a group of individuals that control the world through secret societies. And of course, a protagonist is trying to save the world. Only . . ." Jessie hesitated. "I just finished the outline, and my protagonist fails."

"She doesn't save the world? Well, that's a horrible ending. Change it!" *The Ultimate Conspiracy?* He marveled at the coincidence between Jessie's story and the drama he had become wrapped up in.

"I'll work on the ending, but what can I help you with Steve?"

"I'm going to be in LA in July for a conference. I just wanted to get my reservations in early."

"You know you're welcome anytime, Steve."

On Sunday morning, Steve arrived at the House of the Temple. He had heard from the brethren how impressive the structure was, but words did not do it justice. The building stood high above Sixteenth Street, downtown DC. Two sphinxlike creatures bordered an expansive stairway leading to the entrance.

Before Steve scaled the stairway, he moved to one of the sphinxes. The granite lion had a man's head. His neck was entwined with a cobra and decorated with an ancient Egyptian symbol, the ankh. Steve journeyed up the granite stairs. The absence of windows made the building cold and uninviting.

High above the entrance was a series of huge pillars. As Steve walked closer he realized that an image was concealed behind the columns. Moving his line of vision he saw the illustration of Ra, the Egyptian sun god, bordered by six snakes.

Steve continued toward the lofty bronze doors. Carved in the stone in front of the doorway were two Egyptian swords with winding blades. In between the blades, brass letters set in the stone revealed "The Temple of the Supreme Council of the Thirty-Third and Last Degree of the Ancient and Accepted Scottish Rite." Above the bronze doors, etched in stone was "Freemasonry Builds Its Temples in the Hearts of Men and Among Nations."

As Steve finished reading, he felt sick to his stomach. He knew that his life would never be the same. He drew near the door and felt the hair stand on the back of his neck as he tapped the lion's head doorknocker three times.

It was close to two that Wednesday afternoon when Rachel's cell phone rang. She inserted the earphone into her ear and pressed the answer button as she made her way toward her office. "Rachel Addison."

"We need to see each other as soon as possible."

Rachel ducked into her office and closed the door. She barely recognized his voice, "Steve? Is that you?"

"Rachel . . . it's big. It's bigger than you can imagine. It's the ultimate conspiracy. . . . My God, it's going to change everything. . . . Don't trust anyone, do you understand?"

"Are you okay, Steve?"

"I'm going home. I need to get some things, and then I'm heading to the cabin. It'll be late by the time I get there. Probably close to midnight. . . . Meet me there. A spare key is under the planter on the deck. Please meet me there," he whispered.

"I will. I promise."

Six

Jessie was stuck. She had worked all week on her new project but the story just wasn't coming together. Piles of paper and books cluttered her desk along with two empty coffee mugs and a crumpled bag of tortilla chips. She had never experienced writer's block this bad. Stepping away from her desk, she paced her office, brainstorming ideas for a new ending of her conspiracy novel.

The forty-two-year-old glanced at the framed book-covers hanging on the walls for inspiration. Her eyes settled on *Beyond Paradise* and *Deceptions*. Both had made the *New York Times* Bestseller List and were made into motion pictures. *Deceptions* was the easiest novel she had written. She suspected that *The Ultimate Conspiracy* would be the most challenging. Jessie lifted a mug from her desk and was about to fetch another cup of coffee when the phone rang.

"Hello."

"Is Jessie Mercer there?" a man asked.

"Who's calling, please?"

"This is Detective Hopkins from the Scarsdale Police Department."

Jessie felt a lump in her throat. "This is Jessie Mercer. How can I help you?"

"I have some bad news, I'm afraid. It's about your brother, Steve. There's no easy way to say this. . . . I'm sorry. Your brother is dead."

Jessie couldn't speak. She closed her eyes and darkness came upon her.

"Miss Mercer, are you okay?"

"How?" she whispered. "What happened?"

"The preliminary evidence suggests suicide. He shot himself."

"Suicide? Is this some type of sick joke? My brother wouldn't have killed himself. Are you sure it's him?"

"He has been positively identified. He left a note . . . to you. Does he have any family members here in New York?"

Published by The Haworth Press, Inc., 2006. All rights reserved.
doi:10.1300/5721_07

"Our parents have passed on. I have some relatives, upstate. Where is he?"

"He's at the medical examiners', now. They'll need to hear from you. Will you be coming back East to make arrangements?"

Jessie fought to hold back the tears. She bit her lip hoping the pain would take her mind off her grief. Once satisfied that she was in control, "Yes, of course. I have some things I need to tend to here. I'll try to get out tomorrow morning."

"Call me when you settle in. I'll give you an update on the investigation, then."

Jessie took the detective's phone number then rested the handset on the cradle. Stunned by the news, she stared at the phone. How could this have happened? Her eyes wandered to a button on the answering machine, and she pressed "play." A digital voice spoke, "You have one old message."

"Hi, Jessie. It's me," Steve said. "If you're there, pick up. . . . I guess you're out. I'm on my way back from DC. It's a little after two, my time. I'm driving. Call me on my cell. If I don't hear from you, I'll call you tomorrow. There's something I need to run by you. It's about your project, *Among Us.* Let's talk soon. Love you."

Jessie remembered calling Steve after she received the message. His phone was out of the service area. She anguished over the fact that she hadn't kept calling back.

That afternoon, Jessie made flight arrangements to head for New York the following morning. Then she called Taylor's cell phone.

"The customer you have called has traveled outside the service area."

"Shit!" Jessie's frustration surfaced. Taylor's cell service hadn't been fixed yet, and she didn't know where Taylor was.

It was close to six o'clock that evening when the taxi arrived at the Scarsdale house. Jessie paid the fare and made her way to the front door. A yellow and black warning tape, stating CRIME SCENE—DO NOT ENTER, was wrapped around a planter on the front stoop. She dropped her bags, picked up the tape, and angrily crumbled it in her hand. From a pocket, she retrieved a key. She paused momentarily, hoping that she was ready, then opened the door.

Jessie picked up her luggage and moved through the grand foyer. The house was quiet. She had an odd feeling that she was invading her brother's privacy as she walked toward the kitchen.

The ring of a telephone startled her. She set her belongings down, and headed toward her brother's study where she picked up the handset. "Hello." But as she said it, she saw the blood on the wall behind the desk.

"Hello. Is this Jessie?" a man's voice asked.

Jessie couldn't respond. She stood motionless, across from the chair where her brother had pulled the trigger. Blood had splattered over the wall and carpeting. The hair on the back of her neck stood. She closed her eyes to calm herself.

"Hello, is anyone there?" he interrupted.

Jessie opened her eyes. "This is Jessie," she whispered.

"This is Detective Hopkins. I take it you had a key to the house. I was hoping I could meet with you tomorrow morning. Are you staying there tonight?"

"I was planning on it," she whispered, but wondered if she could.

"The criminologists are finished there. We found your brother in the study. I'd hire someone to clean it up and just avoid it until then."

"What time do you want to meet?"

"How's nine o'clock? I can swing by then."

"That's fine. I'll see you in the morning, detective."

As Jessie rested the handset she surveyed the area. Then, as quickly as she had entered, she fled. She grabbed her baggage and climbed the stairwell. On the second level she faltered a bit as nausea hit, then she staggered into the guestroom. She set her laptop on the desk, and threw her suitcase on the bed. She opened the sliding glass door and walked unsteadily onto the private deck. As she gaped over the landscaped backyard, she took deep breaths and tried to rid herself of the sick feeling.

When the nausea subsided, she headed for the bathroom. At the sink she applied a wet facecloth to her face and neck, and studied herself in the mirror. She looked exhausted. Her normally bright brown eyes were dull from fatigue. Her hair was pulled away from her face in a ponytail, revealing a small scar on her cheek. Jessie removed the hair tie and her long brown hair fell loosely past her shoulders.

Jessie called Taylor once again but got the same message. She avoided the study that evening and went to bed early since she'd had a sleepless night the evening before. But, between the creaking of the house and disturbing thoughts of her brother's suicide, she had another sleepless night.

In the morning, with coffee mug in hand, Jessie wandered through the sizeable house. She studied the photographs that were hung from the walls and displayed on the furniture. Most of them were connected with Steve's work at *Over the Edge*. Jessie knew that Steve had worked there going on ten years and that he aspired to replace a retiring anchor person in the year to come. She shifted to a photo of the two field reporters, Rachel Addison and Steve. Jessie knew from her conversations with Steve that the attractive brunette was being considered for the anchor opening also.

The doorbell rang, announcing Detective Hopkins's arrival, and they spoke at the kitchen table.

"Ms. Mercer, when was the last time you saw your brother?"

"Last month, at Easter time."

"Were you close to him?"

"Yes. Our parents died when I was a teenager, and Steve was ten years older than me, so he cared for me after they were gone. We always spent holidays together."

"When was the last time you spoke with him on the phone?"

"He called me last Saturday. He also left a voice mail three days ago."

"That was the day he killed himself. How did he sound?"

"Fine. He said it was about two and he was leaving Washington, DC. He called from his cell phone. I called him back, but his phone was either off or out of range." Jessie was overwhelmed with guilt that she hadn't kept trying. "I left him a message . . . but he never called back."

"Considering your brother's depression, how has he been over the past year?"

"Steve didn't suffer from depression."

"I'm sorry, Ms. Mercer. I assumed you knew. Mr. Mercer had been seeing a psychiatrist for about a year, now. He was being treated for clinical depression."

Jessie ran her fingers through her hair, pulling it away from her face. "I'm sorry, detective. I'm having a difficult time believing that my brother would ever kill himself."

"He obviously was hiding things from you. You missed signs of his depression." The detective extracted a paper from his attaché case. "This, of course, is a copy. We found it on the desk near his body."

He laid the handwritten note on the table. There were dark discolorations over it from blood. Jessie: Forgive me.—*Steve*

She recognized her brother's handwriting and the tears came. Up until this point, she had not believed he was gone. Now, she knew otherwise. She removed a tissue from her pocket and dried her eyes.

"Our handwriting expert has verified that your brother wrote the note."

Jessie tried to pull herself together. "Where did he get the gun? He hated guns."

"He purchased it about three weeks ago. There was a cash receipt in his desk."

"But why? Why would he kill himself?"

"We believe his death was attributed to complications of depression, with the final blow being job related. Apparently, your brother was up for a promotion and he learned last Friday that he didn't get it."

"And you think he killed himself because he didn't get a promotion?" Jessie struggled to control her disbelief and anger. "Does anybody know why he was in DC earlier in the week?"

"We didn't know he was out of town. Perhaps his employer may know."

"Who found his body?"

"Apparently the cleaning lady." Hopkins retrieved his notepad. "Marie Heron cleaned the house every Thursday. From what I understand, she came in around eight o'clock, and we received the call at nine ten."

"Detective Hopkins, would you mind showing me the study and demonstrate what you think happened?"

His eyes met Jessie's. "Ms. Mercer, your brother put a gun to his head and pulled the trigger." His voice was devoid of emotion.

"Is my request that unreasonable?"

Hopkins briskly moved into the study where he dispassionately mimicked Steve sitting in his chair, writing a letter, and then putting a finger to his skull. After pretending to pull a trigger the detective's head slumped backward and his arms dangled lifelessly to both sides of the chair.

His head perked up and he pointed to the floor beside his right arm. "Here is where we found the gun." Jessie saw the stained carpeting where the blood had pooled.

"My brother was left-handed," Jessie said.

"Unfortunately, his less dominant hand worked just as well," he said tactlessly.

Before Hopkins left, he gave Jessie the phone number to the medical examiner's office, so Jessie could make arrangements for the body. He also handed her the numbers for Neil Samson, the executive producer of *Over the Edge*, and Marie Heron.

Later that afternoon, Jessie called the network and left a message for Neil Samson. Within minutes he returned the call. "Jessie, this is Neil Samson. I just got your message. I'm terribly sorry to hear of your loss."

"Thank you, Mr. Samson. I'm sorry to bother you on a Saturday."

"Don't worry about that, and please, call me Neil. I was expecting a call from someone this weekend about services. Is that why you called?"

"Partly. I was hoping that you knew why Steve was in DC earlier this week. Was he there on business?"

"Is that where he went? No, Steve was out on vacation."

"I understand that he didn't get the anchor position."

"Yes. I'm terribly sorry if that announcement could have contributed to his condition. I had a lot of respect for your brother, he was a good man."

"Thank you. May I ask . . . who got the anchor spot on the show?"

Neil thought Jessie's question was a bit unusual. But the circumstances were certainly unusual. "Rachel Addison."

She thanked Neil and gave him the particulars on Steve's memorial service, which was scheduled for Monday morning.

It was close to four o'clock that Saturday afternoon when the doorbell rang. Jessie opened the door and greeted a heavyset man holding a homemade pie.

"Hello, can I help you?" Jessie asked.

"I'm Gary Stonewall. I'm terribly sorry to hear about your loss." He extended the pie to her with his large hands, and Jessie took it.

"Thank you. I'm Jessie Mercer, Steve's sister. I take it you knew him?"

"Oh, very well. He was a good man. We'll miss him down at the Lodge."

"The Lodge?"

"A men's social club. Your brother was an officer. I only hope that his duties didn't contribute to his illness."

Illness? Guilt haunted Jessie. Did everyone know about Steve's condition, except her? "I'm sure they didn't. Thank you for the pie."

"I hate to ask this at such a bad time, but there were things that Steve was responsible for that have slipped. I'm taking over his position and I was hoping I could pick up some Lodge files."

"Well . . . the study hasn't been cleaned up since that night. I'm having a cleaning company take care of it tomorrow. Then the service is Monday. If you come back Tuesday afternoon, I'll try to have the files ready. What's the name of the Lodge?"

"It probably would be best if I could just go through the files myself. I could pick them out in no time. To be honest, I was in Vietnam and blood doesn't bother me at all. Would you mind if I take a shot at it now?"

Jessie gazed back at the man. "Yes. I would mind, very much. You can call me Tuesday morning and let me know what I should be looking for and I'll have the files to you by the end of that day. Have a good day, Mr. Stonewall."

Jessie didn't give Gary Stonewall a chance to object. Fuming, she slammed the door in his face. "The nerve of him! He can't even wait for me to bury Steve—for some lousy files."

Jessie picked up the telephone and pressed some numbers. When she heard the ring she smiled, Taylor's cell service had been restored. After the second ring, the voice mail answered.

"Hi sweetheart, it's me. Could you call me on my cell phone when you get the message? It's important. . . . I love you." Jessie ended the connection.

Early that Sunday morning Jessie was making coffee when she heard the faint chime from her cell phone. "That must be Taylor." She bolted for the stairwell. The cell phone was on the nightstand beside the bed. She counted the rings as she took the steps two at a time. *One. Two.* She knew the call would go into voice mail if it reached four. *Three.* Jessie dived across the bed and pressed the answer button, just in time.

"Hello!" Jessie breathed heavily.

"Jessie?"

"Taylor! I'm so glad to hear your voice," she gasped. "Where are you?"

"In Beijing."

"China?" Jessie's heart sank knowing that Taylor couldn't be much farther away.

"I arrived yesterday, before that . . . the Philippines, Taiwan, and Hong Kong. It's all just running together."

"Your phone hasn't been working."

"I know. I noticed it when I was in Taiwan. It finally cleared up yesterday. I just got your message. Is everything okay? Where are you?"

Jessie sighed. "I'm in New York. Taylor . . . Steve is dead."

"Oh, God! Honey, I'm so sorry. How?" Taylor was shocked.

"I don't believe it, but they claim suicide."

"Jess, I'm on my way to a concert now. I go on in two hours. By the time I get back to the hotel, pack . . . I probably won't be able to get out until the morning. Where should I fly into? Kennedy?"

"No. I don't want to screw up your tour. Besides, the funeral is first thing tomorrow. Even if you got out tonight, you'd miss the service. Continue on your tour. . . . I just needed to hear your voice."

"I hate the thought that you're alone through this, Jess."

"I won't be alone. I know you'll be with me in your thoughts."

"How are you holding up?"

"I'm okay. I don't think it's really hit me yet that he's gone. I'll make whatever arrangements I need to make, and then I'll join you on your tour for a little. Okay?"

Taylor hesitated. "Jessie, I could be with you in a couple of days."

"And I could rendezvous with you in perhaps a week. I'll be fine." Jessie tried to sound convincing. "Really."

"Are you sure about this, Jess?"

"Yes, and I feel better just hearing your voice."

"I love you, Jessie."

"I love you, too. Break a leg tonight. I'll call you tomorrow after the service."

Taylor hesitated. "Okay. Good-bye sweetheart."

Jessie's heart ached as the phone disconnected her from Taylor. It hadn't been two weeks since Taylor had left, but she missed her so much. She wondered how she thought she could ever last eight months without seeing her.

Later that morning, Jessie stood motionless at the entry of her brother's office. From where she was, everything appeared normal, but she knew that if she moved any closer she would see blood. Since her arrival, she had the feeling that something wasn't right. But then again, what would be right? After all, Steve was gone.

Jessie took a deep breath and approached the desk. She hesitated as she sat in her brother's chair. With eyes fixed straight ahead, her mouth watered, and she tasted the unpleasant saltiness. The nausea hit and she closed her eyes, bringing her into darkness. The overwhelming feeling of loss approached like a freight train, and she sobbed.

"Why would you do this Steve?" she cried.

Jessie took a deep breath. *Control yourself.* She tried to collect herself.

She opened the top desk drawer. Steve had always been a neat person, and everything seemed in order. Calendar, paper clips, floppies, CDs, pens, pencils. She picked up a CD from a stand and smiled. The computer-generated label was so neat and orderly compared to the Post-it method she used on her own floppies and CDs. The label simply said "#46." She returned the CD to the stand.

Jessie turned her attention to the filing cabinet. She quickly skimmed through the files. "I don't see files for a social club," she mumbled.

The desktop was also orderly, unlike her desk. She picked up the stone paperweight with an engraving of a V-shaped compass, the kind used for drawing circles, along with a square. A trace of blood was on the object, so she set it down. She leaned backward in the chair and her eyes caught sight of a framed certificate on the wall, stating, STEVE MERCER, WORSHIPFUL MASTER OF BLUE LODGE #46. The certificate displayed the same compass and square logo. *Blue Lodge #46. . . . That must be the club Stonewall referred to.* She picked up the CD labeled "#46." *This must be for the lodge, but where are the files?*

The doorbell interrupted her thoughts. At the door Jessie recognized the woman standing on the front stoop, since she had met her during her recent visit.

"Hi, Marie. Thank you for coming over on a Sunday."

"Oh, don't worry about it. I just wish I could do more. Steve was such a good man, and he was always good to me."

"Could you do me a favor, and let me know if anything strikes you as odd?"

"Odd?"

"Yes. You know—different from usual."

It took Marie a couple hours to clean the study. The bookshelf near the desk was time-consuming as she had to scrub the book spines to remove traces of spattered blood.

Before Marie left, she found Jessie outside on the main-level deck reading the Sunday paper. "There you are. I couldn't remove all the stains. I would just replace the carpet, and paint the walls." She handed Jessie an envelope. "I found this wedged in one of the books."

"What is it?" Jessie opened the envelope and found two tickets for a Caribbean cruise. "Steve must have been going on vacation. My God, the trip is next week. Marie, did you know that he was going out of town?"

"No. But that's not unusual. I've gone a month without seeing your brother because of his traveling. I just know to show up every Thursday. Sometimes, it's obvious that he hadn't been around since my previous cleaning."

"The other ticket is for Julie Harris. Do you know who she is?"

Marie shook her head. "No."

"I should go through his Palm Pilot. I wonder if she knows that he's
. . ." Jessie had difficulty saying the words, "passed on." Then she
changed the subject. "What do I owe you for today?"

"Nothing. Steve always paid me a month at a time. I owe you two
more cleanings. You know, there is one thing that seemed a bit odd.
Maybe the police took it, but there was nothing in the trash basket."

"My brother was out of town most of the week. There was probably
no trash."

"Then the liner would still be in the trashcan. I remove the trash
liner from each wastebasket and replace it with a new liner every
week. The trashcan in the study didn't have a liner or trash in it."

Marie left, and Jessie ventured toward the study. Deep in thought,
she whispered aloud, "It doesn't make any sense. He was going on a
vacation next week. How could it look so bleak that he would take his
own life?" She sat at the desk, removed Steve's Palm Pilot, and
searched for Julie Harris, but there was no one listed by that name.

Seven

The rain beat against the limo's windshield as it traveled from the church to the graveyard. Jessie had been surprised by the turnout for her brother's memorial service. She had sat by herself in the front pew of the crowded Catholic Church and was reminded of how alone she was without her brother. Her heart ached, and in a moment of weakness she wished she had asked Taylor to come be with her.

The limo arrived at the gravesite and Jessie made her way to a small canopy beside the grave. Alongside the casket were two headstones identifying her parents' resting places. To Jessie, there seemed to be an endless delay while the crowd gathered around her beside the coffin. The priest finally continued the service with a prayer that Jessie would never remember. Subsequently, each person tossed a rose on top of the casket, greeted Jessie, and departed. Jessie recognized only Marie Heron and Gary Stonewall. Others introduced themselves, including Neil Samson and members of the TV show.

Jessie recognized Rachel Addison as she waited in line to meet her. She was taller than she appeared on television, but then again, she had on killer pumps. She wore a simple black dress, with dark glasses concealing her eyes. Her long dark hair had been pulled away from her face and clipped low, drawing attention to her cleft chin.

When it was Rachel's turn to greet Jessie, she warmly took Jessie's hand and shook it. "I'm Rachel Addison. I worked with Steve. If there's anything I can do to help, please let me know." Unexpectedly, she embraced Jessie.

Jessie felt her slip something into her jacket pocket.

"Meet me," she whispered into Jessie's ear, and then she retreated.

Preoccupied, Jessie stayed at the casket until everyone disappeared, leaving her with her brother's body. She had been strong this weekend, but as she stood all alone she felt her walls crumble. Then the

Published by The Haworth Press, Inc., 2006. All rights reserved.
doi:10.1300/5721_08

tears came. "Why?" Jessie asked between sobs. "Why did you do this? How come you didn't talk to me? How come everyone knew you were having problems, except me? Was I so self-absorbed that I missed it? I'm sorry if I was. . . . Please . . . forgive me."

Jessie pulled a tissue from her jacket pocket and a piece of paper fell to the ground. Remembering when Rachel Addison embraced her, she picked up the note and read it. "Meet me at the Dobbs Ferry Chart House. Five o'clock. It's important. Rachel Addison."

As Jessie drove to the Chart House that evening, she mulled over why Rachel had been so mysterious about their meeting. She suspected that Rachel felt guilty that her promotion had upset Steve. Jessie parked Steve's cherished BMW and headed into the restaurant.

Rachel greeted Jessie at the hostess station. Both women remained silent until the hostess seated them. Although their table offered a breathtaking view of the Hudson River and Tappan Zee Bridge, neither was interested in the scenery.

To Jessie, Rachel seemed nervous, maybe even a little preoccupied. Frequently, she peeked around the restaurant, inspecting her surroundings. When she finally removed her sunglasses Jessie realized that Rachel was even more attractive in person than on television. Her long dark eyelashes outlined intense grayish-blue eyes.

Jessie spoke first. "I think I know why you wanted to meet."

"You do?" Rachel's voice was husky.

Jessie nodded. "I understand that you and my brother were—"

Rachel grabbed Jessie's hand and without warning she whispered, "Steve didn't commit suicide. He was murdered." She withdrew her hand and diverted her eyes.

The stranger certainly had seized Jessie's attention. "I'm listening."

Rachel sipped her cabernet, and then began. "Have you heard of the Council on Foreign Relations, the Trilaterial Commission, or the Bilderbergers?"

"They're modern secret societies that allegedly strive for one-world government."

Rachel was surprised and hesitated, "That's correct. They're globalist. There is a theory that the world is actually controlled by members of the CFR and Bilderbergers."

"Yes. It's one of the ultimate conspiracy theories. Some speculate that these societies start and stop wars, control the stock market, interest rates, and the politicians that we supposedly elect."

Rachel hesitated again. "You sound well versed in the subject."

"I'm a writer, and I'm presently working on a conspiracy novel. So I've read a couple books on the subject. But . . . what does any of this have to do with Steve?"

Rachel began telling her story. She told Jessie about the investigation she had been doing on secret societies the year before, and how Steve had warned her to drop it. She explained that Steve was a Freemason and had advanced through thirty-two degrees in the Scottish Rite, that he had questioned the integrity of the organization and worked to get an invitation to the Thirty-Third Council. She shared that Steve went to Washington, DC, for the initiation into the thirty-third degree. Apparently he went through his initiation, called Rachel on his way back from DC, and had asked her to meet him at his house in the Catskills.

Rachel tried to hold back the tears as she finished telling her story. "That was the last time I spoke with Steve," Rachel said somberly. "He never showed up that night."

Jessie removed a tissue from her purse and handed it to Rachel.

"Thank you."

"So you think my brother was murdered because of something he learned in DC?"

"It wasn't suicide."

"I was told that Steve was suffering from depression, and that he was upset about not getting the promotion."

"He *wasn't* suffering from depression. And I spoke with him the Friday night before he left for DC. Believe me, he was fine about my promotion."

Jessie was thoughtful and continued to stare at Rachel.

"You don't believe me."

"Actually, your statement that my brother was murdered is probably the most believable thing I've heard since I arrived here." Jessie shook her head. "I'm just struggling with all this secret society stuff. Were the two of you . . . lovers?"

"We were good friends. We were cautious about spending time together and took precautions. I don't think anyone knew we were anything other than co-workers."

Jessie glanced at her watch. They had been at the restaurant going on three hours. "I need to reflect on everything you've told me. Can I call you if I have any questions?"

"Yes, of course."

Rachel handed Jessie her card. "If you need me, call my cell phone. Don't call from your brother's house phone."

"Do you think it's bugged?"

"I wouldn't be surprised."

Jessie was exhausted by the time she returned to the house that night. It had been a long day—the funeral, the gravesite, and then the meeting with Rachel Addison. Before she retired, however, she went into her brother's office and sat at his desk. She turned the computer on and called Taylor as it booted up.

"Hi, it's me," Jessie said when she heard Taylor's voice.

"How are you?"

"Drained."

"What can I do to help?"

Jessie smiled. "Just hearing your voice helps."

The couple spoke briefly about the funeral and Jessie's day, but Jessie never mentioned her meeting with Rachel Addison. As she hung up the telephone, she quickly scanned the computer's hard drive. There were no document files. The download manager was empty, and the recycle bin had been wiped clean.

"CDs," she whispered. She browsed through the CD stand and retrieved the disk labeled "#46." Jessie inserted it into the CPU, only to learn that it was blank, along with the rest of the CDs.

She accessed the backup software, only to learn that the computer was last backed up on the evening Steve was killed, at ten ten p.m. "The medical examiner placed Steve's time of death between seven thirty and nine thirty." The external hard drive used for backing up the computer had the one backup copy on it, with no files.

Jessie was exhausted and the events of the day caught up with her. She began to cry. Sobbing softly, she wandered upstairs to the bedroom. The room was stuffy, so she cracked open the deck door. She crawled on top of the bed, rested her head on the pillow, and cried herself to sleep.

Hours later, a siren pierced the silence. Disoriented, it took Jessie a few seconds to realize that she lay on top of the bed. The house was dark, and something was dreadfully wrong. She tasted soot in the back of her dry throat. Jessie reached for the lamp on the nightstand. The light hurt her eyes and when they adjusted she saw the thick blanket of smoke on the ceiling. "Shit." She rushed into the hallway. The smoke was coming from the stairwell, where flames sprouted from the first floor.

Jessie slammed the bedroom door and ran to the phone. Hastily, she pressed 911.

Seconds later, a woman answered. "What's the nature of the emergency?"

"My house is on fire."

"You're calling from Forty-Three Robin Lane, Scarsdale?"

"Yes."

"Can you get out of the house?"

"I'm in a second-floor bedroom. I'm going to try. Send the fire department."

Jessie hung up then dashed out on the deck. There was a ten-foot drop to the grass below. She leaned over the edge and looked into the downstairs window. Flames pressed angrily against the glass.

She bolted back into the bedroom. The smoke was much thicker than before. Her eyes stung and she gasped for air. She pulled the comforter from the bed, removed the sheets, and retreated to the deck. Jessie tied one corner of a sheet to the deck railing, then coupled the opposite corner to the other sheet, creating a rope. She flung the rope over the banister.

One last time, Jessie scurried into the house, penetrating the now smoke-filled room. Instinctively, she groped to the desk where she found her computer bag. She hung it over her shoulder. "Where's my purse?" She coughed.

She recalled hanging it on the chair by the desk. As Jessie fumbled for the chair, the bottoms of her shoes warmed from the smoldering floor. Swiftly, she grabbed the purse and hurried outside, gasping for air.

Suddenly, an explosion from the first floor shattered the windows just below the deck. Flames sprang up furiously from the windows. Jessie hung the handbag on her shoulder, opposite the computer. She climbed over the railing and yanked firmly on the sheet. She readjusted the computer bag, as it was cutting into her neck. Sirens blasted in the distance and she considered waiting for help, but as she thought about it, flames from below seized the deck and the wood ignited.

She twisted the sheet around one of her hands, took a deep breath, and started down, slowly at first, then more rapidly until her hands were rope burned, and she leaped the remaining distance.

The sirens now blared out piercingly. She sprinted alongside the burning house toward the fire engines. As she passed a door to the garage she noticed the fire had spread. Just as she spotted her brother's prized BMW engulfed in flames, it exploded. Jessie's forearms covered her face as glass shattered from the door window all over her. She toppled backward awkwardly, landing on top of the computer bag that was draped across her shoulder.

Jessie was stunned. The glass had scored her skin, the air was filled with smoke, and the sirens were deafening. She barely noticed the firefighters shuffling her away from the burning house.

In those early morning hours, as an Abbey Richmond paramedic treated her scrapes and burns, Jessie sadly witnessed Steve's house burn to the ground.

Who did this? What the hell did they want? Her mind raced. *My God, Steve, what on earth did you discover?*

Eight

It was going on six a.m. when Jessie reached her Tarrytown hotel room. As she placed her computer bag on the desk, she caught her reflection in the mirror.

"My God, I look like I've been to war." Her long hair was unkempt and she sported a bandage on her forehead, with scrapes on her cheeks. Band-Aids and scratches covered both hands and forearms. Her clothes were dirty, wrinkled, and even frayed in areas. She studied her bloodshot eyes and decided that it was from the smoke. "Or crying," she whispered.

A knock at the door alerted Jessie that her items had arrived. She took a bag from the bellboy, tipped him, and then dropped the bag on the dresser. Jessie was exhausted. She lay on top of the bed, just for a minute, just to rest her eyes before she headed to the shower. But her body had other plans, and she quickly fell asleep.

It was close to noon when she woke. She emptied the contents of the bag the bellboy had delivered onto the bed. From the items she selected toiletries, sweatpants, and a T-shirt, and headed for the bathroom.

While showering, Jessie brooded over the events from the last week. She recalled the phone call announcing her brother's death, the funeral, her conversation with Rachel Addison, followed by the fire.

Now where do I go? Jessie contemplated as the hot water streamed over her body. "What should I do, Steve?" she whispered. For a moment she considered hopping on the next plane and joining Taylor in China. *I can't do that. . . . I'd never forgive myself.*

Soon after, room service delivered lunch and Jessie felt better after she ate. She searched for the business card the arson investigator had given her earlier that morning. As she retrieved his business card from

Published by The Haworth Press, Inc., 2006. All rights reserved.
doi:10.1300/5721_09

her wallet, Rachel Addison's card fell to the carpet. She set the card on the desk and called the detective.

"We haven't finished the investigation," the detective said, "but we suspect it was from faulty electrical wiring."

Jessie pondered as she set the phone down. *It's a new house, and they suspect faulty wiring?* She picked up Rachel's card. *I need to go to Steve's cabin,* she decided. *There's nothing else for me here.* Jessie punched in the numbers to Rachel's cell phone.

"Rachel Addison."

"Hi, Rachel. It's Jessie Mercer." Jessie needed to get right to the point. "I need your help. Can you take me to Steve's mountain house?"

Rachel hesitated. "I probably could take tomorrow off."

"Can we drive up this evening and stay the night?"

"I guess I could do that. Let's meet at the Palisades exit on 87. How's eight o'clock?"

Jessie faltered. "I hate to be an inconvenience, but can you pick me up? Steve's BMW is . . . out of commission."

"What's wrong with it?"

"It exploded. There was a fire at Steve's house last night. Everything was destroyed. There's nothing left."

"My God. Where are you now? I'll pick you up in two hours."

It was around seven o'clock that evening when the women arrived at the cabin. Jessie studied the rustic house as they approached the front stoop. "Are you sure nobody knows about this place?"

"That's what Steve told me a couple months ago." Rachel reached for the key under the planter.

Jessie roamed through the small house, searching for signs that her brother had been there. There were few. His house in Westchester County had been contemporary, which fit him, while the cabin was simple and rustic.

"The house doesn't *feel* like my brother," Jessie said.

"From what I understand, he spent his weekends here."

Jessie finished her tour in the smallest bedroom, which was set up as an office. She sat at a small desk and ran her fingers over the dark wood. "Even the desk. . . . It's an antique." Jessie turned to Rachel. "My brother hated antiques."

"Perhaps, he bought the place furnished."

"Perhaps." Jessie's fingers moved to the computer keyboard. "Steve's computer at his house was wiped clean. There were no documents on the hard drive. His CDs were also empty." Jessie resisted the urge to turn on the computer; instead she changed the subject. "You must be hungry. Is there any food in the fridge?"

In the kitchen the women scrounged for something to eat, then prepared pasta and sauce from a jar. Within a half hour they were seated at the small dining area table with their dinner and some wine.

"Thanks for driving me up here, Rachel."

"What are your plans?"

Jessie sipped her merlot. "I'm not sure."

Rachel curled pasta on her fork. "I'll have to go back tomorrow."

"I understand. I'm going to stay here. I want to go through the house and see if there are any hints to what got Steve killed."

"The two of us have to be careful, Jessie."

Jessie nodded. What an odd turn of events. Only last week she had been home curled up with Taylor on her loveseat. Now, her closest comrade was this stranger sitting beside her.

Rachel recalled Steve's last conversation in her head. *"It's the ultimate conspiracy. . . . My God, it's going to change everything. . . . Don't trust anyone."*

"Your brother told me not to trust anyone. He called it the *ultimate conspiracy.*"

"Steve called me Wednesday on his way back from DC and there was something he said in his message that doesn't make sense."

"What's that?"

"He said that he wanted to run something by me about my new project. Steve and I had spoken the previous weekend and I told him about two projects I had been working on. One of them is *Among Us* and the other—*The Ultimate Conspiracy.*"

"*The Ultimate Conspiracy?*" One of Rachel's dark eyebrows spiked.

"That's not what's strange. His voice message said that he wanted to discuss *Among Us,* not *The Ultimate Conspiracy*—which is my conspiracy project."

"Perhaps he just got his titles mixed up. Let's go shopping tomorrow and get some food for you. I can come up over the weekend and see how you're doing."

The following day, the women left the cabin early. After the grocery store, they stopped at a strip mall where Jessie bought a battery charger for her phone, as her charger was destroyed in the fire. She also purchased a pair of sneakers, since she had only the dress shoes from her escape.

"Do you want to buy some clothes while we're here?" Rachel asked as they passed a clothing store.

"I'd prefer that nobody knows I'm here. I shouldn't use my credit card, and I don't want to deplete my cash. I'm sure there are some clothes at the cabin that I could hang around in."

The women returned to the cabin and Rachel soon left, agreeing to call Jessie later in the week. From the front deck, Jessie watched Rachel's car back out of the bumpy driveway. She waved good-bye, then retreated to Steve's office. She turned on the computer and browsed through a small filing cabinet as the computer booted up.

"Bingo!" She pulled a manila file labeled "Lodge #46." Curious, she perused the documents. *These must have been what Gary Stonewall was looking for when he visited the house. He probably thinks they've been destroyed.*

The bottom file drawer was labeled "expenses." Here she found records relating to the cabin. Oddly though, the bills had been mailed to Brennan Keller at a post office box in Jewett. *Who's Brennan Keller?.* She found auto insurance, utilities, banking statements, even tax returns for the previous year, all in Brennan Keller's name. Then she discovered Brennan Keller's check stubs from the *Syracuse Herald.* She wondered if Steve had been subletting from Brennan, or perhaps Brennan was a roommate.

The computer, which was now ready, lured Jessie from the cabinet. She was relieved when she saw several documents concerning the White Plains lodge. There was a check-writing program for Brennan Keller; the register showed a little over one-year's history. Also, there were articles by Brennan, along with letters to a *Syracuse Herald* editor. Apparently, Brennan was a freelance writer for the paper.

Jessie turned her attention to a small bookshelf where countless books on Freemasonry and other secret societies were stored. A gaudy mug that had been used as a bookend also contained a set of keys. One key appeared to be for the cabin, another for a post office box, and then there was a set for a Ford.

At the front door, Jessie inserted a key in the keyhole, confirming the match. She opened the screen door and stood on the small porch. It was a pleasant May evening. A warm breeze stirred the dense evergreens that surrounded the house. A single chair was placed in the corner of the porch. Jessie drew near the chair and sat, feeling sad that there was only one chair. Steve had always been a loner, valuing his privacy. As she rested, she recalled memories of her brother, reminding her of her loss.

The cry of a crow drew her attention to the property. There was nothing luxurious or elaborate about the house. The driveway wasn't even asphalted. Rather, two dirt paths from tire wear and tear etched across the front of the property.

Jessie followed the tire tracks which led her behind the house to a Ford Mustang. Here, the car was hidden from the road. The car was locked. From her pocket she retrieved the key chain and inserted one of the keys. The doors unlocked.

Jessie sat in the car. She unlocked the glove compartment and retrieved an envelope. The registration and insurance card confirmed that the car belonged to Brennan Keller. As she stuffed the envelope back she spotted a man's wallet. She lifted the eel skin folder and unfolded the wallet. A picture of Steve stared at her from a New York license. Jessie glanced at the name under his picture, "Brennan T. Keller. . . . Oh my God," she whispered. "Steve was Brennan Keller?"

Over the next few days, Jessie ransacked the house. She studied the clues she uncovered, and by the weekend—when Rachel visited—

Jessie had much to share. Rachel was at the cabin only minutes that Sunday morning when Jessie hit her with questions. "What was your relationship with Steve?"

Rachel sat at the dining area table. "I already told you. We were friends."

"You were more than friends, weren't you?" Jessie leaned against the refrigerator, her arms crossed.

"We were friends," Rachel said defensively, "but under different circumstances, I think there would have been more. There was a moment between us."

"A moment?"

"A kiss. But we both agreed that a relationship would be too complicated." Rachel's eyes met Jessie's. "To be honest, I was in love with him, but I never told him."

"Are you Julie Harris?"

"No. But I am aware that Steve purchased cruise tickets and one of them was in that name. He asked me to join him on that trip using that alias."

"Have you ever heard the name Brennan Keller?"

"No. Who is he?"

"It was an alias for Steve." Jessie joined Rachel at the table. "Apparently, over the last year, he has been living another life. His alias has a social security number, a driver's license, and credit. He's been freelancing as a reporter for the *Syracuse Herald*. He even filed tax returns. I don't have a clue how he pulled this off."

Rachel appeared thoughtful. "About two years ago Steve did a report on how easy it was to get a fake ID and assume another identity."

"He started portraying Brennan about a year ago. It looks as if his relationship with the paper was by mail or e-mail. The question is— why would he do it?"

"Something obviously didn't feel right a year ago. That's when he first came to me and insisted that I stop my investigation. Perhaps it was a contingency plan if something went dreadfully wrong, then he'd have a place to start over."

Jessie stared at Rachel, "He must have thought a lot of you and trusted you. He told you about this place. I didn't know it existed."

"Jessie, the only thing Steve conveyed was that he had a second home. He didn't share any of the other stuff. What are you going to do?"

"I'm staying right here. I'm going to learn everything I can about Brennan Keller and this men's secret society he belonged to. Did Steve actually have a second life, or was it a hideaway? Did Brennan have friends? Did he know his neighbors? Did anybody actually see Brennan?"

"Why?"

"I need some answers, Rachel. I owe it to Steve to find out who killed him."

"I understand your grief. But how is learning about Brennan going to get answers?"

"If my hunch is correct, no one actually saw Brennan. My brother was very much a loner. I bet he didn't have friends up here, and I believe his relationship with the newspaper was completely by correspondence."

"I still don't get it, Jessie."

"I'm going to assume Brennan Keller's identity and infiltrate the Freemason lodge."

"Are you off your rocker?"

"I can take on Brennan's identity fairly easily. He has credit, a social security number, resume, employment, shelter, and transportation. He has insurance and a driver's license."

"A driver's license with *Steve's* picture on it."

"Steve and I have a family resemblance." Jessie walked to a small mirror that hung on the wall. She pulled her long brown hair away from her face. "We have the same eyes, chin, and cheekbones."

"Steve's eyes were blue!"

"Contacts can correct that. My biggest challenge is the height and weight. But, I can do this," Jessie said trying to convince herself.

"Timeout! Not to burst your bubble, but when your brother was alive, I jokingly threatened to do the same, and after he laughed hysterically, he said it would never work."

"Rachel, you're very feminine. I don't believe you could impersonate a man. I'm five-ten. I tower over most women, and I've worked out for years, so I already have a muscular build—"

"No! It goes beyond that. Your brother said that as long as I had breasts, I would never make it through the first three initiations. I got the impression that the candidates have to be topless during an initiation."

Jessie wasn't going to allow the challenge to dampen her spirit. "I'll find a way. I'm going to discover what all this secrecy is about and then I'm going to write a novel, revealing the truth about why Steve died," Jessie vowed.

Rachel saw that Jessie was becoming obsessed and drawn into the saga that had consumed her own life over the past year.

That Monday morning, Jessie called Alison Townsend, a friend in California, who was taking care of her cat, Maxwell. "I'm going to be in New York longer than I had expected. Would you mind watching Maxwell longer?"

"No, not at all. Do you need me to stop by your house and check on things?"

"Perhaps. How do you feel about paying my bills while I'm gone?"

Jessie agreed to have her mail forwarded to Alison's house and to add Alison as a signer on her checking account. She would make arrangements to have most of her bills paid electronically and have her royalty payments from her publisher direct deposited. While she was gone, Jessie felt comfortable that Alison could handle things. Alison even agreed to use Jessie's house occasionally as a weekend retreat.

"Terrific. If you need to reach me, call my cell or you can e-mail me. Thanks for your help, Alison."

Later that night when Jessie's cell phone rang, she knew it was Taylor. Jessie wasn't looking forward to this conversation. "Hi, sweetheart. How are you?"

"I'm missing you. When can you join me?" Taylor asked.

"It looks like I have to spend more time here, Taylor. I'm not sure how long yet."

"Why? What's going on?" Taylor sounded disappointed.

"There are some real estate issues that need to be wrapped up." Jessie hated misleading Taylor. "Also, I need to spend more time around Steve's home. I don't believe he killed himself, Taylor. It's hard to explain, sweetheart. I just want to be around where he was living."

Taylor brought to mind when she had lost her fiancé a couple years earlier. She remembered how she had needed her own space to deal with the loss, and how she had withdrawn from her life. "Honey, do whatever you need to."

Jessie's heart warmed from hearing Taylor's words. "Thanks for understanding. Are you checking your e-mail?"

"Maybe once a week, why?"

"I've refrained from calling you many times because of the time difference. I've thought about e-mailing you, but I wasn't sure if you were going online."

"I'll do a better job getting online, Jess. Many times I've wanted to call you, also, but I knew you'd be sleeping."

When their conversation ended that night, Jessie missed having Taylor in her arms. She retreated to Steve's computer, put her feelings in a note, and e-mailed Taylor.

Nine

Over the next week, Jessie crammed any information she could find on Freemasonry. She scrutinized Lodge documents she found in the filing cabinet. There was one letter in particular that intrigued her. Apparently, a member of Steve's Lodge was relocating to California, and Steve wrote to a California Lodge to identify the man as a Master Mason. The California Worshipful Master followed with a letter to Steve requesting a personal meeting with the man when he moved.

"If I had a referral from a Worshipful Master, I could avoid the first three initiations," she speculated. From everything Jessie had studied, she knew the initiations through Master Mason were grueling, and she had already been warned about the threat of having to unclothe during those initiations.

Jessie jolted from the sudden telephone ring. She hadn't heard the cabin telephone before. After two rings, she heard a female voice. "Hello, we can't come to the phone right now. Leave a message after the tone." Beep! Using the voice as a beacon, Jessie traced the answering machine location to a remote kitchen shelf.

A voice was broadcasted from the machine, "Hi Brennan, it's Len Richards. I haven't received a response on my article request. I need it by Friday. Let me know if you can do it. Call me or e-mail back."

"E-mail?" Jessie returned to the computer. She accessed America Online and saw BKeller among the screen names. A password was needed. For a half hour, Jessie speedily keyed in the obvious: birthdays, mother's maiden name, social security number, address, etc. But nothing worked.

Then she closed her eyes. "Steve, what would you use?" she whispered aloud. She didn't hear the password, but she typed the first thing that came to mind—RACHEL. Jessie smiled when the com-

Published by The Haworth Press, Inc., 2006. All rights reserved.
doi:10.1300/5721_10

puter recognized the password. "So big brother, you *did* have feelings for her."

Among the few e-mails to Brennan was a note from Len Richards offering Brennan an assignment to write an article on a company relocating to Syracuse. He had asked Brennan to answer by the previous day.

Jessie reviewed Steve's previous e-mail exchanges and attempted to mimic Steve's writing style in a note: *Dear Len, Sorry for the delay. I've had the flu. I'll do the piece on the Xandex relocation. I'll e-mail it by the end of the week. Brennan.*

For the rest of the week, Jessie studied Freemasonry and surfed the Web collecting information for the article. She scrutinized Brennan's articles to reproduce his writing style. Jessie was surprised by how challenging it was to do the article. *I'll stick with writing novels,* she decided as she e-mailed the article that Friday morning.

Within an hour, Jessie received a note back from Len. In it, he praised the Xandex article and offered another assignment that would be due the following Friday. Jessie surprised herself when she replied by accepting the project.

Using her cell phone, Jessie called Detective Hopkins for an update on Steve's death. The police still believed it was suicide. After talking with Hopkins, she was transferred to the arson investigator, who had concluded that faulty electrical wiring set off the fire. Jessie provided the police department with her e-mail address. "I'm going to be traveling a bit," she told them. "If you need to reach me—try my cell or e-mail."

Later that afternoon, while online, Jessie purchased a scanner with a credit card in Brennan Keller's name. She arranged to have it shipped to the cabin. Then she surfed to LensWorld.com. In the evening she e-mailed Jason, a friend in California. Jason was a cosmetologist and a cross-dresser. Jessie asked for help.

That Monday, the UPS driver set a package by the front door. After the truck left, Jessie emerged and retrieved the carton. It didn't take long for her to install the scanner. In the filing cabinet, she dug out the letter from the California Lodge that had intrigued her. She scanned its letterhead, reproducing the image, and transferred the replica to a Word document.

While online, Jessie searched for the White Plains Freemason Lodge #46. On their Web site she confirmed that Gary Stonewall had replaced Steve. She copied and pasted the Lodge address into the document with the California letterhead. Then, she wrote a referral letter, in which the California Worshipful Master indicated that Brennan Keller, a Master Mason, had relocated to New York and was searching for a Blue Lodge. The letter stated that Brennan would contact Gary in the near future.

After Jessie practiced signing the man's signature a dozen of times, she forged the document. She set it beside the original letter sent to Steve, and smiled. It looked authentic. She inserted the letter into an envelope, addressed and stamped it, then stuffed it in a larger packet with a note: *Hi Alison—Could you drop this letter in the mail? Please? Thanks! Jessie.*

The next day, Jessie mailed the envelope using overnight service. At a department store, she purchased scissors and trimming shears. When she returned to the cabin, she smiled when she saw two packages on the deck.

Jessie poured a glass of wine and headed for the small bedroom. She stopped in front of the full-length mirror, sipped her cabernet, then set it on the nightstand. She looked at the scar on her cheek. With her fingers, she traced the mark, recalling how she had fought for her life in the Grand Canyon the previous year. She grabbed a brush and stroked her long dark hair.

Jessie retrieved scissors from the dresser. She opened the blades and placed them against a clump of hair. Cowardly, she recoiled and sipped her wine. She took a deep breath, pulled a bunch of hair to the side, and opened the sheers so that they edged her hair. Closing her eyes, she severed the large clump. There was no turning back.

A brief time later, Jessie's hair was shorter than she had ever worn it. She drained the last of the wine, then stood back from the mirror, taking in how the haircut altered her appearance. *God, I look butch.*

Jessie opened the box that Jason had shipped to her. She withdrew items and spread them on the bed. There was a padded body suit, artificial facial hair, Ace bandage, and makeup. She removed her T-shirt and bra. With the Ace bandage, she wrapped her breasts, squashing her femininity. She slipped on shoulder pads, which draped from her back to her flattened chest. The padded bodysuit had no bulges and appeared smooth.

She slipped on one of her brother's dress shirts and buttoned it to her neck. The shoulders fit well, but the sleeves were a tad too long. Then she removed her sweatpants and slid on a padded undergarment over her hips. She followed with boxer briefs. The padded insert had accented her buttocks, detracting from her feminine hips.

Jessie slipped into the pants. The extra padding in the butt allowed a perfect waist fit, but the inseam was too long, so she cuffed the hems. She wedged inserts into a pair of Steve's shoes, then tried them on for size. A little large, but they could do in a pinch. She followed with a tie, then jacket.

Jessie stepped back from the mirror. She was stunned. She looked huge. The padded undergarments had expanded her shoulders, making her appear barrel-chested. Between the shoes and inserts, she approached six feet tall.

She stood awkwardly, not knowing exactly how to stand or where to rest her hands. Then she pulled a straight chair in front of the mirror and practiced sitting. It felt foreign and uncomfortable.

Determined to get this right, Jessie stood. One of her hands slid into a pants pocket. She turned slightly so she wasn't directly facing the mirror. "That's better." Without thinking, she smiled, but quickly banished it from her face. She realized that her smile made her look too feminine.

She removed the jacket and tossed it on the bed. She then sat in the chair, critiquing her every move in the mirror. "Legs apart," she whispered, and her legs parted so that they ran parallel to the chair legs. Over and over she practiced sitting, then her stance, until she could do it without thinking.

Jessie picked up the artificial facial hair. It matched her hair color perfectly. It adhered to her face and she stepped away from the mirror. The goatee enhanced her masculine appearance, and somehow, she thought her scar was more fitting for Brennan.

From the bed, Jessie retrieved a small package. Inside, there was a vial containing contact lenses. She inserted the lenses and her brown eyes were now blue.

Jessie started in a low tone, "Hi, I'm Bren—" She cleared her throat, and said even lower, "Hi, I'm Brennan Keller." *This is going to take practice.*

For the rest of the week, Jessie set out as Brennan. She visited the mall, hairstylist, post office, and grocery store. Each day she learned from people's reactions to her disguise. She used Brennan's credit card to purchase new clothing and shoes. She was pleased with her dress rehearsals, but she knew her true test would be her Friday night debut.

As on the previous Friday, Jessie e-mailed another article to the *Syracuse Herald.* Again, she received a note back from Len Richards, complimenting Brennan's work.

Ten

Early that Friday, Rachel received a mysterious voice mail from Jessie. "Hi Rachel. It's Jessie. We need to talk. Meet me at the Westchester Marriot, in the bar, five o'clock."

Rachel arrived at the specified time, which coincided with happy hour and the bar was jammed. Jessie was no place to be found. Rachel waited at an unoccupied table.

Within minutes, a man approached Rachel. "Excuse me," he said. "I'm supposed to meet someone here. One of those electronic blind dates. . . . You wouldn't happen to be her, would you?" The man was stylishly dressed in a black, pin-striped suit.

"No. I'm not her," Rachel said.

"I'm sorry to bother you." Politely, the attractive man retreated to a nearby table.

Rachel ordered a drink. She withdrew a notepad from her purse and tried to review notes on a story she was working on. But the music blared and voices soared, making it difficult to concentrate. Consequently, her eyes wandered around the bar, and she found herself people watching. She noticed the man in the black, pin-striped suit nearby. When he caught her stare, Rachel shyly averted her eyes.

She drained her wine and glanced at her watch. It had been thirty minutes, and still no sign of Jessie. This didn't seem like Jessie. But then again, she hadn't known her very long. She glanced at her phone. There were no messages.

"Hi, beautiful." A man slipped into the seat across from Rachel, not giving her a chance to object. He appeared to be in his mid-twenties.

Rachel smiled at the man. "I'm saving that seat."

"I'm Paul and I've been watching you. If he hasn't arrived yet, he's not coming."

Published by The Haworth Press, Inc., 2006. All rights reserved.
doi:10.1300/5721_11

"I don't mean to be rude, but I'm trying to do a little work," Rachel opened up her notebook and picked up a pen.

"Come on, it's happy hour. Why don't you play for a while?" Paul asked.

"Excuse me, I don't mean to interrupt." The man in the black suit had moved to the table again. "You *are* Rachel, right?"

She gazed at the man. "Yes."

"I *am* supposed to meet you. Didn't you get the message from Jessie?"

"No."

He turned to Paul. "Would you excuse us?"

Paul stood eye-to-eye with the stranger, then turned to Rachel, "See you later."

The man slid into the seat across from Rachel and she couldn't take her eyes off of him. He had intriguing eyes: deep blue with long lashes. Although there was something familiar about him, she couldn't figure it out. "I didn't get a message. Who are you?" she asked coldly.

"A friend," he said mysteriously. "I think I can help find out who killed Steve."

Rachel eyed the man suspiciously. "How do you know Jessie? Where is she? Who are you?"

He grinned, slightly. "Let's start over." He offered Rachel his hand. Just as their hands met, he introduced himself. "I'm Brennan Keller. It's nice to meet you."

It took Rachel a few seconds to process the name *Brennan Keller.* When the epiphany hit, her mouth opened, revealing her shock. Her eyes roamed from Brennan's eyes, to the familiar scar, to his wide shoulders and chest. "What the hell are you doing?" she whispered, her voice lost in the noise of the bar.

"So, what do you think?" Jessie asked in Brennan's low voice.

"I think you're nuts. What are you doing?"

"I'm going to be a Mason."

"You're going to get yourself killed," Rachel said. "I told you what Steve told me. You won't make it through the first initiation."

Jessie leaned closer so that she didn't have to talk so loudly. "I found a way to circumvent the first three initiations." Jessie passed a folded paper to Rachel.

Rachel opened and read the letter Jessie had written. She shook her head, eyeing Jessie with skepticism. "This is too dangerous. Why are you doing this?"

"I owe it to Steve to find out what happened to him."

"You know your brother would never approve of this."

Jessie was careful not to put too much emotion into her voice. "No woman has ever become a Mason. My brother has set me up with an alias, IDs, credit, real estate, even a profession that I can do. I can't pass on this."

"So, you're looking for a story!" Rachel lashed out.

Jessie was surprised by how much Rachel's words hurt. Her eyes met Rachel's. "Aren't you?"

The women stared at each other, each stubbornly not budging. Jessie finally spoke. "I'm willing to give up the rest of the year to find out what happened to Steve and learn about Freemasonry."

"You just want the story. I've been working on this for over a year, now."

"Rachel, I write novels. I don't report the news. Don't you think there's enough here for the two of us to use? Maybe we can approach this from different angles. I'd be happy to share information with you."

"And you expect me to share my information?"

Jessie sighed. This was not the reaction she had expected from Rachel. Perhaps she had overestimated Rachel's friendship with her brother. *She was Steve's friend. She's not mine.* Jessie scratched her goatee. The feel of the facial hair was foreign to her. "Rachel, what would you do if you were in my shoes?"

"That's not a fair question."

"Okay. What if I said I would give you Brennan Keller? Could you play him? Would you be willing to sacrifice the rest of the year to infiltrate the Masons?" As Jessie said it, she wondered herself. *Am I willing to make that much of a sacrifice?*

Rachel analyzed Jessie's portrayal of Brennan—his stylish short hair, trimmed goatee, and thick eyebrows. Brennan sat with broad shoulders and his legs apart. When he spoke, his voice was low, with no feminine character. Jessie had completely fooled her.

Rachel shook her head no. "I don't think I could make those sacrifices," she admitted. "I still think it's too dangerous, Jess," she softened.

Jessie smiled, and then quickly covered the goatee, concealing the grin. "I need to work on that."

Eleven

The following week, Jessie telephoned Gary Stonewall. Her heart pounded faster than usual and her stomach churned as she waited for Stonewall to answer.

"This is Stonewall," he said.

"Worshipful Master, this is Brennan Keller," she said in a low tone.

"Hello, Brennan. I received the referral letter from California yesterday. Are you in New York, already?"

"Yes, I was hoping we could set up a time to meet."

That Thursday evening, Jessie drove to the White Plains Blue Lodge. As she approached the temple, she realized that she was walking in her customary manner. She faltered a bit, remembering that she was dressed as Brennan, and adjusted her stride.

Tiny barred windows with blinds prohibited her from glimpsing the inside of the temple. The building's cold appearance amplified the unpleasant feeling she had in the pit of her stomach.

Jessie opened the heavy door and entered the temple. Her vision was immediately drawn to the black-and-white checkered floor beneath her black wing tips.

"Can I help you?" a man at a receptionist desk asked.

"Yes." She cleared her throat. "I'm Brennan Keller and I have an appointment with Gary Stonewall." Mindful of her walk, she strolled to the desk.

"The Worshipful Master is in the Lodge room. He's expecting you." The man pointed to a door near him.

Hoping her anxiety was inconspicuous, she moved to the door. Based on the information she had studied, she suspected that Stonewall would interrogate her. Jessie knew it was critical to find the altar

Published by The Haworth Press, Inc., 2006. All rights reserved.
doi:10.1300/5721_12

and assess the position of the compass. This would determine how she was expected to greet him. Her hand froze on the knob. She took a deep breath, trying to settle her nerves, and opened the door.

Faint lights adorned the walls and the dimness intensified the ominous feeling in her gut. A stone altar stood in the center of the room. The ceiling was dark and when Jessie's eyes adjusted, she realized that the ceiling was blue. *Is that why it's called a Blue Lodge?* Gary Stonewall's back was to Jessie as he arranged items on the altar. As she advanced, she saw him adjust a compass so that its points were above a square. *Both points above—the Lodge is open to the third degree!* She knew she was expected to salute him with the sign of a Master Mason.

Without warning, Stonewall abruptly turned. "Are you a Master Mason?"

Jessie's heart beat harder. "I am," she said as she approached.

"What induced you to become a Master Mason?"

Jessie froze; she stood speechless. A wave of nausea hit and she feared that she was going to give back her dinner.

"What induced you to become a Master Mason?" Stonewall barked.

She recalled the Master Mason examination she had found on an anti-Masonic Web site. She had rehearsed it repeatedly over the past week. Now when she needed to perform best, she couldn't move.

"Jessie, you can do this," a voice echoed in her head. "Just relax."

Jessie hadn't heard that little voice in such a long time. It sounded foreign to her, and yet, it was comforting. She took a deep breath and began. "That I might obtain the Master's word . . . travel to foreign countries, work, and receive Master's wages, and be thereby better enabled to support myself and family, and contribute to the relief of distressed worthy Master Masons, their widows and orphans."

Stonewall was silent. Then, as if considering his prey before an attack, the stocky man circled around his victim. "What makes you a Master Mason?"

Jessie feared that Stonewall was suspicious. "My Obligation," she answered.

"Where were you made a Master Mason?"

"Within the body of a just and duly constituted Lodge of Master Masons, assembled in a place representing the Sanctum Sanctorum of King Solomon's Temple."

"How may I know you to be a Master Mason?"

"By certain signs and tokens." Her confidence grew.

Stonewall approached Brennan from behind. "What are signs?"

"Right angles, horizontals, and perpendiculars."

"Advance a sign. Has it an allusion?"

"It has; to the position of my hands while taking the Obligation." She extended her hands, palm down. Jessie knew that the initiate's hands were placed on a square, compass, and Bible while taking the Master Mason oath.

"Have you a further sign?"

"I have," Jessie answered with poise.

"Has that an allusion?"

"It has, to the penalty of the Obligation." Her hands were still extended from the due guard and abruptly her left hand fell. She placed her right hand palm down, near her waist on her left side. With her thumb pointing toward her body, she quickly brushed the digit crossways as if severing her body, and then her hand rested by her side. Unaware of what the gestures meant, Jessie mechanically performed them as she had memorized from the Saints Alive in Jesus Web site.

"What are tokens?"

"Certain friendly or brotherly grips whereby one Mason may know another in the dark as in the light."

"Advance and give me a token," Stonewall ordered.

Jessie shook Stonewall's hand. She wrapped her thumb and pinky finger around the edges of his hand, while the remaining fingertips dug into the inside of Stonewall's wrist.

"What is that?" he asked.

"The pass-grip of a Master Mason."

"Has it a name?"

Jessie played out what she thought to be a silly dialogue where she eventually offered the name of the pass-grip, "Tubalcain!"

"Will you be off or from?" Stonewall asked.

"From."

"From what, and to what?"

"From the pass-grip of a Master Mason to the real grip of the same."

"Pass. What is that?"

"The real grip of a Master Mason, or lion's paw."

"Has it a name?"

"It has."

"Will you give it to me?"

"Place yourself in the proper position to receive it and I will."

"What is the proper position to receive it?"

"On the five points of fellowship," Jessie answered.

"What are the five points of fellowship?"

Jessie's right foot stepped alongside Stonewall's; instep-to-instep, her knee was against his and their chests converged. Jessie felt sweat dribble beneath her bodysuit. Her lips approached Stonewall's ear and he laid his hand on Jessie's back. "Foot-to-foot, knee-to-knee, breast-to-breast . . ." The contact with Stonewall distracted her and she lost her place.

"What are the five points of fellowship?" Stonewall repeated.

"Foot-to-foot, knee-to-knee, breast-to-breast, hand-to-back, and cheek-to-cheek, or mouth-to-ear." She paused, and then she whispered, "Ma."

"Ha," Stonewall added.

"Bone," she finished.

Stonewall receded and silently stared at Brennan with scrutinizing eyes. Jessie calmly waited for a reaction. She could feel the perspiration form on her facial hair.

Then, Stonewall grinned. He extended his hand and gave Brennan the pass-grip. "Brother Keller, I presume."

Jessie nodded. "Yes, Worshipful Master."

"Come, let's talk." Stonewall left the Lodge room with Brennan on his heels.

Jessie could feel her pulse slow down as she followed him. With a handkerchief, she wiped the perspiration from around her goatee and fake eyebrows. *I think it worked.* She breathed easier as she followed Stonewall into the lobby, down a hall and into an office with a nameplate WORSHIPFUL MASTER—STEVE MERCER.

"Take a seat," Stonewall pointed to a chair across from a large desk. "So, I understand you're from the West Coast."

"Yes, the LA area."

"What's bringing you here?"

"My parents are upstate. They're getting older. It's best that I'm closer."

"What do you do for a living, Brennan?"

"I write. To help with the East Coast transition, I've been freelancing with the *Syracuse Herald* the last year. But I'd like to get into one of the Westchester or New York City papers. Upstate New York is a bit quiet for me."

"Are you married?"

Jessie shook her head. "No. Never married."

"Girlfriend?"

"Not at the present."

"A good-looking man like yourself—are you gay or something?"

Jessie was surprised by Stonewall's directness. She was careful not to smile too much. "I assure you, Worshipful Master, I am quite attracted to the ladies."

"You can call me Gary."

"I noticed there was another name on the door."

"Yes. Steve Mercer. A fine man, he passed away . . . five weeks ago. A new nameplate is being made as we speak. So, are you settled in the metro area?"

"Not yet. I want to find a more permanent position before I move. In the meantime, I'm staying upstate."

"Have you applied to *The Empire*? They're the second largest New York paper."

"No. Reporting is a new profession for me. I'm not sure a large paper would be interested because of my limited experience. I was thinking of trying to get into the Westchester weekly paper."

"To hell with the little paper," Stonewall picked up a pen and started writing. "I know someone at *The Empire*." He handed Brennan the paper. "His name is Clark Coburn. He's the managing editor. Call him. Tell him I suggested that you call."

"Thanks. I'll do that."

"Are you considering the Scottish or York Rite, or are you just looking for a Blue Lodge?"

"I'm interested in the Scottish Rite."

"I'll be happy to provide you the degree schedule for the Northern Masonic Jurisdiction. Next time you come in, I'll set you up." Stonewall stood, suggesting the meeting was over. "It was nice to meet you, Brennan. I wish you luck."

Jessie stood and extended her hands palm down. She knew she was expected to perform the due-guard when entering and leaving. Abruptly, she dropped her left hand to her side, and mechanically performed the gestures again.

Minutes later Jessie was in the Mustang. She exhaled. *My God, it worked. I'm a Master Mason.* She turned the ignition key, and proceeded for the throughway. Jessie was excited and wanted to share the experience with someone. She removed her phone from the suit-jacket pocket and punched in a number.

"Hello," Rachel answered.

"It worked," Jessie said. "I'm a Mason."

"Congratulations. They didn't suspect?"

"I don't think so."

"Be careful."

Considering her next move, Jessie sipped her coffee at the kitchen table. She stared at the business card that Stonewall had given her the previous night. She flipped it repeatedly between her fingers. Then, she moved to the wall and lifted the phone handset. Jessie decided to use the cabin phone whenever she impersonated Brennan, reserving her cell phone for her life as Jessie.

She hit "0" on the handset and waited for the operator to answer. "Hello, can you tell me the number I'm calling from?"

Moments later she punched in the numbers that she read from the card. She left a voice mail. "Hello, this is Brennan Keller. Gary Stonewall suggested that I call; my phone number is . . ."

Fifteen minutes later, the cabin's phone rang. Jessie cleared her throat. "Hello."

"Hi, is this Brennan Keller?" a woman asked.

"Yes, it is."

"This is Cindy Palmer. I'm Clark Coburn's administrative assistant, from *The Empire*. He asked that I call to set up an interview Monday morning."

An interview? I didn't leave a message why I had called. "What time is convenient for Mr. Coburn?"

"Ten o'clock."

The Empire's headquarters was in Yonkers, off the Deagan Expressway. The contemporary office building reflected sunlight from its mirrorlike windows. The reflective siding reminded Jessie of mirrored sunglasses—from the inside you could people watch without them being aware of it.

It was close to ten o'clock when Brennan entered the lobby. The receptionist handed him a visitor's pass and suggested that he wait for Mr. Coburn's assistant.

Within minutes, a pretty blonde woman greeted him. "Brennan Keller? I'm Cindy Palmer," she shook his hand and smiled flirtatiously, batting her long eyelashes. "Mr. Coburn asked me to escort you to his office."

Jessie resisted smiling, fearing it would reveal her femininity. She forced her eyes away from Cindy's to a familiar checkered floor pattern. *Where have I seen a checkered floor recently?* Then she remembered it was at the Blue Lodge.

Cindy led Brennan into an elevator, and when the doors parted they were at the heart of a newsroom. Dozens of tiny cubicles centered the area while private offices lined the perimeter of the building. People hustled about, phones rang, and printers spewed out paper. Jessie wondered how people could work in such a noisy setting.

Brennan followed Cindy, bordering the activity, to a corner office door. She turned to Brennan. "Well, it was nice to meet you, Brennan," she smiled.

"Likewise."

She knocked gently, and opened the door when a muffled voice from inside welcomed her. A distinguished looking man with gray hair sat behind his desk. He stood as Brennan entered, and Cindy quickly closed the door.

Jessie approached the man and extended her hand. As she shook his hand, his grip quickly changed to the pass-grip of a Master Mason, and Jessie's grasp conformed accordingly.

Clark Coburn's expressionless eyes were fixed on Brennan's. Jessie finally broke the silence. "It's a pleasure meeting you, Mr. Coburn."

"Call me Clark." He released Brennan's hand, and gestured at a chair. "Please, have a seat."

"Thank you for providing me this opportunity to visit with you." Jessie crossed her legs, but soon realized what she had done and shifted in her seat.

"I like your work," Clark said unexpectedly. "I particularly like the last few articles. I understand you're looking for employment in the metro area."

"That's correct."

"We just happen to have a reporter position available. You would need to relocate to the metro area. Commuting from upstate wouldn't be practical. We offer competitive salaries and benefits." Clark scribbled on a piece of paper, folded it, and passed it to Brennan.

Jessie opened the paper and read the figure. She knew it was more than competitive. "That's a very generous offer."

"We take care of *our kind* at *The Empire.*" For the first time, Clark smiled. "Do you need anything from me?"

"If the terms are agreeable, just let Cindy know your start date."

Apparently, Clark Coburn had checked out Brennan Keller's professional background after Gary Stonewall had called about his visit. Nobody ever questioned his sexuality, and everything fell into place. Brennan was welcomed at the White Plains Blue Lodge, and now he had a position with *The Empire,* which connected him to other Freemasons. He rented an apartment in Hartsdale, offering an easy commute to *The Empire,* the Blue Lodge, and New York City.

Twelve

It was going on seven-thirty and Jessie was returning from work. With two handfuls of shopping bags, she made her way into the garden apartment. Quickly, she emptied the bags and put the groceries away. She was exhausted, and couldn't wait to get out of Brennan's attire. She methodically pulled the blinds in every room, ending in her bedroom.

In a flash, she stripped. First the suit jacket, tie, dress shirt and pants came off. Systematically she removed the padded bodysuit, padded insert, and then unwound the Ace bandage from around her chest. She cupped her now sore breasts in her hands, trying to relieve the discomfort. Then she slipped on a T-shirt and sweatpants.

At the mirror she removed her contacts, then peeled off the goatee and eyebrows. Where the facial hair attached, her skin was blotchy. Jessie studied the red blemishes. *Am I going to be able to do this?*

A small bedroom was set up as an office. She turned on the computer. Each evening she looked forward to seeing if Taylor had e-mailed her. The couple had fallen into a routine of a weekly telephone call and e-mailing each other a few times a week. Jessie spotted the flashing light from the answering machine on the desk and she pressed "play."

"Hello, Brennan, this is Gary Stonewall. There's a Master Mason initiation tomorrow night at seven o'clock. We need a Wayfaring Man for the reenactment of Hiram Abiff. You'd only have a couple lines. Call me and let me know if you can do it."

"Can I do it?" Jessie asked. "Where did I put the reenactment?" She moved to the small filing cabinet where she retrieved a script she had found on the Internet. She skimmed through it. "I can do this," she tried to convince herself. Jessie picked up the handset and called the Lodge. "Is the Worshipful Master in?" she asked in her normal voice. The call was transferred.

Published by The Haworth Press, Inc., 2006. All rights reserved.
doi:10.1300/5721_13

A couple minutes later, Stonewall sounded baffled. "Sally?"
Jessie froze. She realized that she had called in her regular voice. *Shit!*
"Sally, are you there?"
Jessie spoke in Brennan's low tone. "This is Keller."
"Keller? Mathew told me a woman was on the line. . . . I assumed it
was my wife."
     "Sorry to disappoint you. You can count me in tomorrow night."
She bit her lip as she hung up the phone. "I have to be more careful."

     Jessie arrived at the Lodge that evening just before seven o'clock.
As she signed in at the reception desk, she noticed a compass and
square on the wall. Both points of the compass were above the square,
indicating that the Lodge was open only to Master Masons. Jessie sa-
luted Stonewall with the due-guard and sign of the Master Mason, as
he approached.
     "Keller, let me introduce you to the others before we begin. Follow
me!"
     Stonewall led Brennan downstairs to a sitting area where eight men
mingled. Here, Brennan was introduced to the men. The names became a blur to her. Most of them were called by a title, like Worshipful
Master, Senior and Junior Deacon, Senior and Junior Warden. Opposite the sitting area, long, black, hooded robes hung from lockerlike
compartments. The men moved into the dressing area where they
stripped away their apparel, down to their underwear.
     Jessie averted her eyes from the partially naked men. She removed
her suit jacket and tie, hung them from a hook, and slipped on the
hooded robe.
     "Keller, you're going to be hot!"
     Jessie turned toward the voice. The Junior Warden stood wearing
only flamboyant boxers. He slipped a robe over his head concealing
his hairy chest and large belly.
     "I'll be fine," Brennan responded.
     Nine men and Jessie moved into the dim Lodge room. Tonight,
only scattered candles lighted the area. The Worshipful Master, Senior

Warden, Junior Warden, Chaplain, Junior Deacon, and Senior Deacon took their places near the altar, while the others moved to the side.

There was a cyclic opening ceremony where passwords were requested to ensure that only Master Masons were present. Then duties of the primary participants were identified. The chaplain prayed to the Great Architect of the Universe, and they all finished with the Pledge of Allegiance.

The opening was quite repetitive and monotonous. Jessie was bored. Uncomfortably warm beneath the heavy robe, she had difficulties keeping her eyes open, and found herself nodding off. Then the initiation began, and Stonewall called upon everyone to participate.

"How should a brother be prepared for the Third Degree of Freemasonry?" Stonewall asked the brothers.

"By being divested of metallic substances," the brothers chanted. "Neither naked nor clothed, barefoot, both knees and breasts bare, hood winked, and with a cable-tow three times around the body, clothed as a Fellow Craft."

Jessie mumbled lightly, trying to appear as if she knew what she was doing. She almost gasped though, when the candidate for initiation appeared in the doorway. He wore pajama-like bottoms that were rolled up above the knees. He was barefoot, and naked from the waist up, with a blue rope wrapped around his body. Blindfolded, he was directed to the center of the room by the Junior Warden.

Jessie was far from bored now. Panic gripped her. She realized that a woman wouldn't make it through a ceremony. For a moment, she wasn't sure if she was fearful of being discovered or the unknown of the ceremony, or perhaps both.

The Senior Deacon approached the candidate. "Brother Henry, when first you entered a Lodge of Free and Accepted Masons, you were received on the point of a sharp instrument piercing your naked left breast. On your second entrance, you were received on the angle of a square applied to your naked right breast.

"I am now commanded to receive you on the extreme points of the compasses, extending from your naked right to your naked left breast," the Senior Deacon held the compass high for all to see the sharp points. "Which is to teach you that as within the breast are contained the most vital parts of man, so between the extreme points of the compasses are contained the most valuable tenets of Freemasonry, which are Friendship, Morality, and Brotherly Love." He abruptly stuck the sharp points into the blindfolded man's chest.

The candidate winced, and blood trickled down his chest.

Jessie couldn't believe that he actually plunged the points into the man's chest!

The ceremony continued with the Chaplain praying. Then the candidate was bestowed the Master Mason password and the Senior Deacon helped him get in position to take the oath. He knelt on bare knees, his body erect. His legs awkwardly formed the shape of a square, while his hands lay on top of the square and compass, and beneath that was the Bible.

The candidate began his oath. "To all of which I do solemnly and sincerely promise and swear, without any hesitation . . ."

Jessie was lost in thought. She couldn't comprehend how Steve was involved in this group. Did she even know her brother? She wondered where this journey would end, and then the candidate's voice brought her back.

"Binding myself under no less a penalty than that of having my body severed in twain, my bowels taken thence, and with my body burned to ashes, and the ashes thereof scattered to the four winds of Heaven."

It hit her. Only then Jessie grasped the sign of the Master Mason. When she ran her thumb across her abdomen, she was gesturing having her body severed in two.

After the candidate's lengthy blood oath, in which he promised not to reveal the secrets of Freemasonry, he kissed the Bible. Constrained by the oath, the Senior Deacon removed the blue rope from his waist. The participants, including Jessie, encircled him.

"Brother Henry," Stonewall began. "In your present situation, what do you most desire?"

To get the hell out of here, Jessie thought.

"Further light in Masonry," the candidate said.

"Let the Brother be brought to light."

Simultaneously, the Senior Deacon yanked off the hoodwink, the overhead lights blinded Henry, and the participants surrounding him clapped in unison. Jessie quickly adapted to the rhythm and joined in the crescendo.

Henry was shown the sign, due-guard, and the pass-grip. Then the Senior Warden instructed him how to wear his apron. "My Brother, you have already been informed that at the building of King Solomon's Temple, the different bands of workmen were distinguished by the manner in which they wore their aprons. Master Masons wore theirs turned down in the form of a square to designate them as Master Masons or overseers of the work."

After his instructions, the candidate left the Lodge room with the Junior Warden. When he returned, Henry was dressed in street clothes with his apron fitted properly and a plumb emblem hung around his neck. Unaware of things to come, he appeared calm now, less nervous, and smiling. But that would quickly change.

The participants, including Jessie, took their places around Henry. Henry was asked to remove his possessions from his pockets, and he was once again blindfolded.

"My Brother," the Senor Deacon instructed, "heretofore you have represented a candidate in search of Light, now you represent a character, none less a personage than our Grand Master Hiram Abiff, Grand Architect at the building of King Solomon's Temple."

Everyone participated in the enactment. Here, Henry played Hiram Abiff, architect of King Solomon's temple, but the Senior Deacon spoke the script of the character. The man was led around the Lodge room, blindfolded. He stumbled and struggled to understand the meaning of the words. In the legend, Hiram Abiff had promised to reveal the mysteries of the Master Mason to the workers when the temple was completed. In the script, three Masons portraying Ruffians approached Henry, and demanded that he reveal the secret word of the Master Mason.

The Junior Warden played the first Ruffian. He grabbed Henry roughly by his collar and shook him. ". . . I therefore demand of you the secrets of a Master Mason."

The Senior Deacon spoke for Henry. "Wait until the temple is finished and then you will have the secrets of a Master Mason."

The Junior Warden asked three times for the secret word. Each time, the Senior Deacon refused, and each time the Junior Warden became more violent. After the Senior Deacon declined the third time, the Junior Warden picked up a twenty-four-inch rod and struck Henry across the throat.

Jessie's heart beat wildly. She never expected the reenactment to include physical violence. Henry fell to the ground clinging to his throat. The Senior Deacon picked him up to face the second Ruffian.

The second Ruffian asked him the same question, three times. And each time, the Senior Deacon refused to cooperate and more cruelty was focused on Henry. The second Ruffian concluded with striking Henry's chest with a square. He stumbled, but the Senior Deacon kept him on his feet.

The last Ruffian repeated the questions. Henry fell blindly to the floor after the Ruffian slapped him. The Senior Deacon picked Henry up again, but panic had gripped him. The man was visibly distressed, fearful and in pain.

Other steward members opened a large canvas behind him.

What the hell are they doing? Jessie wondered.

The Ruffian grabbed Henry violently. From where Jessie stood, she saw the man's saliva spray upon Henry's face as he yelled at him. "Grand Master Hiram, I for the third and last time demand of you the secrets of a Master Mason."

Fearing for his life, light sobbing escaped from Henry's lips and he cowered and held his arms out to protect himself.

The Senior Deacon spoke for Henry. "And I, for the third time, refuse you."

The Ruffian picked up a setting maul and held it up for all to see, except Henry. "If you will not give me the secret word of a Master Mason, then die." Just as he said the word *die* the third Ruffian pounded the maul into Henry's forehead. Henry fell unconscious into the canvas.

Jessie was shocked. Her world was spinning and nausea hit. Without thinking she stepped out of place to see Henry. In that moment his hand moved to his forehead, and he moaned. He was alive. But just then, Jessie realized everyone was staring at her. She took a step back and composed herself.

The rest of the enactment was a blur. Lost in her own thoughts, Jessie almost missed her cue to say the three lines as the Wayfaring man. After the performance, there was a repetitive lecture on Masonic symbols. Hours after the initiation began, it ended with Henry as the newest member of the Master Masons, and everyone crowded around him to congratulate him.

After the ceremony Jessie fled to the lounge where she removed her robe. As an excuse for her baffling behavior, she mentioned how hot she was under the robe. She was actually ill; all she wanted to do was get out of the Lodge, but as she passed through the lobby she ran into Gary Stonewall.

"I was hoping I'd see you before you left," he said. I have the schedule for the Scottish Rite degrees."

"Great," Jessie lied. The last thing she wanted to do was review the schedule, but she did. The initiations were spread out over the tristate area. There were two reunions, one in the fall and one in the spring. "Thank you, Worshipful Master."

"Are you okay?" Stonewall eyed Brennan suspiciously. "You look pale. During the enactment you looked upset."

"Upset? No," Jessie smirked. "I didn't have time for dinner, and I got this low blood sugar thing going. I got a little lightheaded."

Back at the apartment, the silence haunted her. She was lonely. It had been close to one week since she had spoken with Taylor, and she missed her terribly. Jessie was looking forward to picking up Maxwell from the airport the following afternoon. Earlier that week she had made arrangements with Alison to have Maxwell flown out to a friend, Brennan Keller.

As Jessie climbed into her bed that night, her mind replayed the Master Mason initiation. She knew she would be in trouble if the Scottish Rite degrees had similar initiations. No wonder mauls, squares, and compasses came to her in her dreams. At first there was only darkness, then images came slowly, then more quickly, until they changed into geometric signs. Signs that Jessie would not have understood . . .

⁓

She walked the dark temple courtyard. It was lit only by the moonlight from the moon god, Thoth. Jessie was apprehensive; her pace quickened. She thought she heard footsteps near the columns, and stopped. "Mark?" she called out. "Is that you?"

She saw the curved metallic blade gleaming in the moonlight, and Mark Rutledge stepped from the shadows. A sinister smile dressed his lips as he advanced.

He raised the sword above his head. "You have broken your oath. For that, you shall pay with your life." He swung the sword severing her in two.

⁓

"No!" Jessie screamed, waking from her nightmare. Her hand felt her abdomen for blood. "My God. . . . It was too real." Jessie recalled the nightmare she had had right before Taylor left on her tour. They were so similar. Jessie's heart pounded wildly. She sat up, wide eyed, analyzing why she had dreamed of Taylor's former personal manager, Mark Rutledge.

Thirteen

The following evening after work, Jessie drove to LaGuardia and picked up Maxwell. The cat was still groggy from the air travel drugs and slept in the pet carrier all the way back to the Hartsdale apartment. He started meowing when Jessie pulled the carrier from the car. Speaking in Brennan's pitch, she consoled Maxwell as she passed one of her neighbors outside her apartment.

Once in the apartment, Jessie opened the small cage. The feline sauntered from the carrier, and as he stretched his front paws, his hindquarters rose. The cat glanced at Jessie, uninterested, then turned to explore the apartment.

Her disguise had fooled her cat. "Maxwell? It's me." The cat eyed Jessie with curiosity and drew closer. She hadn't pulled the window treatments yet, so she looked around, assuring that she was out of sight, then sat on the floor near the feline. She removed the goatee, and the cat purred and rubbed his chin up against her body.

Jessie had been looking forward to her reunion with Maxwell, but bringing the cat to New York backfired. Rather than bringing her comfort, she realized just how lonesome she was. It had been almost two months since Steve had been murdered, and a little more since Taylor had set out on tour. Jessie had ceased contact with most people, and the few she continued communications with were mostly by e-mail. Once a month, she would touch base with her editor. Although the publisher was waiting for her next book, they were supportive when she told them that she was taking time off and wouldn't have anything until the end of the year. Isolation was just one of her sacrifices to infiltrate Freemasonry, but she was starting to wonder if it was worth it.

Published by The Haworth Press, Inc., 2006. All rights reserved.
doi:10.1300/5721_14

Jessie had long shed her masquerade and was ready to hop in bed. Feeling alone, she picked up her cell phone, and punched in the numbers. She hadn't spoken with Rachel in about a month.

"Hello," Rachel whispered.

"I'm sorry. Did I wake you up?"

"Who is this?" Rachel's voice was groggy.

Jessie had been disguising her voice for so long, she had forgotten to speak naturally. "I'm sorry. It's Jessie," she said in her normal voice.

"Are you okay? What time is it?"

Jessie felt awkward calling and didn't realize how late it was. "Sorry about the time. I was wondering if we could get together this weekend for dinner. . . . I'd like to catch up. I'm going up to Jewett Friday night. Perhaps we can meet at the cabin. I'll cook dinner."

It was three o'clock that Saturday when the Saab's tires rolled to a standstill beside the cabin's porch. As Rachel approached the front entry she remembered her time there with Steve, and for a moment a wave of loss troubled her. She paused for a moment in the July heat, composed herself, and then knocked on the screen door.

"Who's there?" a masculine voice asked from inside the house.

"It's Rachel."

Jessie opened the door. "Come on in," she said as she surveyed the outside. Dressed in shorts and a tank top, her outfit lacked Brennan's bodysuit and facial hair.

"Are you finally coming to your senses and returning to womanhood?"

"I have thought about it, but no. I needed a day away from facial hair and breast harnesses. And my body armor needed a good cleaning."

Rachel shook her head. "I don't know how you do it."

"What would you like to drink? There's wine, beer, or lemonade."

"Chardonnay would be great."

The women moved outside to a patio area off the living room. A picnic table was already set. Although trees and shrubs camouflaged the area, infrequently a car was heard from the road and Jessie would be watchful.

"I have to admit—I've had a tough week and wondered if all this is worth it."

"What have you been up to?" Rachel sliced a piece of cheese to top her cracker.

"I have an apartment in Hartsdale and Brennan has a job at *The Empire.* I'm a reporter."

"How'd you manage that? From everything I've heard they're difficult to get into."

"It was the easiest job I've ever gotten, and all because the managing editor is a Mason!"

"Did he tell you that?"

"No. Believe it or not, there *is* a secret handshake that identifies a person as a Mason."

A thump from inside the cabin got the women's attention. Seconds later, Maxwell pawed at the screen door and Jessie opened it. The cat sauntered over to Rachel.

"When did you get a cat?" Rachel scratched under his chin, instantly winning his affection.

"This is Maxwell. I developed a massive case of homesickness, so I arranged to have him flown out from California." Jessie sipped her wine.

"I'm sure you *are* homesick. Are you in touch with your family through this?"

"Steve was the only biological family I had. Our parents passed away when I was a teenager."

"I'm sorry, I remember Steve mentioned that. How about friends? Have you left a boyfriend behind in California?"

It hit Jessie that Rachel didn't know that she was gay. "I'm sorry, Rachel, I thought you knew this. I'm gay."

"Oh. . . . No, I didn't know."

"I do have a girlfriend, but she's on tour. I haven't seen her since May. She doesn't have a clue what I'm doing."

"On tour? What does she do?"

"She's a singer."

"Can I ask who it is?"

Jessie reminded herself that she was talking to a reporter. "Off the record?"

"Of course."

"It's Taylor Andrews."

"Really? And she doesn't know what you're doing?"

"No. She's overseas, and will be traveling through January. I told her that I'm staying in New York to wrap up Steve's estate. I've mentioned that I'm suspicious about his death, but that's pretty much it. It's getting more difficult not sharing any of this."

"Why don't you tell her?"

Jessie appeared thoughtful. "If this backfires, I don't want her to get hurt."

"You'll have to say something eventually, after all, what about your hair?"

Jessie sighed. "I'm hoping I can wrap this up and start growing it out before I see her again. We had plans for me to meet her in Europe over Thanksgiving. I can't imagine that I'm going to be able to do it, though."

"So, you got a case of homesickness. What else happened that was so bad?"

"I participated in a Master Mason initiation. It was probably the most dehumanizing experience I have ever had."

"What happened?" Rachel was sincerely curious.

"The candidate is blindfolded and brought into the Lodge room half-naked."

"Half-naked?"

"Yes. But that's not the worst of it. The two sharp ends of a compass are stabbed into the candidate's chest while he's blindfolded. Apparently, during the first and second initiations, they stab a compass and square into the candidate's chest, also."

"That's why your brother said I wouldn't have gotten through the first three initiations."

"That's not the worst of it. They do a reenactment of the legend of Hiram Abiff. And during this play, the candidate is struck on his throat with a stick, on the chest with a square, and then in the head with a hammer."

"Are you serious?"

"My God, Rachel, I felt so helpless. When they hit him in the head, the man fell unconscious. Before I knew what I was doing I left my position to see if he was okay. Thank God, he was, but everyone just stared at me."

"I take it you didn't blow your cover?"

"I don't think so. But I did have to make up some excuse about my behavior. I keep wondering what I'm getting into. I'm going into the Scottish Rite in a couple of months. Although none of my research suggests it, I'm afraid that I'm going to be put in a situation where I'll need to strip. Then, I'm afraid that I'll have to memorize more hand-shakes or passwords," Jessie smiled at her humor. "But you know what I wonder about the most?" She became serious.

Rachel shook her head.

"I thought I knew my brother. It just blows my mind that he was involved in this undignified group."

"I wouldn't be so quick to question your brother. He didn't trust them for well over a year before he got killed. I'm sure that's why he set up his alias. It was as if he knew he might need to drop out of sight. Your brother was a very sharp man. By the way, who's Hiram Abiff?"

"He was the architect of King Solomon's Temple. Supposedly, he was a Master Mason who promised to reveal the secrets of Freema-sonry to his workers when the temple was completed. Apparently, he was killed before he could pass on whatever secrets he held."

"King Solomon's Temple? That's where the Ark of the Covenant was buried." Rachel was thoughtful. "I got an anonymous letter three . . . maybe four months ago suggesting that I do a story on the ark. I never pursued it. But I remember the letter was accompanied by an article about the fact that there are *two* arks."

"How could there be two?"

"From what I remember . . . God gave Moses the first two tablets on Mount Sinai and Moses got angry and supposedly broke them. The broken tablets were placed in a golden ark, while two other tab-lets were stored in a wooden ark. From what I remember, the golden ark went to battle and eventually disappeared into Egypt, while the wooden ark was hidden under the Temple of Solomon."

"Interesting." Jessie was reminded of her recent dreams about ancient Egypt. *Coincidence?* "Freemasonry has been linked to ancient Egypt. Do you still have the article?"

"I think so. I'll look for it on Monday."

"How often do you get anonymous suggestions like that?"

Rachel appeared thoughtful. "Come to think of it—that was the only one I received that I thought had any merit. The timing just wasn't good for me to pursue it."

Jessie glanced at her watch. "Let me put the chicken on." She went inside and returned with a plate. She placed marinated chicken breasts on the grill.

"I've been meaning to ask you. . . . Don't you think it's strange that before your brother died you had been researching secret societies and conspiracy theories, then he's murdered, and here you are perhaps wrapped up in one yourself?"

Jessie's eyes met Rachel's. "Yes. What a coincidence. . . . The thought has crossed my mind."

"But Jessie, you know there's no such thing as a coincidence," the voice in her head blurted out. *"Most people don't understand coincidence. Coincidence is the act of coinciding, Jessie. It is a state of synchronicity, of harmony. Never brush anything off as a coincidence,"* the little voice harped.

Jessie never understood that voice that seemed to come from nowhere. At times she found it to be annoying, but since it had helped save her life the year before, she rarely dismissed what it said. Jessie closed the cover to the grill and turned to Rachel.

"Can I confide in you about something? I'm not sure if it's relevant, but I'm starting to wonder."

"What is it?"

Jessie studied Rachel's eyes as she sat on the bench across from her. "I was not only researching secret societies, but I had outlined a conspiracy novel. In my story, I used a TV news reporter to uncover a conspiracy that the world was actually run by a one-world government and these secret societies were in charge."

Rachel was skeptical. "You're not serious."

"I am serious." Jessie wondered how much she should share with Rachel. "There's more." Jessie sighed. "Some time ago, I wrote a book called *Deceptions*—"

"Yes. I've seen the movie."

"Well . . . after I wrote the screenplay and the movie was released, I realized that *Deceptions* was becoming my life."

"What do you mean?"

"I wrote a murder mystery and the next thing I knew—that story became my reality. I was drawn into a murder investigation, and I was one of the key suspects."

"What are you telling me, Jess?"

"Do you know what precognition is?"

"Isn't it being psychic?"

"Some people would call it psychic phenomena. Precognition is knowing future events through other senses."

"Are you telling me that you're psychic?"

"No more psychic than you. I believe that we're all psychic, but some people use it more than others. I'm not sure why, but somehow, when I was writing *Deceptions* I tapped into a future event and I wrote a story about it."

"And you're thinking that the conspiracy story that you outlined is about your future?"

"It's a thought." The sound of a car approaching diverted Jessie's attention away from Rachel, until the revving engine passed the house and faded. "To be honest, since the incident I've been cautious about writing."

Rachel stood and started to pace, but her eyes never left Jessie's. Then she stopped. "Jessie, I don't know what to tell you. I've never really believed in psychic stuff. Destiny? Fate? Absolutely. But . . . assuming you did tap into your future, is there anything else you can tell me that may be helpful?"

Jessie wasn't sure if she should say it. "My protagonist failed."

"What do you mean *failed*?"

"My protagonist is a TV reporter, and she's trying to expose this secret society. In my story, she failed; she actually joins the bad guys."

At first, Rachel was speechless. "Okay, let's just assume for a moment that you did psychically tune into something. Is it possible that you tuned into Steve's life? He was a TV newsperson. He was drawn into investigating the Thirty-Third Council."

Jessie appeared thoughtful. "And you could interpret his death as a failure," Jessie mumbled. "It's possible. But don't you find any of this reminiscent of *your* life?"

"You think *I'm* going to trade allegiances?" Rachel felt as if she had been hit in the head with a two-by-four. "I realize that you don't know me very well, so I'll let that one pass. But to put it bluntly, I'll join their group when hell freezes over."

Fourteen

That Monday afternoon, Rachel returned to her office after wrapping up a story on high school violence. She closed her office door, and moved to a file cabinet, where she skimmed file folder labels. Since the fire in her office had destroyed her files the year before, it didn't take her long to locate the article on the Arks of the Covenant.

Written by Professor West Kerry, the commentary had been published five months earlier. Rachel perused a brief biography of the author. Kerry taught Hebrew and Judaic studies at New York University, College of the Arts and Sciences. He was a Manhattan resident. From the phonebook, Rachel learned that he lived in Chelsea. She punched in the numbers in her phone.

"Hello," a woman answered.

"Good evening, this is Rachel Addison. I'm looking for Professor Kerry."

"One moment, please."

Seconds later, "Hello. This is West Kerry."

"Professor Kerry, this is Rachel Addison from *Over the Edge*. I hope I'm not interrupting your dinner."

"No. I just walked in. How can I help you, Ms. Addison?"

"I found your article on the Arks of the Covenant very interesting. I'm doing some research trying to connect Freemasonry and King Solomon's Temple. I just figured that—with your expertise—you would be an excellent authority on the subject."

"I'd be happy to help. What would you like to know?"

"I've heard about the legend of Hiram Abiff, the architect of Solomon's Temple. I understand he was a Master Mason. Are there any other connections between the temple and Freemasonry?"

"Oh, yes, indeed. But it's very lengthy. I think it would be best to discuss this in person."

Published by The Haworth Press, Inc., 2006. All rights reserved.
doi:10.1300/5721_15

"I agree. When can we meet? Are you free this evening?" The professor remained silent and Rachel hoped that her aggressiveness did not push him away. "I would be happy to come to you, or we could meet at a place of your choice."

"You may stop by after seven-thirty this evening. Do you have my address?"

Rachel arrived at the professor's residence at seven-thirty sharp. A woman in her mid-forties greeted her. Rose Kerry escorted Rachel to the family room where West Kerry was reading.

"Would you like some iced tea?" she asked Rachel.

"No, thank you. I'm fine."

Rose disappeared into the kitchen leaving West Kerry and Rachel alone.

He removed his glasses revealing kind eyes, and smiled warmly. "It's nice to meet you," West offered Rachel his hand. "I've watched *Over the Edge* for years."

"Thank you for meeting with me in such a short notice."

"It's my pleasure. Let's go to my study."

The professor was younger than what Rachel had expected, perhaps in his late forties or early fifties. And yet, he walked with a slight limp, favoring his right leg. He led Rachel down the hall into a small office where floor-to-ceiling bookcases lined the walls. In between the bookcases hung diplomas revealing advanced degrees from two Ivy League schools. The room was small but neat, lit only by a desk lamp, as drapes diffused the last remaining rays of the daylight. The professor motioned for Rachel to sit in a soft chair.

"How can I help you, Ms. Addison?" He sat behind his desk, across from her.

"Please call me Rachel."

"Only if you call me West."

"West, as I mentioned on the phone, I'm interested in connections between Solomon's Temple and Freemasonry."

"The term *Freemasonry* actually originated from ancient Egypt. At that time, architecture was considered an art, and masons had a special status. Records as early as 2000 BC show that masons belonged to special guilds. These groups were organized and sponsored by a secretive brotherhood that practiced mystical traditions and taught the Egyptian mystery schools."

"So, the masons were teachers of the ancient Egyptian mysteries?"

"Not exactly. This secret brotherhood initially taught the mysteries to the mason guilds which have survived down through the centuries. The guilds' members were considered free men, thus came the term *free mason*. Anyway, these groups have continued the mystical traditions, which are carried on today through Freemasonry."

"But how does this relate to King Solomon's Temple?"

"Solomon was a complex individual. Although he's best known for the construction of his temple, he also established ties between the Hebrews and Egyptians. He was an advisor to the Egyptian Pharaoh, Shishak I, and married his daughter. But anyway, while in Egypt, he studied in the brotherhood, the group that taught the Egyptian mysteries. Apparently when he returned to Palestine, he built the temple to accommodate the brotherhood in his own country. But the creation of this temple today, never mind thousands of years ago, would be a monumental architectural accomplishment. He brought in special mason guilds to help design and build the temple."

"Is this where Hiram Abiff comes into the picture?"

"Yes and no. I've heard the story that Hiram Abiff was the architect of the temple. And that he supposedly was killed before he could pass on the secrets of the brotherhood's mystical practices. I have also heard that it's a legend and symbolically represents the execution of one of the Knights of the Temple."

"Wasn't the Knights of the Temple a Christian-military group?"

"Yes. But . . ." A smile came to the professor's lips. "I hate to jump around on you, but let me back up here for a minute. In my article, I explained that there are two arks. The original tablets Moses took from Sinai were damaged, and stored in a chest made of acacia that was overlaid with gold. Now, there was a second set of unbroken tablets. They were put away in a simple wooden ark. The golden ark was carried into battle, and supposedly any group that possessed it was undefeatable, while the other ark was eventually hidden beneath King

Solomon's Temple. It is believed that the golden ark was taken by Shishak and returned to Egypt. That ark's location today remains a mystery. Some believe that it is in Ethiopia. Others believe it's in Egypt, and still several believe it was returned to Solomon's Temple where it remains hidden today."

"Where's the wooden ark?"

The professor smiled, intensifying the smile lines on his cheeks and magnifying his pale blue eyes. "It's also a mystery. However, there's evidence that suggests it's here, in the United States."

"The United States? How?"

"It's possible that the Knights of the Temple, or Knights Templar, brought it here. Let me back up. Originally this group consisted of only nine Frenchmen. They requested permission from King Baldwin of Jerusalem to protect pilgrims traveling to the Holy Land. But they also asked if they could stay in the ruins of Solomon's Temple.

"Oddly enough, Baldwin granted their wishes. He even paid these men a fee for their services. But this group was formed in 1118, and the temple was in ruin. It had been destroyed during the Babylonian conquest around 586 BC. And although it was rebuilt during the life of Jesus, it was destroyed during the Jewish revolt against the Romans. Then there were countless desecrations after that that altered its integrity.

"Anyway, the original nine men lived in the temple for close to ten years. And what were they really doing there?" the professor's eyes gleamed with excitement. "They excavated for treasures deep under the temple as well as on Mount Moriah."

"Did they find the ark?" Rachel asked.

"Excellent question! There's a good likelihood that they did. According to several accounts, they found the tablets, the Ark, as well as scrolls of hidden knowledge."

"What happened to all of these treasures?"

"Another excellent question!"

Rachel could see the enthusiasm in the professor's eyes. She could also feel her own excitement build.

"Whatever they discovered brought them power and recognition from both church and political leaders. For close to ten years there were only nine members. Then in 1129, two members of the Knights Templar, Grand Masters Payens and Montbard, approached the church for official recognition. One of the members of this council was Saint Bernard, who was the nephew of Grand Master Montbard. To make a long story short, the pope and King Baldwin approved the Templars as an official military and religious order.

"The order prospered becoming powerful and wealthy for close to two centuries. Then on Friday, October 13, 1307, a French king and a pope who feared the order's secrets crushed them, giving the ominous meaning to *Friday the thirteenth.*"

"What happened?"

"The Templars were captured, tortured, and burned, eventually even Grand Master Jacques de Molay. And *I* believe the reenactment of Hiram Abiff symbolizes de Molay's death."

"So, the Knights Templars were Freemasons?"

"Not exactly. You see, *Freemasonry* is a descendent of the Templars, along with the Hospitallers, Knights of Malta, Knights of St. John, the Rosicrucians, and there are many others."

"What did the Templars acquire that made them so powerful?"

"The innermost secrets of Christianity! They recovered ancient manuscripts that predated the Gospels. The manuscripts had not been edited by the church, and the Templars could show how the Roman Catholic Church . . . let's just say *misinterpreted* the resurrection and the virgin birth."

"What?"

"The Templars had in their possession the most untainted and unadulterated Christian documents, ever. This is what led to the order's great power as well as demise. France's King Philip IV convinced Pope Clement V that the Templars were plotting the destruction of the church. And the church was receptive because, at the time, it was rumored that the Templars were attempting to restore the Ancient Merovingian kings."

"Who are they?" The information was beginning to overwhelm Rachel. "Why would this upset the church?"

"The Merovingians were descendents of Jesus."

Now Rachel was truly confused. "But Jesus didn't have children."

"According to whom—the Roman Catholic Church?" A smile came to his lips. "We could discuss this for hours. Not that I wouldn't mind chatting with you, but I think you should research the Merovingians. Then I'd be happy to discuss this further."

Rachel had taken a good deal of the professor's time, and so far he had been very gracious. "May I ask you one other question before I leave?"

"Of course."

"What happened to the treasures? The ark . . . where did it all go?"

"Apparently the Templars were tipped off about their premeditated destruction because Jacques de Molay had the Templars' rules and books burned. But also, the treasure that had been stored in a Paris Temple was transferred to La Rochelle, where eighteen ships disappeared, along with the treasure."

"Where'd they go?"

"Some historians have proven that Templars arrived in New England in 1308."

"But that would be close to two hundred years before Columbus even set sail. You believe the Templars brought the ark and treasures here? And they're still in the United States?"

The professor nodded.

Rachel's head was spinning when she left the professor's apartment that night. As she drove back to her apartment, her mind raced, trying to digest what Professor Kerry had told her. The Templars. The Merovingians. The brotherhood. What did it all mean?

Two weeks later, Rachel found a parcel in her mailbox. She had been waiting for it since her meeting with West Kerry. Anxious to get started, she hurried to her fifth-floor apartment and tore open the Internet-bookstore carton. She perused the books' jackets, selected *Rule by Secrecy* by Jim Marrs, and settled in her favorite reading chair. The index directed her to the subject matter that most interested her, specifically, the Merovingian dynasty. She quickly thumbed through the pages to get to the section she wanted, and read aloud:

The Merovingian dynasty of Franks has been traditionally considered the first race of kings in what is now France. France was named for the Franks and their first ruler, Francio, was said to be a descendent of Noah.

"What does that have to do with Jesus?" Rachel mumbled. Realizing that she needed to start from the beginning, she turned to the first page:

Be forewarned. If you are perfectly comfortable and satisfied with your own particular view of humankind, religion, history, and the world, read no further.

As if there wasn't enough foreshadowing in her life, Rachel read the entire collection of books West Kerry had suggested. In her cramming, she stumbled upon various controversial theories, but the one that held her interest the most was about Mary Magdalene.

Contrary to traditional Christian belief, Mary Magdalene was Jesus' wife. Following his crucifixion, Mary and Jesus' children settled in south France. Here, they preserved their bloodline until the fifth century when they intermarried with Frankish royalty creating the Merovingian Dynasty. At the time, the Roman church had full knowledge of the messianic ancestry, but it became fearful of the bloodlines and fuelled the assassinations of Dagobert and Childeric III, the last of the Merovingian kings.

Over the next few months, Rachel became obsessed with discerning the links between ancient secret societies and their connection with Freemasonry. She found the details surrounding Mary Magdalene's life captivating. Although she was impressed by the research that supported such theories, she was baffled that the information had not been conveyed to the public through traditional reporting venues.

Occasionally Rachel would bring to mind her last conversation with Steve Mercer. *"The conspiracy. . . . It's the ultimate conspiracy. . . . My God, it's going to change everything. . . . Don't trust anyone!"*

"My God, Steve! Is this what you stumbled on?"

Fifteen

With no social life or family to go home to, Jessie became engrossed in her work at *The Empire.* She had worked for herself, writing novels, for almost fifteen years, and had forgotten what it was like to be accountable to someone else. Now, three times a week she was committed to writing a column on education.

At the core of the newsroom's commotion was Brennan's small cubicle. It took Jessie a bit to adapt to the noise, but she adjusted.

"I just read your piece for Sunday." Clark Coburn's voice was barely discernable above the noise in Brennan's cubicle. "It's very good."

Jessie motioned for Clark to sit in the chair across from Brennan's small desk. "Thank you, Clark." Jessie wondered why Clark was visiting her.

"It's clear that you're working below your abilities. How would you like to work where the action is?"

Jessie knew that any reporter would jump at an opportunity presented by Clark. But she liked her position. It limited her exposure to the public, which always concerned her. She had been impersonating a man for almost two months, now. Still, her performance was unnatural and proved to be work. Every minute she had to think about how a man would sit or how she should put her legs. She constantly scrutinized her performance: *Is my voice too high? Would a man say it that way?* Frequently she had to remind herself to alter her walk.

On Jessie's first day of work, she had shocked a group of ladies. Without thinking, she barged into the ladies' room. Brennan had stood immobile, dazed, in the heart of the restroom, surrounded by women. When Jessie realized what she had done, a spontaneous smile found her lips, revealing a softness that most women find charming. She blushed and profusely apologized as she retreated to the hallway.

Published by The Haworth Press, Inc., 2006. All rights reserved.
doi:10.1300/5721_16

Now, sitting across from Clark Coburn, she knew she couldn't refuse his offer, but she didn't want a new assignment. "I'm not sure I'm ready for that, Clark."

"I've seen your work. You're ready. On Monday, I want you to start working the political beat of the city. Give me two columns a week on ongoing political activities. I'll arrange with Cindy to get your own office along with your title changed, and of course," he smiled, "an increase to correspond with your promotion."

Jessie was confused. What did she do to earn a promotion?

"Congratulations, Brennan."

Clark stood and Jessie got to her feet also. They shook hands and just as she anticipated, the handshake transitioned into the Mason pass-grip. "Thank you, Clark."

Coburn moved out of the cubicle but poked his head back in. "I heard you're starting the Scottish Rite next month. I also heard you are trying to do it in one reunion."

Jessie nodded. "Yes."

"Your schedule will be grueling. If you need any time off to study or travel, you just take it, do you understand?" He grinned.

"Thank you, Clark." In that moment, Jessie understood Steve's motivation for being a Mason. In a very short time, Brennan had been promoted without deserving it, all because of his association with this group.

"Brennan!" Cindy popped her head into the cubicle. "I just got a phone call from the doctor's office. You missed your employment physical, again."

"I did?" Jessie glanced at her watch and acted surprised. "Oh gees. . . . I completely forgot."

"Here," she handed Brennan a note. "You have another date, next month. Don't forget it. Employees are supposed to start employment *after* their physical. I don't want Human Resources to get on my case."

"No, problem. I won't forget, Cindy."

In September, Jessie got underway with her Scottish Rite degrees. To earn twenty-nine degrees, most candidates would spread them over a fall and a spring reunion, or even years. But Jessie couldn't wait for the spring session. She needed to cram the twenty-nine degrees in one reunion, a monumental feat. She knew it would be extremely difficult, logistically challenging, but not impossible. Each Sunday Jessie traveled throughout the mid-Atlantic and New England states so she would earn the thirty-second degree in January. From nine in the morning until six in the evening she sat through exemplifications or communications, earning multiple degrees each Sunday.

The unknown of each degree—wondering if she would be forced to unclothe and be exposed—sickened her. At the beginning of each session her stomach cramped, followed by nausea, and her heart pounded viciously. Until she was caught up in the lesson of the lecture she was miserable, but once drawn in, she relaxed.

Within each degree, there was always a discussion of finding the *true light* in the higher degrees. But at the end of each initiation, Jessie found herself no closer to understanding the meaning of *true light.* Based on her conversations with some of the other candidates, she knew she wasn't alone.

Jessie was merging onto the Deagan Expressway that Thursday after work when the cell phone that connected her to her real life chimed. She attached the earpiece. "Hello."

"Hi, Jessie," Taylor said.

"Hi, sweetheart, how are you? God, it's great to hear your voice."

"I'm good. I'm in Germany and I was just getting ready for bed. You've been on my mind a lot. Is everything okay?"

Jessie smiled. She wanted to scream, "No! Things aren't okay!" Instead, "Yes. Everything's fine, sweetheart."

"How's your new project coming?"

"Slow," Jessie admitted. "Very slow."

"When are you going to tell me about it, anyway?"

"How's next spring?"

"How about next month? You *are* meeting me in France, aren't you?"

"I'm trying. But I won't have as much time as we originally planned."

"Why not? You make your own schedule. How come you can't finish the tour with me? It's just through New Year's and then I'll be in New York in January."

Jessie's heart sank. How could she explain that she had Scottish Rite degrees to earn? That she had a job as a reporter? Or that she lived her life as a man? How could Taylor understand? The hard part for Jessie was that Taylor *would* understand. Jessie just wasn't willing to compromise Taylor's safety.

"I'll be there for Thanksgiving, Taylor. I promise."

In the morning when Jessie woke, she questioned why she had been so willing to make the sacrifices that she had. For four months she had been involved in the Blue Lodge, and she had been unsuccessful connecting the group to Steve's death. Other than the testosterone-heavy occult rituals, most of the men appeared to be decent.

There was one custom within the Blue Lodge that Jessie found odd. Although Masons frequently prayed from the Bible, they always extracted the name Jesus from the reference. In the Blue Lodge, and from what she was learning in the Scottish Rite higher degrees, all religions were considered equal, but Freemasonry was placed above all.

Up until this point, Jessie had been disappointed in her discoveries of the higher degrees. She felt like she was becoming the princess of the royal secret, but she didn't know what secret she was protecting.

While masquerading as Brennan Keller, Jessie maintained electronic and telephone contact with her publisher and agent. She continued the plot development and research for *The Ultimate Conspiracy.* Over that summer, she had submitted a book proposal for the project to her publisher. She was disappointed when her submission was rejected, but Jessie was too invested in the project, so she continued writing *The Ultimate Conspiracy* using her brother's life as the impetus of the story. Simultaneously, she submitted similar proposals to other publishers, and most recently, the rejection letters continued to come in. Apparently, no one was interested in a conspiracy novel regarding the Freemasons.

Now, Jessie was desperately homesick and she wanted to be with Taylor. Her confidence in her writing and new project marketability was shaken. Only three months away from reaching the thirty-second degree, Jessie had to constantly psych herself into continuing her charade. She couldn't wait to reclaim her life as Jessie Mercer.

That Friday evening, Jessie had agreed to meet with Rachel for dinner. The women hadn't seen each other in almost two months. A restaurant in Paramus, New Jersey, was selected for their get-together.

"Sorry, I'm late," Jessie said as she slipped into the booth across from Rachel. "I got a little lost."

"That's okay." Rachel studied Brennan. There was something different. "Are you okay? You don't look well."

Jessie sighed. She leaned over the table toward Rachel, and whispered. "I'm tired, I'm homesick, and I'm afraid that my breasts are going to be permanently flat."

Although Jessie was very serious, Rachel started to giggle. At first, Jessie didn't know how to react to Rachel's response. She felt as if she were coming apart at the seams and now, her only friend found amusement in her despair. Then Jessie saw Rachel's caring eyes, and she laughed herself.

As Rachel sipped her wine, Jessie spotted an image on the inside of Rachel's wrist. It was familiar. Jessie reached for her hand and the contact surprised Rachel with a start.

"May I?" Jessie asked. Rachel surrendered her hand so Jessie could view the image. Jessie smiled when she recognized the symbol. "You have an ankh tattoo?"

"It's a birthmark."

"A birthmark?" Jessie looked closer. "How odd, it's so close to an ankh."

"I'm not familiar with the symbol."

Jessie traced the dime-size birthmark. "Here's the loop, and the cross is on the bottom. It's the ancient Egyptian symbol for life." Jessie was reminded of the ankh she had found when she visited Salem, Massachusetts, and the pendant that Taylor wore.

Rachel changed the subject. "So how are you? Are you going to make it?"

Jessie sipped her wine. "I've started the Scottish Rite. It's a pretty grueling schedule. Every weekend I'm traveling all over to get the degrees in by January. But each degree has been a disappointment so far."

"How so?"

"They keep promising that we'll find the *true light* in the next degree. I'm up to the tenth degree and I haven't seen any light. It's just very frustrating."

"Can you finish by January?"

"I think so. The alternative is that I would have to wait until June. I have no intention of being Brennan Keller next June." Jessie sipped her wine. "I've got to get to Europe over Thanksgiving."

"Have you told Taylor what you're doing?"

"I said that I'm working on a new project and I need to be in New York for research." Jessie felt terrible that she had misled Taylor and didn't want to talk about it. She changed the subject. "What have you been up to?"

"Mostly reading and studying. I've had a number of very interesting discussions with Professor Kerry, the author of that article I told you about on the arks. I'm in the middle of a project on the ark and the Merovingian dynasty."

"The what?"

Rachel shared with Jessie what she had learned, and after Jessie absorbed Rachel's findings, she tried to summarize them. "So let me get this straight. Freemasonry is what links modern and ancient secret societies. The common thread is that they practice ancient Egyptian mysteries. But it's unclear whether anyone really *knows* the ancient mysteries today." She paused. "Now, that would explain why I'm feeling like the princess of the royal secret."

"It is possible that members of the thirty-third degree have this knowledge."

"And you believe that the Knights Templar discovered that the Roman Catholic Church censored information regarding Jesus?"

"Yes. The concept of the Trinity—the Father, Son and Holy Spirit —was *not* an original Christian concept. Jesus never taught it, but the

Council of Nicaea adopted it in AD 325, establishing the foundation for the Nicene Creed. One year after that, the Roman Emperor Constantine ordered the confiscation of any material that conflicted with the new Trinity orthodoxy."

"But the Father, Son, and Spirit are the cornerstone of the Christian faith!"

"I know, but it wasn't a doctrine from Jesus. Man created the concept. Jesus actually never claimed to be the messiah. Before the church created the Trinity doctrine, Gnosticism flourished. And Gnostics professed to have an intuitive discernment of the mysteries of God. Gnosticism, where people sought personal inner enlightenment, was a fundamental part of the ancient mysteries. Up until the Council of Nicaea, reincarnation had been an acceptable doctrine of the church, but after that, it was considered a heresy."

Rachel paused to sip her wine, and then continued. "There's sufficient evidence that shows Jesus studied in a secret brotherhood during his lost years. He was an Essene. The Essenes were the ancestors of Freemasonry. They were the followers of Pythagoras and sacred geometry. They were known to be keepers of the Covenant."

"*The* Covenant?" This caught Jessie's attention.

"That's right. They were known to have the knowledge of the ancient mysteries, like the Gnostics. Some researchers believe that they were the guardians of Mystic Christianity, the original form of Christianity that was based upon the earliest mysteries. The Essenes were also known as mysterious healers, and actually very little was known about them until the Dead Sea Scrolls were found in 1947."

"Dead Sea Scrolls?"

"In AD 70, when Rome advanced during the Jewish revolt, the Essenes hid their sacred manuscripts in jars in mountain caves. Between 1947 and 1960, almost 800 manuscripts were uncovered, 170 of them contain remnants of the Old Testament.

"Seven of these scrolls were secured by an archeologist and published, but the rest of them were acquired from Jordan by the Rockefeller Archaeological Museum in Palestine. Some believe Israel controls them now, because Israel conquered the location where they were stored during the Six Day War in 1967. Others believe the scrolls were destroyed. But based on the discoveries from the seven scrolls, historians believe that the Essenes had the purest ancient traditions."

Jessie was silent, trying to grasp the information. Then she broached another one of Rachel's theories. "And you believe there's sufficient evidence that suggests Mary Magdalene was the wife or consort of Jesus? And they had children?"

"Yes."

"You think the Roman Catholic Church was afraid of this Merovingian dynasty and was responsible for the assassinations of two kings? And you're doing a report on it?"

"Yes! I've kept this story quiet, so far."

Sixteen

Her new spacious office normally provided plenty of sunlight, but the sun had set and dark had fallen, yet Jessie was still working. A halogen lamp lit the computer keyboard, where her fingers quickly typed. Earlier that day, she had learned that Iraq had, once again, advanced on Kuwait. The news blitzed the media and Jessie found herself watching the developments on CNN throughout the day. Apparently, the United Nations had called an emergency meeting to discuss action against Iraq. The unwelcome distraction had impeded her latest project and she was working late to meet a deadline.

There was a knock on Brennan's door, and Cindy's head popped in. "Hi, Brennan. Still working?"

"With the diversion today, I wasn't able to finish my Sunday column. What about you?"

"Catching up on my filing." She leaned up against the door. "A bunch of women from the office are heading over to Tony's happy hour. Would you like to join us?"

"Thanks for the invite. Can I take a rain check? I really need to finish this."

"Next time, I won't let you off so easily," Cindy smiled flirtatiously. "I understand you missed your doctor's physical again." Her eyes studied Brennan. "I think I know your little secret, Mr. Keller."

Jessie looked up at Cindy; she had been caught once more. Her heart skipped a beat. "And what is that, Ms. Palmer?"

"You're using and you can't have the drug test now."

Jessie breathed a little easier. "Actually, I'm just really busy right now."

"It's okay," she said. "How much longer do you need to pass the drug screen?"

Jessie sighed. "My schedule lightens up after the holidays. Why don't you schedule me an appointment around the first of February."

Published by The Haworth Press, Inc., 2006. All rights reserved.
doi:10.1300/5721_17

"Consider it done." She dropped an envelope on his desk. "This was in your mailbox." She left.

Jessie picked up the envelope. It was addressed to "Brennan Keller and Guest." She craned her neck to see if Cindy was lurking outside her office door. Satisfied that Cindy had gone, she opened the envelope. It was an invitation to an annual party sponsored by the Broadcasting Corporation of America (BCA), an organization that supported the media. Jessie was baffled. Generally, this was an exclusive event attended by only the highest echelon in the industry. The affair was scheduled a week before Thanksgiving.

It was the first Sunday in November and Jessie had just completed the fourteenth degree. To commemorate the occasion, the candidates were awarded the official Masonic ring, a gold band with the Hebrew letter "YOD."

As Jessie and the other initiates left the Pennsylvania lodge that evening, they were bombarded with heckles from demonstrators outside the lodge. "Go away, devil worshippers!" the crowd chanted. "Go away, Satan worshippers!"

Jessie was puzzled. She had been involved in Freemasonry since June and had never even heard the devil's name mentioned. Crude jeers were barked at the initiates all the way to the parking lot where Jessie found sanctuary in the Mustang.

On the Sunday that followed, Jessie was initiated into the fifteenth, sixteenth, and seventeenth degrees. During the exemplification of the seventeenth degree the term Abaddon was expressed. Although the ceremony did not explain who Abaddon was, he was conveyed as a sacred being.

The next morning, while at Brennan's desk, Jessie went online and searched for "Abaddon." To her surprise thousands of references were noted. She hit the first link, leading her to the book of Revelation.

And they had a king over them, which is the angel of the bottomless pit, whose name in the Hebrew tongue is Abaddon, but in the Greek tongue hath his name Apollyon.

Revelation 9:11

"So, Abaddon is the angel of the bottomless pit?" Jessie mumbled as she searched for another reference. Most of the links directed her to similar Biblical references. Then she clicked the link to an online dictionary. "Abaddon," she started to read. *Oh, my God . . .* "The Devil, Hell; literally destruction (Revelation 9:11)." Queasiness hit. Was it a coincidence that Revelation 9:11 alluded to the events of September 11, 2001?

In no time the BCA event arrived. Jessie's legwork uncovered that it was Clark Coburn who had arranged to get Brennan an invitation. He had also prearranged a limo to transport Brennan to and from the affair.

Jessie had showered and slipped on the undergarments that obscured her femininity. Her attention was on the TV as she dressed in the pleated French-cuffed shirt, black wool pants, and lavender Bellisimo vest.

"With no place to go," the CNN correspondent reported, "it appears that the United Nations is heading for an impasse concerning how to proceed against Iraq."

Jessie flicked the remote control and the television faded. She picked up the black silk bowtie and fastened it around the wing-tipped collar. Then she stepped into her dress shoes and finished with the black tuxedo jacket.

She walked in front of the full-length mirror that hung from the closet door. Stunned by her reflection, she approached the mirror and straightened the bowtie. The lavender vest added the right touch of color to the conventional black tuxedo. She had never seen Brennan look so handsome. The doorbell buzzed, alerting her that her limo had arrived.

As Jessie strolled the Silver Corridor of the Waldorf Astoria, she admired the polished marble floor. The black and white checkered pattern sidetracked her from the extraordinary passageway where magnificent chandeliers hung from soaring arched ceilings. She was en route to the banquet room, lost in the checkered design, when she heard the familiar voice from behind her.

"Hello, Brennan."

Jessie's eyes left the floor. Clark Coburn approached with an attractive, younger woman. "Clark. Good evening." Jessie shook his hand.

"Brennan, this is my wife, Michelle. Michelle, this is Brennan Keller." Jessie took her hand. "It's a pleasure to meet you."

"Likewise," she smiled. "Clark, I need to find the little girls' room." Her eyes on Brennan, "Would you excuse me?" Michelle left them alone.

Clark and Brennan headed down the corridor, toward a grand piano where a man skillfully stroked the keyboard. "Brennan, tonight will be a good opportunity to meet some very influential people."

"I've been looking forward to this evening for some time, Clark."

As they neared the end of the corridor, the piano amplified, and the rhythm of a social gathering drew them into a small banquet room. Ten round tables were elegantly set, dressed with white linen tablecloths. Candles, and long-stemmed roses in gold vases, adorned the tables, creating an intimate atmosphere.

A group mingled in the center of the room, near a bar. As Clark made his way through the crowd, he introduced Brennan to the CEO of one broadcasting company, the president of another, and finally the CFO of a third. By the time they reached the bar, Jessie's mind raced.

"Scotch on crushed ice," Jessie told the bartender.

Clark fingered through a box of cigars at the bar. He selected one, smelled it, then picked another. With the two cigars he gestured to Brennan, "After dinner."

Jessie nodded, and decided to get right to the point. "Clark, why am I here?" She looked around the room. "These people, like yourself, have great achievements in the broadcasting world . . . but, why am I here?"

Clark grinned. "Because I like you, Brennan. Because my gut tells me you are capable of great things. I told you once before that we take care of *our* kind. We do. Continue getting your degrees, Brennan. . . . Stay on our side, and you will become a very powerful man."

"Here you are, Clark," Michelle interrupted them.

Clark handed his wife a drink, but ignored her. He directed Brennan away, leaving Michelle, who quickly engaged herself in conversation with others.

"Brennan, there is someone I want you to meet," Clark said as he led him to a tall and slim man. But the stranger was talking with someone else, so Clark waited patiently for an opening.

The man engaged Clark when his conversation ended. "Clark, how are you this fine evening?"

"Michael, I'd like you to meet Brennan Keller. Brennan, this is Michael Whitman."

Michael's dark eyes studied Brennan intently. Jessie placed Michael in his late fifties or early sixties.

She shook his hand. "It's a pleasure to meet you, Michael."

"Likewise, Brennan. So, you're the new reporter that's been writing the New York City political beat?"

"Yes."

His eyes narrowed on Brennan. "I want you to do a story on me after Thanksgiving. Clark will give you the details. Would you excuse me?" Whitman abruptly left to greet a younger woman.

"We'll talk later. There's someone else I want you to meet." Clark directed Brennan toward a small group that Michelle had connected with. "Neil, how are you?"

Neil Samson turned toward Clark, then Brennan. Jessie's pulse quickened slightly as she stood face-to-face with her brother's previous boss.

"Neil, I want you to meet Brennan Keller."

Neil smiled, and then shook Brennan's hand. "It's a pleasure to meet you, Brennan. I've heard a lot about you."

"The pleasure is mine." Jessie found it odd that Neil, like Clark, had turned his back on his companion, giving Brennan his undivided attention.

Clark, Neil, and Brennan had been speaking about five minutes when Jessie became aware of Neil's eyes on her. She resisted showing her unease.

It was Neil who broached subject. "Brennan, have we met before?"

Jessie's heart skipped and she shook her head. "I don't believe so, Neil."

"Maybe you just remind me of someone I once knew." There was a flicker of dissonance in his eyes.

In Jessie's peripheral vision, she glimpsed a long, black, shapely gown. Without giving it any thought, Jessie turned to admire the fleeting woman, only to see her backside, and long dark hair braided in a chignon.

Neil and Clark noticed Brennan's gaze. "Have you met her?" Neil asked.

Jessie's skin heated from embarrassment. She realized that she must have looked like a teenage boy in heat, and didn't know what to say.

"Have you met Rachel Addison? She works for me," Neil continued.

Rachel? Jessie's heartbeat quickened. She had never expected to see her, and she didn't want to surprise her, after all, it could blow her cover. "Excuse me," Jessie said seriously. "I didn't mean to seem disrespectful."

"Disrespectful?" Clark eyed Michelle chatting with Neil's wife. In a low tone, "Rachel's the most beautiful woman in the hotel."

"Here she comes. I'll be happy to introduce you." Neil turned away from the group and gestured to Rachel.

Rachel in everyday attire looked beautiful, but tonight, she was absolutely stunning. Her gown draped from one shoulder, baring the other, while side slits revealed just the right portion of thigh.

Jessie didn't know what to do. She turned away from the advancing Rachel.

"Rachel, I'd like to introduce you to some people. This is my very good friend from *The Empire*, Clark Coburn."

"Clark, it's a pleasure," she said.

Neil continued, "And this is his upcoming star reporter, Brennan Keller."

Rachel's eyes peered into Jessie's. There was the slightest falter before Rachel offered to shake Brennan's hand. "It's a pleasure to meet you, Brennan," she said, her eyes not leaving Brennan's.

People were starting to sit for dinner, and Neil suggested that they get a table. "Why don't we take the table in the corner?" He pointed to a table away from where musician's equipment had been set up. "Rachel and Brennan, why don't you join us?"

"Excellent idea," Clark said.

The round tables had place settings for six. It was Jessie who objected. "I'm sure Ms. Addison has an escort. I would be happy to find another table."

Rachel, still digesting Jessie's appearance, remained uncomfortably quiet.

Neil was direct, "Rachel, is Stanley here tonight?"

"He's out of the country. There's enough room, Mr. Keller." Rachel's seemingly cold eyes bore into Jessie. "If you would excuse me, though, I would like a drink." She headed away from the small group leaving Brennan watching her backside.

Neil laughed. "She must like you, Brennan."

Brennan Keller's presence at the BCA event threw Rachel. It had been only the past two years that she had been deemed worthy enough to earn an invitation herself, and only recently felt welcomed by the old-boy network. But somehow, Brennan Keller managed to stroll into the business and get an invitation to the most exclusive event of the year. Consequently, Brennan's attendance undermined her feeling of accomplishment.

To Jessie the dinner was awkward and uncomfortable. On her left was Michelle, Clark's chatty wife, and Rachel was on her right. Rachel snubbed Brennan most of the evening.

Over dessert, a band started performing and Rachel broke her silence. "So . . . Brennan . . . was that your name? *Brennan?*"

Jessie was getting the feeling that Rachel enjoyed this way too much. "Yes. Brennan Keller."

"You're a reporter for *The Empire?*"

"Yes." Jessie sipped her cabernet. She noticed that Neil was eavesdropping on their conversation. "I've been there since July. Congratulations on your promotion, by the way. I read that you will be taking over an anchor spot next season."

"Thank you."

"Oh, I just love to dance," Michelle's voice escalated over their conversation. The comment was clearly directed toward Brennan.

Jessie glanced at Clark and was surprised when he made eye contact and cocked his head toward the dance floor. Clark remained sitting with his arms folded.

Does he want me to dance with his wife? Brennan flashed a questioning look.

As if reading Brennan's mind, Clark directed his vision on Michelle, then back to Brennan. He nodded at Brennan.

Jessie reluctantly took Clark's cue. She turned to Rachel, who had been witnessing the eye exchange. "Excuse me." To Michelle, "Would you like to dance?"

Brennan led Michelle to the dance floor. They danced three songs and returned to the table when the music slowed, and Brennan continued idle chitchat with Rachel.

After one song, Michelle voiced her opinion, "Oh, I just *love* to slow dance."

This time, Jessie didn't dare look at Clark, for fear that she would be asked to slow dance with his wife. Instead, Jessie turned to Rachel. "Would you like to dance?

To Jessie, Rachel's pause felt like an eternity rather than the few seconds of hesitation. Then Rachel nodded, Brennan took her hand and led her to the dance floor.

Once among the other couples, Jessie pulled her so that they were only inches apart. "I'm sorry, Rachel," Jessie whispered in her ear. "I didn't want to slow dance with Michelle."

"You afraid she's going to feel you up?" Rachel's voice had a detached ring to it.

Yeah. Actually I am, Jessie thought. "This is a bit awkward tonight. Wouldn't you agree?"

Rachel backed away from Jessie and their eyes met. "Very awkward!"

Jessie noticed that at the far corner of the room Neil's and Clark's eyes were glued on them. "Can we have a truce? It's obvious that my presence has upset you. I'm sorry I didn't warn you. It just slipped my mind that you might be here."

Rachel didn't respond and danced rigidly.

"Can you relax? You're stiff as a board." Rachel's arm braced Jessie, placing Brennan at a distance.

"Am I?" Rachel slowed to almost a stop.

It was just a whisper. "Please don't blow my cover."

As if there was a ceasefire, Rachel's arm journeyed up to Jessie's shoulder, closing the gap between them.

"Thank you," Jessie whispered. The couple continued to slow dance. "So your *boyfriend* . . . is out of the country? I didn't realize you were seeing anyone."

"I have for the last couple of months."

"Can I ask who it is?"

"Stanley Chancellor."

"From the Fed?" Jessie knew Stanley worked for the Federal Reserve. "Isn't he a member of the Trilateral Commission?"

"Yes." Rachel said.

Jessie introduced more space between them so she could better see Rachel's eyes. "Do you know what you're doing?"

Rachel nodded. "Yes."

Instinctively, Jessie squeezed Rachel's hand, and pulled her closer. Her lips brushed against the loose strands of hair. "Be careful," she whispered in her ear.

Rachel's demeanor softened a bit, and she changed the subject. "Are you still going to Europe for Thanksgiving?"

"Yes. I can't wait to see Taylor. I leave on Tuesday."

Rachel saw how Jessie's eyes lit up when she spoke of Taylor. "I hope you have a good trip. Any news from the lodge?"

"I went through the seventeenth degree last weekend," Jessie twirled Rachel around. "One of the sacred names used during the lecture was Abaddon."

"Abaddon? What does that mean?"

"The devil," Jessie answered as the song came to an end.

Seventeen

Jessie had longed for this day for such a long time. At noon on Tuesday, she left *The Empire* and headed to the Catskills. When she arrived she found three boxes by the front door of the cabin. She quickly lugged the packages inside and opened them. They contained women's clothing, shoes, and cosmetics.

After a quick shower, Jessie dressed in woman's clothing for the first time since she could remember. Her makeup application felt foreign to her. She squeezed the gel in her hand, massaged it into her short hair, then quickly blew it dry. She backed away from the mirror so that she could take in her appearance. It surprised her that her hair actually looked stylish. It had nothing to do with her hair. She could have been bald, she decided. She was just delighted to be herself.

Jessie bolted out of the house with a small bag. She hopped in the Mustang and drove to Syracuse Airport. There, she caught a flight to Boston. In Boston she connected to Brussels and in Brussels she took a plane to Nice. She was so exhausted on the last leg of her journey that she fell asleep, only to be awakened by the jet wheels screeching to a stop at 11:30 the following morning.

Jessie waited for the other travelers to disembark before she retrieved her carry-on bag and moved to the exit. As she followed the signs to the baggage claim she realized that she was dawdling. Why? She was nervous. She hadn't seen Taylor in seven months, and she had missed her so much. What if Taylor wasn't looking forward to this visit as much as she was? What if she hated her hair? After dressing like a man for so long, she felt unattractive. She had never felt so insecure in their relationship before.

As Jessie entered the baggage area, she searched the unfamiliar faces, but she didn't see Taylor so she proceeded to the carousel. She didn't get very far before she stopped. She hadn't seen Taylor, or

this

Published by The Haworth Press, Inc., 2006. All rights reserved.
doi:10.1300/5721_18

heard her, but something made her glance behind. That's when she saw Taylor's familiar back, her long dark hair, but she was waiting at the wrong carousel. Jessie paused about thirty feet from her; she admired her backside.

It didn't take Taylor long to feel Jessie's eyes upon her. For no logical reason, Taylor turned, catching sight of Jessie. She smiled, ran to Jessie and flung herself into Jessie's open arms. All of Jessie's nagging concerns had been answered.

Taylor drove from the airport. She picked up the motorway, exited past Monaco, and followed signs to Eze-Le Col. Eze, a 1,000 year-old medieval village, sits 1,300 feet above the Mediterranean Sea. From its central square, Taylor turned onto a small winding road. The sporty Mercedes convertible hugged the twisting roads that led up the mountain until they could go no further. A valet took the keys from Taylor and removed Jessie's bag from the trunk, leaving the women to hike the remaining distance to the Chateau Eza.

Jessie resisted taking Taylor's hand as the couple ascended the cobblestone passageways, passing cavelike restaurants and boutiques. The ancient castle, now an exclusive ten-room hotel, clung to the cliff's rock walls. At the path's summit, the ancient stone pathway forked. Taylor's hand slipped into Jessie's and she led her down a stone walkway to the room's private entrance.

Moments later, Jessie was taking in the view of the Mediterranean Sea from their private balcony. She marveled at the postcard-like surroundings of the blue sea and nearby mountainous cliffs. "It's absolutely beautiful." Jessie felt Taylor's arms wrap around her waist from behind, and her chin rest on Jessie's shoulder. Jessie closed her eyes, welcoming the safe feeling.

"It is," Taylor whispered.

Jessie turned to meet Taylor's familiar eyes. Their lips met and they kissed. When they parted Jessie whispered, "God, I've missed you."

Taylor smiled. "I've missed you, too." Her hand moved to Jessie's hair. She pulled it and smiled. "Is there anything you want to tell me?"

Jessie had been so anxious about their meeting—it slipped her mind. "Well, you see there was this drag contest and . . . let's just say I didn't want to lose. You hate it?"

Taylor backed away to study it. "No . . . I don't hate it. It's just going to take a little getting used to."

"Do I look too butch?" Jessie smiled.

Taylor laughed. "You could never look butch."

Jessie laughed out loud. If she only knew.

"You must be exhausted. We have dinner reservations at eight. Do you want to take a nap?"

"Eventually." Jessie stepped closer to Taylor. "But first," she kissed her forehead. "I want to take a shower. Then I want to hold you," her lips moved to Taylor's lips, "and love you," she nibbled Taylor's neck, "and please you." Jessie's eyes returned to Taylor's. With her index finger, she slowly traced Taylor's seductive lips, and when she came to a complete circle, her mouth found Taylor's. "And then I want to rest my head on your shoulder," Jessie wrapped her arms around her, "listen to your heartbeat, and fall asleep in your arms."

Even without a nap, Jessie felt like a new person by dinner. The couple strolled to the hotel's restaurant, Gastronomic. They were seated on a romantic balcony, overlooking the spectacular French Riviera. Each table was dressed with white lace tablecloths and lighted candles that gently flickered in the Mediterranean breeze. The ambiance was delightful, consistent with their romantic afternoon.

It was Taylor who changed the mood as they sipped wine before their entrees were served. "Jess? Why don't you stay with me the rest of the tour? Or at least through New Year's?"

Jessie had feared the subject would come up. "There's nothing more that I'd rather do. But I can't."

"What are you working on that's so important? Or, do you have a new romantic interest in New York?" Although Taylor smiled, there was seriousness in her eyes.

"Taylor, I assure you, my only romantic interest is right here." She reached for her hand. "I'm working on a conspiracy novel, and I'm using my brother's life as the impetus for the story."

"What do you mean?"

Jessie paused, deciding what she could tell her lover. "Remember how I wrote *Deceptions,* and years later the story became our reality?"

"How can I forget?" It was only the year before that Taylor had gone back to Salem.

"Before Steve died, I was working on a story about conspiracy theories."

Taylor recalled the night that Jessie had had the nightmare. Jessie had told her about the projects she was working on, but she couldn't remember the details.

"I was writing a story about a woman—a TV news reporter—who is attempting to uncover that the world is actually ruled by a few powerful people."

"Jess, what's this got to do with Steve?"

"Taylor," it was more like a whisper. "You can't repeat any of this to anyone."

Taylor saw something in Jessie's eyes. "You're scaring me, Jess. What the hell is going on?"

"Steve didn't commit suicide. He was involved in a secret men's group. He suspected that the senior hierarchy of this organization was involved in a globalist agenda and controlled the world. He had started his own investigation and then he was murdered. The authorities don't seem to give a damn. So, I've been attempting to piece together what happened to him. And I'm using his story as the basis of my new project."

"My God, Jessie! This sounds dangerous."

"I'm taking every precaution. But I have appointments lined up in December and January. I just can't stop right now. I need to finish this. Taylor . . . this is important."

Taylor was quiet. Something troubled her but she couldn't put her finger on it. But what could she say? She just stared back at Jessie. "Jess, I don't have a good feeling about this . . . at all. Please . . . don't go back to New York."

"I'm sorry, Taylor. I have to."

"You think the story you were working on before Steve died was precognitive, don't you?"

"I don't think it's a glimpse of *my* future, Taylor." Jessie tried to relieve her. "I've wondered if somehow, I psychically tapped into what Steve was mixed up in."

"Why do you want to write about this, anyway?"

"I have to do this. Maybe it's my way of seeking closure on Steve's death." Jessie tried to explain further. "Taylor, years ago, when you walked into my life and auditioned for the role in *Deceptions,* I asked you why you wanted the role so badly. Do you remember what you said?"

Taylor recalled the moment. "I said that . . . the role felt like my destiny."

"Taylor, I need to do this. Somehow I feel like this is *my* destiny. I assure you, I'm taking every precaution. When you return to the states I will be wrapping this up. Then we can go home and continue where we left off."

Both agreed not to discuss Jessie's project the rest of their vacation, and the week flew. Their days were spent hiking, sailing, horseback riding, or just relaxing in the sun. During the evenings, they feasted on the best food of the French Riviera, and at night they took pleasure in each other's arms.

Two days before Jessie was scheduled to leave, she was in the hotel lobby browsing through tourist brochures, trying to decide what they'd do on her last day. She came across one for Rennes-le-Chateau. There was a picture of an old church and on the back of the brochure it said, *"Explore the mysteries of Rennes-le-Chateau. Were treasures from the Merovingian dynasty hidden here?"*

Around noon the following day, Jessie and Taylor arrived at Rennes-le-Chateau. The church itself was architecturally impressive, and considering its age, it was in surprisingly good condition. A guide greeted them, holding the gate open as they made their way toward the entrance.

"Bonjour," he said.

"Bonjour," the women echoed.

Above the entrance was a statue of a woman. Jessie slowed to read the inscription. It was a statue of Mary Magdalene, to whom the church was dedicated. Beneath it was another message. Jessie stopped and in poor French, she attempted to verbalize it, *"Terribilis est?"*

"Oui! Terribilis est!" the guide corrected her pronunciation.

"What does that mean?" Jessie asked.

"It means—this place is terrible!" The man said with a smile.

"What an odd thing to say at the entrance of a church," Taylor mumbled as she entered. She quickly recoiled when she saw the statue that greeted them, a frightening, cowering demon. "My God! What kind of church is this?"

The guide, still holding the door, "That's Asmodeus—the demon that King Solomon allegedly tamed." The baptismal font was just above the devil's head. "I was just running out for a bite to eat. I should be back in a half hour, or so. Enjoy your visit." The guide ran off, leaving Jessie and Taylor to explore the ancient church.

Later that afternoon, Taylor and Jessie stopped at a quaint café in town for lunch. An elderly man escorted them to an outdoor table.

"How's your new manager?" Jessie asked as they were seated.

"Sidney? I think she'll work out fine. She's very different from Mark, though."

"How so?" Jessie recalled the dream she'd had of Mark Rutledge, Taylor's former manager, only weeks earlier.

"She works on the opposite side of the county, for one. But also, Mark was involved in my personal life, not only my business. Sidney is more . . . detached."

"Don't you think that's a good thing?"

"Yes. Don't get me wrong. She's very professional. She's admitted from the beginning that she's here to make me money, not to make friends. Mark's priorities were obviously a little different."

After Jessie and Taylor had finished their lunch, an elderly man brought them coffee. "Did you go up to the church?" he asked in perfect English.

"Yes," Taylor answered. "Parts of it were quite beautiful. Other areas were baffling."

"You mean the Devil?" the man asked.

Taylor nodded, then sipped her coffee.

"I was a little disappointed," Jessie admitted. "I was hoping for a more in-depth discussion with the guide."

"The guides are generally very good."

"He was running out to lunch when we arrived."

"My name is Joseph. I'm no guide but I've lived here most of my life. Maybe I can answer some of your questions. What interests you about Rennes-le-Chateau?"

"Was the church connected to the Merovingian Dynasty?" Jessie asked.

"Oh, yes. Some believe that the Knights Templar hid treasures there—including the Ark of the Covenant—before their demise, while others speculate that ancient scrolls which include the genealogy of the Merovingian Dynasty were hidden there."

"What's the Merovingian Dynasty?" Taylor asked naively.

"The descendants of Jesus," Jessie answered.

"But Jesus didn't have children."

"That is indeed one theory." The man continued, "Another theory suggests that Jesus didn't die on the cross but moved to Rennes with Mary Magdalene where they had a child, and Jesus later died peacefully here, in Rennes. Some even believe that Jesus is buried under Cardou Mount or Corpus Christi, meaning the corpse of Christ."

"Interesting," Jessie said. "Your English is very good, by the way."

"I was born and raised in Connecticut. I moved here after the war." The man smiled. "I take it you're Americans. Travel safe, ladies. I heard the United Nations admitted stalemate yesterday, and there was an incident at the American Embassy in Germany as well as at Kennedy Airport."

Jessie had heard that the United Nations stepped away from discussions. "What happened in Germany and at Kennedy?"

"There was a suicide bombing at the Embassy and apparently intelligence uncovered a bomb threat at the airport. They closed Kennedy yesterday and from what I understand there was rioting and looting while security attempted to clear the terminals. Well, ladies," he smiled. "I hope I answered some of your questions."

"You have. Thanks for the information," Jessie said kindly.

"Excuse me. I need to get back to my other customers."

The couple walked silently side by side as they approached the security checkpoint. The guard asked for Jessie's ticket, and she handed it to him with her passport. As he fumbled through her papers, Jessie turned to Taylor. She had had a wonderful week with her and didn't want to say goodbye. Jessie hugged her silently. She didn't want to let her go.

"Here you are, Ms. Mercer," the guard said. She was expected to move into the security area, the point at which the women had to separate.

Jessie released Taylor and looked into her eyes. She didn't say anything, and kissed her.

"Don't go," Taylor pleaded as Jessie started to leave.

"You know I have to," she whispered. "I love you." Jessie would never forget Taylor's eyes, as they pleaded with her to stay. Getting on that plane was one of the hardest things Jessie had ever done.

Eighteen

Rachel pulled the scarf around her neck shielding herself from the bitter December wind. She hurried alongside Washington Square Park searching the NYU campus for Heyman Hall. Here, West Kerry was giving a lecture, and she wanted to meet him before the period was over. Once inside the building, she scanned the directory, which directed her to a second-floor auditorium. She entered the rear of the lecture hall while Kerry was addressing his attentive students.

West did a double take as Rachel moved to a seat in the rear row. His motion caused the students to look in her direction. She nodded at him, smiled, and then he continued his lecture.

"In Genesis, the serpent plummets from grace. He falls from the tree of life and is forced to stay on earth, banished from the heavens." Professor Kerry flashed an overhead showing an Egyptian woman standing beside a raised snake with four loops in its tail. At its mouth was an ankh.

Rachel pushed up her sleeve, revealing the birthmark on her wrist. Even she admitted that it resembled an ankh.

The professor removed his glasses and set them on the podium, then strolled with his slight limp to the wall near the slide's projection. "This illustration is on the tomb of Thutmose III," he pointed to the projection. "The ancient Egyptians believed that the greatest achievement was to raise the serpent. The looping tail signifies the spiritual centers within each of us that are affected as we raise the life force, or Kundalini energy. According to the mystery teachings and the Eastern tradition, this is how we reach enlightenment."

Although Rachel was baffled with the subject matter, she enjoyed watching West strut, tall and slim beside the Egyptian image.

West referred to his notes at the podium. "Even Jesus told Nicodemus, 'as Moses raised the serpent in the desert so must I be raised

Published by The Haworth Press, Inc., 2006. All rights reserved.
doi:10.1300/5721_19

up to eternal life.'" Using a pointer, the professor pointed at the ankh near the mouth of the snake. "Eternal life. It was the ancient Egyptians' belief that while they were here, they needed to raise this energy to fully realize their *true nature* and find eternal life." As West finished his lecture, he glanced at his watch. "Our time is up. Same time and place on Tuesday."

Rachel waited while the students scattered. The men quickly disappeared while an entourage of the women lingered behind, flirting with the professor. Eventually he excused himself and climbed the auditorium stairs to where Rachel was seated.

"You have quite a following, West." Rachel gestured at the young women now leaving the auditorium.

He smiled, reflecting a boyish grin. "To what do I owe the pleasure of your visit? I thought the project was finished."

"It is. There's something else I was hoping you could help me with."

"This was my last lecture today." He glanced at his watch. "It's going on four o'clock. Would you be interested in getting a bite to eat? I missed lunch."

Within a half-hour, Rachel and West were seated at a small restaurant near the campus. There were few customers eating at this time of day.

"When is the Merovingian piece airing?" West asked.

"After the first of the year. It turned out very well. Thank you, West."

"It was my pleasure. You're working on something else I can help you with?"

Rachel smiled at the thought of working with the professor on another piece. "Maybe," she cleared her mind. "I'm still poking around at Freemasonry. I heard something and I was wondering if there was anything to it." She glanced around, assuring that nobody was listening. "I heard that Freemasonry is devil worship."

"Oh . . . I've heard that angle before, also."

"Is there anything to it?" Rachel asked, urging him on.

"There are thousands of Freemasons. I've known many personally over the years. I just can't believe that all these men would be involved in devil worship."

"I've heard that one of the sacred names used in an initiation is Abaddon."

"Ah. The angel of the bottomless pit! Abaddon *is* referenced in Revelation and *does* imply the devil. Are you familiar with Sumeria, though?"

"Wasn't it an ancient society, predating the Egyptian dynasties?"

"Yes. You've been doing your homework. It was an advanced society that existed between 5000 and 3500 BC in the Mesopotamian region, actually Iraq. Interestingly enough, nothing was known about Sumer until about one hundred sixty years ago. That's when archeologists found buried cities and palaces, and retrieved thousands of clay tablets that detailed Sumerian life. It's very well possible that one day we'll know more about the Sumerians than we know about the Romans, Greeks, or Egyptians."

"Why?"

"The other civilizations used papyrus to write on—thin strips of plant pressed together. Unfortunately it disintegrates over time, so much of the Roman, Greek, and Egyptian documentation was lost through aging, as well as fires from wars. But the Sumerians inscribed their records on wet clay tablets. Then they dried and baked them, and stored them in huge libraries. From what I've read, they've uncovered about a half million of these tablets."

"A half million?"

"Yes. And many have not been translated, yet. This was an extremely advanced society that seemingly showed up from nowhere and lived for about two thousand years. We owe the concept of spherical astronomy, our timekeeping system, and the modern zodiac system of twelve astrological gods to them. One thing that is quite fascinating is that the Sumerians had an uncanny knowledge of the solar system. They correctly recorded our solar system with the exception of a tenth planet. The strange thing is that in 1981 scientists started theorizing the existence of a tenth planet based upon a telescopic sighting."

"How is that possible?" Rachel found it hard to believe. Of course, much of what West told her was that way. But she still sat and listened, engrossed as always.

"If you think that's strange . . . even though the Sumerians only lasted about 2,000 years, they recorded a celestial cycle that takes about 26,000 years to complete."

Now he truly had her attention. "How? How come we don't hear more about the Sumerians?"

"Probably because the loonies in the field believe that the Sumerians were created by little green men from outer space to be a slave race. So much of the information is not taken seriously. But mostly because their civilization conflicts with our own; they were a polytheistic society."

"They believed in many gods?"

"That's correct. And . . . let's just say there has always been a filter that screens out undesirable data regarding scientific discoveries."

"You're not serious."

"Very serious. Think about it, the National Geographic Society and the Smithsonian were started by influential groups whose interests were to discourage mankind's pursuit of our true creation."

West retrieved a notepad from his jacket and jotted down names of books. "There's a lot of information available on the Sumerians. Some of the more controversial theories are represented in the works of Immanuel Velikovsky and Zecharia Sitchin." He handed Rachel the slip of paper. "In case you ever lack good reading material."

The waiter brought their salads and Rachel mulled over the information until he was gone. "This is all very interesting, but what does any of this have to do with devil worship and Freemasonry?"

He smiled, then sipped his wine. He enjoyed having such an attentive audience, and Rachel had become his favorite student. "The Mesopotamian tablets tell stories similar to those you would find in the Bible. There is a creation story, the story of Adam and Eve, the great flood, the tower of Babel, and so on. But . . . the Sumerian tablets have different twists to these stories.

"For example, like the Bible, the Mesopotamian story of Adam and Eve is believed to be symbolic, not literal. In their story, it was believed that Adam and Eve— or the first man and woman—were created to till the soil and tend to the gardens of the gods. Remember? They were polytheistic. As long as they accepted their servant status, their needs were met and they were able to remain in a paradise. But . . . there was one thing they were warned never to do. Never to seek certain types of knowledge, and this is symbolized in their story as two trees, the tree of knowledge of good and evil and the tree of life. Or in other words, they were warned never to seek spiritual freedom and immortality. Now, in the story, Adam and Eve live in material bliss until a third party gets involved. This person is represented by the snake."

"The devil?" Rachel took a bite of her salad.

"In the Bible—yes. According to the Mesopotamian tablets, however, the snake represents one of the gods by the name of Enki. Anyway, Enki suggested that Eve involve herself in the fruit of a tree, the tree of knowledge of good and evil. And she does, as well as Adam. This angers the other gods, because the last thing they want is for mankind to seek spiritual immortality. They want mankind to remain servants, forever."

"So, the gods send Adam and Eve from their paradise."

"Yes, so their lives are consumed with maintaining their physical survival, and there is little time to seek spiritual enlightenment. The Sumerian's recorded that Enki was banished to earth, forever, by the other gods, who exposed him as being the source of all evil. It's recorded that the gods called him Prince of Darkness, and he was referred to as Satan, Lucifer, Ea, the devil, and Abaddon."

"Interesting twist."

"Remember when we first spoke, I told you about this secret brotherhood that was formed in Ancient Egypt? They taught the ancient mysteries and organized the masons into special groups?"

"Yes, I remember," Rachel said, and took another bite of her salad.

"It is believed that Enki formed this brotherhood. It was known as the Brotherhood of the Snake."

For a second Rachel had difficulty swallowing the food lodged in her throat. She coughed to clear her passageway. "Excuse me. . . . So, according to the Mesopotamian text it *is* possible that Freemasonry could be devil worship?"

"Yes. But the term *devil* is generally perceived as being evil. According to Egyptian writing, this brotherhood was committed to the teaching of spiritual freedom."

"You make it sound like he was a good guy."

"I wouldn't exactly say *good*. Eventually, the brotherhood became corrupt, and the dissemination of knowledge became restrictive to the point where it became a tool of spiritual repression. Only pharaohs, priests, and a select few were admitted into the mystery schools. And according to Egyptian lore, the teachings became distorted by Enki's son, Marduk."

Beeping interrupted them. "Excuse me." West removed the pager from his belt and peeked at the number. "I need to call home."

Rachel removed her cell phone from her purse. "Would you like to use mine?"

He smiled. "Thank you. Everyone tells me I need to come into the twenty-first century and get one of these." He punched buttons on the phone. "Hi, Rose."

Rachel tried to appear uninterested in the professor's conversation, but that was furthest from the truth.

"No, Rose. Eat without me." He glanced at his watch. "Yes, I should be home in about an hour. I'll see you then." He disconnected the line and handed the phone to Rachel. "Thank you."

"Everything okay?"

"Yes. Rose has been so nervous since the Kennedy Airport riot and the United Nations turmoil. Have you heard the latest?"

"The United Nations reconvened discussions this morning."

"Yes, and it sounds like the member states are acting like children. The countries are dividing allegiances, and they've completely lost sight that Iraq continues to advance upon Kuwait." West shook his head.

Now it was Rachel's turn to change the subject. "How long have you been married?"

"I'm not married."

"Sorry for being presumptuous. How long have you and Rose been together?"

West smiled warmly. "Rachel, Rose and I aren't *together*. Rose is my sister. She's going through a divorce, and she's staying with me until things are resolved."

Rachel felt her face heat from embarrassment. "I apologize, I just thought . . ."

"I've been meaning to ask, how's it going between you and Stanley Chancellor?"

"He's been out of the country for weeks now."

"I see. Are you guys . . . serious?"

Rachel smiled. "No."

Nineteen

Since Jessie had returned from France, she was having the hardest time concentrating on work. She turned away from her monitor and gazed out her office window. She couldn't get Taylor off her mind. She knew that her request to remain with her through the holidays was a reasonable one. She relived their airport parting over and over again, each time, analyzing what she saw in Taylor's eyes. Then it hit her; it was so simple. It was disappointment.

The knock at her office door jolted her back to reality. "Come in," but her voice was too high and she coughed to clear her throat. "Come in."

The door creaked ajar and Clark Coburn stepped in. "Good afternoon, Brennan. How was your vacation?"

"Too short, Clark, and your Thanksgiving?"

"Fine." Coburn closed the office door behind him. "I have a special assignment for you. I need an editorial on Michael Whitman, endorsing him for the senate race." Coburn dropped a file on Brennan's desk. "All the information you'll need is right here."

"When do you want the article?"

"A week from today."

"Consider it done."

Coburn moved to the door. "I knew I could count on you."

With her fork, Jessie scraped the crumbs of her TV dinner from the bottom of its plastic container. *Hardly enough,* she thought as she ate the last bite. She set the empty plate on the coffee table beside her. From the nearby attaché case, she retrieved the Whitman file. She fluffed the throw pillow on the couch behind her, nestled into it, and opened the manila folder.

Published by The Haworth Press, Inc., 2006. All rights reserved.
doi:10.1300/5721_20

Jessie scanned through the file. There were numerous editorials on Whitman's humanitarian works, which highlighted generous donations to hospitals, homeless shelters, and schools. Apparently, he had taken over the family business when he was in his mid-thirties and built Whitman Industries into a thriving empire. At the age of forty-five, he was listed as one of the top ten wealthiest men in the world. Now, according to the articles, he intended to step away from his empire to become a public servant.

The information was presented in such a manner that most would easily endorse the man. But Jessie was unlike most reporters. She set the file folder down. "This is just too squeaky clean," she concluded.

Thoughtful, she moved into her home office and sat at her computer. Maxwell jumped on her lap and rubbed his chin up against Jessie's arm. He settled down and lay purring on Jessie's legs.

She typed *Michael Whitman* at the search engine prompt, modified her criteria to remove duplicate URLs and clicked go. Almost 200 Internet references were listed. For hours, Jessie skimmed the material. Most of the information was similar to what she had already read. She was just about ready to call it quits when she saw the hyperlink "Billionaire Sues Ex-Wife for Custody of Son." Here, she learned that in the 1990s Whitman had sued for full custody of his son, alleging his wife was unfit to raise their child because she was a homosexual. "My kind of guy!"

Jessie read the article aloud: "Behind closed doors, Michael Whitman and his former wife, Sidney Marcum, agreed . . ." Jessie stopped. *Sidney Marcum? Could it be?* She returned to the article. ". . . agreed upon a settlement regarding the custodial arrangement of their twelve-year-old son. Ms. Marcum is an entertainment manager; her clients have included Anastasia—"

"Sidney Marcum is Taylor's new manager." Jessie pondered the connection. "What a coincidence."

"Jessie, you know there's no such thing as a coincidence."

Jessie ignored the faint voice in her head. After another five minutes of searching, she came across, "Whitman Loses the Governor Race." Jessie clicked the hyperlink. The article indicated that in the early 1980s Whitman ran for New York governor, and lost.

"My God, how old *is* this guy?"

Jessie read aloud: "Whitman's failure to hold his marriage together with Marcum crippled his chances of winning this election—." Jessie whispered, "Marcum strikes again!" It was getting late and she was tired. Her mouse pointer approached the X to exit.

"Jessie, keep going," that little voice pestered her.

Jessie stopped from exiting. "Where have you been?" she asked out loud. "I don't hear from you often anymore."

"I'm here, you just haven't been listening."

"Who are you?"

"A friend."

For a moment, Jessie wondered if she was going crazy. "Do you have a name?"

"You can call me Charlie."

"Are you a ghost, Charlie?"

"I am a spirit."

"Why are you with me?"

"I told you. . . . I am a friend."

"Do I know you?"

"You know me very well. We have known each other in many other lifetimes, Jessie. We were supposed to know each other here, but my life was taken prematurely."

"Why are you with me, Charlie?"

"To finish our business together."

"What business?"

"It is not time for it to come to fruition."

Jessie's vision returned to the monitor. "What should I be looking for?"

"Patience and you will find it."

In the early morning hours, Jessie found one more article of interest. The title of the commentary said it all, "Whitman Industries Acquires *The Empire*." Jessie learned that Whitman had purchased the newspaper five years earlier.

Jessie knew how to play the game. Within a week she had her article finished and on Coburn's desk. The article summarized the information in Whitman's original file, excluding the extras Jessie had learned.

Twenty

Jessie was typing in Brennan's office when the phone rang. "Hello," she answered in her masculine voice.

"Hi, Brennan," a familiar voice said. "This is Rachel Addison. How are you?"

"Hi, Rach—" she started in her normal voice. She coughed. Rachel's call to *Brennan's* phone confused her. "Excuse me. I'm fine, and how are you, Rachel?"

"I was wondering if you wanted to join me for lunch, sometime."

"Lunch would be nice." Jessie was taken aback by the call. *Why are you calling, Rachel?* "But I'm swamped this week for lunch. Would you consider dinner, instead?"

It was seven o'clock when Rachel neared the hostess station at the Chart House. This time, Brennan greeted her. "Good evening, Rachel." Brennan was dressed handsomely in a tailored Calvin Klein suit. Jessie's tinted blue eyes searched Rachel's as she drew near. Awkwardly, Rachel extended her hand, and Jessie shook it.

The hostess led the couple to a table with a view of the Hudson River. But nearby parties were too close for comfort.

"Excuse me, Miss? May we sit over there?" Jessie pointed at a vacant table across the room.

"Of course." She left them with menus.

"You do realize that my office phone is probably tapped," Jessie started.

Rachel nodded. "I didn't think there would be anything wrong with a single woman asking a single man to lunch."

"Aren't you seeing Chancellor?"

Published by The Haworth Press, Inc., 2006. All rights reserved.
doi:10.1300/5721_21

"I haven't since our first couple of dates. He travels a lot. . . . He's guarded about developing a relationship, so I've backed away."

"That's probably best." Jessie glanced around, making a mental note of the parties.

Rachel changed the subject. "I saw your commentary on Whitman, and wanted to talk with you about it. Whitman is a Bilderberger."

A waiter greeted them. They ordered a bottle of wine, and he disappeared.

"That's interesting. My article didn't say this, but Whitman owns *The Empire.*"

"I know," Rachel said. "That's not *all* he owns. He's the controlling stockholder of WABS. The network that carries *Over the Edge.*"

Jessie absorbed the new information. "He must be a Mason."

A waiter brought a bottle of wine. He displayed the label to Brennan, uncorked it, and poured a splash for Brennan to sample. Jessie sipped, nodded at the waiter, and he poured two glasses. The waiter took their orders and left.

"How was France?"

A smile came to Jessie's lips, and her eyes lit up. "Too short."

"What are your plans?"

"I'm back earning my degrees. I'm on schedule for the thirty-second in mid-January. Taylor comes back to the states shortly after that. I'm not sure what I'll do. . . . What have you been up to?" Jessie changed the subject.

"I did this incredible piece on the Merovingian Dynasty. It's great, Jes—." She corrected herself. "Brennan." She shook her head. "It went to Neil for review last week. I learned yesterday that he won't air it. He said it was too controversial."

"What was in your project?"

"It was about the theory that Jesus and Mary Magdalene had children and how the church was not only aware of the lineage, but how they supported the assassination of two of the last Merovingian kings. I showed that there exist today endless manuscripts that suggest the Church misled us about the virgin birth and resurrection. I documented the rise and fall of the Knights Templar and how the Knights Malta took over their military orders after the Templars were destroyed."

"The Knights Malta?"

"While Freemasonry is one descendent of the Knights Templar, others are the Hospitallers, Knights of St. John, the Rosicrucians, and the Knights of Malta. The Knights Malta watched the demise of, and in some cases even contributed to the Templars' destruction, and then they took over their military orders. Today, they're supervised by the Vatican and are the primary contact between the Vatican and the CIA. Some believe the Knights of Malta are involved with the Bilderbergers."

"Well, if what you said is true, they wouldn't air it. Think about it. Whitman is one of the owners of WABS—he's a Bilderberger, which means he has indirect ties to the Vatican—and he can dictate what can be aired at the network."

"Of course! And the last group that would want this to be aired is the Vatican." Rachel took a sip of her wine. "Sometimes I'm so close to something I can't see it. . . . If what you're suggesting is true, it would be a losing battle to fight him to air it."

"That would be correct."

"And if he's not going to show this piece, he's certainly not going to air my new project. I'm exploring the angle that Freemasonry is devil worship."

"And?" Jessie's curiosity was piqued.

"I've learned about this ancient civilization known as the Sumerians."

"I'm a little familiar with the Sumerians. But I didn't think they were connected to Freemasonry."

"Indirectly they are. Apparently, the Sumerians were a polytheistic society and one of the gods, named Enki, chose to give the first man and woman the ability to seek their spiritual freedom. This pissed off the other gods; they banished him to earth and called him Abaddon or the Prince of Darkness. According to Egyptian lore, Enki or Abaddon, formed the Brotherhood of the Snake, the group that formed the mason guilds and taught the mysteries."

Jessie listened intently to Rachel, and when she finished, she didn't know what to say. "I assure you, if Neil objected to your Merovingian piece, he's going to object to that one."

"Sometimes I wonder why I'm a reporter. My work is always edited and, in some cases, censored. And yet, the network has always been patient with me. What am I going to tell West?"

"West?"

"West Kerry, the professor from NYU." There was a sparkle in Rachel's eyes. "He was instrumental on the Merovingian piece and the devil-worship project. How can I tell him the network isn't going to air it? He put in so much energy into it."

Rachel and Jessie finished their dinner. They had been at the restaurant for over two hours. Jessie, on the alert, had watched all the tables in the room turn over, all except for one. At that table sat two men. They each appeared to be in their early thirties. Both were dressed in black suits with white shirts and conservative ties. They were attractive and clean-shaven. Silently, they sat, each nursing a cup of coffee.

Jessie casually sipped her coffee. "I think we're being watched."

"Really?" Rachel sipped her after-dinner drink. "Where?"

"There are two men sitting behind you. They've been here since we arrived."

"What makes you think they're watching us?"

"Two men, dressed in business suits, having a very leisurely dinner, and not talking with each other?"

"That doesn't mean they're watching us. Perhaps you're just being paranoid."

Jessie paid for their dinner and claimed their coats near the front door. She caught Rachel by surprise when she helped her into her coat. Jessie slipped on the Ralph Lauren trench coat and held the door for Rachel. As Rachel passed through, Jessie's eyes darted to the table where the men had sat at. It was vacant.

Still not accustomed to short hair, Jessie pulled the wool collar around her neck. "Brr," she rubbed her hands together to warm them. "Where'd you park?"

Rachel's head nodded toward the end of a dark parking lot, where a streetlamp was mysteriously unlit. The couple made their way across the pavement, passing Brennan's Mustang. They were three parking spots from Rachel's car when the sound of footsteps alerted them.

"Keep your eyes open." Her breath in the moonlight exposed Jessie's whisper. Casually, Jessie glanced behind. Without the light from the streetlamp, she could see only two dark silhouettes approach a car on the other side of the pathway.

"Is it them?" Rachel whispered.

"I think so."

An interior car light lit, revealing that the men sat in a car across from them. The light dimmed when both doors slammed shut. Jessie escorted Rachel to her Saab where they stood awkwardly, knowing that they were being watched.

"Rachel, get in your car and leave."

"I'm not leaving you here, alone. You better come up with a better plan than that." Her eyes revealed a stubborn side.

"Drive over to my car, then park." Jessie whispered. "When I've started my car, leave, and I'll follow you out."

Rachel hesitated. She took a step forward closing the gap between the two. She whispered, "Kiss me."

"Excuse me?" Jessie was taken back by the suggestion.

"You heard me. We're supposed to be on a date. It'll look suspicious if you don't at least kiss me goodnight," Rachel whispered.

Kissing Rachel was the furthest thing from Jessie's mind. It's wasn't that Rachel was unattractive, because she was a knockout. And it wasn't because she didn't like her, because she did. But Jessie was committed to Taylor's lips. And here, in the cold, dark parking lot along the Hudson River, she was torn. In the end, she realized that Rachel's safety was more important than her discomfort, and Jessie approached Rachel's moist lips. Then she withdrew. "Get in your car," Jessie whispered.

Rachel opened the door, started the ignition, and put the Saab in drive. But abruptly, she slammed the car into park, and hopped out of the car. She had her arms wrapped around Jessie's neck and back. While Rachel pressed her shapely body against Jessie, giving the appearance that she wanted Brennan, Rachel's lips moved to Jessie's ear. "Get in the car," she whispered. "It's safer that we leave together."

"Fine," Jessie succumbed. She walked around the car and got into the Saab.

As Rachel drove slowly through the parking lot, Jessie's eyes were fixed on the side-view mirror. They were just about to the road when Jessie saw headlights. "Here they come."

"What should I do?" Rachel asked.

"Head north, stay within the speed limit. I don't want to tip them off." Rachel complied, and the shadowing car maintained an inconspicuous tail.

"Who would be following us?" Rachel asked. "What's wrong with me asking you out?"

"Nothing. Unless they're onto one of us."

Now in Tarrytown, the car approached the entrance to the Cross Westchester Expressway. "What do I do?"

"Take 287 and see if the car follows."

As suggested, Rachel merged onto the highway, and the other car followed. "Where's your apartment? I'm not going to spend all night driving around."

"That's my spot over there," Jessie pointed to the assigned parking space.

Rachel cut the engine. "Do you see them yet?" Their pursuer had fallen out of sight after they turned off the main road.

"No. Not yet. Let's get inside."

Jessie led Rachel down the walkway to the lighted apartment entrance. As they climbed the exterior stairs, she spied the parking lot. Nothing seemed out of the ordinary. She opened the door and cut the entry light. Jessie permitted Rachel to enter but something caught Jessie's eye as she closed the door. The dark sedan was making its way toward the apartment with headlights off.

"They've arrived," Jessie shut the door and dead-bolted it.

Jessie knew that their pursuers had seen them enter the apartment. She hit the light switches for the kitchen and living room. Rachel was on Jessie's heels as she moved into her dark bedroom. At the window she searched for the car. "There they are," Jessie pointed at the dark car parked outside the apartment.

"Now what?" Rachel asked.

"Let's wait and see."

The women waited. But the car wasn't leaving anytime soon, so just after midnight Jessie suggested that Rachel spend the night. When Jessie undressed for bed that night, she didn't remove the body suit or facial hair. She needed to be prepared. While she tossed and turned uncomfortably in her bed, Rachel remained restless on the sofa.

In the morning the car was gone. It had left sometime in the early morning hours. Rachel drove Jessie to her car, then headed for her own apartment for a change of clothes.

The abrupt rap on Brennan's door diverted Jessie's eyes from the monitor. Without giving her a chance to respond, Coburn stuck his head in Brennan's office.

"Brennan, we need to talk."

Jessie knew something had gone amiss; the man was pale. "Come in, Clark."

Coburn closed the door behind him. "Brennan," his eyes on the floor, "it's been brought to my attention that you have been *seeing* Rachel Addison."

Jessie knew it would be pointless to deny it. "We saw each other last night."

Clark's eyes finally met Brennan's. "You must stop."

"Why?"

"*Why* isn't important. It's just important that you stop seeing her."

Jessie was curious and pressed him. "If you were in my shoes, wouldn't you be unsatisfied with that answer?"

Clark nodded. "Yes . . . of course. Brennan, I'm not asking you, I'm telling you. You *must* stop seeing her."

At lunchtime, Jessie left *The Empire* and drove to a nearby restaurant. She scanned her surroundings as she strolled the busy sidewalk. Satisfied that she hadn't been followed, she punched in Rachel's cell number.

Rachel recognized Jessie's number. "Hi."

"I was warned today by Clark Coburn to stop seeing you."

"Why?"

"He wouldn't give me a reason."

While driving back to the office after lunch, Jessie punched in the Manhattan phone number. The call was answered on its third ring.

"Good afternoon, Marcum Productions," a woman answered.

"Good afternoon. Is Sidney Marcum in?" Jessie asked in her normal voice.

"She hasn't returned from lunch yet; can I help you?"

Jessie hesitated. "I understand that Sidney will be seeing my partner, Taylor Andrews, in Europe next week."

"Oh, you must be Jessie Mercer. I'm Natalie."

"Hi, Natalie. I hate to be an inconvenience, but I was hoping that Sidney wouldn't mind delivering a small Christmas gift to Taylor for me."

"I'm sure Sidney would be happy to help."

"A friend of mine will be near your office later this afternoon. If it's okay, I'd like to have him just drop the gift off."

"Shouldn't be a problem," she said warmly. "What's your friend's name?"

"Brennan Keller."

Jessie left work early that day and headed into Manhattan. Taylor had been a moving target since Jessie left her in France, so Jessie convinced herself that Sidney Marcum would be a more reliable means to transport her Christmas gift.

When Brennan arrived at Marcum Productions, Inc., the receptionist greeted him. "Hello, can I help you?"

Jessie unfastened the top few buttons of the trench coat, and smoothed out Brennan's hair. "Yes. Is Sidney Marcum in?"

From behind the desk, an attractive African-American woman pushed through swinging glass doors that separated the lobby from the offices. She smiled at Brennan as she dropped a pile of mail in an Out box.

"She's in meetings all afternoon. Do you have an appointment?"

"No. I was asked to deliver a package to her for Taylor Andrews."

"Oh, you must be Brennan," the woman of color interrupted. "Hi, I'm Natalie." She shook Brennan's hand. "You have a package from Jessie Mercer for Taylor, right?"

"That's correct."

"I gave Sidney Jessie's message. She's happy to help out, and I'll make sure that she gets it," Natalie said warmly.

Jessie left the small package with Natalie. As she left the building she realized the real motivation for dropping the gift off—she wanted to meet Michael Whitman's ex-wife.

Twenty-One

It was late that Sunday night when Jessie returned from the Freemason initiation. Maxwell greeted her at the door, weaving between her legs. She had just spent the previous three hours in the car, and she was exhausted. She removed the suit jacket and hung it in the coat closet. She loosened her tie and undid the top buttons of her shirt.

Today's initiation had been the last of the year. She had been looking forward to the break, and it was here at last. Jessie retrieved her cell phone from the charger on the kitchen counter. She wanted to call Taylor. "One missed call" was displayed, so she retrieved her message.

"Hello, Jessie. This is Sidney Marcum. Sorry it has taken me a few days to get back with you. I just wanted to let you know that I received your package. I'm flying out on Tuesday and plan on seeing Taylor Wednesday. I hope you have a nice holiday. Good-bye."

Jessie deleted the message. "Sidney sounds much younger than Whitman." She set the phone on the counter and wandered into the living room, where she parked on the couch.

Although she was bushed, she was wound up from the trip. She needed to clear her mind. A quick glance around the room verified that the blinds were still drawn from the previous evening. She peeled the artificial facial hair from her face, and laid it on the coffee table beside her. Jessie removed her shoes, rested her feet on the couch, and then closed her eyes.

Relax, she told herself. It didn't take long for her body to unwind, but her mind kept replaying activities from that day, that month, and that year. Unexpectedly, Jessie's thoughts drifted to other images. Images foreign to her, or at least, so she thought. At first, the geometric patterns came so quickly that she couldn't see them. Then they slowed—circles, triangles, pentagrams, hexagrams, tetrahedrons, and others—but they were still meaningless to Jessie.

Published by The Haworth Press, Inc., 2006. All rights reserved.
doi:10.1300/5721_22

⁊⁊

The sand scorched the bottom of Jessie's bare feet. She quickened her pace; somehow knowing that relief was just beyond the peak of the sandbank. She knew she was being chased, making her sprint even faster. Her swiftness and ease dashing up hot sand surprised her. Almost effortlessly, the strong, youthful legs carried her up the crest and over, and then she saw her destination. She bolted down the embankment, and at the base of the dune her feet plunged into a small pool of water, relieving her searing skin.

She sighed as the tepid water doused her feet, then laughed, but her voice seemed foreign. An abrupt splash from behind surprised her. She turned. A young girl with an olive complexion was dancing in the shallow water. Although her ankle-length linen dress was pulled to her knees so the bottom wouldn't get wet, she splattered the water so much that the top of the short-sleeve dress was soaked.

The girl laughed at Jessie. "I almost beat you that time, Lukeman. Let us try one more time." The girl ran up the mound of sand.

Lukeman? Jessie gazed into the pool surrounding her. Before the water calmed, she glimpsed a white kilt draping just below the knee, then her olive-colored legs standing in the shallow pond. She leaned over, closer to the water, waiting for the ripples to still. When they did, she gazed into the dark-brown eyes of a ten-year-old boy.

His hand felt the smooth bald head. With the exception of a small patch of hair tied on his right side, his head had been shaven. With his hands he explored the dark skin of his upper torso, the lean but firm abdominal muscles and developing pectoral muscles. It was indeed the body of a boy.

Echoes of laughter thrust him from this memory, to a future event.

A blast of sand brushed against his face. The air was hot and dry. He squinted, waiting for the wind to subside. When it did, his gaze returned to the rock face carved on the body of a lion. Although it was huge, behind it a massive pyramid soared above the landscape. He observed the causeway that connected the sphinx and the pyramid.

Throughout his life, clairvoyant images had revealed his future. Today, his visions showed that his initiation would begin in the temple of the great sphinx. Here he would begin his transformation, then proceed through the causeway to the funerary temple at the east side of the pyramid. After another initiation he would advance to the north entrance of the pyramid. Once inside, he *would* master ceremony after ceremony, progressing through chambers that few had known, until he would conquer the final initiation, finding eternal life.

A footstep alerted him of her presence, catapulting him back to his present. He felt her energy before she touched him and he smiled. "Hello, Mother."

Eshe moved to his side and set her hand on his shoulder. He found the warm smile on his mother's face. Like the young girl, she wore an ankle-length linen dress with straps.

"Hello, Lukeman. Are you seeing your future?" Her neckline was adorned with a broad collar shining of gold and precious stones. Her earrings glittered gems, and matching dual bracelets dressed her upper arms.

"Mother, why are only a select few able to learn the secrets to eternal life?"

"I wish I had a good answer, but I don't. The gods and pharaohs believe that only a few chosen souls can seek the mysteries of our creators. This is how we have lived and died for many lifetimes."

"But you know—it is not right."

Eshe smiled. She admired the insight and strength of her firstborn. Her arms embraced the strong boy. "You are correct. It is not right."

Darkness came, and with it brought anger and sorrow. The echoes of her cry brought him to a new place.

At first it was so faint that Lukeman didn't know what it was. Then he recognized his sister's distress. With more urgency he searched the palace until he found Dalila, sitting against the hard chamber wall. She was sobbing.

"What is wrong?" Lukeman asked.

Dalila's tear-filled eyes met Lukeman's, and his heart ached sensing his sister's sorrow. Then he heard the yelling, and he understood. His mother and father were arguing again, but it was different this time. Lukeman approached the curtain that separated the chambers. He peeked through a tiny crevice.

His father, Oba, paced back and forth, and his mother knelt on the ground near him. Oba seemed enormous compared to his mother's cowering body.

"You are a disgrace to this family," Oba screamed.

"Please . . . the children," she stood up calmly, blood trickling from her lip.

"You don't want them to know their mother is tainted? You didn't think I would find out? I'm Oba, the vizier, the pharaoh's closest advisor. Of all the souls in Egypt . . . you will pay dearly for this act of weakness." Abruptly, he slapped her face with the back of his hand.

"No," Lukeman screamed, rushing to his mother's side. He placed his body in front of Eshe stopping another blow.

Oba loomed over the boy, and with an unwavering stare he said, "Wish your mother good-bye, Lukeman."

Desolation added to the darkness and sorrow. This time the echoes of sobbing were of his mother's, and they brought Lukeman again to his future.

Lukeman didn't know why his father sent him to the dungeon, but when Oba asked him to go, he obeyed. One of the servants escorted him down the dark passageways. Turn after turn, Lukeman trekked through the mazelike corridors until they arrived at the dungeon door. The servant lifted the beam, permitting access to the cell. He nodded at Lukeman.

Naive about what lay behind the door, Lukeman opened it. Instantly, his stomach churned from the putrid smell of dying flesh. He covered his mouth and nose, fearing he would vomit. He stepped into the dark cell, lit only by tiny holes to the outside world. He couldn't fathom why his father had sent him here, and then her saw her lying on a thin blanket.

"Dear god," Lukeman rushed to her side. He barely recognized her. She had withered to skin and bones. "Mother?" he swept her in his arms, and held her the way she had embraced him, so many years earlier.

Eshe stirred and opened her eyes. "Lukeman?"

"Yes, it is I, Mother." Tears came to his eyes.

Eshe gasped for air. "You have grown."

"Mother . . . I didn't know you were here. Father told me you went far away. He has held you here all these years?"

"I needed to see you before I go." Eshe coughed. "Your father has given me a gift."

"My father should burn in netherworld." As a boy, he had never understood why his mother was sent away. "What happened, Mother? Why did he do this to you?"

"I fell in love . . . with a servant . . . Jahi. He was . . . untouchable."

Lukeman felt the life energy seep from her frail body. "Mother, don't leave. Not now that I have found you."

"The baby. . . . Find the baby, Lukeman. When I was put here, I was with child."

"You had a baby?"

"A girl. It's Jahi's. Find Jahi and tell him . . ." Eshe closed her eyes.

"Mother? Don't go! Stay! Please."

The words were barely audible. "It is my time. I love you." Eshe's body stilled.

She was gone. Lukeman cradled her, and wept for their lost years. Rage fueled his soul, a feeling so foreign to him, and dangerous if not harnessed.

Lukeman left the dungeon and hunted for his father. He raged through the palace, seeking the man who had killed his mother. He found Oba in the food preparation area nibbling on grapes and pome-granates.

Lukeman's stormy entrance alerted Oba. Though he saw the rage in his son's eyes, he was unthreatened by it and popped a grape in his mouth.

Lukeman struggled to control his feelings. "How could you do that to her?" he screamed, clenching both hands. "You killed her."

"Punishment for women who commit adultery is death," Oba said matter-of-factly.

"Yet, it is no crime for you to seek the companionship of another woman?"

"Men may have many wives, as long as they can afford them."

"Mother said she was with child. What happened to the baby?"

"It died in childbirth."

"Father . . . you must provide her with a proper funeral."

"I mourned her passing six years ago," Oba said coldly.

Lukeman could barely control his emotions. "Father, I have *never* liked you," tears of anger filled his eyes. "I have always respected you for the great man that you are. But I cannot anymore. I have never felt hatred, until now." Lukeman moved to the exit. "I will leave here, before I do something that I will regret for eternity . . . before I kill you." Lukeman dashed from the palace.

Although her body was here, Jessie's mind was back in Egypt thousands of years ago. But when her cell phone chimed, it severed the connection with her distant past, and she struggled to find her way home. Like an unwelcome friend, Lukeman's rage followed her back. Jessie woke disoriented. Abruptly she stood, the dizziness hit, and her heart pounded wildly. She stumbled back on the couch, feeling Lukeman's anger caged inside her.

"What happened to me?" she said.

"You are remembering," Charlie answered in Jessie's mind.

"Remembering what?" Jessie murmured, almost inaudibly.

Twenty-Two

It was a few days before Christmas. With no initiations, and no reason to go to the office, Jessie was on sabbatical from Brennan. She had stocked up on food and intended to hang out in her apartment with Maxwell through Christmas. After her Egypt experience, Jessie needed a break.

She had set up her laptop at the kitchen table. Her fingers quickly stroked away at the keyboard. Her story, *The Ultimate Conspiracy,* was finally coming together. In between moments of clarity, she'd grab a handful of dry cereal and munch. Her attire lacked her body suit and her face was hairless. She felt more peaceful since she recognized that Lukeman's displaced anger was not Jessie's. But was it?

The cell phone that connected her to her real life chimed. Knowing that it was probably Taylor, she smiled and grabbed it without looking at the display. "Hello."

"Jessie, it's Rachel. What are you up to these days?"

"Hi, Rachel." Jessie hoped Rachel didn't hear her disappointment. "I'm writing."

"Would you like to get together for dinner tomorrow night?"

Jessie hesitated. The last thing she wanted was to cut short her life as a recluse. She recalled their last meeting. "After last time, do you think that's wise?"

"If either one of us has a tail, let's abort. There's a decent restaurant in Tappan."

Jessie wanted to scream, *"NO, THANK YOU!"* But she also knew she was starving for human contact. "Do we need reservations?"

Once again dressed in Brennan's garb, Jessie headed out. After being out of the body suit for a few days, her breasts were now sore by

Published by The Haworth Press, Inc., 2006. All rights reserved.
doi:10.1300/5721_23

their containment. As she crossed the Hudson River, she listened to the radio. A newscaster reviewed UN discussions regarding the Iraqi invasion of Kuwait.

"Today, behavior of the United Nation members was baffling. Like children, the delegates resorted to name-calling, and three countries announced their withdrawals from discussions. According to representatives of at least two member states, a significant portion of the UN is opposed to taking any action against Iraq. Apparently, their reluctance is triggered by the United States' and coalition force's failure to uncover Saddam Hussein's weapons of mass destruction in the earlier—"

Jessie turned the radio off. She shook her head. "I can't believe this has dragged on this long," she mumbled.

Jessie drove past the restaurant, monitoring the traffic behind her, then turned again and watched. After ten minutes of futile zigzagging, she arrived promptly at seven o'clock. The parking lot was packed.

A hostess greeted Brennan. "Can I help you, sir?"

Even after all this time, Jessie was still not accustomed to being greeted as a man. Eying Rachel at a table against a wall, she pointed. "I see my party."

The waiter took their menus and hurried off to the kitchen.

"I've been meaning to ask you," Rachel's voice was low. "Have you had any other warnings about seeing me?"

Jessie shook her head. "No. Coburn never brought it up after that one time."

"Do you think they're onto us?"

Jessie lowered her voice, "I think if they suspected that I wasn't who I appear to be, they would have pursued it confrontationally. They knew about your investigation into secret societies last year. Maybe they just don't want Brennan to get mixed up with the *wrong* people." She smiled.

Rachel changed the subject, "Do you have any plans for the holidays?"

"You mean other than missing Taylor and feeling sorry for myself? I just want to spend a few days writing, and being my old self." Jessie was thoughtful. "Actually, this will be my first Christmas, ever, without being with my brother."

"Steve was a special guy," Rachel admitted. "In some ways, I was closer to him than any of the men I've ever dated, and yet, we never dated."

Jessie realized that Rachel was the closest person in her life, and yet, she knew very little about her, personally. "What's your story? Ever married?"

"No, never married. Never really been in a serious relationship. . . . I don't think I've ever really even fallen in love."

The waiter returned with their soup. Jessie sipped her wine considering what Rachel had said. "I find that odd. I mean . . . you're attractive, intelligent, have a great career, from what I've learned about you, Rachel, you're a nice person. I would think that there would be a healthy line of gentlemen callers."

Rachel plunged her spoon into the French onion soup, skimming cheese. She smiled. "I'm not saying I don't have my fair share of dates. I just haven't dated anyone special for any great length of time. Usually, we go out on a first and maybe a second date and then . . . things change."

Jessie was a little uncomfortable suggesting it. "Are you, perhaps, picky?"

"No. It usually isn't my choice to stop seeing them. Perhaps it's my job, which does entail an incredible amount of time. I've wondered if it's because I've placed my father on a pedestal, and maybe they feel that they just can't compete with a ghost. Then there are times when I've guessed that they wanted to get me in bed, and then the challenge is over . . ." Rachel shrugged her shoulders. "Whatever the reason is—I just can't take it personally."

Jessie changed the subject. "How about you? Do you have any plans for the holidays?"

"I'm leaving tomorrow to visit my mother for a few days. She's in Maryland."

"I don't think you've mentioned her before. Do you see her often?"

Rachel shook her head. "No," her eyes fixed on a glass of water, avoided contact. "My mother hasn't been the same since my father's death."

Jessie clearly saw Rachel's pain, and instinctively placed her hand on top of Rachel's. "I'm sorry, Rachel." She lightly squeezed her hand and withdrew.

"She's hospitalized. It breaks my heart seeing her, so . . . I don't go very often. They think she's crazy."

"And you?" Jessie's eyes softened.

Rachel sighed. "I think my father's death traumatized her. She's been in therapy since he died. And . . . about ten years ago, she started talking about seeing him."

"Seeing your father?"

"Yeah. She said that he started visiting her and shared that with her therapist. I'm sure you can figure out the rest. She's been institutionalized for close to ten years. I've tried to get her out, but whenever she makes progress, she has a setback."

"Like what?"

"She sees him. So, they increase her medication. So she's over-medicated."

"I'm sorry, Rachel. What do you think? Do you think she's crazy?"

Rachel shook her head. "No. I think she sees my father's spirit. Perhaps he has not been able to transition because of the circumstances of his death. Maybe he's stuck here until there's closure."

"You've always suspected foul play regarding his death. Now I have a better idea why this is so personal. If your suspicions are correct, this Freemason group is not only responsible for your losing your father . . . but also your mother."

Rachel nodded.

The holidays passed. Between the loss of her brother, and being away from her partner, Jessie was terribly lonely. Taylor called her on Christmas day. She loved the necklace that Jessie had sent through Sidney Marcum. Taylor was scheduled to perform in New York City on her return to the states, in three weeks.

Jessie resumed her initiations after the first of the year. There were two more Sundays before she would graduate to thirty-two degrees of Freemasonry. The first Sunday passed without incident.

Jessie wrapped her coat collar around her neck to protect her from the bitter wind as she approached the Grand Lodge on Twenty-third Street. Once inside, Brennan was directed to the Chapter Room which had soaring ceilings and an aged chandelier. Drapes on both sides of the room were hung from ceiling to floor, and tied against the walls. Earthy tones and Egyptian decor added to the dated feeling of the room.

There were two rows of leather-upholstered benches along the longer sides of the room. Elevated staged areas were situated along the shorter walls, where three chairs were situated. A small altar centered the room.

Jessie, anxious to experience this final Masonic degree, arrived a few minutes early. She removed the trench coat and sat in the back row of the refinished benches. Soon, other candidates filtered in.

Throughout the Scottish Rite levels, Jessie had been led to believe that she would find the light in subsequent degrees. Here, she was in the thirty-second degree, and this afternoon, she expected to find *the light.*

Jessie no longer feared that she would be forced to remove her clothes during an initiation. Her anxiety was finally gone. In the higher-level initiations, a Degree Master and degree cast were prearranged to perform the complex rituals. The candidates observed but did not directly participate in the ceremonies.

As she waited, she found herself drawn to cobra figures that lined the wall across from her. She realized that the snake sculptures surrounded the room.

"Hello, Brennan," a vaguely familiar voice called to her.

Michael Whitman stood in front of her. She rose, extended her hand, and their handshake transitioned into the Master Mason pass grip. "Mr. Whitman. It's nice to see you again." Her speculation about Whitman's association with Freemasonry had been answered.

"I enjoyed your feature story last month. Well done."

Michael's dark eyes had a mesmerizing effect on her. She couldn't focus. Though she knew she must bring her attention back, it was a monumental task. She shook her head, attempting to shake off the stupor. "Thank you. I wish you the best in the senate race." She hoped that her trance had been inconspicuous.

"Good luck, Brennan. I hope you find the lecture . . . enlightening." A sinister smile came to his lips, and then he disappeared outside the hall.

The meeting room slowly filled with other candidates. Observers, wearing white or black Masonic caps, also sat. Then two cast members sat on the east stage. Jessie couldn't see their faces, but they were dressed in full costume, with robes, caps, broad collar trinkets, and regalia.

One of the cast members stood and addressed the audience. "Good morning, gentlemen. I have some disappointing news. Our Thirty-Second Degree Master has become ill." Sighs of disappointment echoed throughout the large hall. "But we're fortunate to be in New York City, where a former Thirty-Second Degree Master resides. Mr. Michael Whitman has graciously agreed to deliver the lecture this morning."

The man in the center chair stood, and moved to the platform's edge. It was Whitman in full costume, including a violet cap. "Good morning."

The lights dimmed, and a spotlight illuminated him as he read the pages of the thirty-second degree lecture. "You are here to learn, if you can learn, and to remember what you have been taught. In the Scottish Rite you will be taught that our ancient ancestors who knew all the mysteries left enough traces so that we today, with diligent labor and teaching, may renew them and bring them to light for your enlightenment." He lingered a moment, then, "We now come to the great symbol of Pythagoras."

Suddenly, directly above Michael, a three-dimensional triangle in black light emerged. Its appearance was subtle, yet gripping. "Our symbols have descended to us from the Aryans, and many were invented by Pythagoras, who studied in Egypt and Babylon."

The black light faded and the triangle transformed into a pentagram, a five-pointed star. "In order to preserve the great truths learned from the profane, there were invented some of our symbols that represent the profoundest of truths descended to us from our white ancestors."

The pentagram swiftly changed to a six-pointed then seven-pointed star. The stars faded, then Masonic symbols appeared in black light: the square and compass, the Bible, the letter "G," and the Hebrew letter "yod."

The collective effect of Whitman's mesmerizing voice and the visuals of the Masonic symbols had a hypnotizing effect on Jessie. She closed her eyes, only for a second, to shed the stupor that had fallen upon her. In that second, the darkness swallowed her, and with her mind's eye she saw the geometric patterns. At first they appeared rapidly, then they slowed, this time seeming more familiar than the last time.

At sixteen, Lukeman fled his father's home. The notion that his mother had lived in that dungeon, isolated, for six years haunted him. She had been alone and sick. He would never forgive his father for punishing her so. But, he would never exonerate himself for not questioning his father more about his mother's disappearance.

It upset him to leave his sister, Dalila, but he knew she was safe with his father's second wife. Besides, she had grown fond of Zuka, Lukeman's half brother, who had just turned five.

After living in the comfort of the Great House, Lukeman left the fortress for the Memphis streets. Soon, rumors circulated that the vizier's undisciplined son had left the nest of his rightful legacy. Many nights he slept in the alleyways of the workers' village, and days passed without food. Because of the gossip, people feared repercussions from Oba if they helped Lukeman.

Asim was exhausted. His muscles ached from the toil of a long and difficult day. As he left the Great House, thoughts of his family lured him through the Memphis streets, back to the workers' dwellings. Today was his ninth day of work. Tomorrow he rested. With that thought, he smiled.

It was faint. At first Asim thought nothing of it, but then it repeated, and he stopped. He cocked his head, listening for the groan. A distressed cry was coming from a narrow alleyway.

It was approaching sundown, and the alley's walls blocked the remaining rays of sunlight. When Asim's eyes adjusted to the dark alley, he saw a figure against the far wall. He drew to the shadow, and recognized the vizier's son. He had heard gossip about the young man but would never turn his back on a person in need.

"Are you hurt?" he asked softly. "Can you walk?" With that he pulled Lukeman to his feet, wrapping his arm snugly around Lukeman's waist. Slowly, he carried him from the dark alleyway.

Lukeman was close to starvation when Asim found him that night. Asim, being the kind and gentle soul that he was, welcomed Lukeman into his home. To Lukeman, Asim had the ideal family. He was a loving husband who had a devoted wife and four children, three teenage boys, and a five-year-old girl named Jamila.

Lukeman was grateful to Asim, and as soon as he was strong enough, he searched for work. Since Asim and his sons worked in the palace kitchen, Asim introduced Lukeman to his superior, Mosi.

Mosi, of course, recognized Lukeman and consulted with his superior. Eventually, the plea for work advanced to Oba. Unknown to Lukeman, he was granted work after Oba sanctioned the request.

Memphis was situated along the Nile, in Lower Egypt. Away from the palace and grand courtyard was the crowded village. Here the working caste lived and died in small, barrack-like compartments strung together, with narrow alleys separating the clay-brick dwellings.

Asim's home was in the center of a ten-unit cluster. There were three rooms to his quarters, and in the front, goats were sheltered. A small kitchen and storage area was in the rear, and a reception area was in the center. Here, Asim, his wife Femi, and Jamila slept while

Lukeman slept with Asim's boys on the rooftop, where the family also ate and cooked.

Although the living accommodations were overcrowded, Lukeman was touched that Asim's family welcomed him. Asim's boys revered Lukeman as an older brother, while Jamila shadowed Lukeman, longing for his attention. Eventually, a small chamber opened across the alley from Asim's dwelling and Lukeman moved.

Lukeman crushed the pestle against the mortar. Scrapes and abrasions marred his knuckles, making it painful to grind the grain, but he continued pressing. He still wasn't accustomed to the workload expected of him from his superiors. He was exhausted. While living at the palace, he had never realized how difficult it was for the lower class. Lukeman labored for nine days, on the tenth day he rested, then the cycle began again. He was compensated for his hard work with grain, and Asim taught him how to barter to satisfy his other needs.

As Lukeman applied pressure on the pestle, his sore knuckles slammed into the side of the mortar. A shriek escaped his lips and hastily he shook his hand. Lukeman heard the tread of sandals from behind. He glanced at the worker across from him, whose eyes were focused over Lukeman's shoulder, confirming that someone had entered the kitchen. Anticipating his superior, Lukeman returned to work, ignoring his pain.

"This is not your destiny, Lukeman." An unfamiliar voice resounded behind him.

Lukeman turned. A tall man loomed over him. Dressed in a long, white, hooded robe, the man's eyes bored into his soul. He was unlike most Egyptians. His skin color was less red and his eyes had an unusual bluish tint.

Eyes of the Nile, Lukeman thought.

Stubble grew in the recess of his chin, creating a shadow of facial hair, which was uncommon for Egyptian men.

Lukeman knew Kek only by reputation. As the founder of the great brotherhood, Kek would have been his teacher if he were still living the life of a chosen one. Out of respect, Lukeman bowed his head, but returned to his work.

"Lukeman, walk with me," the man instructed.

"But I can't. If I don't produce my part, I will not earn my grain."

Kek reached for Lukeman's sore hand. Warmth emanated from his touch. "Walk with me. Today, you have earned your keep."

Lukeman returned the tool to the bowl and followed Kek from the kitchen. They exited into an expansive courtyard bordered by soaring brick walls. The intense sun beat on them as Kek strolled the court, with Lukeman on his heels. Nearing a boundary wall, a sizeable shadow was cast, and here, Kek found relief from the scorching afternoon sun. He stopped, turned, and his eyes meandered over Lukeman. He removed his hood, revealing the shaven head.

There was something about Kek's presence that Lukeman didn't understand. He was atypical from most Egyptian men. Although attractive, there was an entrancing quality that drew people to him.

"You are not destined to be a servant, Lukeman."

Lukeman heed the charismatic words. "It is the only way I know to get fed."

"Go home. Your father would still welcome you."

"I will *never* return to my father."

"Lukeman, I know you have the vision. You know your destiny is to become a high priest. How can you fulfill it if you live among the profane? How are you to become the great teacher that you are predestined to be?"

"Worshipful Master," Lukeman bowed his head. "There is nothing that I want more than to attend the mystery school. I am at a loss as to how I can do it."

Kek eyed the young man. He knew that the boy's stubbornness could preempt his fate, impacting the brotherhood. "You will work in the kitchen, mornings as usual, for your grain. You are more valuable to the pharaoh if you become a priest." Kek placed his hand on Lukeman's shoulder. "You will study the mysteries with me in the afternoons and evenings. You *will* become a priest. This is how you will pay the pharaoh's tax."

For the first time in weeks, Lukeman felt something that was foreign to him. It took him a moment to comprehend what it was. Then
he realized—it was hope. Lukeman bowed his head to the benevolent
offer. "How can I repay you?"

"Never disappoint me. And *never* betray me."

Kek's words echoed in Lukeman's ears.

Lukeman's life became meaningful. In the mornings he toiled in
the kitchen. During the afternoon and evenings he studied with Kek.
Lukeman quickly advanced and in no time was initiated into the mysteries.

He knew the brotherhood was exclusive, and what a privilege it
was to partake. It had become Egyptian tradition that the mysteries
be entrusted to the chosen ones. Only the pharaoh, his heirs, the
priests, and a select few were privy to the secrets of divine wisdom.
But also, one of the fundamental directives was that the secrets were
never to be shared with the uninitiated or profane. The penalty for
such was death.

The sanctuary was set away from the Great House and cramped
village. As in the human body, the temple consisted of three chambers: the abdominal, pulmonary and cranial cavities. The chambers
represented the three states of consciousness: conscious, subconscious,
and superconscious, along with the three dimensions of life: physical,
mental, and spiritual.

As the abdomen, the courtyard was open and used for ritual purity,
eliminating self-centered thoughts and desires. Symbolizing the ribs
of a pulmonary cavity, huge pillars bordered the hypostyle hall off the
courtyard. Within this passageway, a priest or priestess elevated their
meditations from the conscious to the subconscious. From the narrow
passage they emerged into the sanctuary, which, like the brain, was
divided into two sections: the holy place and the holy of holies. In the
holy place, the priest further prepared for spiritual enlightenment, so
they were worthy to meet God in the Holy of Holies, where a shrine
for Ptah, god of Memphis, was housed.

After Lukeman was ordained, he served religious duty at the temple four times a year. During each one-month stint, he shaved off all bodily hair, including eyebrows, and abstained from sexual activity. He was allowed to dress only in white linen cloth and papyrus sandals, as animal products were unclean. Normally, priests spent the remainder of their year in their natural professions. Lukeman, however, studied full-time with Kek the rest of the year.

Shortly after Lukeman was initiated into the priesthood, the pharaoh pressured him to leave his diminutive living quarters for the comfort of the Great House. But, as long as Oba remained alive, Lukeman refused to live at the palace. It was Kek who reasoned with the pharaoh when Lukeman disobeyed the request and continued living among the uninitiated.

Twenty-Three

Lukeman grew into a strong and handsome man. He demonstrated an uncanny knowledge of the mysteries. The other priests were envious of his ability to grasp the complex concepts of sacred geometry, divine wisdom, and spiritual enlightenment. He advanced quickly and, with the endorsement of Kek, became the youngest Hem Neter of Memphis. As the High Priest, Lukeman acted as the chief ceremonialist in all the processions, unless, of course, the pharaoh desired to preside.

It was a festival day honoring Ptah, universal architect god, patron of masons, and the great god of Memphis. During this celebration, nobody worked, not even the servants. The smell of incense filled the air. The statue of Ptah, veiled from common eyes, was paraded through the courtyard. Lukeman led the procession, while other priests fanned around the statue, protecting Ptah from Ra's sunrays with ostrich plumes. The Kher-Heb, or lector priest, followed Lukeman, carrying a sacred book on his shoulder. The procession reached the temple in the courtyard and the statue of Ptah was set on the altar where Lukeman performed the ritual for all people of Memphis to observe.

Sometime later, the scent of roasted gazelle and baked bread replaced the odor of incense. Laughter, rather than chanting, was heard throughout the courtyard. And instead of water streaming from ritual vessels for libation offerings, pitchers of beer ran copiously through the crowd.

In the midst of the festivities, Lukeman strolled through the crowded courtyard beside his dear friend, Asim. Since Asim had found Lukeman near death, twelve years earlier, their friendship had been unending. Asim and his family were Lukeman's family.

Published by The Haworth Press, Inc., 2006. All rights reserved.
doi:10.1300/5721_24

"My, how things have changed for you," Asim said as he sauntered a step behind Lukeman, "from kitchen worker to high priest, responsible for the god's needs and salvation of Memphis."

"I am still the same person," Lukeman slowed so his friend walked beside him.

Asim was so proud of Lukeman. He smiled. "In some ways you are the same."

Just barely above the rhythm of the crowd, a woman called out. "Father?"

Asim and Lukeman stopped. They turned toward an approaching young woman. Her long, white dress emphasized her shapely figure and reminded Lukeman of the seasons that had passed. Her light brown eyes were wide, bright, and playful. She hugged Asim, and then turned toward Lukeman. "Lukeman, how are you?"

Lukeman hadn't seen Jamila in months. With each passing encounter, he marveled at her beauty. He smiled. "I am very well, Jamila. And how are you this day?"

"Very well." Jamila looked at Asim. "Father, Mother would like to show you some baskets. She's on the south side of the courtyard." She pointed across the square.

Asim's eyes met Lukeman's. "Would you excuse us?"

"Can't Jamila walk with me a little? I haven't seen her in months." Although his words were for Asim, Lukeman watched Jamila.

"That would be up to Jamila." Uncharacteristically, Asim turned and left them.

Jamila hesitated, then walked with Lukeman.

"I don't see you often, anymore," Lukeman said. "I realize that I'm at the temple from time to time, but when I'm home," his eyes met hers, "you're usually away."

"You are a busy man, now that you are the Hem Neter," she said distantly.

"I liked it when we shared more time together."

"Things are different now." There was distance in her tone.

Lukeman sensed her detachment. "Are you avoiding me?"

The courtyard was bustling with activity. Jamila knew that this was not the place to have a personal discussion with the Hem Neter.

Mindful of eyes on both of them, she bowed. "Perhaps we can speak about this another time."

"Walk with me, tonight, after sunset."

Jamila hesitated. "I'm sorry, Lukeman, I cannot. I have things I need to tend to."

Lukeman stepped closer to Jamila. "I *will* call upon you after sunset." He was serious, and then he softened with a smile. "I hope you will join me."

Jamila avoided eye contact. "I'll see what I can do." She slipped into the crowd.

Lukeman watched her disappear into the festivities. Thoughtful, he moved through the crowd, returning greetings and good wishes. As the Hem Neter, he was well known, and since he lived among the working class, he was well liked. To many, he represented hope. He nodded, smiled, or expressed words of comfort as he passed the common people. For those who needed healing, he reached for them, channeling the universe's energy. Without judgment, he trusted the cosmos to send the force to the life dimension in need, whether physical, mental, or spiritual.

Lukeman had just finished comforting an older woman. He backed into the crowd, turned, and saw her. He stood motionless, searching her familiar eyes. Silently, they remained face-to-face. Although he had seen her from afar over the years, they hadn't been within an arm's length of each other in over twelve years.

Tears of joy formed. The moment he opened his arms, she nestled against his chest, and he held her silently. "My Dalila! How are you?" He whispered.

Dalila withdrew from her brother's arms and smiled. "Lukeman. I am *so* proud of you. For everything you have achieved." She slipped her arm under his, and rested her other hand on top of his forearm.

Dalila had grown into a striking woman. The resemblance to their mother was uncanny. Even the jewels that adorned her neckline reminded Lukeman of Eshe. With a finger he stroked a familiar gem hanging from her neck. His eyes darted to her eyes.

As if understanding his question, she nodded. "It was mother's." She took his hand in hers. The siblings recalled memories of their mother. For Lukeman, it was mixed emotion without closure.

"Are the two of you finished?" a young man asked with a nasal voice.

Lukeman had been so distracted at stumbling upon his sister he hadn't realized that she had an escort. A young man possessively attached his arm to her waist. At first Lukeman didn't recognize his half brother; then he saw Oba's eyes. "Zuka?" Lukeman asked.

"Yes, it is I, Lukeman." Zuka turned to his sister. "Come, Dalila. Let us go."

"Zuka, give me a moment."

Zuka faltered, then he moved away from his siblings in a huff.

Lukeman was sure that Zuka couldn't hear them above the crowd's noise. "You . . . and Zuka?" He didn't believe it, but he had seen Zuka had put his arms around her.

Dalila nodded. "Yes. We will marry after Shemu, our harvest. It's been arranged by Father."

Lukeman wasn't sure what he was feeling. Sadness? Anger? Or was it jealousy? "I'm sorry, Dalila. I guess I should have expected it, but somehow, it is a shock."

"You know Father believes it is critical to maintain the bloodline." Dalila's eyes were on Lukeman's. "Over the years, I had hoped you would have returned for me."

Lukeman smiled. What could he say to her? His eyes wandered to his half brother. He was much shorter than Lukeman, and much thinner. Compared to Lukeman's developed pectorals, he had a sunken chest. The young man was clearly annoyed that he was waiting on Dalila. He stood arrogantly with his nose in the air, ignoring the commoners as they passed between them, enjoying their day of pleasure.

He sighed, took Dalila's hand, and moved to Zuka where he embraced his brother. "It is nice to see you, Zuka. How old are you, now? Sixteen?"

Zuka huffed. "I'm seventeen."

"Seventeen? When are you starting the mystery schools?"

"Before peret, before the fields are sowed." Zuka's hand possessively took hold of Dalila's. "We are also to be married next year."

Lukeman's heart ached, but he forced a weak smile. "Congratulations, Zuka. I wish both of you much happiness."

That evening was perfect. The hot sun of Ra had long set, and the moon god, Thoth, provided sufficient light. Deep in thought, Lukeman sauntered the narrow passageway that divided the dwellings. He approached the familiar door. He had been here so many times, and knew he was always welcome. He knocked.

Moments later Asim opened the door. "Lukeman." Asim uncharacteristically avoided eye contact and gestured for Lukeman to enter. The men moved through the stall into the middle room. Asim's home was less cramped now that his sons had moved out.

Something didn't feel right to Lukeman. This was the second time his friend had treated him distantly that day. "Asim, is everything all right?"

Asim hesitated, and then he stuck his head in the back room entry. "Jamila?"

Jamila appeared, but as her father had done, she evaded eye contact with Lukeman. She didn't acknowledge him; rather, she exited through the stall.

Lukeman shot a questioning look at Asim, hoping for some answers to their peculiar behavior.

"Good evening," Asim said and retreated to the kitchen.

Lukeman watched Jamila as she walked toward the Nile. He trailed her, trying to sort out why his extended family was acting so detached from him.

Jamila knew Lukeman was following her. When she reached the riverbank, she stopped, allowing him to draw near.

He stopped short by a man's length. "Are you well?" Her eyes met his and he knew something was amiss. "Tell me, Jamila. What is wrong?" He stepped closer.

"Lukeman . . ." Jamila stopped. She searched for the right words, but the only thing that left her mouth was, "I cannot see you. We should not be seen together."

Lukeman, now close to her, eyed her. He felt her pain, but was confused by its source. "So . . . you *are* avoiding me." He reached for one of her hands. It was soft and warm. "What happened?"

Jamila mustered up every ounce of strength she could find. "We are of two worlds. You are the Hem Neter and I am a servant's daughter. You know that spending time with me could only bring you pain."

"Jamila, we are friends. A title will never change my friendship with you. I will always value it, as well as your father's."

Although Lukeman was undoubtedly brilliant, he was naive regarding matters of the heart. Sensing this, Jamila didn't know what else to say.

Lukeman changed the subject, "Can we walk for a little?" He led her down the riverbank. Both, so preoccupied with their own thoughts, failed to notice the exquisiteness of the moon's reflection in the streaming water. At last, he broke the silence. "I saw my sister at the festival today."

Jamila sensed he needed to talk. She stopped. "And?"

"I was reminded of a sacrifice she has made, because I left home. And I've been troubled by that."

"What sacrifice?"

"If I had stayed," his eyes darted to the river, "Dalila and I would have married. I would eventually have become the vizier. But now . . . she is to wed my half brother."

"Are you sad that she is marrying someone else? Or are you sad that you have chosen a life of celibacy?"

Lukeman smiled. His queries exactly! He had spent so much time debating this philosophical subject matter. As a priest, he had been required to be celibate during his monthly temple shifts, because of ritual purity. The prevailing acceptance of marriage for high priests seemed contradictory to him. As a high priest, responsible for three services each day, where ritual purity was essential, celibacy seemed to be the only option. How could he be married and not copulate? How other priests had dealt with marriage and celibacy was their matter. It was too duplicitous for him. Besides, his clairvoyant visions always lacked female companionship. This was his best indicator that he was not meant to have a wife, and celibacy was his only choice.

"You are very wise, Jamila. The same questions pester me."

"I know we've never talked about this, but why did you leave the Great House?" Her robe fluttered in the gentle breeze, and the moonlight revealed her feminine figure.

Lukeman closed his eyes, recalling the horrid memories. "When I was a boy, my mother fell in love with a servant. My father discovered it and punished her. I believed she had been sent away. But for six years, he held her captive in a dungeon cell, here, in Memphis. In her dying moments, my father sent me to her. She died a slow and painful death. Alone."

Lukeman opened his eyes and Jamila saw his hatred. "But you were with her, when it mattered." Her words were gentle and sensing his pain, Jamila impulsively took Lukeman's hand.

He felt the warmth of her energy radiate from her core.

"I am so sorry for bringing up these memories." Without warning, Jamila wrapped her arms around his hard body. She held him, feeling his pain. Then she withdrew and whispered, "You need to let go of the hatred, Lukeman. It will kill you."

Lukeman knew she was right. He smiled sadly. "How did you become so wise, my little Jamila?"

But Jamila was not so little anymore. Lukeman's eyesight wandered over her face. She had the most intense eyes he had ever seen; moreover, the moonlight reflected in them luminously. She was indeed stunning. His eyes strayed to her full lips. Without contemplating what was happening, he drew to her mouth, and they kissed. Fervently, his lips parted and his tongue slipped alongside hers. As the flesh in their mouths converged, their souls touched.

Suddenly, Jamila backed away, her hand over her mouth.

"I'm so sorry, Jamila," he whispered hoarsely. How could this have happened? This was his best friend's daughter, and his thoughts were so impure. "Forgive me," he hung his head. "It will never happen again. You have my word."

Emotion overtook Jamila. "This is why we should not be together, Lukeman." Tears swelled in her eyes. "It is too hard to be your friend.

I'm not a little girl anymore. I am a woman. My feelings for you could beget trouble."

"Feelings?"

"All those years . . . getting to know you . . . friendship, companionship," she sobbed, "of falling in love with you." Tears streamed down her face. "Father and I have spoken of this." She backed away. "Please do not call upon me anymore. It hurts too much, Lukeman." She turned and scurried off.

Lukeman watched her go. "What have I done?" he whispered. He was confused. Could he have feelings for this woman? For a second he pondered the adverse reaction of the pharaoh if he learned Lukeman was seen with a servant's girl. He shook the thought from his head. He had made a commitment to become the Hem Neter, and had dedicated himself to a life of service. He knew his soul's purpose was to provide for the spiritual needs of Memphis. As he watched Jamila's silhouette disappear into the shadows, he knew these corporeal feelings betrayed his divine aspirations.

Twenty-Four

Lukeman put time and distance between himself and Jamila. Temporarily, he left his dwelling and lived at the temple, seeking comfort through meditation. He realized how insensitive he had been to continually seek Jamila's friendship, placing her in a painful situation. He tried to pinpoint over the years when her feelings became more complicated. This is how he realized that his feelings went beyond friendship. Through meditation and prayer he convinced himself that his physical and emotional feelings for Jamila were immaterial, and he was to serve a higher purpose. By the time the fields were seeded, he returned to his humble dwelling, living again among the profane.

Over the year, Zuka entered the mystery school. Although Zuka never showed interest in learning the mysteries, Kek took a personal interest in the vizier's son. After the harvest, and from afar, Lukeman watched Dalila marry their half brother. Lukeman's interaction with the pharaoh increased dramatically. It was only a matter of time before he would be expected to have dealings with the vizier, his father.

The Royal Offering ritual was performed to soothe troubled spirits of necropolis, the city of the dead. The pharaoh anticipated the passing of his brother and Lukeman stood before the altar at the temple's shrine performing the ritual. Facing the altar was a tomb with a statue of Ka. Baskets of fresh bread, pitchers of beer, and plates of roasted meat surrounded him. Lukeman with right hand extended, chanted in a strange voice:

> Send forth thy voice to grant refreshment: she is given a thousand of bread, she is given a thousand of beer, a thousand of oxen and fowl, fine ointment and clothing. She is given all things good and pure, all things on which the Neteru live.

Published by The Haworth Press, Inc., 2006. All rights reserved.
doi:10.1300/5721_25

Lukeman's praying ceased, the sacrifices were presented, and the spirits had been appeased. The pharaoh thanked Lukeman for performing the powerful rite, then the king's party left him. After meditating, Lukeman left the sanctuary and entered the hypostyle hallway. He walked the narrow passageway, bordered by tall pillars. It was dark and the limestone columns cast eerie shadows.

"Lukeman. Let us talk." A nearby voice startled him.

Instinctively, his adrenaline spiked. From the corner of his eye, he saw a silhouette amid the pillars. Although it had been over thirteen years since he had spoken directly with him, Lukeman would never forget his father's voice. He spoke calmly. "I have nothing to say to you."

"You are now the prophet of the Neter, Lukeman. You are expected to interact with the Royal House regarding divinatory matters. You cannot hide from me forever."

"I am not hiding from you." Lukeman's fists were clenched as he tried to control his caged anger.

"For the good of Egypt—move on. You are responsible for the spiritual needs of our land. You cannot serve Egypt if you refuse to speak to me."

"When I need to speak with the pharoah, I will go directly to him."

"You will not," Oba's voice escalated. "You owe me and will show me respect."

"I owe you nothing. I show respect to those who deserve it."

"You owe me *everything*. How do you think you got into the mystery school? How do you think you became Hem Neter?"

Lukeman tried to grasp the implication of his questions. Surely his father could not have manipulated his life. "You're lying. I earned Hem Neter."

"You may have earned it, but you never would have attained it without my endorsement. You would have nothing! Not the work in the kitchen when you left the palace, or your miserable dwelling, or the mystery school, and certainly not Hem Neter. Without me, you are nothing! So don't be so self-righteous. Show some respect. If not because I'm your father . . . because I'm the vizier."

Lukeman couldn't say a word. He felt the sweat in his clenched fists and the rage swelling within him. He closed his eyes to pray, to control his anger, but it was too hard. When he sensed he was losing to the dark energy, abruptly, he turned and disappeared into the night.

It was Asim who noticed that Lukeman was missing. He hadn't seen him for over a week, so early that morning, before he was expected at the Great House, he knocked on Lukeman's door. When there was no answer, he whacked it harder.

The door beside Lukeman's quarters creaked open, and a man appeared. "I don't believe anyone is there. I have not seen anyone come or go since I arrived."

Asim turned to the stranger. "And how long has that been?"

"Today is my tenth day here." The man stepped forward and offered him his hand. "My friends call me Ja." He smiled warmly.

"Ja." Asim shook his hand. "My friend, Lukeman, lives here."

"The Hem Neter?"

"Yes." Asim guessed that Ja was about his own age. There was something familiar about him, but he couldn't place it. "You are new here?"

"I lived here years ago. I've been away."

"Are you a servant at the palace?"

"Yes." Facial lines revealed remnants of a kind smile.

"I thought so, you look familiar." Asim peeked behind Ja. "Do you have family?"

"I am not married, and since my return, I've learned that my parents passed on."

"I'm sorry. Would you like to dine with my family this evening?"

The kind smile returned. "That would be very considerate." He pointed back at Lukeman's door. "What about the Hem Neter?"

Asim opened the door and toured the small compartment. Lukeman was nowhere to be found. He returned to Ja in the alleyway. "He does from time to time stay at the temple for long periods," he mumbled. "He usually tells me when he leaves, though. I will go to the temple and check on him."

Later that afternoon, Asim visited the temple. Because he was uninitiated, he was not allowed beyond the courtyard, but an eyebrowless priest told him that the Hem Neter had vanished.

Femi and Jamila had prepared a special dinner to welcome the new neighbor, but the mood was not so festive. The small group gathered around a table on the roof of Asim's home. Though the scent of roasted fowl and fresh baked bread filled the air, their attention was on the discussion.

"Where could he be?" Femi asked, clearly concerned.

"I do not know. It doesn't feel right." Asim turned to his daughter. "When did you see him last, Jamila?"

Jamila's eyes met her father's. "You know I haven't seen him in over a year. What are we going to do?"

"Wouldn't the pharaoh be doing all he could to find his Hem Neter?" Ja offered.

"The pharaoh must have a search party looking for him," Asim agreed.

Jamila rose and moved to the roof ledge. "I hope they know where to look," she said thoughtfully. She retrieved a pitcher of beer, topped everyone's cup, then returned the jug to the ledge. As she set the pitcher down, she closed her eyes, and prayed. *Goddess Isis, give me insight to see my Lukeman.* Although she didn't see her friend, she had a childhood memory of when Lukeman had taken her and her brothers one special day to his favorite place, an oasis north of Memphis.

"Ja, where are you from?" Femi changed the subject, which drew Jamila back.

"Originally, here. I've just returned from Thebes."

"That is far. Did you travel by foot?"

"I have a camel."

Although the food was delicious, the conversation was less than celebratory, and the small party broke shortly after dinner. Ja graciously thanked Asim and his family for their hospitality and left. With some daylight remaining, Jamila offered to fetch water from the village well, and she went off with a bucket.

Ja returned to his home, delighted that he had the fortune to meet Asim. He found a comfortable corner in his reception room and sat. He closed his eyes and, with palms up, he meditated. His session was interrupted with an abrupt bang at the door. He opened the door and to his surprise, Jamila stood before him, a bucket of water by her feet.

"Ja, excuse my forwardness, but may I borrow your camel tomorrow?"

He was taken aback by the question. "What do you want with my camel?"

Jamila wondered if she could trust him. "I may know where Lukeman is."

"And if a camel isn't a possibility?"

"It's not an impossible trek by foot. It would be easier though, by camel."

"Your father does not know that you are here, does he?"

She connected with the man's kind eyes. "No."

He hesitated. "Tomorrow is my day of rest. I will take you, myself."

"I cannot ask you to do that."

"It would not be right if I let you run off in the desert by yourself. Come here tomorrow morning after your father goes to the Great House."

The sun was just peeking over the horizon—its reflection shimmering across the river—when Jamila and Ja headed out on the camel. Ja led the dromedary and Jamila rode her. They journeyed over dunes of rippled sand and near rock hills. Occasionally, they passed heaps of animal bones, reminding them of the perils of desert travel.

For the longest time, they traveled silently, heading north along the Nile. It was Ja who finally spoke. "Where do you think the Hem Neter is?"

"When I was younger, Lukeman took me to that mountain." She pointed to an elevated peak that rose in the distance. "There is a beautiful oasis there. I remember a cave, a small pond, and a couple tall trees. He called it his little paradise. It's just a feeling . . . but I think he's there."

Although it was still early morning, the sun was scorching. She wiped her brow with the sleeve of her robe. "Let us switch now. I can walk," she offered.

Ja halted the camel. "If you don't mind, I can ride her also."

Jamila sloped forward, so that Ja sat behind her, and they continued their trek across the desert toward the mountain.

Unending hills of sand and time passed before Ja broke the silence. "I could not help overhearing," it was almost whispered in her ear, "that you haven't seen the Hem Neter in over a year. I don't intend to pry . . ."

Under most circumstances, Jamila would have ignored the remark. But there was something about Ja. He had a calming effect on her that she didn't understand. His direct, yet unobtrusive comment worked. "When I was a child, Lukeman came to live with us for a short time. He became a member of our family. Over the years, I had fallen in love with him. I hid it for such a long time, until it hurt too much to see him. Then, about a year ago, I told him . . . and I explained that I couldn't see him anymore."

"And your father knows?"

"Yes. It was his idea. He doesn't want Lukeman to be hurt, anymore than I."

"And he would be hurt because you are a servant's daughter?"

"Yes! He is committed to Memphis. He doesn't need the strife."

The camel neared the base of the mountain, and Jamila spotted a small patch of greenery. "Look, there's the pond over there." Leading to the foot of a ravine where water pooled, the topography changed from sand to wild weed to scrub. Two modest-size trees bordered a tiny pond. Here, they descended the camel and brought her to the water.

Jamila studied the area. "This is it. Let me go up the ravine and see if he's here."

"You want to go up alone?" his voice sincere with concern.

"Yes. I will be fine. I'd like time to talk with him a bit."

He hesitated, and then agreed. He sat alone in the shade, beside the pond.

Jamila hiked the ravine trail. Sections of it were familiar from her visit years earlier. The higher she climbed, the more nervous she became. What if she were wrong? She had dragged Ja into the desert on his day of rest. Worse yet, what if she found Lukeman, and he didn't want to be discovered? As she reached the trail summit, she spotted him, and stopped. He sat against a stone outcropping, near the entrance of a cave. The ravine's walls shaded the rocky area. He was meditating. He looked so thin.

As Jamila approached, his eyes flew open. She stopped and he got to his feet. The couple remained awkwardly apart, staring at each other. Lukeman broke the silence. "How did you find me?"

"Isis. Are you all right?" Jamila saw the sadness in his eyes. Guardedly, she approached. "What is wrong? Why are you here? How long have you been here?"

"A while. I'm not sure how long."

"You could come to us if you're in trouble. Don't shut us out."

"I couldn't come to you," Lukeman lowered his eyes. "Not after what happened."

Jamila sat on the rocky surface. "Lukeman, please sit. Tell me what is wrong."

Lukeman rested beside her. "I saw my father. He told me that the only reason I became the Hem Neter was because of him."

"You didn't believe him, did you?"

"At first I didn't. But now . . . the more I think about it—it makes sense."

Jamila could feel Lukeman's pain. She reached for one of his hands and held it tightly. "Lukeman, *you* did it. Not your father, but you."

"It's not that simple. It's so difficult to get into the mystery school. It's so exclusive. I should have known that a servant would not have been accepted."

"But you were not born a servant."

"I thought it was because Kek believed in me." Lukeman shook his head, "He didn't believe in me . . . he did it for my father."

"What are you doing out here?"

"Thinking. Meditating. *Uaa.* Praying. *Qakh.* How can I be the Hem Neter when I know that my father gave it to me?"

She squeezed his hand. "You're the Hem Neter because you earned it. Perhaps your father helped get you into the school, but you went through the initiations. You were chosen by the pharaoh because you were most worthy."

"I have so much hatred inside," Lukeman's eyes met Jamila's. "It scared me. I thought I was going to kill him. . . . I needed to leave. I didn't know where to go."

"You should have come to us. To me! I'm sorry if what I had said made me unapproachable. But I'm well now, Lukeman."

Lukeman saw Jamila's strength. He wished he were well. He wished he had never tasted her sweet lips. He wished he could purge his visions of holding her in his arms, touching her skin, converging their bodies and souls.

"When did you eat last?"

Lukeman shook his head. "I don't know."

"We have a camel. It will take you back to Memphis."

"We?"

Ja paced the area anxiously. He had expected Jamila back by now and wondered if he had done the right thing, allowing her to seek Lukeman on her own. Just then, Jamila and Lukeman emerged from the trail. Jamila's arm was snuggly wrapped around Lukeman's waist, assisting his descent as he appeared emaciated and weak.

Ja rushed to Lukeman's side. He helped direct Lukeman to the large boulder by the pond. As Lukeman rested, Ja introduced himself. "Hem Neter, I am Ja."

"Please, call me Lukeman." He was trembling.

"Lukeman needs food," Jamila said. "Do—." Before Jamila had finished the request, Ja had retrieved bread from a bag on the camel's back and offered it to Lukeman.

"Thank you." Lukeman, famished, tore a piece and thrust it into his mouth, trying to satisfy the insatiable hunger. Ja passed a vessel of beer to Lukeman. He gulped of the warm beverage, but his eyes didn't leave Ja's face. "Ja, you look familiar, have we met?"

Ja shook his head. "I don't believe so."

"Ja worked at the palace years ago," Jamila offered.

Ja nodded. "I moved away close to twenty years ago. I couldn't imagine that you would have remembered me."

"Whom did you work for at the palace?"

Ja hesitated; his eyes met Lukeman's. "For the vizier."

"That is my father. That is why you look familiar. I was certain I had seen you before." He bit off another piece of bread. "I don't remember the name Ja, though."

"Ja is what my friends call me. I was known in the palace as Jahi."

At first, Lukeman missed the significance of his name. *Jahi?* Lukeman stopped chewing. His face paled and he swallowed hard. "Did you say *Jahi?*" Lukeman stood unsteadily. He stared at Ja, sizing him up.

"Lukeman, what is wrong?" Jamila's arm helped steady him.

Ja also stood, but remained calm. "Yes, Jahi."

Lukeman's eyes pored over the man of almost fifty seasons. "It was you," Lukeman whispered. "My mother was with you?" Lukeman's head throbbed. It felt as if it was going to burst. The ache from hunger was now the furthest thing from his mind. He didn't know what to do. This was the man that his mother had died for.

"How did you know?" Ja asked.

Lukeman recalled his mother's words, *"I fell in love . . . with a servant . . . Jahi. He was . . . untouchable."* Jahi, Jahi, Jahi, echoed in his ears. "She told me."

"Where is she? I need to see her."

This even got Jamila's attention; she stared at him with open mouth.

Lukeman looked Jahi in the eye for the longest time, and then he understood. "You don't know," Lukeman said.

"I don't know what?" There was concern in Ja's voice. "I have been away."

"My mother has passed on." Lukeman recognized the shadow of pain that flashed through Ja's eyes. "What happened to you?" Lukeman tried to keep his voice calm.

Ja didn't answer; he couldn't speak.

"Where did you go?" Lukeman's poise was wearing.

"She's gone," Ja whispered. He was shaking and retreated to the large rock that Lukeman had been sitting on. Tears brimmed his eyes. He concealed his face in his hands. "I prayed she was well," he sobbed, "Oh, how I prayed."

Lukeman softened. He rested his hand on Ja's shoulder. "Ja, what happened?"

For a moment Ja prayed silently. Then, he told his story. "Almost twenty years ago, I was awakened in the middle of the night. A group of the pharaoh's soldiers removed me from my home. They flogged me, tied me up, and dragged me behind a camel into the desert.

"I was left there, to die, but a drifter found me and nursed me back to health. He brought me to Upper Egypt where I was sold into slavery and sent to Thebes. I served my master until he died, just after last Shemu. My master was a priest. With his death, I was granted my freedom and the few assets that he owned, including his camel. All these years, I had pledged to come back to Eshe."

Lukeman's hand tightened on Ja's shoulder.

"How did she die?"

Lukeman took a deep breath, and began his story. "About twenty years ago, my mother and father had a terrible fight. I was just a boy. I was told that she moved away. For six years I believed she had chosen another life, another family. Then, when I was sixteen, my father sent me to her. . . . He had imprisoned her for being unfaithful to him. I had only minutes with her before she passed on."

Lukeman recognized the horror in Ja's eyes. "Before she died, she told me about you. She asked me to find you and tell you—." He wavered a moment. "When she was imprisoned she was with child. My mother said that the baby was yours. She claimed to have had a baby girl while she was in prison—."

"A baby?"

"As soon as my mother died, I confronted my father. He claimed that the baby died in childbirth. I asked around the dwellings for you. Some remembered you, but they didn't know what happened to you."

The small group returned to Memphis. Asim was overjoyed to see his friend return. With the help of Femi, Lukeman was nourished back to good health, and returned to his duty as Hem Neter. Though Asim was disappointed that Jamila had searched for Lukeman in secret, because of the outcome he could not remain displeased.

Strangely enough, Lukeman and Ja became friends. Their love for Eshe, and hatred for Oba, pulled them together. Being neighbors facilitated many late-night discussions. At first, they just wanted to get to know each other, and then surprisingly, their discussions evolved into philosophical deliberations. Lukeman was impressed with Ja's quick mind and spiritual approach to life.

Late one night, Lukeman lay on a mat of woven twine. He had finished his meditation and prayers, and closed his eyes, to rest. On the brink of sleep, he heard chanting, or *kai*, a form of spiritual meditation. While at the temple, he was accustomed to falling asleep while listening to priests' chants as they elevated their subconscious to know the divinity. But here, in the dwellings of the profane, he was baffled at where the prayer was coming from.

His eyes flew open. Abruptly he sat up. He cocked his head and struggled to pinpoint the source of the sound. He slipped on a robe and moved into the alleyway. Since he resided in the end dwelling, he walked toward the center of the units, but he quickly realized that he was heading away from the sound. He turned back and swiftly isolated the chanting coming from Ja's quarters.

"Ja?" he whispered to himself outside of Ja's door. He knocked, and the chanting stopped. Moments later Ja jostled open the door.

"Lukeman! What is wrong?"

Lukeman brushed past his friend, into the dwelling lit only by a candle. His eyes moved to Ja's. "You know the prayer of mekh neter! How is that possible?"

Ja lowered his eyes. "My former master was a priest. He taught me some of the sacred beliefs."

Lukeman was astonished. "Your master took an oath. He was never to share these beliefs with the uninitiated. The penalty for doing such is death!"

"I am aware of that. He took me through the first transformation."

Lukeman didn't know what to think. He was reminded of a conversation he had with his mother so many years ago.

"Mother, why are only a select few able to learn the secrets to eternal life?"

"The gods and pharaohs believe that only a few chosen souls can seek the mysteries of our creators. This is how we have lived and died for many lifetimes."

"But you know—it is not right. It is not right. It is not right."

As Lukeman stood there, he was reminded of his youthful feelings. It wasn't right! As a child he knew it, how could he have forgotten? How could he have spent his life overlooking his soul's true purpose? Why should only the elite be given the opportunity to understand mankind's origins and seek eternal life? By excluding people, wasn't he oppressing the spirituality of Memphis?

With newly found inspiration, he set out to fulfill his destiny. He abandoned the blood oath he had taken more that a decade earlier. And, behind closed doors, Lukeman taught Ja and others the secrets to the ancient mysteries.

Twenty-Five

Jamila left the palace kitchen and was crossing the courtyard. From across the square, she saw Zuka, second son of Oba, approach. Since servants were not allowed to cast their eyes on the elite, she lowered them as he drew near.

This wasn't the first time Zuka had spotted the servant girl. He was delighted at the opportunity to meet her. As he expected, she passed him without making eye contact, and he turned and trailed her.

Jamila felt his aura near her, so she wasn't surprised when she heard his voice from behind.

"And what is your name?"

She stopped, turned, and spoke, avoiding eye contact. "I am Jamila."

Zuka circled her, his hands clasped behind his back, extending his bloated stomach. "What a beautiful name," his eyes combed her body, "for a beautiful woman. I am Zuka, son of the vizier."

"Yes. I know." Jamila lowered her head.

Zuka's ego inflated, she knew who he was! "What business do you have at the palace?"

"My father is a servant. I brought him some coriander tea for poor health."

"I see. It must be hard being a servant's girl." Zuka's hand touched Jamila's chin, he directed her head so that their eyes met. She was more beautiful than he had imagined. His eyes left her face and scoured her body. "You *could* have a life of ease. I could assure you of that."

"Take your hand off her!" Lukeman's voice bellowed behind him. "Jamila! Go home!" Jamila scurried away.

Zuka watched after the fleeing girl. "Who are you to tell *me* what to do?"

"You are with Dalila. Is that not enough?"

Published by The Haworth Press, Inc., 2006. All rights reserved.
doi:10.1300/5721_26

"Dalila and I have our own arrangement, which is none of your concern."

"Keep your hands off Jamila."

Zuka eyed Lukeman. What was he missing? A sinister smile came to his lips. "Could an untouchable be keeping the Hem Neter's bed warm?"

Lukeman stepped into Zuka's space. Even with his inflated gut from indolence, Zuka shrank as Lukeman's presence beset the younger brother. "Stay away from her," Lukeman said and he left.

Later that evening, as Zuka and Oba gorged their faces with fresh fruit, Zuka discussed his confrontation with Lukeman. "Father, I'm telling you, Lukeman is interested in this servant girl, Jamila," Zuka whined. "How can a Hem Neter be with an untouchable and still be pure enough for Ptah's needs?"

"Perhaps you are overreacting," Oba said.

"No . . . there is something there. I wouldn't fault him, though. She truly is stunning, Father. The highest cheekbones I've ever seen, and golden-brown eyes."

Something pestered Oba about Zuka's accusation. He couldn't put his finger on it, but like parasites breeding in the Nile, it gnawed away at his gut until he no longer could stand it. He knew the women would be washing clothing at the river this time of day, so this is where he journeyed.

Accompanied by the pharaoh's soldiers, the vizier walked the river-bank, surveying women. He seemingly sifted through them as they scrubbed clothing. Occasionally, he would point to one, and a guard would retrieve her from the water. He would inspect her face, nod "no," and she was freed to return to the water. Oba continued downstream, advancing toward Jamila.

Standing in knee-deep water, Jamila rinsed a vessel. Murmurs from other women near by drew her attention to the unusual sight.

Not daring to lay her eyes on the vizier, Jamila continued her chores. From her peripheral vision, she saw that he had stopped at the shoreline near her. She sensed his eyes on her. Then she heard the rising and falling of feet plunging through the water.

"What is your name?"

Anticipating a soldier would drag her from the water, she took a deep breath, and turned. The vizier stood in the water beside her. "I am Jamila."

Oba couldn't take his eyes off of her. He recognized her distinct cheekbones, haunting eyes, and full lips. She was indeed beautiful. "Who are your parents?"

"My father is Asim and my mother is Femi."

Oba nodded pensively, then trudged back to the shore.

Later that evening, Jamila embarked to find Lukeman. She knew that he routinely strolled the riverbank just after sunset. Occasionally, she and Mosi, her gentleman caller, would happen upon him by the river. Her encounter with Oba troubled her. She had debated whether to tell him; in the end, she decided that she ought to mention it.

It wasn't long before she glimpsed the familiar silhouette by the river's edge. He was leisurely walking, taking in the charm of the Nile. "Lukeman?"

He turned. "Jamila? Is that you?"

She emerged from the shadows. "It is. May I walk with you a little?"

"Of course," he glanced around. "Are you alone? You are not with Mosi?"

"I am alone."

He sensed something was amiss. "Is everything well?"

"I had an unusual encounter today. I was at the river and I met your father."

Lukeman stopped, his aura noticeably changed, exuding the heat of anger. "My father? What did he want?" His voice shot up.

"I'm not quite sure. It was very strange, Lukeman. He strolled the bank, had his guards pull young women from the water. He just looked at them, and then sent them back to work. When he came upon me, he walked to me in the water."

"What did he say?"

"He asked my name, and who my parents are. Then he just left."

With fists clenched he asked, "Did he touch you?"

A crazed look in his eyes scared Jamila. She took his fists in her tiny hands. "No. He didn't touch me." But Lukeman was gone. "Lukeman, come back to me," she pleaded. "Lukeman?" she called louder. He didn't respond and Jamila slapped his cheek.

He caressed his face, and the noticeable anger in his eyes dissipated.

"I'm sorry, Lukeman. You scared me."

That was the last thing he wanted to do. "Why would he approach you?"

"Could it have anything to do with my encounter with Zuka? I had never met either one. And within one day, I've met both. Isn't that odd?"

"Yes. I'm going to my father and find out what's going on." Lukeman brushed past her, heading away from the riverbank.

"No!" Jamila, normally soft-spoken, raised her voice and chased after him. She grabbed his hand. "You cannot see your father, Lukeman. You need to be in a better place before you do. That hatred of yours will consume you if you're not careful."

Lukeman knew she was right; he could feel the rage swell within him, waiting to erupt. His eyes settled on hers. "You're right. I don't know how to purge it."

"Let this go." Jamila still holding onto one of his hands squeezed it. "Promise me that you won't see your father until you have vanquished this fury."

He felt her strength, tenderness, and love emanate from her ethereal body. Lukeman's eyes found hers. "I promise," he whispered. Instinctively, he swept her in his arms and held her, silently. He didn't dare to look back into her eyes for fear that he would take her. Instead, he marveled at how right it felt to have her in his arms, to feel her heart beat next to his, and her soft skin against him. He wouldn't take her, not because he didn't want to, or because she was an untouchable and he was the Hem Neter. He couldn't because he had seen his future through clairvoyant visions, and his involvement in her life would only bring sorrow. But as he held her, he was awed by the feeling that she always left him wanting more.

The other man's voice was foreign to Jessie, so that when he conveyed the final words, they severed her subconscious from her past.

"You have reached the mountain peak of Masonic instruction, a peak covered by a mist, which *you* in search for further light can penetrate only by your own efforts."

Jessie's eyes flew open. Everything was blurry, from where her two realities merged. She shut her eyes, then opened them, this time noticing a stranger standing beside Whitman on a platform. *Where am I?* She was dazed.

"You are here. Back to the present," Charlie said.

Present? Jessie's heart was beating wildly.

"Now we hope you will study diligently the lessons of all our degrees so that there will be nurtured within you a consuming desire to pierce the pure white light of Masonic wisdom."

What happened? Jessie's heart still beat rapidly. She wondered if she was having a heart attack. She closed her eyes.

"Relax, Jessie," Charlie told her.

"And before we let you go, let me give you a hint and that is all that the greatest Mystics ever give. The hint is the Royal Secret, it is there that you may learn to find that light. Yes, brothers, the hint is the Royal Secret. The true word—Man, born of a double nature finds the purpose of his being *only when these two natures are in perfect harmony.*"

Images of black-and-white checkerboard flashed through Jessie's mind, and the instructor's words *born of a double nature* echoed in her head.

As if awakening from a dream and its memory drifting from her, Jessie kept her eyes closed and tried to cling to her experience. But soon, the intricacies of her life as an Egyptian high priest were a blur. She reached for her notepad and pen beside her and jotted down details of that life, before they slipped from her grasp.

"Harmony, my brethren, Harmony, is the true word and the Royal Secret which makes possible *the empire* of true Masonic Brotherhood."

The Empire?

"Harmony, Jessie," Charlie repeated.

Twenty-Six

Jessie wandered the sidewalk disoriented. In one hand, she clutched a men's attaché case, in the other a black silk cap. Not really knowing what she was doing, she stuffed the cap inside her trench coat. Being in Manhattan, most didn't find Brennan's swerving between pedestrians or feminine walk peculiar. Still lightheaded, she passed the parking lot where she had parked, seemingly, lifetimes earlier. She staggered five blocks before she realized her error.

Sometime later, she started the cold Mustang. She needed to share her experience with someone, but had never felt so alone. From her coat pocket, she retrieved her phone and punched in some numbers.

"I need to see you," Jessie murmured.

An hour later, Jessie pulled into the parking lot of the Paramus Park Mall. She searched for the suggested meeting place and parked. She cut the engine and stepped from the car. Studying the surrounding area, she walked the row of cars until she reached the Saab, opened its door, and sat in the passenger seat.

"My God! You look like shit!" Rachel said. "Are you okay?"

Jessie pulled the vanity mirror from the visor. She was pale and her eyes were bloodshot. Her hair was uncombed and her goatee had become loosened on one side. She pressed the corner of the goatee, adhering it to her skin.

In the mirror's reflection, she saw the black silk protrude from her trench coat. She pulled out a crumpled Master of the Royal Secret cap. It was black, trimmed in gold, with a gold double-headed eagle surmounted by a red equalateral triangle inscribed with "32°" in gold. The ceremony where Brennan received the cap was a blur.

"Today was your last initiation?"

Jessie nodded. She was still grasping at bits and pieces of her Egyptian experience. Now it felt like a dream. "Something happened," al-

Published by The Haworth Press, Inc., 2006. All rights reserved.
doi:10.1300/5721_27

though she spoke in her normal voice, it sounded foreign to her. "I don't know how." She didn't know where to begin. *She's going to think I'm crazy.* As she sat there, all she wanted to do was run to Taylor.

"What happened?"

Jessie began to tell her story. "Right before Christmas, I was meditating, and I think I had a past-life memory."

"Why would you think that?"

"I had a vision, and in it I was a young Egyptian boy. My father was in the government. My mother. . . ." Jessie seemed to be lost in a world of her own. She stared distantly into the darkening parking lot.

"Your mother?"

Jessie shook off the stupor. "My mother was unfaithful to my father and was imprisoned. Years later, I was sent to her. . . . She died in my arms." Jessie felt the hatred surge within her. It startled her. "Today . . . when Whitman gave the lecture—"

"Michael Whitman?" Rachel was curious.

"Yes. His voice had a hypnotic effect on me. And when they showed the geometric and Masonic symbols, I was back in Egypt." Jessie wondered if Rachel thought she was nuts. Then she remembered that her mother saw ghosts, so she proceeded. "Some time ago, I had another past-life experience, but in that situation I had a past-life regression and remembered parts of a lifetime during the Salem witch trials.

"Our subconscious mind is a reservoir of our past-life memories. One way to access it is through past-life regressions, another is through meditation . . . but I meditate all the time. This was different. What would trigger something like this?" she mumbled.

Rachel was skeptical. "What exactly happened?"

"I had a memory of the same Egyptian boy. He left his father and lived among the lower caste. He went into the ancient mystery school and became a high priest."

"*The* mystery school? The one that Freemasonry was based upon? Isn't it possible that this Freemasonry stuff is going to your head?" Rachel suggested.

Jessie could not ignore the possibility. "It's possible."

Although skeptical, Rachel was genuinely curious. "What else happened?"

"My name was Lukeman. Kek was my teacher. He started the brotherhood. And Jamila was . . . it was complicated. But I started teaching the uninitiated."

"What do you mean?"

"The mystery school was restricted to the elite class. I befriended an untouchable and started teaching him, and others."

"If you were a high priest, what do you remember of the mysteries?"

"That part is fuzzy. I remember bits and pieces of rituals. They believed that we needed to free our soul from our physical existence to reach eternal life. But it's like a dream that keeps slipping away, then every once in a while I remember something."

"Do you remember the thirty-second initiation?"

This was the most upsetting piece. She shook her head. "Not much. I remember the introduction and the conclusion and that's it. Everything else is gone." She was so angry. She had invested all this time studying Freemasonry. She had been anxious to experience the thirty-second degree, and now she had missed it.

Jessie spotted the doubt in Rachel's eyes. "You don't believe me."

"I believe something happened to you, Jess. Maybe this Freemasonry stuff is brainwashing you or something. But I don't believe you had a past-life memory."

"Do you believe in past lives?" Jessie saw Rachel's skepticism. "Weren't you the one who told me that even the early church believed in reincarnation?"

"That doesn't mean I believe in it. To be honest, I don't know what to believe."

Jessie felt lost. "Don't you find some irony in that—here I am, in this lifetime, attempting to uncover the ancient mysteries through Freemasonry . . . when in the past, I knew the mysteries and realized that the elite suppressed them. Rachel, the Thirty-Third Council could still be doing it today. I must have failed then, and that's why this is happening to me." Jessie stopped. She realized that she was rambling on, and probably sounded crazy. "I don't know what I'm saying. I'm sorry."

Rachel started the car engine and music filtered through the speakers. She lowered the volume, and jacked up the heat.

"Where are you going?"

"No place." Rachel rubbed her hands together. "I'm just getting cold."

"I'm sorry. I shouldn't have dragged you out on a Sunday night." Dusk had almost set, and Jessie still felt lost. *I should never have called her.* "I should go."

"Jessie, relax," Rachel knew that Jessie was upset. "Do you know what you're going to do now? Do you have what you need?"

Jessie felt like she was falling apart. "I don't know what I'm doing anymore. I'm so confused! I'm not any closer to solving Steve's murder than when I started. Taylor is coming to New York City next weekend. I just want my life back. . . . How come it's so complicated?" Jessie's voice cracked. She wiped away tears.

Rachel reached for Jessie's free hand and held it.

With great effort, Jessie pulled herself together. She took a deep breath and cleared her throat. "Sorry."

"Don't be sorry. I don't know how you've lasted this long. Go home with Taylor when she leaves."

"I can't just walk away. I would waste almost a year of my life. I need closure."

Rachel, still holding Jessie's hand, squeezed it. Her hands were so soft. There was a familiarity to Rachel's touch that Jessie drew comfort from. Her eyes migrated to Rachel's newly manicured hands, her familiar ankh-like birthmark, and wool dress-coat sleeve. Only then did she realize that Rachel was dressed up.

"Did I interrupt anything this evening?"

"No. I'm going out to dinner with West." Rachel smiled.

"Please don't tell me I messed up your date."

"No, not at all. We pushed it back an hour."

The song that had been playing on the stereo came to an end and a newscaster announced a special news broadcast. It was an occupational habit for Rachel to raise the volume to hear the news.

"The United Nations once again walked away from discussions regarding Iraq. In an unprecedented move, England took the opposing position to the United States' desire to move forces into the Middle

East. This is the third time in these proceedings that a U.S. ally has taken an unexpected stance to refrain from taking aggressive action upon Iraqi forces. Discussions will resume Wednesday; in the interim, as of last Friday the price of crude oil was up three hundred fifty-seven percent since. . . ."

Rachel lowered the volume on the stereo. "Wow. When was the last time the United States and England have been on different sides of the fence?"

Jessie shook her head. The last thing she could fathom was this Iraq mess.

Twenty-Seven

Rachel refused to allow her minor delay with Jessie dampen her spirits. She had looked forward to her date all week. She returned to her apartment with just enough time to look over herself in the mirror. She reapplied her lipstick, fluffed her hair, and sprayed perfume into the open recess of her blouse.

The doorbell rang.

An hour later the couple sat at a local Italian restaurant. Rachel had decided that she wouldn't discuss the subject matters that had pulled them together: secret societies, the Merovingians, or Satan.

The waiter served them wine, then left, giving them time to peruse the menu.

West raised his glass of cabernet. "May I propose a toast?" He paused. "To our third date, and I hope there'll be plenty more."

"Likewise," she tapped his glass, and they sipped their wine. Rachel had thoroughly enjoyed getting to know West. It had been a long time since she had had the companionship of a man who interested her.

"May I ask . . ." West started. "Are you seeing anyone else?"

There was a part of Rachel that didn't want to answer. She didn't want to sound lonely or desperate. "No. Why?"

He smiled, "I was just wondering. A lovely woman like yourself—it's hard to imagine that there isn't a long line of gentlemen callers." He retrieved his eyeglasses from his jacket pocket, and returned to the menu.

Dinner was delightful. They chatted about sports, the theater, movies, and growing up. Neither one brought up the documentaries that West had assisted Rachel with. Throughout dinner, Rachel found herself drawn to him. For a moment, she wondered if her interest in the controversial topics was fate. Could her curiosity have developed to bring the two of them together?

Published by The Haworth Press, Inc., 2006. All rights reserved.
doi:10.1300/5721_28

Rachel felt the effects of the wine as West escorted her to her apartment. She had had a wonderful time and didn't want the evening to end. They silently made their way to her apartment door. She was nervous. She liked West, and he seemingly liked her. *You don't want to lose this one!* Something always changed after she slept with them; even after years of therapy it still baffled her. *Don't invite him in!* She lectured herself.

At the door, Rachel inserted a key into the keyhole and turned it so that the door cracked open. She turned back to West, and smiled. "I had a nice time."

"I did too." He leaned up against the doorframe. "May I call you tomorrow?"

Rachel caught a scent of his cologne. She nodded.

As in the closing moments of their previous dates, West brushed his lips upon Rachel's cheek. He lingered just a moment, long enough to sense her soft skin and perfume arousing him. He withdrew and with great effort whispered, "Good night."

As West backed away, Rachel seized one of his warm hands, luring him to her. She stepped closer, and brought her lips toward his mouth, firmly planting them on his. He kissed her back and held her intimately in his arms. Their kiss ceased momentarily, and their eyes met, giving each an opportunity to consider their next move.

With the back of her foot, Rachel jostled open the door. Her eyes settled upon his lips, and her mouth met his again. Rachel's lips parted and her tongue invited him in.

Monday morning came too quickly. When Rachel woke, she reached for West between the smooth satin sheets, but he wasn't beside her. Then she felt his wet lips on the back of her neck. He nibbled at her skin, moving down her back, stirring her senses.

"Good morning," she whispered.

He stopped kissing her back. "It's a wonderful morning," he agreed.

Rachel rolled onto her back. To her surprise, West was fully dressed sitting beside her on the bed.

He reached for something on the nightstand, then handed her a coffee mug. "I made some coffee. It's black. I wasn't sure how you like it." He propped up a pillow behind her.

She sipped. "It's perfect. Thank you. How long have you been up?"

"A little while. I've made breakfast. Hungry?"

Rachel retrieved her robe and slippers, and joined West in the kitchen. She eyed pancakes with caution. "It's pretty scary thinking that anything edible could have come out of my refrigerator."

"I did notice that pickings were slim around here, but I think this is safe." He moved to the table with his subtle limp, and pulled the oak chair out for Rachel.

Rachel wasn't used to the attention. "Thank you." She sat at the small dinette set. "What time do you have to be at the school?"

"Not until ten." He offered her some syrup.

"Thanks. It's only six-thirty! Why are you up so early?"

"I wasn't sure what time you had to be in."

"My calendar is clear until lunch," she took a bite. "Thank you for breakfast."

"I should have let you sleep in."

"I usually get up early, anyway."

"Even after being up most of the night?" His blue eyes sparkled.

Rachel was tired. It had been only a few hours since they had fallen asleep in each other's arms. She smelled a trace of his cologne on her skin, almost veiled by the scent of sex.

"Do you realize that last night was the first time we hadn't discussed Freemasonry, or the Merovingian Dynasty, or even Satan?"

"And look what happened," he reached for Rachel's hand. "Thank you."

Rachel was uneasy. Half of her relationships ended after her first intimate encounter. She needed to walk a fine line between being interested and indifferent. She smiled, sipped her coffee, and then changed the subject. "A friend of mine came across a couple of names. She wondered if they were Egyptian. Would you know?"

"It depends. What names?"

Rachel recalled her discussion with Jessie. "Lukeman and Kek."

West removed a pen and pad from his tweed jacket. He jotted down the names. "I believe they are. Would you like to meet for dinner, and I'll let you know for sure?"

"Dinner?" Rachel didn't know how she should respond.

"There's a great Thai restaurant in midtown. . . . I can't remember its name. Do you have a Zagat's Guide? That is of course, if you'd like."

Rachel hesitated. Then she rummaged through the pantry and drawers. Clearly, she hadn't spent a lot of time in her kitchen. "I'm not sure where it is." She pulled a phonebook from a drawer instead.

"That will work." He speedily retrieved the location and phone number of the restaurant. Post-it tabs that stuck out of the book drew his attention to the church section. Here, handwritten notes were spread throughout multiple pages.

"Are you doing a story on religions or churches?" he asked.

"No." Rachel took the phonebook from him.

West eyed Rachel inquisitively. "Personal interest?" he pressed.

"In a way," she admitted. "I was never raised in an organized religion. Although my father was a spiritual man, I didn't have the opportunity to study different faiths. So, over the years, I've set out to do so."

"And I thought I had strange pastimes," he smiled.

"Do you consider yourself a religious man?"

West shook his head, "No. I used to be Methodist."

"What happened?"

"Because of my work, I've had to dissect the Bible. . . . I just don't believe that the God, or Jehovah, in the Bible is our supreme God. At least not *my* God!"

"Why not?"

"I vowed never to discuss religion or politics on my dates." West peeked at the clock, then smiled. "Are you sure you want to get into this?"

Rachel nodded. "Absolutely."

"Do you have a Bible?"

Rachel left the kitchen, and when she returned she placed a Bible in front of him.

He picked up the book and cracked the spine. "I don't have to go very far into the Old Testament to question whether Jehovah deserves my devotion." He leafed through the new pages. "You haven't read this?"

"Not entirely. Certainly the readings during services."

"The ones the church *selects* for you to read. Let's start with the story of Moses. When the Hebrews were still slaves in Egypt, Jehovah asked Moses to go to the pharaoh to ask him to free the slaves. Right? But Jehovah warned Moses that he would make him say no. Here, this is Exodus 10:

> And the Lord said to Moses, "Go to the Pharaoh: for I have hardened his heart, and the heart of his servants, that I might show these signs before him."

"So Moses, of course, goes to the pharaoh, and asks him to free his people. And time after time, the pharaoh refuses because Jehovah has *hardened his heart.* And each time, Jehovah punishes the Egyptians, from vermin infestations, to plagues, to boils, and finally . . . the murder of the eldest sons.

"Anyway, the Hebrews are freed! They leave Egypt and go to Mount Sinai where Moses is given the Ten Commandments on two stone tablets, which interestingly enough, Moses breaks! Then he's given a second set of tablets. The Bible points out that no one was permitted on the mountaintop with Jehovah except a select few, which included Moses and Aaron. Jehovah even threatened to kill anyone else who tried to see him. Now, through the commandments, they were given very specific moral teachings. To start, they shouldn't kill, steal, or want their neighbor's possessions, right?"

Rachel nodded. "I'm following you."

"Well, Jehovah demanded obedience from them as they journeyed to the Promised Land. Unfortunately, not all were compliant, so according to the Bible, Jehovah killed up to fourteen thousand people.

"Then, they reach Canaan, and settle in their new homeland. But Jehovah sends them on a mission, under Joshua, to depopulate the area. The first city they cross is Jericho." He leafed through the pages. "This is Joshua 6:21." He read again:

And they utterly destroyed all that was in the city, both man and woman, young and old, and ox, and sheep, and ass, with the edge of the sword.

His finger skipped through a few more paragraphs, and he continued:

they burnt the city with fire, and all that was therein: only the silver, and the gold, and the vessels of brass and of iron, they put into the treasury of the house of the Lord.

"The next city was Ai which had thousands living in it . . . and Jehovah ordered all twelve thousand to be butchered. This is Joshua 10:40:

So Joshua smote all the country of the hills, and of the south, and of the vale, and of the springs, and all their kings: he left none remaining, but utterly destroyed all that breathed, as the Lord God of Israel commanded.

"This army went on a seven-year holocaust under the direction of Jehovah and killed thousands of innocent men, women, children, and animals. But what's really barbaric is that the Bible actually explains why most resisted Joshua's army. This is still Joshua:

There was not a city that made peace with the children of Israel, save the Hivites the inhabitants of Gibeon: all others they took in battle.
For it was of the Lord to harden their hearts, that they should come against Israel in battle, that he might destroy them utterly, and that they might have no favor, but that he might destroy them, as the Lord commanded Moses.

"Jehovah *hardens their hearts,* so that they resist him, and he can have them slaughtered. And this is supposed to be a loving God? In my opinion, Jehovah is undeserving of my love and devotion." Clearly angry and fervent about the subject, he slammed the Bible shut. He took a deep breath, and softened a bit. "I'm sorry."

"No need for an apology. I find this interesting. Do you consider yourself atheist?"

"No. I very much believe in God; just not the god of the Old Testament."

"If Jehovah isn't God, though, then who is he? He's clearly an advanced presence."

West smiled. "That certainly is another topic for conversation, perhaps tonight?"

Rachel left her lunch meeting and headed back to her office. Something was different. She was humming. She turned west on Forty-ninth Street, and found herself smiling as she dodged the hustle of New Yorkers rushing back to their offices. West didn't stray far from her mind. Memories of their previous evening replayed in her head, and Rachel looked forward to her date later that evening.

West strolled the drafty university hallway. His mind wandered from the task at hand, which was to grade exams. Reminiscences of his previous evening drifted into his head: Rachel straddling him, their bodies coupled, sweating, surging, and collapsing in each other's arms. With only a couple hours of sleep, he should have been exhausted, but thoughts of their date kept him going. Occasionally, he considered that he hadn't been completely forthcoming with Rachel, and feelings of guilt pestered him.

He unlocked a wooden office door with WEST KERRY stenciled on an opaque glass panel. The glass clattered as he closed the door, echoing within the room's tall ceilings. He dropped a stack of exams on his desk, beside a galvanized statue of an Egyptian man with a falcon head. The inscription on the base of the sculpture was RA—SUN GOD. A flashing light on the telephone indicated that he had voicemail. He sat behind the large desk, his back against a drafty tall window. Beneath the window was an old-fashioned cast iron radiator that knocked from use. He lifted the handset and pressed a few buttons.

A digital voice said, "You have . . . two messages."

West pulled the top exam from the stack of papers and started to evaluate it. But he stopped as soon as he heard her inviting, husky voice.

"It's Rachel. I just wanted to say thanks for last night. I'm looking forward to this evening. See you then."

A smile came to his lips. Almost instantly, he was lost in the feel of her soft skin. But the smile quickly vanished.

"I told you to stay away from Rachel Addison!" The haunting voice bellowed through the handset. "You were warned." Dial tone sounded.

"Who the hell is that?" West whispered as he rested the handset. "She told me she wasn't seeing anyone."

Preoccupied, West returned to the exam in front of him. He pulled open his desk drawer to retrieve the red marker he always used to grade papers, but hissing came from beneath the desk. Slowly, he closed the drawer and gasped. A king cobra's head had reared up between his legs. The yellow-bellied serpent flattened its neck ribs into a hood. The snake hissed madly, exposing the half-inch venomous fangs.

How could this tropical snake find its way into his office? West knew that if he moved, it would strike, and cobra's venom could kill an elephant. His heart pounded wildly. He eyed the galvanized statue on the right side of his desk. It must have been thirty pounds. *Can I reach it?* Even if he could, the movement alone would prompt an attack.

His adrenaline surged, and his movements were swift. He thrust away from the desk and sprang to his feet, twisting his body to grab the heavy piece. The movement exposed a leg, and the snake lunged. He hoisted the sculpture above his head, took aim, and heaved it downward, as the venomous fangs plunged into his calf. The iron statue simultaneously crushed the snake's head and West's leg, toppling him to the ground where he hit his head on the radiator. All went dark.

It was seven o'clock when she arrived at the restaurant. Rachel was surprised that West wasn't there yet, but asked to be seated. As she waited, she eyed her Gucci watch. At ten minutes after the hour she checked her phone. There was no message. Something wasn't right.

Rachel could feel it. Just as she pressed the speed dial button, jingling alerted her that the front door had opened.

It was West. His subtle limp was now obvious, and he shuffled with a cane. He peered around the room, scrutinizing other diners. Then he slid into the seat across from Rachel. There was an air of unease about him.

"What happened?"

"Are you seeing someone else?" he asked unexpectedly.

"You asked me this last night. No, I'm not! What happened to your leg?"

A glass dropped at a nearby table and West jumped. Impulsively, he raised the cane to protect himself. It was then that Rachel noticed the bandage at the base of his skull.

"What happened to your head?"

It was barely a whisper. "You were seeing Stanley Chancellor . . ."

"Yes. It ended very soon after it started. What's going on?"

West spoke softly, "Before our date last night, I received a call from a man. He warned me to stay away from you."

"Away from me?"

"Yes. And today—" The jingle bells on the front door distracted him. He sighed when he saw the old couple enter. "Today I got a phone message, pretty much reiterating the warning, and someone planted a king cobra in my office."

"You're not serious."

"I am serious."

"My God, West. Did you get bit?"

"Yes and no," West's eyes met Rachel's. "Look, I'm not proud of this, but I haven't been completely honest with you about something." He stuck his leg away from the table for Rachel to view. He lifted the pants from the bottom of his left leg. An artificial limb was wedged into his shoe.

Rachel shot a questioning look at West. As if reading her mind, "This is temporary. My prosthetic is much more *natural* looking."

"That's why you left my bed so early this morning?"

He nodded, "I'm sorry."

"That doesn't matter, West. Are you telling me the snake bit your prosthetic?"

He grinned for the first time that evening. "Yeah. Then I bashed its head with an iron statue. . . . Unfortunately, it totaled my leg. I fell and hit my head."

Rachel pondered the situation. She remembered how Jessie had been warned not to see her. "I'm so sorry, but I honestly don't know who would do this."

West put their situation in perspective. "Someone doesn't want me to see you, Rachel. A minute doesn't go by when I haven't thought of you," his voice softened. "What are we going to do?"

Rachel felt lost. Why was this happening? She shook her head. "We shouldn't see each other." Her heart sank at her own suggestion.

"I don't intimidate that easily, Rachel."

"Until I know what's going on, I don't see any other choice. The last thing I want is for you to get hurt. Please, just leave."

West knew she was right. He reached for her hand. "I have information on your names, Lukeman and Kek."

"Are they Egyptian?" Rachel was curious.

"Very much so. The name Lukeman means *a prophet*. There was once a high priest of Egypt whose name was Lukeman. He was a teacher of the mysteries; apparently, he was murdered after he was caught teaching the mysteries to untouchables."

"Untouchables?"

"The lower caste, the uninitiated . . . the profane."

Rachel marveled at the coincidence. "And the name Kek?"

"Kek means the god of darkness."

"The god of darkness?" she whispered. "Like the devil?"

West nodded. "Yes, like the devil, like Abaddon."

Twenty-Eight

It was around ten o'clock that morning when Jessie arrived at the cabin. She grabbed the packages from the rear seat. She hadn't been there in weeks, and a half-foot of snow had accumulated on the front porch. With her foot, she brushed the snow away from the entry. While balancing the packages in one hand, she opened the door.

Jessie dropped the mail-order items on the table. "Brr," she rubbed her hands together, then jacked up the thermostat. The small furnace flared to life. She glanced at her watch. "I've got to get out of here in two hours."

She had agreed to meet Taylor that evening at the Hudson Hotel in New York City. The cabin was the only place she felt safe to transition back to her real life. Without wasting time, she gathered the packages and headed for the upstairs bedroom. She opened the parcels of women's clothing and shoes and arranged them on the bed.

Jessie removed her jacket and tie. As she unbuttoned her shirt she spotted her reflection in the dresser mirror, and approached the glass. Brennan's appearance was now familiar. She rubbed the facial hair—it no longer felt foreign to her. She peeled the goatee from her face, exposing her feminine skin. There was a noticeable color difference where the goatee stopped the sunrays from the rest of her bronze skin. "Nothing a little makeup can't cure!"

Within a couple hours Jessie had transitioned back to her old self. Now, as she stood in front of the mirror, she realized that her innate feminine mannerisms were no longer natural to her. What an awkward place to be, but she didn't have time to dwell on it. She packed a small bag for the weekend, and headed for Newark Airport where she had reserved a car rental in her name.

As she headed south, she listened to the news on the car radio:

Published by The Haworth Press, Inc., 2006. All rights reserved.
doi:10.1300/5721_29

In international news today, anti-U.S. protestors demonstrated in Ottawa, outside of Rideau Hall as the president met with the Canadian governor general. Some political experts believe that the president is attempting to ascertain Canada's position regarding the Iraqi situation. This is especially critical with the recent loss of England as a U.S. ally. Most authorities believe that Canada will follow Britain's lead. In other fronts, during UN discussions, England officially warned that if the United States takes an aggressive action against Iraq they would retaliate. That wraps up this report on Desert Disaster.

Jessie turned the radio off. "This just becomes more and more bizarre each day."

By the time she arrived at the Hudson Hotel, it was close to seven o'clock and she was exhausted. Although she had longed for this rendezvous for two months, she had hoped it would be under different circumstances. So many thoughts ran through her mind. She wanted to be here, in her own life, but Brennan's life kept seeping into her mind. As the elevator doors opened, she faced a mirror. Jessie approached it. There were noticeable dark circles beneath her eyes. She hadn't been able to sleep since her last Egypt experience. Now, effects from her sleepless nights blemished her face.

She looked like hell and wondered what Taylor would think as she approached the hotel door. She lingered a moment, then knocked.

The door opened. Taylor smiled at Jessie, "Come in. I'm just finishing a phone call." She retreated to a phone on a stainless steel nightstand beside the bed.

As Taylor continued her conversation, Jessie stood opposite the bed, in a small sitting area. Dark paneled walls offset the white curtains and linens. At a window she viewed the subtle landscape lights in a park. As she waited for Taylor to finish the call, her self-confidence waned. What would a person like Taylor Andrews see in Jessie? Taylor was beautiful and successful. Jessie felt as if she had aged twenty years since their last encounter. With each passing moment, her anxiety grew.

"Dinner after the concert would be nice. . . . Yes, she just came in." Taylor glanced at Jessie. "She's looking forward to meeting you too. . . . Good night."

Taylor placed the handset on the cradle then turned toward Jessie.

Although they were only ten feet apart, to Jessie, it felt as if they were in different countries. Taylor's eyes were on her, but Jessie couldn't read them. Then, Taylor moved to her so that they were within reach of each other. Jessie needed Taylor to say something. Anything! Instead, Taylor's expressionless eyes remained fixed on her.

Jessie waited for what seemed to be an eternity for a response. Then Taylor made her move. She stepped forward and brushed the back of her soft fingers along Jessie's cheek. Her eyes followed the stroke until they reached Jessie's scar beneath her eye. Taylor delicately kissed the flaw.

Jessie tilted her head, bringing their mouths to each other. Ever so gently, Jessie kissed her. The feel of her moist lips and sweet tongue awakened feelings she had cast aside when she left France. In that moment, Brennan's life was silenced. She desired her.

Jessie needed the feel of her skin, and the safety of her arms. The wonder of her shadows always took her breath away. She craved Taylor's hands over her body and the sweat amid their skins. She ached for Taylor's mouth on her breasts and needed her deep inside of her. Jessie yearned to run her tongue over her skin, to taste her, to hear the subtle change in her breathing. Building. Surging. Cresting. Jessie had never wanted Taylor more.

As if sensing Jessie's needs, Taylor thrust Jessie toward the bed where she pressed her to the mattress.

Taylor's head had found that perfect spot on Jessie's chest. The one that made everything feel right. Their bodies fitted seamlessly together as Jessie held Taylor closely in her arms. The rhythm of Jessie's heartbeat, normally, would put her to sleep. Tonight, though, she savored every moment of being near Jessie. "God, I've missed you," Taylor whispered.

"I've missed you, too." Jessie sighed. "More than you'll ever know."

Taylor lifted her head to look into Jessie's eyes. "Are you okay? You look tired. You're not sick, are you?"

"I'm not sick. I am tired, though. I haven't been sleeping well."

"How come?"

"I had a strange experience last weekend." Jessie and Taylor had gone through so much together the previous year during their Salem incident. If Jessie couldn't share it with Taylor, whom could she share it with? "I think I had a past-life memory."

"Really? From Salem?"

"No. It was Egypt."

"Egypt? What a coincidence. I was talking with Sidney Marcum last week. . . . Oh, by the way, we're having dinner with them after the concert. Is that okay?"

Jessie wasn't sure if she wanted to meet Michael Whitman's ex-wife now. She had sampled her old life and didn't want anything to do with Brennan. Perhaps she didn't need closure from her experience. Being back with Taylor was enough. Jessie knew, however, that dinner with Taylor's personal manager was more political than social. "That's fine, sweetheart."

"Anyway," Taylor continued, "Sidney and her partner, Anastasia, knew each other during an ancient Egyptian life. But what's going on with you?"

Jessie shifted the pillows. She tugged at a bra that she had been lying on and tossed it on the floor, near the other garments that had been stripped from their bodies. "I started seeing geometric symbols that progressed into, what I believe to be, past-life visions. But anyway, since the experience, I haven't slept real well. I keep having nightmares. I see a sword, then there's blood everywhere."

"Past-life memories or dreams usually occur when we're faced with a similar situation. It kind of gives us a chance to do things differently. Have you been able to isolate what should be done differently?"

She must have failed in Egypt, Jessie thought. Failed at what, though? Teaching the profane the secrets to eternal life? How could that relate to this lifetime? Did her project, *The Ultimate Conspiracy,* foreshadow her own failure?

"No. I haven't been able to relate it to anything in this life."

Taylor nuzzled into Jessie's shoulder. "How's your project coming?"

Jessie had been hoping to avoid the subject. "This is a tough one," she admitted. "I may need to let this one go, at least for now."

"I can't say I'm disappointed. The project hasn't felt right from the beginning. I'm going home on Tuesday. Can we go back together?"

There were so many loose ends. The cabin. The apartment. *The Empire.* Maxwell. What about Rachel? "I'll need a few days to wrap up things. I'll be home next weekend. I promise."

Twenty-Nine

Up until the concert the following evening, Jessie and Taylor remained in their hotel suite. They indulged in room service, soaked in steaming hot baths, slept in each other's arms, and made love. For Jessie, it was a wonderful initiation back into her life.

It was seven o'clock when Taylor and Jessie entered Taylor's private dressing room at Radio City Music Hall.

"How do you feel about the tour coming to an end?" Jessie asked as Taylor opened a wardrobe bag.

"I have never been so happy to see a tour end. This was *way* too long."

Jessie's thoughts exactly! The day she had spent with Taylor only reinforced that she was ready to leave Brennan's life. A knock sounded, disrupting her thoughts.

"Come in," Taylor said.

A woman appeared at the door. She stopped when she saw Jessie. "Excuse me! Is this a bad time?"

"Hi Andrea, would you mind giving me a minute?"

"Sure." Andrea smiled, and closed the door.

Jessie moved to Taylor. "You look great. I'll leave you alone with your makeup lady." Her gaze settled on Taylor's lips, and she kissed them. She turned toward the door, but stopped. Something didn't feel right. She couldn't put her finger on it, though. Abruptly, Jessie turned back and gently wrapped her arms around Taylor.

"What's this for?" Taylor always found comfort in her embrace.

Jessie wasn't sure, but she had an overwhelming need to hold her. She looked into her incredible blue eyes. "I love you, Taylor. I love sharing my life with you. Thank you for being so patient with me."

"Are you okay, Jess?"

Published by The Haworth Press, Inc., 2006. All rights reserved.
doi:10.1300/5721_30

"I'm great." As Jessie held her close, she marveled at the feeling. She always left her wanting more. *Déjà vu?* It was such a familiar feeling. She wondered where she had felt it before. Then she remembered. *It was in Egypt . . . with Jamila.*

Andrea had waited outside the dressing room. When Jessie emerged, the makeup artist smiled at her. "I just wanted to let you know how much I enjoy your stories."

It had been a long time since she had been recognized as Jessie Mercer. "Thank you."

With time to kill before the concert, Jessie roamed the drafty backstage halls. Taylor crossed her mind, and a smile lit up her face. Their reunion had been just what she needed.

The tall ceilings and dark walls dimmed the effect of the hallway lights. Footsteps from the opposite end of the hallway drew Jessie's attention to an approaching woman. There was an aura of dignity about her. She projected a classy professional image with black wool pants, tan silk blouse, and a wool jacket.

As they approached each other Jessie was drawn to the woman's necklace. It was an ankh, very similar to Taylor's pendant. Jessie slowed, and their eyes met. Spontaneously, warmth intensified around her heart and face. A heart connection! This was a sensation she had not experienced since she had met Taylor. Suddenly, from Jessie's third eye she glimpsed a Sphinx and pyramid. Then she saw her. It was Lukeman's mother, Eshe. The images flashed, and then swiftly disappeared.

Jessie shook free of her trance. She stood beside this woman whose familiar brown eyes gazed upon her.

"Do I know you?" she asked.

Jessie didn't know what to say.

A door slammed in the hallway behind her. Then, a man's voice, "There you are! We need to talk."

Jessie turned toward the voice. Michael Whitman stormed toward them. He slowed when his eyes met Jessie's, and her third eye sparked to life. She glimpsed a raised hand; it struck a face—the face of Eshe, Lukeman's mother. Then she saw him: Lukeman's father, Oba.

Jessie closed her eyes and shook her head, clearing the images from her psyche. Lightheaded, she turned from Michael and rushed past the woman.

"Who . . ." Michael started.

Although the woman remained silent, Jessie felt her eyes burrow into her soul, strengthening their link. She hoped that Whitman had not recognized her as she fled. At the end of the hall, Jessie turned a doorknob, and stepped through. As she closed the door, she heard Whitman again. "Sidney, who the hell was that?"

The door shut. To say the room was spinning would have been an understatement. The spiraling in her head reflected in her walk as Jessie staggered aimlessly down another hallway. She opened another door, expelling her into the midst of stagehands preparing the stage for the evening's event.

"Who are you?" a man asked who worked on lights.

"You shouldn't be here," someone said as they checked a microphone.

Without heeding their words, Jessie roamed across the stage where she exited into another hallway, and moved away from the flurry of activity.

She was entranced. *That was Sidney Marcum. What the hell does this mean?* Were Sidney and Whitman her parents in Egypt?

She recalled listening to Whitman's voice at the initiation. "It was Whitman's voice that sent me back," she mumbled, barely able to contain herself. Jessie's hand moved to her chest where she could still sense her heart connection with Sidney.

"I've only felt this with Taylor."

Thirty

The opening act was a blur. Although the noise in the concert hall was deafening, and she had a front row seat, Jessie was barely cognizant of it. Then Taylor went on, and Jessie's connection to her grounded her. She was so beautiful and talented. Jessie considered herself the luckiest person alive as she admired Taylor from the foot of the stage.

About thirty minutes into Taylor's performance, Jessie's phone vibrated. As Jessie moved to a nearby exit, she could feel Taylor's eyes upon her.

A guard opened the door permitting Jessie through.

"Hello." But Jessie couldn't hear anything. "Hold on." She walked away from the doorway, waiting for the door to close behind her. "Hello?"

"I need your help!"

Jessie heard panic in Rachel's voice. "Rachel?"

"God, we were so stupid."

"Rachel, are you hurt?"

"I'm afraid something terrible has happened. Where are you?"

"I'm at Radio City Music Hall."

"Good! You're in Manhattan. I'll meet you out front in twenty minutes." Rachel disconnected the phone.

Jessie hoped that Taylor wouldn't notice her absence. She retrieved her coat in the dressing room, then watched for Rachel in the lobby. Flashing lights from the sign on the front of the building illuminated the street. Soon, she saw the glowing Saab double-parked and she moved out into the bitter January air. She hopped into the passenger seat.

Rachel, startled by Jessie's feminine appearance, gasped. "My God, Jessie. I was expecting Brennan."

Published by The Haworth Press, Inc., 2006. All rights reserved.
doi:10.1300/5721_31

"Taylor is in the city for the weekend." Jessie knew something was wrong. Rachel should have known that, after all, Taylor was the headliner tonight, her name flashing above their heads. "What's going on?"

"We did something totally foolish." Hastily, Rachel sped away from the curve.

"We did?"

"Not us. West and me."

"What happened? Where are we going?" Jessie became sadder as they moved further and further away from Radio City Music Hall.

Rachel took a deep breath and spoke quickly. "West and I had been dating. Last Sunday, he spent the night. On Monday, someone called and threatened him to stay away from me. Then a king cobra was planted in his office.

"I was warned to stay away from you after we *appeared* to be on a date."

"I thought of that also. West and I agreed to stop seeing each other until this was sorted out." Rachel sighed. "He showed up at my apartment late last night. He said he wasn't afraid." Rachel paused.

"And?"

"We were foolish and weak. Our hormones kicked in and he spent the night. I called his home. . . . His sister said that he hadn't come home yet. There's no answer at NYU. Jessie, I can't explain it, but I have a terrible feeling about this."

Jessie could sense it also.

The Saab sped to the heart of Greenwich Village, where Rachel parked illegally alongside Washington Square Park. She placed a press pass on the dashboard. The women stepped from the car. Because of the cold, there was no activity in the park. Across the street was a dark red brick building, with a tall stooped entrance.

"His sister says his office is on the second floor," Rachel said.

"Do you have a key?" Jessie asked as they topped the entrance stairway. "I can't imagine the door would be unlocked at this hour."

Rachel squeezed the handle set, and the door opened. She dashed a look at Jessie.

"Odd," Jessie admitted.

Once inside, they headed up a stairwell to the second floor. A hallway was lit only by the red light from the EXIT signs on each end of the floor. Rachel and Jessie scanned the names on office doors. The building was ominously quiet.

They were halfway down the hallway. "Here it is," Rachel said. The frosted glass window on the door was dark. Rachel tried the doorknob. "It's locked." She knocked on the door; it echoed loudly.

Jessie retrieved a credit card from her wallet and inserted it in the gap between the doorjamb and the door.

"What are you doing?" Rachel was surprised.

"It's a cheap lock; it shouldn't be—" there was a loud click. Jessie turned the doorknob and the door creaked ajar. "It shouldn't be tough."

"That's breaking in!"

Jessie backed away from the door. "You don't want to go in?"

Rachel pushed open the door. The room was dark. She searched the wall for a light switch. A fluorescent overhead fixture blinked on. From the doorway, the woman spotted a mug on top of his desk, resting on its side. Spilled coffee surrounded the cup. Rachel and Jessie glanced at each other, then cautiously approached the desk.

Beside the coffee spill were two opened books. One was the Bible. Jessie focused on reading the other title upside down, *Myths from Mesopotamia.*

"Oh my God," Rachel cried.

Her shriek startled Jessie. She moved to Rachel's side and gasped. Lying in a pool of blood, behind the desk, was a man. She faltered a bit, knelt by his side, and felt for a pulse. His hand was cold. Blood oozed from an abdominal wound. "He's dead," Jessie whispered. "Is it West?"

Tears welled up in Rachel's eyes as she gazed at her lover's body. She was in shock. "My God, what have I done?" Rachel mumbled.

"You didn't do this. We've got to call the police," Jessie said.

Rachel, visibly shaken, stooped beside Jessie. "He didn't deserve this. It's my fault," she said between sobs.

"This isn't your fault." Jessie embraced her. "Let's call the police."

"Steve got killed—because of me," Rachel rambled on.

Jessie held her closer. "You don't know what you're saying."

As Rachel looked upon West's body, her anger grew. Who could have done this? She wiped her eyes, and mascara smeared both cheeks. It was then that she noticed that one of his fingertips was bloodstained. On the floor beside his hand was a letter sketched in blood. She cleared her throat. "I think he was writing something."

Jessie removed a tissue from a box on West's desk. Using the tissue, she repositioned a desk lamp and turned it on.

"He *was*," Rachel said. The letter K was visible just to the left of his hand.

Jessie squatted beside Rachel, and picked up the cold hand. She couldn't see beneath it. "What did he write?"

Rachel moved so she could make out West's last clue. "Oh my God!"

"What is it?" Jessie pulled the hand so that she could view it. "Shit!" escaped from her lips. Stunned, she dropped the hand. It fell beside the bloodstained floor, so that the name *Kek* was ominously visible. "Kek?" But how could that be? Jessie couldn't comprehend the coincidence.

A noise from the hallway drew their attention away from the body. "Who's that?" Rachel asked.

They ventured from the office and peered down the hallway where two silhouettes were illuminated from the glow of the EXIT sign.

"This doesn't feel right," Jessie whispered. "Let's go to the other stairwell." They turned and rushed away as the men watched them. About ten feet from the other exit, the stairwell door suddenly opened and two men emerged, blocking that exit.

"Now what?" Rachel whispered.

Jessie reached for a doorknob to an office beside her. It was locked. Rachel took one side, while Jessie tried the other. The women moved away from the men searching for an escape. All the while, the men watched.

"Jess, what if they're all locked? Are we trapped?"

"There's a window in West's office," Jessie whispered.

As if reading each other's mind, they darted toward the office.

"Do *not* hurt Addison!" One of the men ordered, and they dashed toward them.

Rachel and Jessie sprinted into the office. Jessie slammed the door, locked it, and jammed a chair against the door.

"This isn't going to hold long." With that, there was an abrupt bang on the door.

Rachel scurried around West. She tried to open the window. It wouldn't budge. There was a resounding blow to the door. Jessie grabbed a large book from West's desk. She dog-eared the page that it was opened to and then lunged it through the glass, shattering the window. She cleared the jagged edges with the book and tossed it out the second-story window.

The glass in the office door shattered behind them.

"Rachel, quick!" Jessie assisted Rachel to the window's edge, where she wavered. It must have been a ten-foot plunge, and she couldn't see the ground. But when she heard the chair against the door being thrust forward, she jumped, falling uncontrollably to the frozen ground.

Jessie, right behind her, leaped from the window. But her escape was impeded when her overcoat shoulders were snatched by one of the pursuers. She dangled in midair.

"If that's Addison, don't hurt her," a man's voice ordered.

"I don't know who it is," another man said.

Jessie was being yanked upward. She unfastened the top button, then another, and another. One more would do it—but it wouldn't come. Inches away from their arms, she ripped the last button free. With arms raised skyward, she plunged from the overcoat. Tumbling to earth, she jolted her knees and scraped her hands in a pile of snow and ice.

Rachel grabbed Jessie's arm, "Are you okay?"

"Let's get out of here." Jessie grabbed the book she had tossed from the window.

The women sprinted toward the Saab as two men watched from the second-story window. Rachel clicked the keyless remote, flashing the lights and unlocking the doors. Just as they reached the car, the front door of the building burst open. Two men charged down the entrance stairway into the street.

Rachel and Jessie hopped in. Rachel fumbled nervously with the keys and they fell to the floor. Jessie tried to grab them, and their heads collided.

"I got them!" Rachel sputtered.

"Let's get out of here!" Jessie locked the doors while Rachel started the car.

An antagonist hammered his fist into Jessie's window. "Floor it!" Jessie ordered.

She did. Tires screeched and the Saab sped into the street slamming against another adversary. Rachel's pressure on the gas pedal waned when she realized that she had hit the man.

"No! Keep going!" Jessie peered out the back window. The man was getting to his feet. "He's fine. Let's get out of here."

The back end of the car fishtailed as Rachel made a sharp turn. "Are they following us?" She floored the accelerator.

Jessie watched the back window. "I don't think so. Just keep go-ing." She tried to sort everything out—but none of it made sense. Her heart pounded wildly and her head throbbed. "What the hell is going on, Rachel?"

"You think *I* know?"

"They said 'don't hurt Addison.'" Jessie's voice rose. "They knew it was you!"

A pedestrian came from the shadows into the road, startling both of them. Rachel swerved to avoid hitting the man and almost collided with a passing car. Both exhaled when the Saab screeched by without smashing into anything.

Jessie knew it wasn't the time or place to discuss this. "I'm sorry. Let's get to the police!"

Thirty-One

Minutes later, Rachel had circled back to the Village police station. As the Saab approached, Jessie rested her hand on Rachel's shoulder. "Don't stop!"

A group of men had gathered across from the station. A man with a wrapped fist caught Jessie's eye. It was the guy that had struck her window. The men that had chased them were engaged in a heated conversation with police officers.

Jessie ducked, and Rachel obstructed her face with her hand. "Do we try another station?" Rachel asked as they drove by undetected.

"Let's get out of the city," Jessie shivered.

Realizing that Jessie must have been frozen, Rachel cranked the heat. Jessie had lost her coat and was dressed in a thin silk blouse.

Jessie's head throbbed. She massaged her temples. "Rachel, he wrote *Kek.* That was a name from my past-life memory. How could that have happened?"

"I ran the names you mentioned from your past life by West."

"Why?"

"I wondered if they were truly Egyptian. They are. The meaning of Lukeman is 'a prophet.'"

"A prophet?" Jessie whispered. Echoes of a distant past whispered in her ear: *"You are now the prophet of the Neter, Lukeman. You are expected to interact with the Royal House regarding divinatory matters. You cannot hide from me forever."*

Jessie shook from the daze, trying to purge the unresolved memory.

"That's not all," Rachel interrupted. "West told me there actually was a high priest named Lukeman. Jessie, he was murdered because he taught the ancient mysteries to the lower class."

Jessie's headache worsened. The Egyptian life did happen. It wasn't a hallucination. "That explains my dreams. The sword and all the blood."

Published by The Haworth Press, Inc., 2006. All rights reserved.
doi:10.1300/5721_32

"He also told me that Kek means 'Prince of Darkness.'"

"Prince of Darkness? You mean Satan?"

"Yes. Satan, the Devil, Abaddon, Lucifer."

Jessie felt as if her heart was lodged in her throat. "Do you think there's something demonic going on here?"

A chill ran up Rachel's spine. She shuddered at the possibility. "I'm merely relaying what West told me. There's more. Some time ago I researched the premise that Freemasonry could actually be devil worship. There's documentation that suggests that the founder of the mystery schools, the one who formed the Brotherhood, was a Satan-like individual."

"And Freemasonry is based on the ancient mysteries." Jessie's heart thumped. The hair on the back of her neck stood. "There was a book about Mesopotamia on West's desk." She reached for the volume that she had used to break the glass. "I grabbed the Bible." She turned to the dog-eared page. "He was reading Ezekiel."

"Jess, where should we go? I'm sure they know where I live."

"Assuming we don't have a tail, let's head for the cabin. I need to call Taylor. What am I going to tell her?" Jessie reached for her phone. "Oh, shit. My phone and wallet were in my overcoat."

Rachel handed Jessie her phone.

Jessie glanced at her watch. There was a good chance that Taylor was still onstage. She punched in the number and left a message. "Hi, Sweetheart. I'm sorry I had to run out on your concert. Something came up. I wish I could explain. I'll call you when I can. Please have patience with me. I love you." She was heartsick leaving the message, knowing that Taylor deserved better.

When Taylor listened to the message that night, she couldn't believe her ears. "What the hell is going on?" She punched in Jessie's number. The call went into voice mail after five rings. She hung up.

Taylor sensed that Jessie had shut her out. She pulled Jessie's overnight bag from the closet and laid it on the bed. A wave of guilt hit as she removed articles of clothing. Nothing seemed unusual, except that all the clothes appeared new.

From a side compartment, Taylor retrieved a man's eel-skinned wallet. She opened the fold and removed a stack of cards. On top, there was a business card for Rachel Addison, from *Over the Edge.* Taylor recalled that Steve had worked with Ms. Addison.

Next, there was a handful of calling cards from a reporter at *The Empire.* "Brennan Keller," she read the name aloud. Then, there were a credit card and social security card in Brennan's name. "Odd!"

About halfway through the stack of cards was a New York driver's license. Taylor recognized Steve Mercer's picture on it. She gasped when she read the name. "Brennan Keller? Steve what were you involved in?" Taylor, being familiar with the Catskill Mountains, recognized the town of Jewett on the license.

She sat on the bed beside Jessie's belongings. *Jessie, what are you involved in?* Her attention returned to other items in the wallet.

It was close to one o'clock when Jessie and Rachel arrived at the cabin that morning. Throughout the trip, Rachel detoured from the highway and picked up secondary roads, assuring that they weren't being followed. Then, they passed the cabin twice before they finally stopped. Once inside the house, they crashed from exhaustion.

Just before nine o'clock the following morning Rachel found Jessie reading and sipping coffee in the kitchen.

"I see you found the sweat suit I laid out for you." Jessie wore similar attire. "Women's clothing is rare around here. It's the smallest one I had. Will it work?"

Rachel held out her arms, demonstrating the baggy workout suit. "It'll do."

"There's coffee in the decanter," she pointed to the counter.

Rachel poured a cup and moved to a window. The ground was freshly covered with a blanket of snow. She joined Jessie at the table. "I need to apologize. I don't know what's going on. But after last night, I realize there's a good chance that Steve would still be alive, if it weren't for me." Tears welled in Rachel's eyes as she relived the loss of West and Steve.

"You don't know that." Jessie reached for her hand and squeezed it.

Rachel saw the Bible opened in front of Jessie. "What are you reading?"

"Ezekiel. I didn't see it last night, but West had highlighted a section of the story of when Ezekiel meets God. Here, let me read it to you."

As Jessie read from the great book, Rachel meandered back to the window.

> And I looked, and, behold, a whirlwind came out of the north, a great cloud, and a fire unfolding itself, and a brightness was about it, and out of the midst thereof as the color of amber, out of the midst of the fire.

"I don't like this!" Rachel blurted out, staring out the window. The color from her face was gone.

"What's wrong?" Jessie moved toward her.

"Look!" She pointed to a set of tire tracks in the driveway. It looked as if a car had pulled into the driveway, then backed out. There was no sign of the car. "They weren't there a couple minutes ago."

"There are no footprints."

From behind them glass shattered from the deck's sliding-glass door. Two men stormed through the opening. Jessie snatched the keys from the table and was on Rachel's heels for the front door. Rachel halted abruptly, stopping Jessie in her tracks, as two other men pounded open the door. The women positioned themselves between the sets of men.

"Who are you?" Jessie asked.

They didn't answer. One of them approached Jessie. His fist was bandaged with blood-stained gauze. He pointed at the couch.

"What are you doing here?" Rachel demanded.

Another man moved toward Rachel. He shoved her toward the couch. Both men gestured for the women to sit, and they did. One man stood in front of them, while the other shifted to the rear of the couch. A third man repositioned himself by the deck doorway, while a fourth closed the front door and guarded it. Oddly, they all stood silently, and were dressed in black suits with black trench coats. They were clean-shaven, had short hair, all in their late twenties or early thirties.

"Is somebody going to tell us what the hell is going on?" Jessie asked.

They didn't respond. They stood watching them.

A frigid breeze gusted through the shattered glass opening.

"How did they find us?" Rachel whispered.

"There must be a tracking device on your car."

Why? Rachel wondered. Had her research uncovered something so outrageous to justify this assault? To justify West's murder?

The man who guarded the front door retrieved his phone. He punched in a speed dial number. "Situation contained," he said in a cold, detached voice.

Although the cabin's tiny furnace blasted, the room was freezing. To test the men's reaction, Jessie stood and walked toward a nearby chair. The closest guard grabbed her and forcefully shoved her back toward the couch. Remaining calm, she pointed to an afghan on the back of the chair. As she spoke the words, she could see her breath. "If you haven't noticed, it's a bit chilly in here."

The man hurled the blanket at her.

"Thank you!" Jessie sat beside Rachel and wrapped the blanket around them.

"What do you think is going on?" Rachel asked Jessie.

"I think we're waiting for their leader." Then loudly, "If any of you are handy with a hammer, there's plywood under the bed." She pointed at the guest bedroom. When the men didn't respond, "I'd be happy to do it myself."

A couple hours passed. Jessie and Rachel were still being held against their will. Although the room was drafty, as Jessie had suggested, their captors boarded up the glass door. The men never said a word.

The sound of an approaching car engine brought one of their captors to the window. The motor cut. Moments later the thud of footsteps came from the porch. Apparently, someone had entered, but from where they sat they couldn't see. To the women, it seemed as if they waited forever. Then the man moved into the living area.

"Whitman!" escaped Jessie's lips.

Rachel knew him mostly by reputation. "What is the meaning of this?"

One of the men assisted Whitman with his overcoat. He stepped in front of Rachel. "Ms. Addison, in time you will have your answers," his voice was raspy. Then he moved to Jessie, and stared at her intently.

Fearing that he might recognize Brennan, Jessie wouldn't look him in the eye.

He removed a cell phone and a wallet from his jacket pocket. "Well Ms. Jessica Mercer, where have we met before?"

While on the inside Jessie's heart pounded, on the outside she remained calm. Then suddenly, like a volcano erupting after centuries of slumber, hatred exploded within her. The malevolent feeling shocked her, then she remembered that *Whitman was Oba!*

He studied Jessie. Where had he met her? He was drawn to the scar on her cheek. Somehow, it seemed familiar. "What were you doing with my ex-wife last night?"

Jessie's eyes remained on the floor.

"We have ways to make you answer. I just don't know why you would want to make it so difficult on yourself."

Whitman turned and wandered around the room, inspecting the surroundings. When he meandered past the living room, Jessie and Rachel couldn't see him. So Jessie stood, but the injured-fist guy roughly shoved her down on the couch.

As Whitman explored the cabin, the women waited for what seemed to be hours. In reality though, only minutes passed. And when he returned, Jessie knew something was horribly wrong. His cold dark eyes would not leave Jessie's face. Then she saw the mail-order box in his hand and she understood.

He read the name on the package. "Brennan Keller . . . Hartsdale, New York."

"And your issue is?" Jessie was desperate. "Brennan's my cousin. He works for *The Empire.* Do you know him?"

Whitman smiled. "Stand up," he ordered. "Face me!"

When Jessie ignored the demand, a guard dragged her roughly to her feet.

"What's the meaning of this?" Rachel sprang up.

"Ms. Addison, if you don't sit calmly and quietly, I will have you removed." With that, another man thrust her downward on the couch.

Whitman returned to Jessie. Abruptly, he positioned the goatee to Jessie's face. He paled when his newest suspicion was confirmed. "My God," he uttered. He stepped backward, his eyes combing Jessie's body. "How did you do this? How the hell did you become a Mason?"

Jessie's heart pounded wildly. Her masquerade had been blown.

Whitman pulled a phone from his jacket. He pressed a speed dial number and waited for the connection. "We have a situation," he said. His eyes were so dark, Jessie couldn't tell where the pupil began and the iris ended. "Yes! This warrants your attention."

Just as Whitman disconnected, a guard by the front announced, "We have a visitor. White Buick Century. A woman is in the car. She's getting out and heading toward the house. . . . It's Taylor Andrews."

"Shit," Whitman said. "Another casualty."

Fearful for Taylor's safety, Jessie lunged toward Whitman. "No!" She yelled. A guard advanced upon her. But she dodged him, coming within inches of Whitman.

Jessie stopped as she heard the safeties on three pistols disengage, and they were all aimed at her. She knew she would be no help to Taylor if she were shot. She needed to appeal to the man's logic. A guard pinned her arms.

"Whitman, I can get rid of her," she said desperately. "I can make her go away. You don't want her involved in this. The press will be all over it if you hurt her."

Whitman was quiet. He seemed to be considering, and after an eternal pause, he nodded at the guard pinning Jessie's arms. He released her. To that guard, "Downstairs bedroom with Addison," Whitman ordered. To the other men, "Spread out, and keep out of sight!"

He pulled Jessie toward the front door. "Let me set the stage. I'll be with Ms. Addison," he pointed at the bedroom. "The door will be open. I will hear *every* word. If I don't—Ms. Andrews will be shot. If you speak cryptically, she will die. You have five minutes to get rid of her, or she's leaving in a body bag. Do we understand each other?"

Jessie heard footsteps on the porch. She nodded. She understood too well. How could she have gotten into such a precarious situation? Whitman disappeared into the bedroom, leaving the door ajar.

Jessie opened the front door preempting Taylor from seeing the damage to it. Without saying a word, Taylor brushed past her and went into the kitchen.

"What's going on, Jess?" Taylor eyed the surroundings.

Still holding the door open, Jessie said sternly, "You need to leave! Go back to the city. I'll meet you there tonight. We'll talk about this, then."

Taylor eyed Jessie. "I'm not leaving until I get an explanation." She sat at the kitchen table. "Are you going to shut the door? It's drafty in here. Are you in trouble?"

Jessie remained at the door. "You need to leave now!" Her voice was harsh.

Taylor stood. "And I told you—I'm not leaving without an explanation! What is it?"

Jessie noticed the bedroom door gap widen. Her heart pounded. It wasn't working. She had hoped that her uncharacteristic aggression would have sent Taylor off. A shadow from inside the bedroom loomed. She needed to change her strategy.

"What, are you blind?" Jessie shouted. "I wanted to tell you this later. Damn it Taylor . . ." the words were so painful for her to say, tears filled her eyes. "I'm not in love with you anymore. I'm in love with someone else." The pain in Taylor's eyes was almost overwhelming to Jessie.

"I don't believe you," Taylor whispered.

"You're so blind," Jessie continued. "Why do you think I've been in New York the last eight months? I'm in love with someone else. Please just leave."

Taylor looked around. Unexpectedly, she moved toward the bedroom door.

"Taylor, no!" Jessie's heart pounded so hard, it hurt.

Taylor was within inches of the door. She turned toward Jessie. "She's here?" Tears welled in her eyes.

Jessie couldn't look at her, fearing her eyes would betray her. There, Taylor waited what felt like an eternity, standing inches from Whitman. Jessie thought she was going to be sick.

Finally, Taylor stepped to the doorway, only inches away from Jessie. She looked outside. Now she knew why there were two cars. She turned to Jessie, but didn't say a thing. Her pain-filled eyes burrowed deep into Jessie's soul. Behind tears of heartache was distrust.

Jessie knew those eyes would haunt her until her dying day. Taylor left, and Jessie closed the door. At a window, Jessie watched her walk away. Tears welled up. She loved her so much. *Forgive me.* Jessie's feelings and thoughts must have betrayed her, because Taylor stopped in her tracks and turned back.

Jessie's heart beat harder. *No, Taylor, go. You must leave.*

Footsteps behind her indicated that Whitman had returned. She didn't care. The only thing that mattered was Taylor. From the corner of her eye, Jessie saw the long needle plunge into her neck. She pulled it out, but it was too late. The chemical stung as it entered her bloodstream. Darkness overwhelmed her and she fell unconscious to the floor.

Outside the cabin, Taylor stood puzzled. The blowing January air was bitter. Her feelings were confusing. For a brief moment, she thought she had felt Jessie's love. Then she turned back toward the cabin, but now she felt only emptiness. The warmth in her heart she typically felt when she thought of Jessie was gone. Their heart connection had been severed.

Taylor got into the car, her face wet with tears. She started the engine and peeled out of the driveway, her tires scattering snow and dirt. How could she have been so blind?

Thirty-Two

Jessie danced with unconsciousness. She never heard Rachel talk to her as they rode to the airport. She never felt Rachel hold her hand during the flight. Most of the time, her senses were numb. But during brief moments of waking, she thought her head had split open. Light hurt her eyes, so she kept them closed, and within seconds of consciousness, she always passed out.

While Jessie was oblivious to what was happening, Rachel was cognizant. The aerial view of Washington, DC, from the private jet window triggered the ill feeling in her stomach.

A stretch limo met the plane at the private airport. One of the guards heaved Jessie's unresponsive body into the backseat. Rachel moved in beside her. With care, she lifted her friend upright and fastened a seatbelt around her, stopping her from tumbling over.

Rachel had given up asking questions. The more she had asked the more Whitman shut down. As on the flight, Whitman and his thugs drove along in silence. It didn't take long before they were in downtown Washington, DC. They turned on Sixteenth Street. Then, she recognized the House of the Temple standing high above the curb. She expected the car to turn, but it passed the temple.

A couple blocks later, the car turned, then again. It pulled up to a wrought iron gate where a man guarded a tiny security house. He apparently was cut from the same mold as Whitman's other bodyguards, as he wore a black suit, white shirt, unexciting tie, and dark sunglasses.

While the driver waited for the security guard to approach the limo, Rachel studied the property. Like a fortress, a tall stone wall seemingly bordered the land, and mature greenery obstructed the view beyond the security gate. She wondered whose house or building was being hidden.

After a verbal exchange between the driver and the security guard, the gate opened, permitting the limo to enter. They drove into a park-

Published by The Haworth Press, Inc., 2006. All rights reserved.
doi:10.1300/5721_33

like setting where lush pines, conifers, and spruces towered above them. Interestingly enough, the property lacked deciduous trees or bushes. Only evergreens, plants that retained their greenery year-round land-scaped the property.

The car maneuvered the winding gardens, turn after turn, until it entered a cluster of huge Ponderosa Pine. The trees obscured the sun from the limo, leaving them in shadows. The car parked. The men didn't move or say a thing.

Rachel peered out the window. The vegetation was so dense that she couldn't see the stone wall bordering the property. Intermittent tiny patches of blue sky were barely visible through the trees' limbs. A window between the driver and herself silenced his phone call. Rachel became anxious. Why had they brought her here? What were they going to do to her? She rubbed her sweaty palms on her pants.

Without warning, the limo jerked, and unconsciously Rachel grabbed Jessie's hand. Was it an earthquake? Then, the car steadily lowered into the ground, swallowed by the earth. They must have descended thirty-five feet before they came to a standstill. Through the limo's skylight, Rachel saw the rectangular hole from where they sank. This opening provided their only light source.

The car pulled forward, perhaps twenty feet, then parked again. A hum from behind them drew Rachel's attention to the rear window, where she glimpsed four columns. It was a hydraulic car lift. A platform lifted skyward until it had closed up the rectangular hole, leaving them in total darkness. A wave of anxiety swept upon her. *Now what?* Her heart beat so hard that her throat ached.

Unexpectedly, brilliant halogen lights flooded the area. The limo was parked in a large circular space. Rachel couldn't see past the lights. Then flashing red lights, similar to those on airport runways, flickered around them. The halogen lights dimmed, revealing five tunnels sur-rounding them. Red lights glowed from the ceiling of each tunnel.

Still, the limo remained stationary, engine idling. The lights on one of the tunnels started flashing red and green. Then the red lights dimmed leaving two rows of green lights on the walls of one tunnel. The limo entered the green-lit tunnel.

Rachel wasn't sure if she was more frightened or bewildered. She studied the tunnel as the car sped through the underground road beneath Washington, DC. The passageway was the width of two lanes. Narrow curbs hugged the concrete walls. They were only a couple minutes into the ride when they reached a turnaround. The limo pulled over and the men got out.

Whitman turned to Rachel before he stepped from the car. "Follow me, Ms. Addison. Try not to do anything stupid. We've come this far."

One of the bodyguards removed Jessie's limp body and followed Whitman. Rachel trailed them with another guard on her tail. Commotion from above drew her attention to the concrete ceiling supported by steel I-beams. The disturbance was seemingly approaching, as the rattling intensified, and the ground on which Rachel stood vibrated. The noise and shaking peaked, then, gradually disappeared.

"What was that?" Rachel asked not really expecting a response from anyone.

"Commuter train," Whitman answered.

How could they do this? Rachel wondered. How could they build streets under the city? Then she wondered why it had seemed so far-fetched, after all, we had been building tunnels for close to 200 years. Rachel realized that she was much more fascinated now with what was happening than she was scared.

Whitman approached an iron door. He keyed in a password on the security pad, and pressed his eye against an optical scan. Within seconds, the door unlocked, leading them to a stairwell. At the top of the stairs, there was a similar security scan.

They entered a long hallway, at the end of which was a third security scan. From here, the group stepped into a large atrium set up like a courtyard of an ancient temple. The floor was paved with polished marble. Eight huge pillars of polished green granite bordered two sides of the room. An imposing stairway with Egyptian statues at the foot of the stairs faced them. A large marble table centered the hall and the walls were white limestone reaching to expansive ceiling beams.

Rachel recognized the room from pictures. "We're at the House of the Temple?"

Whitman ignored her and led them to a door that was positioned behind two columns, then down another hallway, to another door. He opened it and the man carrying Jessie entered. Whitman nodded at Rachel to follow, and she did. Oddly, the room resembled a hotel suite. The guard laid Jessie on a couch and left. Whitman followed.

"You're just going to leave us? Is somebody going to tell me what the hell is going on?" Rachel was clearly frustrated.

Whitman stared at her for the longest time, then a sinister smile came to his lips. "Yes." But he stepped into the hallway.

"Is Jessie going to be okay?"

"For now. She's been sedated. She'll be awake in a few hours." Whitman's dark eyes remained on Rachel as he closed the door.

Rachel rushed for the doorknob. "Damn," it was locked. She turned, and explored the suite. There were no other exits. No windows. In the front room, where Jessie lay unconscious, there was a couch, a small refrigerator, and a desk. The back room had a bed and dresser.

A couple hours had passed, when Rachel heard a soft moan. She almost missed it. A glance at Jessie verified that the sedative was wearing off.

Jessie's head felt like it had exploded. She put her hand to her head to confirm that it was still attached. Her eyes opened to blurry surroundings. She didn't recognize the shadow kneeling beside her. It was the voice that clued her in.

"Jessie? Are you okay?"

"Rachel?" The images were still fuzzy.

"Yes, it's me!"

"My head is splitting." Jessie tried to sit up, but everything darkened, and she laid her head back down. "What happened?"

"They gave you a sedative."

"They?" Jessie could see Rachel now.

"Remember the cabin . . . with Whitman?"

Bit by bit, Jessie's memory returned. First she recalled the men with black suits raiding the cabin. Then Whitman. Fear crept into her eyes. "Whitman discovered that I'm Brennan."

Rachel nodded. "Is that all you remember?"

Just as Rachel asked, it hit her. "Oh, my God!" it was barely a whisper. Jessie looked Rachel in the eye. Unsteadily she sat up. "Is Taylor safe?"

"Yes. She left the cabin."

Jessie's hands screened her face as the painful memory returned. "I told her I wasn't in love with her anymore. I told her I was seeing someone else." She sobbed. She removed her hands. Her eyes were red, tears welling. "I hurt her so much."

"You did what you needed to keep her safe."

"How will she ever forgive me?"

"After we're out of this mess, we'll straighten it all out. I promise."

Jessie felt only emptiness. She couldn't feel Taylor, only resistance. Their heart connection had been severed. Her vision had almost returned, and she didn't recognize the surroundings. "Where are we?"

"In DC, at the House of the Temple. It's bizarre, Jess." Rachel described what she had seen: flying into DC, the limo, the ride through the tunnels, and the atrium.

"Why are we here?" Jessie was puzzled.

Unexpectedly, the door opened, and Whitman entered. "I see that you're awake, Ms. Mercer." One of Whitman's thugs came in behind him and stood beside Jessie. "He will show you to your accommodations," Whitman said.

The guard grabbed Jessie's upper arm and dragged her to the door.

"I would prefer that she stay here," Rachel said as Jessie was manhandled through the doorway. Rachel, now alone with Whitman, said "What the hell is going on?"

"Ms. Addison, let's take a tour."

Whitman and Rachel were back in the tunnel. She spotted taillights from a car driving away from them and wondered if Jessie was in the vehicle. Rachel sat in the backseat of another limo with Whitman beside her. The car sped through the tunnel back to the circular pad where they had entered. The five passageways, now lit with a single row of red lights, were visible. The car parked.

"This is a good a time to start," Whitman began. "Rachel, you have an innate curiosity about power. Over the years, you've worked on a number of projects on this subject. Some you've finished, others not; some have even been sabotaged."

"By you?"

"Let me address some of your suspicions. There *is* a one-world government, and you are sitting at the heart of it. Within these tunnels are connections to the most powerful people and organizations in the world. This is where it all comes together, the Trilateral Commission, the Council on Foreign Relations, the Bilderbergers, the Vatican, the Federal Reserve—"

"And the Freemasons?"

"And the Supreme Council of the thirty-third degree, along with so many other groups, I cannot begin to mention." Flickering from one of the tunnels drew Rachel's attention to red and green flashing lights. As before, red lights dimmed leaving a green-lit tunnel. The limo entered it.

"Why am I here? What do you want from me?"

"You will learn that soon," Whitman said as the car came to another dead end.

To Rachel, there was little distinction between the area they had just left and this one. Whitman led her from the limo to another door. Beside the door was polished marble with hieroglyphics etched in the slab. One of the images caught her eye. It was an Egyptian woman who stood beside a snake. The snake was raised with four loops in its tail. At its mouth was an ankh. Rachel knew she had seen the image before, she glanced at her wrist, and remembered that it was during West's lecture.

After a security scan they entered a huge, bright, sterile room. The walls, ceiling, and floor were white. The only furniture in the lobbylike area was a desk, where a man stood out in his customary black suit. Since they were below ground, there were no outside windows. Instead, on the side walls there were multiple doors, some of which were open. A clipboard hung beside each door.

As Rachel passed one of the open doors, she glimpsed inside. A medical examination table centered the room with an assortment of ultramodern equipment. When she passed the next door, she spotted a woman in a chair. Rachel slowed for a closer inspection. It was Jessie!

She was strapped to the chair and electrodes crowned her head. "Jessie?" Rachel blurted out as she rushed toward the door.

Whitman seized Rachel's upper arm roughly and tried to drag her away from the doorway. She surprised not only him, but surprised herself when she kicked him in the shin. He released his grip, and she sprang toward the door, but the man who had been at the desk stood in her path. She eyed the man. Attacking Whitman was one thing; this was a young, large man, with a gun in a holster.

Whitman hobbled toward her. He was plain mad. "You *cannot* disturb the specimens in these chambers." Roughly, he grabbed her arm and dragged her a few doors down. "Let's wait in here," he opened the door. The room was different from the other rooms she had seen. The walls were decorated with colorful murals illustrating ancient Egyptian customs. Under different circumstances, Rachel may have been quite fascinated by their beauty.

Whitman pointed at a couch and two soft chairs. "Sit," he ordered.

Adhesive from electrodes pulled at Jessie's hair near her forehead. Her wrists were strapped to the arms of the chair, and her ankles fastened to its front legs. Restrained, she faced a white empty wall. Although it was a tiny room, the ceiling must have been twenty-feet tall.

From behind, Jessie heard Rachel call to her. She strained to see her but couldn't. She never saw the man stop her or Whitman lead her away. Then, minutes passed with silence, until the door was pulled shut. Then the lights abruptly went out, leaving her in complete darkness. Her pulse quickened.

Unexpectedly, an image appeared in front of her. It must have been fifteen-feet high and ten-feet wide. Jessie leaned backward to take it all in. It appeared to be a bird, similar to an eagle, except it had a longer neck, and was very colorful. For a second, she could have sworn that it moved. She closed her eyes, then opened them. It indeed moved. It was three-dimensional and seemed so real. She wondered if she reached out and touched it, if she could feel its feathers. Then she could have sworn that she felt the force of the bird's wings as they fluttered. It must have been her imagination. The bird rested upon twigs, singing a melodious five-note song.

She heard a crackling sound. *What was that?* From beneath the bird the twigs flared to life, rapidly engulfing it. Jessie felt intense heat from the flame. Her skin felt scorched. The bird shrieked, suffering, its burning flesh reeking. Live cinders jumped out at Jessie, burning her skin and clothing.

Desperately, but to no avail, she yanked at the straps to free herself. Her heart now pounded fiercely as her sweatpants ignited. Just when she believed that she would light up like a torch, the flames weakened. The fire had consumed the bird, and now, without fuel to feed it, its blaze dwindled to a glow at her feet. The fire burned out and all that remained was a pile of gray ashes and red embers.

Just when her heart rate recovered, something caught her eye in the pile. A tiny gray worm emerged from the cinders, and right before her eyes the worm slowly transformed into the same bird that had appeared before her eyes, singing its song.

As Jessie watched the large bird ascend over her again, she realized that she had experienced the reenactment of the legend of the phoenix. The phoenix was first introduced by the Brotherhood of the Snake. According to legend, the great sun god Ra enjoyed the sweet music of the phoenix every morning. The bird would incinerate itself every 500 to 600 years, and its reincarnated self would gather the ashes and deliver them to Ra's altar.

Jessie wasn't sure how, but she knew that the legend of the phoenix represented resurrection, spiritual survival, and how we reach eternal life. Baffled by how she concluded this, she suddenly realized the true meaning of the ankh. It didn't just represent life or reincarnation, as she previously believed. The ankh signified eternal life, the greatest of the ancient mysteries. The insight of a high priest was coming back to her.

"Jessica Mercer!" An ominous voice took her from stupor.

The image of the bird vanished, and darkness changed to brilliant light, hurting her eyes. Squinting, she looked at her hands and legs. There was no indication that her pants had ever caught fire. Jessie was confused. She had felt the pain from the fire. *How could that be?*

"Resides outside of LA, author of numerous novels and screenplays!"

Jessie listened to the man's deep voice. There was something hazily familiar about it, but she couldn't place it. "Brother of Steve Mercer, former employee of *Over the Edge* who suddenly took his own life last—"

"You and I both know that is not true! Why did you kill him?"

From behind, the man whispered in her ear. "I appear to have hit a nerve. I'm asking the questions. How did you infiltrate the Masons?" The man strutted in front of Jessie, his back to her. "How did you do it, Ms. Mercer?"

From behind, Jessie didn't recognize him. He was slim, tall, had short, dark hair, and was dressed in khakis and a sweater. She didn't speak.

Her silence infuriated him. Abruptly, he turned and roared, "How?"

It took Jessie a moment to place where she had seen those eyes. *Eyes of the Nile!* Last time his head was shaven. She closed her eyes and shook her head, knowing she must have been hallucinating. But when he remained, his name escaped from her lips, "Kek!"

Jessie's recognition took him equally by surprise. And he was rarely surprised. The man circled her, assessing her. "Who are you?"

Jessie remained quiet, staring at the ground. Her head throbbed. She was totally confused. Kek would have lived over 3,000 years earlier.

"Who the hell are you?" his deep voice echoed. "Tell me! Now!"

Fearing that Kek may recognize her through the windows of her soul, Jessie shut her eyes. But with darkness, her reality slipped, as images of freshly carved hieroglyphics flashed in her third eye.

The man whispered into her ear. "You don't want to know what I do to people who have disappointed me."

The word "disappointed" echoed in her mind; she was unable to sustain this reality as the word "disappointed" jerked her consciousness back to Egypt.

Thirty-Three

Lukeman admired the image of creation carved on the wall of the temple's inner court. He reflected on the symbolism of the scarab, Isis, Nephthys, the boat, the solar disk, and the raised serpent. As he contemplated their meaning, a feeling of darkness and despair overtook him. Something was dreadfully wrong.

In his peripheral vision, he saw something stir. About ten feet away, behind a column, a figure lurked in the shadows. He wore a black-hooded robe. Lukeman stepped toward him. "Who is there?"

Kek emerged. "I warned you—never betray me and never *disappoint* me."

There was a chilling tone in Kek's voice that Lukeman had never heard before. "And I have disappointed you?"

"Do you deny teaching the profane?"

Lukeman shook his head. "No, I have taught the uninitiated."

"This is contemptible. You know what the punishment is for your disgrace."

"I do." He not only knew it, he had seen clairvoyant images of his demise.

"Why did you do this? I've given you everything."

"You are a great teacher, Worshipful Master. But it is wrong to deny the mysteries to all. As Hem Neter, I am responsible for the spiritual salvation of *all* Memphis, not just the elite."

"I have given the chosen ones an opportunity to find salvation. If it were up to the other gods no one would find eternal life."

"You know the others are wrong. What gives anyone the right to determine who is worthy of salvation? What has been done for centuries is wrong. You started with good intentions, but the mystery school has become a tool of spiritual repression. All people should have the opportunity to seek eternal life."

Published by The Haworth Press, Inc., 2006. All rights reserved.
doi:10.1300/5721_34

To Lukeman it was clear. He knew his soul's purpose was to make known the truth. Lukeman pointed to the beautiful mural. "All people should be given the opportunity to understand our creation, to know who we truly are."

"I wash my hands of you, Lukeman. Your disgrace will live forever, and you will pay for your failure with your life." Kek stomped into the darkness.

Lukeman remained at the temple to prepare for his death. He meditated in the Holy Place, elevating his consciousness before he moved into the Holy of Holies, the innermost room of the temple. He knew that his presence here would be defiant, as access was restricted to once a year. Only on Yom Kippur was the Hem Neter permitted in the Holy of Holies, where the Ark of the Covenant had been stored. Then, he would take blood of a goat and perform a ritual on behalf of the sins of his people.

Tonight, in the Holy of Holies, Lukeman sat in front of the Ark. His legs were crossed and folded neatly together, spine straight, and arms elevated with palms up. His Kundalini energy rose from the reservoir at the base of his spine and exited through his crown chakra on top of his head. The energy fused with the divine, turning from red-orange to silver, and showered over him. In these moments, Lukeman met God, he encountered the self-divine, he knew oneness, and understood *true light.*

The sound of footsteps hurled him from his trance, back to his situation. He maintained his position with his eyes closed, feeling his spirit return to his body. Anticipating his punishment, he opened his eyes. His father stood on holy ground.

"I am surprised *you* have been sent." Lukeman remained seated.

"I have not been sent. I heard of your failure and I wanted to give you an opportunity to seek closure."

Lukeman knew if he could face death and love his father there would be finality. Without resolution, he wouldn't evolve to the next level, and their breach would follow him into other lifetimes. Of course, other opportunities for closure would be provided in future lifetimes, but the choices would be more difficult.

Just coming from an elevated place of consciousness, Lukeman was stunned at how quickly hatred filled his heart. He knew there would be no closure this lifetime. "Still now, Father, I cannot forgive you for what you did to Mother."

"This unresolved hatred will follow you into the afterlife," Oba said.

"Yes. I know."

Oba started to leave.

"Would you tell me one thing before you go?" His father turned toward him. "What is your interest in the servant girl named Jamila?"

Oba considered the question thoroughly. "Years ago when your mother was imprisoned, she was with child."

"Yes. You told me that the baby was stillborn." As Lukeman said it, even he noted the ring of untruth. Slowly, Lukeman stood, facing his father's cold dark eyes. "That is not the truth. Jamila was the baby?"

"The newborn was given to a trusted servant, who placed her with Asim and Femi." Oba turned, leaving Lukeman alone in the tabernacle.

With sudden purpose, Lukeman set out before it was too late.

She was usually there by now, and Kek paced his bedroom chamber, waiting for her. He wondered what delayed her. He was angered by Lukeman's betrayal. He had called a meeting with Zuka, and he wouldn't have much time with her. Over the year, he had become dependent on her. Only she had been able to satisfy his needs.

She slipped into his chamber from a terrace. But she knew something was wrong. He was preoccupied. He didn't notice her standing there. "Kek?"

He rushed to her, his mouth hungrily finding hers. "We don't have much time!" He lowered the straps from her shoulders, finding the valley between her breasts with his mouth.

She desired him, as much as he needed her.

With one hand he urgently swept up her long dress and caressed her. His eyes returned to hers. "Zuka will be here any minute."

Fervently, she lifted Kek's Kalasiris, exposing him. Her arms wrapped around his neck, he hoisted her off the ground, sliding her smoothly to his hardness. A moan of pleasure escaped her lips, increasing his excitement. With her legs wrapped around his lean waist, he propped her against the clay wall. Their carnal rhythm, although familiar, was still exciting and passionate. Moans of desire escalated to cries of pleasure as they brought each other to climax.

Spent, knees weak, he backed away, repositioning his Kalasiris.

She tidied her clothing. Still sensing something was wrong, she approached, her hands stroking his developed chest. "Why did you call a meeting with Zuka?"

Kek's eyes met Dalila's. "Zuka brought to my attention that I've been betrayed. I need to take care of it." He kissed her lips. "Go. Plan on coming tomorrow, we will have more time then. I'm sure Zuka has arrived."

Dalila departed through the access she had used over the past year. But something wasn't right. She could feel it. She stopped in her tracks, and then turned back. As she wandered through his bedroom, she caught the scent of their lovemaking only minutes earlier, and shuddered. She had never been satisfied with Zuka, and just the thought of Kek's hands on her skin excited her. She shook her head, and focused on finding him.

The next room was empty, but voices drew her to the curtain that separated the chambers. She peeked through a gap and eavesdropped.

"*You* will take care of his demise," Kek ordered.

"You want me to kill my own brother?" Zuka panicked.

"It was you who turned him in. You knew what his fate would be," Kek said.

Dalila gasped. She covered her mouth so the sound wouldn't carry beyond her own ears. Without delay, she fled. She had to warn Lukeman.

Thirty-Four

It was just after sunset, and the moon had not risen yet. Lukeman sensed the eerie feeling the night had brought. He knew his fate. He couldn't change it. But he was compelled to do one more thing before his death. In the darkness, he hurried along the narrow alleyway. When he reached the door, he knocked loudly.

Femi opened it, and Lukeman brushed by her, moving into the reception room where Asim sat. "Lukeman? What is wrong?" Femi asked from behind him.

When Asim saw his face he knew something was terribly wrong, and stood.

"Is Jamila here?" Lukeman asked.

"No! She is walking with Mosi," Asim said.

"I've come across information," Lukeman said. "Jamila. She is not your natural born."

"How do you know that?" Asim was surprised.

"My father told me. My mother was with child when she was imprisoned. All these years I thought the baby died in childbirth. I learned tonight that it was Jamila."

"Jamila is your sister!" Asim was shocked. "We didn't know."

"She believes we are her parents," Femi said.

"And you are. Just for a moment, though, think of Ja. He's alone. He lost his only love! But something good came from their love—Jamila. Perhaps he has a right to know." Lukeman had said what he needed to.

Asim took Femi's hand. "We need to talk about this."

"I understand." Lukeman hugged Asim, "You have always been my family." He embraced Femi. "I love you both. I am late for a service. I must leave." Tears shed from his eyes as he rushed out of their home.

Published by The Haworth Press, Inc., 2006. All rights reserved.
doi:10.1300/5721_35

If Asim hadn't had Jamila on his mind, he may have been alerted by the odd departure.

Dalila paced her bedroom, waiting for Zuka to return from his meeting with Kek. Her emotions were torn. Her husband had been ordered by her lover to murder her brother. She had to stop Zuka, no matter what the cost. She opened the chest and retrieved a dagger. Her heart beat wildly as she considered the possibilities, then she concealed the knife in her robe.

Mumbling from the nearby chamber brought her to the curtain that separated the rooms. She peeked. Zuka paced, cusing under his breath. He chewed the fruit in his mouth, then drank his beer quickly.

Dalila stepped into the room. "We need to talk!"

He rested his cup on a table, then waved a hand at her, showing his lack of interest in speaking to her. "This is not a good time." He was pale.

"I know that Kek ordered you to kill Lukeman," she blurted out.

"And how exactly would you know that? I just left him," he yelled.

"That doesn't matter. You can't kill him, Zuka."

"I have no choice." Zuka paced the room, resting a hand on his hip. "If I don't, my bowels will be fed to the lions for breakfast. Wait! The only way you could have known that—is if you were there. It is Kek that you are sleeping with?"

"Who I'm sleeping with is irrelevant to this conversation. I never ask who you sleep with. This is about Lukeman, and you are not going to harm him."

Zuka laughed. "And who is going to stop me?"

Dalila removed the dagger from her robe. "Don't make me use this, Zuka. He's our brother. . . . You cannot kill him."

Zuka didn't believe his eyes. He approached her. "And I'm your brother *and* husband, you're not going to kill me." Swiftly, he smacked the back of his hand across her face, the blade falling from her grip. She fell against the table, and downward to the floor. Dalila eyed the dagger, only inches from her grasp. She reached for it! His foot stomped her hand. Dalila groaned. Her hand was visibly broken.

Zuka kicked the knife and propelled it across the floor, out of her reach.

Dalila, kneeling and cradling her injured hand, rose to her feet. She eyed her husband. His smug smile enraged her. She charged at him raising her good hand, but he grabbed her wrist.

From within his robe, he extracted something, and pressed lightly against her chest. It pricked her. She couldn't believe her eyes. A dagger had pierced her skin.

A sinister smile came to Zuka's lips. He twisted her arm behind her, and embraced her pushing the blade slightly further. "You cannot beat me," he whispered in her ear. Abruptly, he thrust the dagger deep into her chest.

As Lukeman departed from Asim's home, he was surprised that he didn't have a sense of completion. Something just wasn't right. Dalila came to mind, and he wanted to wish her well, so he set out for the palace. But when a servant searched for her to announce his arrival, a shrill scream confirmed that something was amiss.

Lukeman raced to the chamber where he found her body in a pool of blood. He knelt beside her. A dagger was imbedded in her chest. He yanked the blade from her heart and angrily hurled it against the wall. "Who did this?" he cried, tears streaming down his face. He cradled her like a child, warm blood trickling onto his chest. Placing his cheek along hers, he whispered, "Who did this?" Lukeman didn't need to hear an answer, he knew it was Zuka. "I will take you to the temple, my Dalila."

Barely cognizant of his surroundings, he trudged through the palace cradling his sister's body, his face wet with tears. Lost in his thoughts, he missed those individuals that recoiled at the sight of them. Out into the courtyard, he headed for the south exit. The moon had risen now, and Thoth illuminated his passage.

Still carrying Dalila, he circled the temple's courtyard, praying to purge his soul of selfish thoughts and urges. Beside the hypostyle, he plodded, chanting aloud to prepare her for transformation. "In the morning rays of Ra—you are a child, in Thoth's evening moon-beams—an old man, at the beginning of the year—a newborn."

Lukeman was so distraught that he never heard the footsteps following him from the palace. Nor was he conscious of the movement behind the hypostyle's columns. He certainly missed the eerie shadows cast by the tall pillars. It was the reflection of a metal sword in the moonlight, however, that caught his eye. He turned toward the advancing man. Zuka waved a sword over his head, the blade whizzing through the air.

"Put her down, Lukeman, and prepare to die," Zuka ordered.

"I need to take her to the funerary temple." Lukeman continued his march.

Zuka stood before him, blocking his path. He pressed the tip of the blade against Lukeman's chest, forcing him to stop.

The blood on Zuka's hand and robe confirmed Lukeman's suspicions. "Why did you do this, Zuka?" His eyes on his sister's face, "She was innocent in this."

"She tried to kill me," he whined.

"Help me prepare her for the afterlife, and then you may fulfill your destiny." Lukeman recoiled from the sword and headed toward the hypostyle entrance.

Zuka followed him. "My destiny is to kill you, here, and now." In a flash, Zuka impaled Lukeman from behind.

The sword plunged through Lukeman's back, exiting his abdomen. The blade also penetrated Dalila's body. Eyes wide, he gasped from the sudden pain. Then the blade was jerked haphazardly from their bodies, intensifying his agony. Warm blood streamed from his back and abdomen. He stumbled to his knees, and couldn't hold her any longer. He set her down on the hard surface and rested next to her, laying his head on her shoulder.

He reached for Dalila's hand and whispered to her, "I will see you soon." His heart was heavy. He had failed. He couldn't prepare her for the afterlife. He couldn't absolve his father. He had failed at offering humankind the opportunity to seek eternal life, to know true light, and to understand the royal secret.

A shadowy figure emerged from the hypostyle. It was Kek. He faltered when he saw Dalila's body, and then fell to his knees beside her. "What's happened?" he roared.

"*Oh Great Architect of the Universe,*" Zuka said, pointing at Lukeman, "he killed her."

Kek knew that Lukeman would never kill Dalila, besides Zuka's shimmering aura announced that he had lied. Kek's lips met Dalila's. "I will prepare you for the afterlife, my love," he whispered. "And I will *never* allow anyone to harm you again. *Never!*"

Lukeman heard Kek's eternal pledge to protect Dalila.

Kek got to his feet, his rage swelling inside of him. "Zuka, prepare to die."

Nervously, Zuka raised the weapon to protect himself. "But I didn't do it," he backed away, whimpering.

Crazed, Kek advanced on Zuka. Just within arm's length of each other, Zuka's blade crashed down toward Kek's head. He leaped from the blade's path. It collided with the ground, and Kek lunged for Zuka's wrist, disarming him. The sword clattered on the stone floor.

Desperate and scared, Zuka was in tears. He yanked a dagger from his robe, the same knife that Dalila had pulled on him. He considered slicing his own throat. But Kek approached, and Zuka lunged at him, scratching Kek's chest.

Kek grabbed Zuka's hand. Being stronger than Zuka, he smoothly swiveled the weapon toward Zuka. He savored that moment, then thrust the blade into Zuka's chest.

The shriek could have wakened Ra from his slumber. "Zuka!" Oba cried.

As Zuka had lunged at Kek, Oba emerged from the temple. Now, he watched his son stumble and fall lifelessly to the ground. Oba rushed to his youngest born. As he knelt beside him, he saw the two other bodies nearby. He stood. Could one of the bodies be Lukeman? How could he lose two sons in one day? Steadily, he approached them, and when he saw it was Lukeman *and* Dalila, he stopped in his tracks. Slowly, he staggered from the bodies of his three children, lost, and he wailed.

Kek approached Oba. He gazed into Oba's pain-filled eyes. No person should bear that agony. He laid a hand on Oba's head, closed his eyes, and chanted. Moments later, Kek withdrew his hand. "No man should ever feel your pain," Kek said. With that, Oba's pain was relieved, because Kek had eternally hardened his heart.

Lukeman felt his life force slip from his body. The images of Kek and his father disappeared, and darkness engulfed him. Then suddenly a brilliant light surrounded him and his faith in the afterlife was confirmed.

Disoriented and confused Jessie was back, strapped in the chair. Her head pounded. She heard the door slam behind her, conveying that Kek had just left the chamber.

Thirty-Five

Rachel paced the mural room for close to a half hour. All along, Whitman remained silent and studied her from the couch. Finally, she sat down facing him, her back to the door. "My patience is wearing," she said. "You promised me answers. When will I get them?"

Unknown to Rachel, Kek had entered the doorway. Kek gestured for silence with a finger to his lips. He cocked his head, suggesting that Whitman leave.

"You will get your answers soon," Whitman said. He stood. "I will be back." Whitman passed Kek and shut the door on his way out.

Rachel was frustrated. She needed answers. She sighed, and then ran her fingers through her long hair.

"Hello, Rachel," Kek said from behind her.

Rachel's heart thumped. She had thought that she was alone. She refrained from showing her unease. Instead, she acted unruffled. "Are you here to give me answers?"

"I am indeed."

"It's about time." Rachel stood and looked at her adversary. Her knees weakened when she caught sight of him. Her heart raced and dizziness overwhelmed her. She closed her eyes and shook her head to dispel the hallucination, but a second look confirmed who was staring at her.

"Daddy? Is that you?" Her voice was meek, no longer unruffled.

"It is, Rachel." He smiled and took a step toward her; his arms opened to embrace her.

Rachel retreated. "You're not my father! He died over twenty-five years ago!"

"I didn't die, sweetheart. My death was staged."

"My father would be in his sixties. You look like . . . you haven't aged a day."

Published by The Haworth Press, Inc., 2006. All rights reserved.
doi:10.1300/5721_36

"We have much to discuss, Rachel."

Rachel was shocked. She continued to distance herself from him, until she was backed against the wall.

He stopped. "I'm not going to hurt you, Rachel. I brought you here to tell you about your heritage. You have the birthright to sit with me and rule the world."

"What?" Her head throbbed. Tears sprang from her eyes. "Did you kill West?"

"West became a threat; he was a very smart man. Too smart for his own good."

"Steve? You killed Steve too?"

"Mercer somehow recognized me as Charles Addison. He knew that I supposedly was killed years earlier."

"He saw your picture in my office," Rachel mumbled. She recalled the last phone call she had with Steve: *"It's the ultimate conspiracy. . . . Don't trust anyone."*

"Apparently Mercer spent his initiation snooping around. We were never clear on what he had surmised."

Rachel was afraid to ask. "Are you Kek?"

Now how would she know me by that name? "I have been called many names. Kek is one of them."

She didn't believe it. She crept along the wall, inching further and further away from her father. "You *are* Kek? The prince of darkness?" It was only a whisper.

Kek nodded. "I have been called that."

"The devil? Satan?"

"Yes. I have been called many names over the centuries. Lucifer, Abaddon . . . even Charles." He stepped toward her.

The room spun. "Stay away from me. I'm the daughter of Satan? You killed them. You killed West and Steve, and you killed Mom."

"You know that's not true. She's alive."

"Some life! She's living in a nuthouse all because she claims to still see you." Rachel stared intently into her father's eyes. "You bastard! You visit her, don't you?" Tears welled in her eyes.

Kek pressed a button on his watch and spoke into it. "I need a sedative."

Rachel laughed. She wondered if she were losing her mind. "All these years I blamed that damn Freemason group for taking your life. I was determined to uncover the evil that existed there so I could have closure and move on."

A man entered carrying a syringe. He advanced on Rachel, who was still backed up against the wall. She dodged him, only to fall prey to Kek's grasp.

"Let go of me!" she screamed. As Rachel tried to twist free of Kek's clutch, the man injected the sedative. Her arm stung. The room dimmed, and the light was gone.

Kek caught her as she collapsed. Tenderly, he carried her to the couch.

Whitman, hearing the commotion, had entered and moved to the couch where Rachel was out cold. "I take it she didn't handle it well."

"Not very. I didn't tell her much, though. She has so much more to learn before she can make her decision."

"You really think she'll join you?"

"She always has."

"We do have another option. My sons."

"They're not ready. We need to ensure the family remains in power, now. We can't wait for them."

Whitman changed the subject. "What about Mercer?"

"I don't get her." Kek's eyes met Whitman's. "She knew me by the name *Kek.*"

Thirty-Six

Hours later Rachel woke. She sat up on the couch. Her head pounded and she was lightheaded. Her first image was the Egyptian mural. As she sat there, recalling the outrageous turn of events, her anger grew. She moved to the door and confirmed that is was locked. Rachel struck the door, announcing that she had awakened.

Within minutes, the door was unlocked and opened. Kek lingered in the doorway. "Let me be direct, Rachel. You cannot beat me. You cannot break out of here. My desire is to introduce you to my life."

"Why?"

"You have a decision to make—whether to join me and rule the world . . . or not."

"And if I don't?"

"Let's take this one step at a time." He backed into the lobby. "Let's walk."

Rachel stepped into the sterile area. With its lofty ceiling and size, it was reminiscent of a gymnasium. She walked beside him. "You are the devil, aren't you?"

"Yes . . . and no."

"Oh, come on. You've got to give me some straight answers. How did you meet Mother?"

"You know that story. I met her through a congregation member at a church she had been attending."

"How would the *devil* meet someone in church?"

Kek stopped walking. "Once a generation, I set out to build a family. I selected your mother for a number of reasons, none of which are important right now. Since I wanted her, it was only logical that I meet her in a nonthreatening place. Church was only logical. We met, married, and we had you. In each family that I set out to build, I stay

Published by The Haworth Press, Inc., 2006. All rights reserved.
doi:10.1300/5721_37

with the family ten to fifteen years. Because I don't age in the manner that you age, I need to move on before my youth draws attention."

Kek continued his pace and Rachel followed. "So you move on and destroy lives, including Mother's."

"I adore your mother, and I know I made a huge mistake. When you graduated from Princeton, I wanted to be there. What were the chances that your mother would have seen me amid the thousands attending? Not very good! At least, that's what I thought." He sighed. "We literally bumped into each other on the front lawn of Nassau Hall! I wish I could do it over again, but I can't. It was really unfortunate. After that I had no recourse but to have her institutionalized."

"You're a bastard."

"Let me continue. As my children have grown, I have always approached them to see if they have the same quest for power and interest to rule the world."

"And do they always join you?"

"There have been a few rare exceptions."

"And I'll be one of them."

Kek smiled, admiring her spunk. They had walked full circle around the large vestibule and returned to the mural room. He pointed at the couch suggesting that Rachel sit. Instead, she stood with arms staunchly crossed. He sat in a soft chair.

Rachel changed the subject. "Have you chased off all the men in my life?"

"I don't expect that you'd understand this yet, but it's important to maintain the bloodline. If someone has expressed interest in you and hasn't met with my approval, they have simply been *persuaded* to leave you alone. I assure you that my interest has been solely to protect you."

"Protect me? Who was responsible for cutting my brake line a couple years ago when I started investigating secret societies?"

"That was truly unfortunate for you and Albert Robbins. I assure you, he paid for his mistake."

Rachel recalled the conversation with Neil Samson about his friend, Albert Robbins, who was found dead in his bed from snakebite. "I don't believe this."

"Rachel, you must start believing."

She shook her head. "Okay. Amuse me. How could you ever control the world from a hell hole beneath DC?"

"It's really quite simple. The key to our success has been to maintain our concealment. Other than a select few, nobody knows I'm here. Although I'm the head of the Thirty-Third Council, only two people report to me, and they're family."

"Yes. I'm familiar with pyramid chain of command."

"Only family, and of course the Secret Service know I am here. The Secret Service runs this complex for me."

"That may explain how your identity has been kept secret, but how do you control the world?"

"Every secret group's objectives, plans, motives are indirectly manipulated by me, because they're connected to the Thirty-Third Council. This includes the Bilderbergers, the Council on Foreign Relations, Trilateral Commission, along with any secret-based group you can think of. We control everything, Rachel. If I want a war to break out, it will. If I want the market to crumble, it does. If I want an incurable disease that destroys the immune system, it appears."

"This is sick. All your examples are about destruction and suffering."

"Not for all," he smiled. "I assure you, there are thirty-three members of the council who will benefit from any of these examples. We control the major banks, insurance companies, major corporations, and politicians."

"You can't have everyone. The United States is a democracy; you can't tell me you control every politician including the president."

"You're absolutely right! Although most of the time the candidate that we endorse wins, there are times when he doesn't. Then, there are the even more bizarre times. Take a look at the 2000 election between Bush and Gore."

"Who did you support?"

"That's the funny part. We didn't endorse either one, and look what happened. The country went into a stalemate. For over a month, it was unclear who the next leader of the country would be."

"Why wouldn't you endorse someone?"

"I didn't need to. Both candidates were connected to a group. Either way I won."

"What happens when a president is not *connected?*" Rachel was curious now.

"I have the technology to manipulate thoughts. We would meet regularly with the president and brainwash him."

"With the Secret Service, how could you do something like that?"

"I told you, I control the Secret Service. They work for me!" He smiled. "Come with me." He left the room with Rachel on his heels. In the lobby, he strolled to a nearby closed door and removed the clipboard that hung beside the door. He examined paperwork clamped to it.

"There is a congressman inside whose vote is needed by the tobacco industry." Kek keyed in a code on the security pad beside the door, and a viewing window materialized. Inside, a man lay in what appeared to be a dentist chair. Flashing monitors surrounded him. His eyes were closed. He appeared asleep with earphones and electrodes attached to his head.

"First the man will go through a very simple brainwashing program. Here we implant the desired outcome through audio and electrical stimulation in the brain's cortex. Then the man's short-term memory is rewritten using a similar power of suggestion technique."

"Memory tampering?" Rachel recalled the report she did the previous year. "The CIA has this technology, doesn't it?"

"The CIA? The CIA reports through me. It has since its inception. How do you think Mr. Congressman here will get home?"

Rachel didn't want to believe him. She was hoping this was a nightmare, and kept telling herself to wake up. It didn't work.

"Over the years, I'm sure, you've heard of those people claiming to be abducted by UFOs. They allege to have had their brain scanned and body probed. . . ." He smiled.

"You bastard! You abduct people and make them believe they were accosted by UFOs?" Rachel was incredulous.

"That's not our intent. Most of the time the person has no recollection of what happened." He pointed to the doors that ran alongside the lobby. "Here we can manipulate a specimen's thoughts, or retrieve the information that we may need. When we're finished, their memory of the abduction is erased. There are incidences though, when it

doesn't completely work, because I read about it in the tabloids occasionally."

Rachel's head throbbed. The thought of global control did not surprise her. The knowledge that there was a demonic being ruling the
world, who claimed to be her father, was too much to take in. She
needed to change the subject. "Where's Jessie?"

"She's contained."

"What's going to happen to her?"

"There are two types of people that we bring here. The first are those
we need information or some deed from. The others are problems. How
we determine their release depends on how they came here. Jessie has
been a problem from the start."

"I want to see her."

"That's out of the question."

"Let me see her." When Rachel sensed that he wasn't going to
budge, she said, "For God's sake, what are you afraid of? You think
we're going to escape or something?"

The Secret Service man flicked the switch, stopping electrical stimulation to Jessie's brain. The monitor went black. He knew it would
be a couple minutes before she would wake. He peeled the electrodes
from her forehead, temples, and the base of her skull. Then he unfastened the straps on her wrists and legs, and waited.

When Jessie's eyes opened, he wasted no time. "Follow me!"

Jessie was led into the lobby where she squinted to filter the excess
light. She was groggy and moved slowly along the wall. Where was
she? She followed the man about thirty feet, before he led her into the
mural room, where she stood, eyes glazed over.

"Jessie!" Rachel rushed to her and took her hand, but she knew
something was wrong. She turned to Kek who stood in the corner of
the room. "What did you do to her?"

"I've been scanning her brain for hours, now. Sedation is required
for the procedure." What he didn't tell her was that he had been unsuccessful and had hoped that he would get some answers now. "The
sedative should wear off shortly."

When Jessie heard Kek's deep voice, she faced him. Then she leaned her head forward, and held her face in her hands.

"Jessie, are you okay?" Rachel directed her toward a chair.

Jessie, more cognizant now, shook her head. "I want to stand." Her body was stiff from being strapped to the chair. She stretched the muscles in her back. Her mind was clearing, and she had so much to share with Rachel, but she didn't know where to begin. "It wasn't Steve, it *was* you, Rachel," Jessie whispered.

"What are you talking about Jess?"

"*The Ultimate Conspiracy,* I tuned in to you," she mumbled.

Rachel tried to recall what Jessie had told her about her project.

"Did he tell you why you've been brought here?" Her voice was a little stronger.

"I can't believe it. I haven't had a chance to fully grasp what all this means."

"What exactly did he tell you?"

"Jess . . . he says he's my father. I don't want to believe him!"

Jessie reached for Rachel's wrist, eyeing the birthmark. It made sense. "I know this is hard . . . but he *is* your father, Rachel."

Tears welled in Rachel's eyes, and she rested on the couch.

Jessie sat beside her. "What else has he told you?"

Rachel started to cry and Jessie wrapped her arms around her. She shuddered, and her tear-filled eyes met Jessie's. "He runs the world, and he's brought me here to join him." Rachel trembled.

"Rachel, how has he explained his perceived immortality?"

Fresh tears flowed from her eyes; she wiped them away with her hand. She was so confused. She couldn't fathom what all this meant. "I don't know how to deal with this," she cried as she spoke. "Jess . . . I'm the daughter of Satan."

"Satan?" Jessie's eyes met Kek's cold eyes. "Is that what he told you?" Her attention returned to Rachel. "I'm sorry to give you more bad news, but it gets worse."

Rachel trembled. "What do you mean?"

"Kek is our creator."

Thirty-Seven

"Creator?" Rachel stood. "What the hell are you talking about?" Rachel's body language grabbed Kek's attention. He shifted closer. Jessie stood calmly beside her and repeated, "Kek is our creator."

"He can't be God!" Rachel clearly didn't believe Jessie.

"I didn't say he was God. I said he was our creator."

Kek overheard the conversation, and an evil smile came to his lips. It had been a long time since he'd had a mysterious challenge like Jessie. "Who are you?" he asked.

"Why don't you tell her everything?" Jessie's eyes avoided meeting Kek's. She turned to Rachel. "Did he tell you why he has protected you?"

"I assumed it was because . . ." The words were so hard to say, "He's my father."

Jessie brought to mind when her head, as Lukeman, rested on Dalila's shoulder. Kek's pledge echoed in her head: "*I will prepare you for the afterlife my love. And I will* never *allow anyone to harm you again. Never!*"

"It's not that simple, is it Kek?" Jessie spoke over her shoulder. To Rachel, "He has pledged to protect you eternally from harm."

Kek's smile disappeared and his tone was ominous. "How do you know that?"

"Rachel, it began when you were Dalila. He has pulled you into his life, lifetime after lifetime, because of a vow. You don't have to allow it to happen."

Rachel didn't understand any of this. She backed away from both of them.

"How do you know that?" Kek yelled, his eyes glaring with anger at Jessie.

"I was there, Kek." For the first time, she allowed him to meet her eyes.

Published by The Haworth Press, Inc., 2006. All rights reserved.
doi:10.1300/5721_38

It didn't take long for him to see it. "Lukeman?" He circled her slowly. "And you remember!" From behind he asked in her ear. "How much do you remember?"

"Everything, Kek. Even Nibiru."

His eyes narrowed and his jaw tightened. Abruptly, he jabbed a needle in her neck.

Instantly, Jessie lost consciousness. Her knees buckled and she fell to the floor.

It all happened too fast for Rachel. She tried to catch her, but she wasn't quick enough. "What did you do?" Rachel yelled as she leaned over her body.

Kek pressed a button on his watch and said, "I have a code thirty-two."

Seconds later, the door opened and two men entered. Effortlessly, they grabbed Jessie's arms and dragged her from the room.

"What are you doing?" Rachel yelled at the men. "Leave her alone. Don't hurt her!" But nothing she said mattered.

Kek followed the men out of the room, slamming the door in Rachel's face. As she had expected, the door was locked.

"Nibiru? Who the hell is Nibiru?"

Thirty-Eight

Alone again. Rachel retreated to the couch. Although scared and confused, she didn't have time to dwell on it. She was the key to their freedom. She needed to sort out what had just transpired. Jessie had confirmed her worst fears—Kek was indeed Rachel's father. What did Jessie know that made him so angry? She recalled the details of Jessie's project, *The Ultimate Conspiracy.* Jessie had psychically tuned in to *Rachel's* future when she conceived the story. Her protagonist failed, and traded allegiances. *Is that my future? My destiny?* she wondered. *Can destiny be changed? It has to change—I'd never join him!*

Two hours later the door opened and Kek stood silently in the doorway.

"Where's Jessie? What are you doing to her?" Rachel demanded.

"That depends on you. Come. I need to show you some things, then you have a decision to make."

A golf cart was parked outside the door. Kek hopped in the driver's seat, but Rachel didn't move. He looked at her. "I assure you, our time is precious."

Rachel sat beside Kek. He handed her a hoodwink. "Put this on!"

"Why?"

"Don't ask questions. Just put it on."

She pulled the blindfold over her head.

He tightened a drawstring around her neck. "Don't remove this until I've instructed."

The little cart sped away. Kek made two full circles in the lobby, then a figure eight. When he passed the mural room for the third time, he floored the pedal and the small vehicle sped toward a blank wall with no doors or windows.

Beneath the blindfold, Rachel felt an increase in velocity, accelerating her heart rate.

Published by The Haworth Press, Inc., 2006. All rights reserved.
doi:10.1300/5721_39

Kek didn't slow down as he neared the wall. Just when it seemed the cart would crash into the concrete wall, it disappeared and they accessed another room. Kek braced his arm in front of Rachel and slammed on the brakes.

Her body lurched forward as the cart skidded to a standstill. She felt Kek loosen the string around her neck, and she pulled the blindfold from her head. The vehicle was parked in the center of a dimly lit room. Rachel stepped from the cart; her motion activated recessed lighting and the room brightened. There were no windows or doors. She felt as if they were in a box. Behind the cart, there were skid marks on the white floor. She followed the rubber to the wall where the cart had emerged. She touched the wall's surface. It was concrete. "How did we come through the wall?"

"I have three things to show you, and then I need your decision," he said.

"What decision?"

"Whether you will assume your role and rule the world with me."

"And if I don't?"

"I'll inform you of the consequences when the time is appropriate." His voice was cool, emotionless, and detached. He approached the wall to the right of the cart. With a wave of his hand, an arched entrance to another room mysteriously appeared. The room was dark, yet lights gradually illuminated the area.

At first, she saw a massive shadow in the center. Then, as the area brightened she made out sharp angles surrounding the object. It was a septagram, a seven-pointed star. The core of the star consisted of a golden disk; it must have been over ten feet wide. As the room brightened, the star actually shimmered with sparkling light. Rachel inched closer, discerning that the brilliant light was emitted from thousands of diamonds that shaped the star.

Rachel studied the luminous object. It looked like a celestial art piece. The expense to manufacture the item was inconceivable to her. It couldn't be real gold or diamonds. Could it? Encircling the star, at the extreme points, were seven smaller disks. She glanced around the circular room, then above the star. She felt as if she were standing in a barrel. She couldn't see the top. There was a low-frequency hum.

"What is this?"

"The BeMER machine. Behavior Modification through Electro-magnetic Radiation."

There was a part of her that was afraid to ask. "What does it do?"

"Without getting into specifics, it modifies behavior of every person on earth."

"How?" she whispered.

"By modulating the frequency of the planet, we stay in control. Then there are times when we need more drastic results. In which case the frequency and wavelength is modified which affects humankind's seven ganglionic nerve centers. This we don't do often, but when we do . . ." He smiled with evil in his eyes. "The results are effective."

"Give me an example of when you've done that."

"World Wars I and II."

It struck Rachel. Impulsively she turned to her father. "You asshole! That's why the UN members are acting so unpredictable. Are you trying to start World War III?"

He smiled. "Yes, my dear. That was merely a slight increase in radiation while they were in negotiations. You haven't seen anything, yet."

"Why are you doing this?"

"It's part of the plan, Rachel. Just take a look at the price of oil. Trust me, we're becoming wealthier by the second. And if we go to war, do you have any idea how profitable it will be?"

"You're sick!"

Kek strolled back to the golf cart. To Rachel, the room now felt more like a hallway. He moved to the wall directly in front of the golf cart. With a wave of his hand, another archway magically appeared. As in the BeMER room, the area lit gradually. But unlike the previous area, there were vessels overflowing with treasures. Kek followed a narrow pathway in the midst of chests of ancient gold coins, urns of precious gems, and vases of priceless treasures. This room was substantially larger than the last.

"Here I have gold from the lost continents of Mu and Atlantis." He pointed to chests brimming with gold pieces. "There's gold, silver, gems, and other precious minerals from every ancient civilization.

About a mile from this spot we have a warehouse of precious metals and stones."

Speechless, she followed. The room was about the size of a gymnasium. One thing toward the back wall caught her eye and she passed Kek. Here a wooden chest rested on a platform. Beside it lay a golden pot, and a rod. Two long bars were affixed to the sides of the chest. Over the cover were two cherubs. The chubby children knelt facing each other, their wings stretched to cover the trunk. "Is this what I think it is?"

"It's the Ark of the Covenant."

"How did you get it?"

"For the most part, I've always had it. It belongs to me."

Rachel pointed to the artifacts that lay beside the ark. "The gold pot?"

"It's from the story in Exodus, the golden pot of hidden manna. The staff is Aaron's rod as told in Numbers."

She couldn't fathom the value of the treasures that surrounded her. Her attention turned to the wall behind the platform. Here, there were shelves that stored plastic cylinders. She realized that the book-cases must have been eight feet tall and ran the entire length of the back wall. There were thousands of these plastic tubes neatly stacked.

Rachel moved to a shelf behind the platform and lifted a tube. Rolled inside the polyethylene cylinder was a parchment. "What are these?"

"Scrolls of hidden knowledge."

She raised another tube that had been neatly stacked within a matrix.

"That group is from the Dead Sea Scrolls."

"*You* have them?" She moved along the expansive shelf unit. Kek followed closely. About ten feet down she lifted another cylinder.

"The Roman Emperor Constantine confiscated those in AD 326," he said.

"That was the year after the Council of Nicaea." The scrolls were priceless, but that wasn't why he possessed them she speculated. She turned to him. "They communicate concepts that you don't want people to be aware of, don't they?"

Kek nodded. "True."

"Why didn't you just destroy them?"

Kek smiled. How could he express that he had a soft spot for humankind's emergent philosophies? "They're priceless!"

"Why are you showing me this?"

"Come."

Rachel followed him through the treasures to the entry, where the golf cart was parked. "I'm showing you this, because I want you to be very clear about your choices." He pointed at the BeMER machine. "If you choose not to join me, I cannot protect you from it. But, if you join me, I can give you treasures beyond your wildest dreams. Anything you want can be yours. You want to be in charge of the network? It could be yours. You want to be the first woman U.S. president? I can give you that, though I do have someone in mind for that job."

"And what happens if I say no?" Rachel asked. "Are you going to kill me?"

"No! Your memory will be erased and you'll return to your life as you knew it before. You will have no recollection of any of this. But before you make your decision there is one more thing I need to show you." He approached the wall to the left of the cart. With a wave of his hand, a third archway appeared. The room lit instantly.

"Oh, my God," she whispered. In the midst of a laboratory, Jessie lay on a gurney. Her eyes were closed and electrodes crowned her head. Surrounding her were electronic instruments and monitors. Rachel stepped toward her, but Kek seized her arm.

"Let me go," she tried to twist free. "What have you done to her?"

Kek calmly said, "When you've heard what I need to tell you, you can go to her."

Rachel's resistance disappeared. "What have you done to her?"

Kek released her. "Nothing . . . yet. But if you *don't* join me, Jessie will die."

Rachel was horrified. "What? You expect to gain my loyalty with blackmail?"

"I'll take it any way I can get it. I need your answer."

"Now?" Rachel turned toward Jessie. "Let me go to her. Can't I have a little time to think about this?"

Showing that he wasn't completely heartless, he considered. "You can go to her. She's sedated. I doubt she'll even be able to hear you. But when I return, I'll need your answer. Don't do anything stupid. If you try to move her, she *will* die." Then he pointed at the wall beside him. "The only way out of here is through that wall." He sat in the cart and turned the vehicle around. "You have thirty minutes." He floored the accelerator.

Rachel thought the car would crash, but instead, it sped through the concrete wall. She rushed to where the cart had exited and felt the cold, hard surface. There was no indication that the cart had even bumped it. "I don't have much time." She hurried into the lab and approached the gurney. "Jessie, can you hear me?" She picked up a limp hand. "Jessie?"

Jessie stirred, and her eyes fluttered. "Rachel?" she murmured.

"Yes. It's me, Jess. Are you in pain?"

"No. I'm so tired." Jessie's eyes remained shut. "Turn this contraption off."

Rachel studied the instrument that Jessie was connected to. Leads from the electrodes on her head linked to a computer like instrument.

"My father . . . Kek told me that if I moved you—you would die."

It took so much strength for Jessie to talk. "It's frying my brain. If you don't turn it off . . . I'm going to die."

Rachel studied the instrument. There was an LCD display with dials that referred to volts and a frequency control that was set on one minute. A neuroimaging monitor on the opposite side of the bed seemingly reflected her brain's activity. Abruptly, Jessie jolted. The scale on the monitor spiked, recording her brain's response to the electrical stimulation.

"I don't have much time," Rachel said as Jessie's body calmed. "I need to decide whether or not to join him."

"Don't." It was a whisper.

"They'll be consequences if I don't."

Jessie's eyes opened and met Rachel's. Using all her energy, she said, "Kek won't hurt you. Don't join him. You always have. That's how he keeps pulling you into his life. . . . Say no."

Rachel's eyes filled with tears. Her lips met Jessie's limp hand. "I just keep hoping this is a nightmare and I'll wake up and it'll all be over."

"Has he told you . . . about Nibiru?" Jessie's body jolted as the electrical current zapped her.

"Jess? Who's Nibiru?"

She was so tired. She took a deep breath. "The ark will explain." She could barely speak. "He has it." Jessie fell into unconsciousness.

"The Ark of the Covenant?"

Jessie didn't respond.

Rachel turned to the machine that Jessie was connected to. There were two controls, one for electric stimulation, the other frequency. She turned the red dial until it read 0 VOLTS. When the frequency clock approached the one-minute mark, Jessie's body didn't jump.

Thirty-Nine

Rachel watched as Jessie slept calmly. "The ark will explain Ni-biru?" Rachel squeezed Jessie's hand. "I'll be back, Jess. I promise." She hurried from the lab into the now-empty entryway. Eyeing the storage room of treasures, she rushed through the archway to the rear of the storage area. "The ark will give me the answers," she mumbled. She stepped upon the stage and approached it. "But how?"

Soon Rachel realized that she was trembling. Was she nervous? "This is ridiculous. It's only a chest." She took a deep breath and felt the aged acacia. It was smoother than she had expected. She tried to remove the cover, but the span of the cherubs' wings made it difficult for her to grasp the lid. Then she lifted the wings and, surprisingly, the cover came free.

"Now what?" Rachel stared at the lid in her hands. She backed away from the chest and set it down. If Rachel had had more time to consider what she was doing, she may have become more nervous, or even scared. But she didn't have the luxury of time. She needed to fig-ure out this piece before Kek returned.

Rachel peered over the edge of the ark. Two flat slabs of stone were stacked together on the bottom of the chest. Carefully, she lifted the tablets and laid them beside the ark. They were much heavier than she had expected. Etched in the stones were markings. Although she couldn't read it, she assumed it was the Ten Commandments.

She looked into the chest. Inside, there were two slots, one on each end. They appeared to be about the same size as a tablet's width and depth. Near one of the slots, there was a symbol. She inched closer. It was an ankh. She inspected the opposite end and found a snake. "What does that mean? Who is Nibiru? How can the ark help?"

She examined the relic thoroughly, getting more frustrated by the minute. Then she turned to the tablets but their markings were inde-

Published by The Haworth Press, Inc., 2006. All rights reserved.
doi:10.1300/5721_40

cipherable. She spotted an ankh on the far corner of one. On the oppo-site corner of the other stone, there was the snake.

Could this be something? She lifted a tablet, and brought it to the chest. Sliding it into a slot she confirmed that the ankh on the tablet and the one in the chest aligned perfectly. With the second tablet, she lined up the snakes. Another perfect fit.

"Now what?" To Rachel, it seemed as if she waited an eternity, but it was really only a couple minutes. Nothing happened. Feeling the pressure of being forced to make a decision, she turned away to re-trieve the cover, but as she leaned over, a soft continuous noise rose from behind her.

Rachel turned. The sound was coming from the ark. She moved to-ward it, but stopped when a high-frequency pulse reverberated from within the chest. What was happening? Rachel's pulse raced. She was close enough to witness the ark's floor shift. Unpredictably, a futuris-tic apparatus with a lens emerged. The pupil on the lens dilated and light spewed above the chest, forming a holographic, sparkling globe.

Within the sphere was a small object. She had to move closer to see it. It was a bright circular light. Surrounding the light were smaller spheres randomly dispersed. It was a three-dimensional model of the solar system. The miniature lights moved faster and faster, becoming blurry. Abruptly, the lights dimmed and the globe went dark.

"Now what?" Rachel waited for what seemed to be forever.

"And who's there?" a deep voice echoed.

Rachel's heartbeat quickened. She looked around the storage room. "Over here!"

Rachel gasped. The voice was coming from the orb. Cautiously, she moved toward it. Many researchers and theologians have speculated that the Ark of the Covenant was a communication device with God. *Could it be?* On one hand, it made sense. Kek's incarceration of it pre-vented humankind from communicating with God.

"I still cannot see you, come closer," the male voice commanded.

She drew closer to the orb, and about two feet away, an image came into focus. It was a man wearing a toga, perhaps in his mid-twenties, with golden, shoulder-length hair.

"There you are," he said. "Why Rachel, I didn't realize you had joined Kek yet."

"You know who I am?" she inched closer to view the man. He had a familiar cleft chin and sky blue eyes.

"Of course I do."

The celestial aura about him prompted her, "And you are . . . God?"

The man laughed. "I have been called that. But my family calls me Marduk. Or you can call me Ra."

"Ra?"

"Hasn't Kek explained everything to you?"

"I haven't completely grasped it all yet. I still have many questions."

"Any I can help you with?"

"Yes. Who is Nibiru?"

"Nibiru is not a person. It's our home, the tenth planet of the solar system."

Rachel's head spun. "The tenth . . . planet?"

"That's correct." Kek's haunting voice came from over her shoulder, startling her.

Forty

Kek's cold eyes bore down on Rachel. Holding back his anger, his jawline tightened, and his face flushed. He approached the orb. "Marduk, I need to speak to your sister." Abruptly, he withdrew one of the tablets from the chest. The globe disappeared, and the humming ceased. "I must give you credit, Rachel. I don't know anyone who has so hastily figured out how to communicate with the ark. Most don't even dare to open it."

Rachel's head throbbed. She watched Kek arrange the tablets in the position she had found them. "It's a transmitter and receiver," she mumbled. "The tablets function as a power source to communicate with. . . . You told me you were Satan."

"I agreed that I have been called by many names, including Satan."

"I thought you were the demonic Satan referenced in the Bible." Not that it made any difference, because in Rachel's heart she believed he was the devil.

Kek stared into his daughter's eyes. "I am the Satan referenced in the Bible."

She sat on the stage, closed her eyes and rubbed her temples. In a flash she looked at Kek. "How can you be Satan and . . . what exactly are you?" Tears swelled in her eyes. "Are you an alien? I'm part alien?"

Kek put the cover back on the ark. "Yes."

"This has *not* been a good day." She thought she was losing her mind. "When were you going to tell me?"

"I was planning to take you through the ancient mystery teachings. That approach seems to have worked the best over the centuries."

"How can I be part alien? I look like everybody else."

"And I don't?"

Rachel eyed her father. "You *do* look like everyone else. How can that be?"

Published by The Haworth Press, Inc., 2006. All rights reserved.
doi:10.1300/5721_41

"We don't have a lot of time," Kek said urgently. "The longer you stay out of your life, the more complicated it becomes getting you back. Come with me."

He led her to the golf cart and tossed her the hoodwink. "Get in and put this on."

"Are you serious?" But the look in her father's eyes answered her question.

While she was blindfolded, Kek maneuvered the tiny cart in full circles, so that Rachel became disoriented, and then he drove through the wall. "You can take it off," Kek instructed.

She removed the blindfold. The cart was back in the vestibule parked in front of a door. Kek opened it, and nodded at Rachel to enter. As in the lobby, the walls were white. With the exception of two soft chairs and a coffee table, the room was barren.

"Please sit," he instructed. He picked up a remote control from the table. "I'm going to tell you *our* story, Rachel."

He pressed a button on the remote; the lights dimmed, and the room became pitch black. Over the coffee table in front of them, a three-dimensional image of the solar system appeared.

Rachel was impressed by the illustrative display. Glowing dust particles from the ceiling provided the only clue to where the projection equipment was mounted.

"This is our solar system." Standing partly within the image itself, Kek pointed out the various planets and their orbits around the sun. "And *this* is Nibiru." He identified a planet about three times the size of Earth. He quickly demonstrated its orbit, and then slowed it down. "As you can see, Nibiru travels between Mars and Jupiter, then proceeds on its elliptical path taking it far outside our solar system before the gravitational force pulls it back." The other planets' orbits revolved much quicker than Nibiru. "In the time it takes Nibiru to orbit the sun once, the earth revolves around the sun thirty-six hundred times.

"Thousands of years ago, when Nibiru was in close proximity to Earth, my father—your grandfather—organized a mission to colonize Earth. My brother, Enlil, and I were responsible for the actual migration. Enlil was the commanding officer while I was the chief science officer. We settled in the Persian Gulf, in Mesopotamia. Today this area is known as Iraq. It was chosen because of the vast availability of fossil fuel and water."

It hit Rachel. "You're behind the turmoil in Iraq?"

"I'm behind most turmoil, Rachel. I was responsible for building irrigation systems. Thousands of years passed and a second Nibirian ship arrived with reinforcements, this time under the leadership of my son, Marduk."

"Ra?"

"Yes. The Egyptians called him Ra. My Nibirian name is Enki."

"Why did you come to Earth?" Rachel was curious.

Kek pressed a button on his remote and Nibiru grew. "Nibiru was experiencing a problem that Earth is now facing. Hydrofluorocarbons were destroying the ozone layer. We needed gold."

"Gold?"

"To patch the hole in Nibiru's ozonosphere, we needed to disperse tiny particles of gold into the upper atmosphere."

"One minute. *Over the Edge* did a report on *our* ozone problem. If I remember correctly, scientists believe that if we were ever required to repair our problem, dispersing gold into our atmosphere was the best option."

"Where do you think they got the idea?"

Rachel looked into her father's eyes. "Continue."

Kek pressed a button on the remote and the display disappeared. Lights came on. He sat in the chair opposite her. "The Nibirians mined Earth for years. It was an incredible task we had undertaken. And it didn't look like we were going to make it on time. If we were going to save Nibiru, we needed to speed things up. The only way I knew how to do that was to have a slave force. And since my education was biogenetics, I proposed to clone primitive workers and use them to mine gold.

"My proposal was approved by the governing Nibirian body. At the time, there were primitive humanoids in Africa. To understand the species, we experimented. We produced a variety of mutated creatures such as lions and bulls with human heads, apes and humanoids with goat feet, winged horses, along with other variations."

"Were these creatures the basis of the mythological legends?"

He nodded yes. "Then we took a reproductive egg from the primitive African humanoid and fertilized it with the sperm of a young Anunnaki male."

"Anunnaki?"

"I'm sorry. I know this is confusing. Anunnaki and Nibirians are synonymous. Anyway, the fertilized egg was then placed inside an Anunnaki female. Basically, *Adamu* was the first test-tube baby. He was created in *our image*."

"You're telling me that you *did* create man?"

"Yes. Mankind as we know it today."

"I don't believe it." Rachel stood up. She was angry. "You're lying."

"Why would I lie? Our people were far more technologically advanced than humans are today. I could understand if this was a hundred years ago and you didn't believe me. But face it, humankind now has the ability to clone and has been producing test-tube babies since 1978."

"Why would you be so advanced?"

"To you, I may appear to be a man of forty-five years, correct? I am forty-five in Anunnaki years. In Earth years, I'm over one hundred sixty thousand years old."

"Are you immortal?"

He shook his head. "No. I will die just like everyone else. But it's likely that I will live over three hundred thousand Earth years. I believe our species has been able to evolve quicker because of the longer lifetime."

It was barely a whisper. "How long will *I* live?"

"You won't live thousands of years, Rachel. But it is possible that you will exist into your early hundreds. If you take a look at some of the biblical characters, many of them lived hundreds of years, as St. Germain did."

"Are you telling me that they were also aliens?"

"Rachel, they were part Anunnaki, which contributed to their longevity, as it will play a role in your own.

Rachel was still trying to take it all in. "Let me get this straight—you created mankind to be your slave?"

"Yes. And they served their purpose well for thousands of years."

"No wonder you've been called Satan."

Laughter from a distant past echoed in Kek's ears. He was reminded of when his brother banished him from E.DIN, the day he had first earned his demonic reference. *"You will never be a leader, Enki. My work will rise above you, and you will be called Abaddon, and from where I will put you . . . you will be the keeper of the bottomless pit."*

Kek shook the memory from his head. "But that's not how I earned the nickname Satan. The irony is—I wanted something more for mankind. As slaves, their lives were meaningless; they worked and were treated badly by the Anunnaki. Most were cruel, incestuous, and hateful. After watching generations of first-man and woman live their pathetic lives, I selected a few and offered them an opportunity to seek eternal salvation and spiritual freedom.

"Because of this, I was banished by my people. My punishment was to stay here, on earth. I was condemned for committing *the original sin.* Somehow, humankind interpreted my shortcoming as their weakness. At the time Enlil dubbed me Abaddon.

"So . . . the Anunnaki left you here?"

"Let me continue. About thirteen thousand years ago, Enlil knew that Nibiru's orbit would brush too closely to Earth, creating catastrophic climate changes. At the time, Enlil was angry at the rapid population growth and the interbreeding between the Anunnaki and the humans. He convinced the ruling assembly to allow the anticipated natural disasters to wipe out humankind. After all, at this point they had mined all the gold they needed. But I learned of his plan. I warned one of my human assistants, and instructed him how to build an ark. Sound familiar?"

"Noah?"

Kek nodded. "His real name was Utnapishtim. On the ark, three culturally diverse wives accompanied him. They ultimately produced the three ethnic groups of the world. And contrary to the biblical account, he brought DNA samples of most living creatures, not the actual animals. The boat was a floating genetics laboratory.

"But he wouldn't have the knowledge to clone living creatures from DNA."

"You're right, Rachel. While my brother, Enlil, and the rest of the Anunnaki were safely aboard their spaceships, waiting for the storms to subside, I was with Utnapishtim in the ark. Remember? I had been banished to Earth.

"We survived, and perhaps Enlil even felt remorse over not warning mankind. He permitted me to bring life back to Earth. So, Earth was repopulated. But after the great flood mankind's existence was different. The Anunnaki that had remained with me had no need for gold anymore, so we taught agriculture, and humankind became farmers. During this era, man worshipped the gods, which were actually the Anunnaki."

"The ancient Egyptian gods were Anunnaki? Were the pharaohs Anunnaki, also?"

"The pharaohs were usually male children of an Anunnaki and a humanoid."

Rachel had been dying to ask, and yet was afraid to. "Where does God fit into all this? There is a God, right?"

"There is a Divine Being. And that is part of our teaching in the mysteries. The Nibirians have known how to become one with God for thousands of years. This will be part of your wisdom, should you choose to join us."

"Was Jehovah, in the Old Testament, God?"

Kek laughed. "Jehovah was my brother, Enlil. Apparently, Moses realized that Jehovah was not an all-loving God, and he had other plans for *his* people. When Moses was first presented the tablets on Mount Sinai, he was distraught. He had been handed the ten elements of their destiny, not the Ten Commandments. Their destiny was to help Enlil rise above my work. The original tablets foretold the seven-year holocaust where they would kill thousands of innocent people. Moses was instructed to hold onto the ark, because the combination of the chest and tablets would be a channel to communicate with Jehovah.

"Moses left Sinai disenchanted. He had led his people out of bondage from the pharaoh, into oppression with Enlil. *This* was the reason he broke the first set of tablets. But when Enlil discovered what he did, Moses was instructed to return to Sinai. Enlil needed Moses. He said, 'Moses, if you were God, what ten directives would you bestow upon your people.' Then Moses was instructed to etch them into the stone.

"Now, Moses was a moral man. To him, right and wrong were easy to differentiate. So, Moses actually authored the Ten Commandments. Then, Enlil brainwashed him. We have the technology not only to erase, but alter memories. Moses was reprogrammed to believe that the commandments were from Jehovah. To him, they made so much sense and he pledged his unwavering loyalty. So, Moses took the Ark of the Covenant, never really understanding its significance."

"But you have it."

"Yes. After my son, Marduk, left Earth, I realized the ark would be my only means to communicate with him. I've controlled it through the brotherhood that I formed thousands of years ago."

"If the God in the Old Testament is a fraud," Rachel wasn't sure if she wanted to know. "What about the New Testament? If Jesus is the son of God, does that make him Anunnaki?"

"Both Mary and Jesus were products of artificial insemination. In Mary's case, her mother was human and she was artificially insemi-nated with Anunnaki sperm. So, indeed, Mary was half Anunnaki, and she was inseminated, while still a virgin."

"Making Jesus mostly Anunnaki," Rachel whispered. "So it is true that the Roman Catholic Church misinterpreted the virgin birth."

Kek laughed. "The church didn't misinterpret anything. I control the church, I always have."

"I don't understand. Are you telling me that the Vatican is a sup-porter of yours?"

"I wouldn't put it that way. But I can say that the Vatican is a pawn of mine."

"The Roman Catholic Church is the strongest church in the world; how would this benefit you?"

Kek smiled. "Two simple words—spiritual repression. In ancient times, I was able to suppress people from seeking spiritual salvation by limiting admission to the mystery schools. The Roman Catholic Church gives people false hope for spiritual salvation." Kek grinned. "It keeps them from seeking the truth."

"I don't get it. How do you benefit?"

"As long as humankind remains spiritually ignorant, they won't evolve, and I remain in control."

Rachel stood. She wandered around the small room staring at her father. She felt lost, she didn't want to believe him, but somehow, she knew he conveyed the truth. "I don't know what to think about all this."

"Rachel, look at three significant segments of humankind's development: first farming, 11,000 BC; then prehistoric culture, 7500 BC; and finally civilization, 3800 BC. They all occur about thirty-six hundred years apart. There is no coincidence that it takes Nibiru thirty-six hundred years to approach earth."

"So . . . the Anunnaki visit every thirty-six hundred years?"

"The Anunnaki send reinforcements every thirty-six hundred years. The Great Pyramid of Cheops was built to be a space beacon. To this day it still serves its purpose. My people have never completely left."

"There are others, here?"

"There are millions here. Some are the most powerful people in the world, while others just blend in and exist. I'm their leader. Take a look at the life expectancy of humans over time. It isn't just medicine that's increased humankind's lifespan."

Rachel didn't know what to think. "Is Whitman Anunnaki?"

Kek smiled. "Michael has always shown great promise. He serves on the Supreme Council and is one of the two that report to me. But he is not one hundred percent Anunnaki. I am Michael's great-grandfather; I guess that makes you his great-aunt."

"Who's the other one that reports to you on the Supreme Council?"

"He's a member of the existing administration, but enough of this. It is important that family members rule with me. Although Michael is young at heart, he's aging and we need to prepare someone to succeed him. What's your decision?"

"My decision?" she asked calmly. "Let me get this straight. First, I discover that I'm the daughter of some demon, and now I'm informed I'm part alien. My alien father created us to be slaves, and has attempted to spiritually suppress humankind since the beginning of our existence. He zaps people and sends them off to war whenever—"

Buzz!

Rachel jumped. The loud noise from Kek's watchband startled her. "What's that?" she asked.

Kek glanced at his watch. "That was your last call, Rachel. Ms. Mercer is dying. She's connected to a heart monitor." Kek showed her the display on his watch. "She just flatlined."

Rachel's heart skipped. Had she compromised Jessie's health by changing the voltage setting on the instrument? She was horrified.

Forty-One

The moments that followed were a blur. While blindfolded, Rachel passed through the wall. The abrupt surge forward announced their arrival, she yanked the hoodwink from her head and tossed it to the floor. She rushed to Jessie's side.

Kek was right behind her and moved to the opposite side of the gurney. He felt her wrist. "She's still alive." Why would the EKG indicate otherwise? Kek traced the lead from the clothespin-shaped gadget on Jessie's finger to the electrocardiograph. The plug was partially dislodged from its socket. He pushed the plug back into the notch and the EKG instantly transmitted Jessie's heartbeat.

"Now how would the cable become displaced?" Suspicious, Kek's eyes combed the area. Although they had been there a couple of minutes, and the electro-current machine was on, Jessie hadn't jolted. Then he saw the "VOLTS" on the output display.

"How did this happen?" His voice rose.

"I turned it down," Rachel admitted.

Kek's patience was now gone. From a nearby cabinet, he retrieved a syringe. "I need your answer."

"What?"

Systematically, Kek rubbed a vial of venom between his palms, mixing the solution. He removed a syringe from the package, stabbed the needle into the venom, and filled the hypodermic. He set the vial on the counter and approached Jessie.

"Rachel, I need your answer, now! Join me and Jessie will live." He moved closer to Jessie and lowered the needle, waiting for an answer. "If you don't join me, it will be painless for her. You will return to your life not recalling any of this."

"You are an ass!" Rachel griped.

Published by The Haworth Press, Inc., 2006. All rights reserved.
doi:10.1300/5721_42

Out of nowhere a needle struck Kek's neck. "I'll give you an answer!" Jessie shouted as she struggled to inject him. She had waited for him to approach so that she could assault him with the needle she had concealed underneath the sheet.

Kek released his syringe, and it fell to the floor. With one hand, he grabbed her throat. He yanked the other needle from his neck. Angrily, he chucked the syringe on the floor. He flew into a rage. With both hands he seized Jessie's neck. Relentlessly, he squeezed with all his strength, stopping the air from reaching Jessie's lungs. The vein on his forehead bulged and his face, red with anger, hovered over Jessie.

Jessie lashed out at him, catching him in the face, in the arms, in the chest. The electrodes that Jessie had re-stuck to her forehead fell off. She was no match for his powerful grip. She couldn't breath and grew fainter with each passing second. Her resistance weakened, and on the brink of passing out, her arms fell lifeless to her sides.

Kek watched the life force slip from her body. On the verge of contentment, his sinister smile emerged but quickly vanished when he felt the sharp sting of a needle. His eyes widened from disbelief. *Rachel couldn't have done this!*

He fell lifelessly with a syringe jutting from his back, sprawled on top of Jessie. Rachel yanked his arm, and his body tumbled limply to the floor. With the sudden cease of pressure on Jessie's trachea, she gasped, restoring oxygen to her lungs.

"Are you okay?" Rachel helped Jessie from the gurney.

Jessie coughed. "I think so." Her throat throbbed from where Kek's fingers had jabbed. She felt for Kek's pulse.

"Is he okay?" Rachel asked.

"He has a pulse," her voice hoarse. Lightheaded, she staggered to the cabinet. Here she found the vial that she had used to fill her syringe. She read the label, "Diprivan. It's a sedative." Jessie picked up the other vial that Kek had used for his needle. "The other vial is snake venom. Do you know which syringe you grabbed?"

Rachel nodded no. "So, I either put him to sleep or killed him." There was no sense of loss as she stared at her father's body. There was no closure, either. "He has this machine that he's been using to influence the UN discussions. Jess, he's leading us to world war. We need to destroy it!"

"Where is it?"

"Come!" Rachel rushed across the entry into the BeMER room. Their motion set off the light and the massive star of destruction illuminated.

"My God! It still works!" Jessie mumbled.

"You know what it is?"

"It modifies behavior by bringing out our darkest sides. Ra built it. That's how he earned the name sun god. The people never knew that it was a death machine." Jessie approached the enormous machine. She had forgotten how beautiful it was. She fingered a diamond's pointed edge. "When the slaves mined gold for Nibiru, Ra stashed so much away to make this. Then when there was sufficient gold, he had the slaves mine diamonds."

It *was* real gold and diamonds. "We need to destroy it!" Rachel had urgency in her voice. "In today's economy, rebuilding this machine would be economically impossible."

Jessie knew she was right. What she didn't tell Rachel was that there were more of these machines scattered all over Earth, perhaps a half-dozen or so. How could she explain that the machines modified the frequency of the earth preventing light or wisdom from reaching humankind? How could she make clear that the machines prevented humankind's evolvement by broadcasting humankind's emotional turmoil?

Without time on her side, she said, "We need explosives." Jessie turned back into the hallway. Across from them was the laboratory. She pointed to the now-dark warehouse. "What's in there?"

"Treasures. Silver, gold, gems, ancient scrolls, and religious relics. No weapons."

"Relics?" Jessie was thoughtful. "Is the Ark there?"

"Yes. You were right. The Ark is a communication device, that's how I learned about Nibiru."

"That's not all it is. Show me where it is."

Rachel didn't question her. "Come!" She entered the dark storage area, their movement setting off the lights. She led Jessie through magnificent treasures, to the Ark.

Jessie recognized it along with Aaron's rod and the golden pot of manna. She lifted its cover with the cherubs' wings, and set it beside the chest. Then she placed the golden pot within the ark and replaced the lid.

"What are you doing?" Rachel asked.

"We need the tablets, pot, and rod." Jessie picked up the staff. "Would you give me a hand?" She grabbed the wooden poles on one side of the ark. Rachel took the other side and the women lugged the chest, facing each other, through the storage room.

"Jessie, do you know what you're doing?" Rachel's eyes searched Jessie's as they hauled the heavy chest.

"Yes. I remember being a high priest."

"What exactly are we doing?"

"The Ark is not only a communication device. Within it is an incredible energy that can be used for great things such as healing . . . as well as destruction."

They moved into the BeMER room and Jessie worked quickly. She lifted the Ark's cover and emptied it. As Rachel had figured out earlier, by matching the symbols on the tablets and in the chest, the Ark became a communication device. This time, Jessie mismatched the symbols, aligning the snakes with the ankhs.

Jessie set the second tablet in the chest. "We can produce an electric current by changing the magnetic field. The tablets look like stone, but insulated within them are strands of metal."

A soft noise vibrated from the chest. The floor of the chest shifted and the lens emerged, but this time it didn't spew light. Jessie covered the lens with the pot.

"Manna was the food that Moses and the Hebrews fed on during their forty-year trek to Canaan. Every morning they gathered it before sunrise, because once light hit it, it became inedible. On the sixth day, they gathered extra for the Sabbath. Enlil, Kek's brother, told Moses to fill this vessel with manna and save it as a memorial to how God had fed them." Jessie pointed at the pot. "The truth is, without it they couldn't create electromagnetic induction. Gold is an effective electrical conductor."

Jessie grabbed the cherubs' wings and set the lid on the ark. She lifted Aaron's rod. "During their journey, there was a challenge to Moses' and Aaron's leadership. Enlil couldn't afford to lose his leaders. He was furious. He punished them with a plague, killing thousands. To demonstrate that Aaron had been chosen to succeed Moses, Enlil asked Moses to leave Aaron's rod overnight at the Ark. When Moses returned, Aaron's rod had blossomed. This showed the people that Aaron was God's choice. Enlil told Moses to always keep the rod with the Ark."

"There's more," she pointed between the two winged children. The cherubs faced each other, their hands stretching to touch. "In the Bible, it's speculated that God's presence did not dwell *inside* the chest, but *in between* the cherubs. Here God housed unapproachable light. Even as a high priest, I had to shield my eyes because I would not live if I saw *the light*."

Jessie raised Aaron's rod. "The rod is a conduit." She inserted its handle between the cherubs' hands. A perfect fit. The little angels now held the rod. Jessie nudged the ark so that the rod pointed at the heart of the BeMER machine.

"Now what?" Rachel asked.

"It'll take about ten, maybe fifteen minutes, until the rod ignites. When it does—we can't see the flare! Let's get out of here!"

They rushed into the hallway. It was Rachel who noticed that something was different. "Shit! The cart's missing!"

Instinctively, they darted into the lab. Jessie's pulse quickened when she saw that Kek was no longer there. "You didn't kill him. Let's get out of here!" Jessie said with more urgency.

"That's just it, Jess. I don't know how to without the cart."

"What do you mean?"

The hum from the Ark had amplified. Rachel pointed at the wall. "That's our exit. That's where I've come in and left. But we've always gone through the wall with the cart." Rachel picked up the hoodwink from where she had tossed it earlier. "And I've always been blindfolded."

Jessie approached the wall. She placed her hands on the cold concrete, then turned to Rachel. "The cart went through the wall? Where?"

Rachel shook her head. "I don't think it was any place special, Jess. It just drove through the wall. Look at the two sets of skid marks." Rachel pointed to rubber marks on the floor. "They're at least six feet apart. We came through in different spots."

The humming noise was now louder, making it difficult for Jessie to concentrate. How could a cart drive through a concrete wall? The humming was also now accompanied by the sound of electrical discharge. Jessie rushed to the archway of the BeMER room. Sparks flashed around the Cherubs' fingers.

"We have only minutes before detonation," Jessie hurried back to the wall.

Rachel was behind her. "Jess, can't you abort the Ark?"

She shook her head. "No."

They needed help. Jessie closed her eyes, bringing her to the darkness. She hoped that her higher self would offer some intuitive guidance, but there were no insightful flashes. No answers. Desperate, she called for help.

Charlie? Are you there? I need your help. . . . Charlie?

"Jessie, I am here."

How do I get out of here?

"The wall is like Aaron's budding rod. It's like the legend of the phoenix."

I don't understand.

"It's a virtual reality. Aaron's rod never budded; it only appeared to*. The fire that burned the phoenix never existed, but in your mind it did, so it* appeared *real, and burned."*

Are you telling me the wall isn't there?

"Jess, what are we going to do?" Rachel's voice and the sound of angry sparks brought her back.

She grabbed the hoodwink in Rachel's hand. "I need you to trust me, Rachel. We don't have much time." She slipped the blindfold over her head. "Walk with me. I'll take you out of here," she spoke calmly.

It would be easy to get Rachel out. All she needed to do was disorient her and walk her through the wall. For Jessie however, it was a mind game. She needed to convince herself that the wall didn't exist. Anything short of that would bar her from bringing them to safety.

Holding Rachel's hand, she circled the area. She was reminded of her meditative walks through the temple's hypostyle, where she elevated her thoughts to higher ideals. Using the same principles she surrendered to her higher self, knowing that it would see beyond the wall.

As she approached the wall on her second rotation, for a split second, she glimpsed the sterile lobby on the other side. The vision increased her confidence, disarming the concrete wall. Steadily, she stepped through it with Rachel by her side.

It was like stepping from a dark room into the sunlight. The bright lobby was deserted. Jessie yanked the blindfold from Rachel's head. She tugged her, and spoke urgently. "We need to run!"

The sudden bright light hurt Rachel's eyes. She was in the lobby. She slowed, and glimpsed the concrete wall behind them. "How?" she murmured.

"Come!" Jessie was forceful, and dragged her as she explained. "The wall isn't there. When the Ark ignites, there's nothing to protect us."

The women bolted. They sprinted through the lobby, just past the vacant receptionist desk when the Ark detonated.

Jessie hauled Rachel face down on the ground. She wrapped her arm over Rachel's head, covering her eyes. "Don't look at the light," she yelled. Sudden blasts of hot violent wind rushed over their bodies. Then, superfluous lightning bolts fired into the lobby, above their heads.

A deafening roar followed with rumbling of exploding debris. Continuous hot blasts shot fragments of crystallized carbon at the women, scoring their exposed skin. To Rachel and Jessie, it felt as if hurricane-force winds hurled shattered glass at them. All at once, the hot gusts and lightening ceased. Falling wreckage rumbled, and the sprinkling of smashed diamonds sounded around them. And then—silence.

Jessie lifted her head. Her neck was raw from where her bare skin had been exposed to the razor-sharp fragments. The back of her right hand was covered in blood from similar scoring. Rachel shifted beneath Jessie's left arm. She raised her head.

The women got to their feet, shaking slivers of glasslike particles from their sweat suits. Rachel had similar slices on her skin, but to a lesser degree since Jessie had covered her head. The right side of Jessie's face was badly scratched.

The room was not so bright and sterile anymore. Only half the lights remained illuminated. The imaginary stone wall that had separated the lobby from the hidden areas was now gone. Instead, the room had doubled in size, with debris and wreckage cluttering the far end of the area.

Rachel started laughing softly. "We did it, Jess! We destroyed it."

Jessie knew they didn't have time to relish their victory. "Let's get out of here" She grabbed Rachel's hand and they ran stiffly to the door that would lead to the tunnels. Jessie's bleeding hand turned the lever, but as she opened the door, two Secret Service agents stepped inside. With guns drawn, they blocked their exit.

Rachel and Jessie turned only to see Kek and Whitman emerge from one of the specimen rooms. Jessie had seen the same anger and disappointment in Kek's eyes before. The last time, she had paid with her life.

"Do you know what you have done?" Kek's voice, once resonating, was now weary.

"Something that should have been done a long time ago," Rachel said defiantly.

Kek staggered, and Whitman supported his arm. Jessie wondered if his unsteady walk was from the devastation of losing the BeMER machine, or the sedative.

"We don't need her," Whitman said. "We have my sons for succession."

"We certainly don't need *her,*" Kek pointed at Jessie and nodded to one of the men behind her.

Almost simultaneously, Jessie felt a sting on her back and she fell into darkness.

Rachel grabbed her arm as Jessie plummeted to the floor. "No!" she screamed. She saw the dart lodged in her back, and plucked it out.

"Destroy her!" Kek ordered, his voice now stronger.

One of the Secret Service men attempted to lift Jessie, but Rachel lashed out, kicking and slapping him. "No! Get away from her!" she screamed. Strong arms grabbed her from behind, pinning her arms.

The other agent hoisted Jessie over a shoulder like a sack of potatoes.

"Destroy her," Kek said with pleasure.

The man nodded, and carried Jessie's unresponsive body toward one of the labs.

Rachel squirmed in the other agent's arms. She tried kicking the man's shins and biting his forearm, but he was just too strong, and the more she struggled, the tighter his clutch became. She felt helpless and desperate. What could she do? She couldn't believe the words as they escaped her lips. "I'll do it. Damn you, Daddy. I'll join you, I'll be your pawn, just don't kill her." There was emptiness in Rachel's heart as she pledged her devotion to her father.

"We don't need her," Whitman said convincingly to Kek.

"But you *do* need me. Without me, there'll be a fault in succession. You need blood to maintain your reign. Daddy, without me, your control is vulnerable."

The man that was carrying Jessie had opened the door to one of the labs.

"Daddy, if you kill her—you'll never have me. Send her back safely and I'll promise you my loyalty." Tears ran down her cheeks. She realized that she had once again joined Abaddon, and made a pact with the devil.

Forty-Two

Daylight filtered through the venetian blinds and into her eyes. She covered her face, trying to stop the ray of sunlight from penetrating her reality.

"Good afternoon. It's good to see you stir," an unfamiliar voice said.

Jessie opened her eyes and squinted. "Who are you?"

"I'm Barbara." She was dressed in white. "I'm your nurse today."

"Nurse?" Jessie was confused. "Where am I?" She looked around the small room. She was lying in a hospital bed.

"Oh, you don't remember?"

Jessie shook her head, quickly realizing something was different. She lifted her hands—they were so heavy. Her fingers moved through her hair. "What happened to my hair?"

"What do you mean, dear?"

"What do I mean?" Jessie stepped from the bed. Her legs buckled and she toppled to the floor. Her limbs felt as if they weren't part of her body.

Barbara rushed to her with a walker. She helped her to her feet. "Dear, you've been in bed for a week. You're going to need some PT before you start jumping around."

Jessie was stunned. What was wrong with her body? Feebly, she took the walker and approached a wall-mounted mirror. She gazed into a stranger's eyes and gasped.

"You should be in bed, dear," the nurse said.

"Someone cut my hair," Jessie mumbled. Her hair was short, lacking style. There was something else. She was pale. When had she ever been pale living in southern California? She was thinner. But also, crow's-feet blemished her skin around her eyes. And there was a visible streak of gray hair above her forehead.

Published by The Haworth Press, Inc., 2006. All rights reserved.
doi:10.1300/5721_43

"Your hair was that way when you arrived. You've been through a traumatic experience. Perhaps you should lie down." The nurse led Jessie back to the bed.

"Where am I?"

"Holloman Hospital, dear."

"For the mentally disturbed? What the hell am *I* doing here?"

"You're awake," a man's voice came from the doorway. "Barbara, why don't you let me speak with Ms. Mercer for a few minutes?" With that said, the nurse left.

"Who are you?" Jessie asked suspiciously.

"I'm Dr. Lenore. Jessica, what is the last thing you remember?"

"What I remember about what?" But just then, memories of her brother's funeral flooded back. "Oh, my God!" It was only a whisper, "Steve died."

The doctor nodded. "Is that the last thing you remember?"

Tears came to her eyes. "I was at his funeral in the church." Jessie rubbed the tears away. "What am I doing here? What happened to my hair?"

"Ms. Mercer, this is going to be a shock for you. But your brother passed away over a year ago. You've had a nervous breakdown, and most recently you're recovering from a suicide attempt."

Hours later, Jessie was lying in bed. She was mulling over her conversation with Dr. Lenore. It didn't make any sense. Although the loss of her brother had occurred over a year ago, it felt as if it had happened yesterday. *What happened to me? What happened to the missing year?*

Alison stood in the doorway and knocked. "Jessie, how are you feeling?"

"It's nice to see a familiar face," Jessie gestured for her to enter.

Alison smiled. She approached Jessie's bed. "Do you mind if I sit?" She hopped on the bed. She was shocked at how awful Jessie looked. Then again, she had just attempted suicide. How was she supposed to have looked? "You really had me scared, Jessie. You should have told me you were back in town. We could have done dinner or something. I felt just terrible when I saw the report on the news."

"What report?"

"You know . . . when you tried to kill yourself."

"I didn't try to kill myself," Jessie said defensively. Clearly frustrated, she confided in her friend. "To be honest, I don't remember any of it. The last year is gone. How did I *supposedly* try to kill myself, anyway?"

"Sleeping pills."

"God . . . I wish I could remember."

"Do you remember Desert Disaster? The Iraqi invasion of Kuwait, and the United Nations almost bringing us into World War III?"

"The United Nations almost brought us to world war?" She nodded, "No."

"It's probably just as well. People were just crazy, especially the UN members."

"When did all this happen?"

"It climaxed in late January. It didn't look good. England and the United States were on opposing sides, and then overnight everyone just seemed to come to their senses. Personally, I think it had to do with the stars or voodoo."

Jessie changed the subject. "I haven't seen Taylor, yet. How did she take it?"

"Girl, you'll be lucky if Taylor ever gives you the time of day."

Jessie's heart thumped. "Why?"

"You don't remember?"

"Alison, I swear the last thing I remember was being at Steve's funeral."

"Jessie . . . you met someone in New York. From what I've heard, you dumped Taylor in January. It's the middle of May."

Jessie's heart felt sick. She shook her head, tears welling in her eyes.

An hour passed and Barbara brought in a tray of food. She handed Jessie a small paper cup. "Here, take your medication first."

Jessie studied the pills in her palm. "Medication? What is it?"

"Sedatives and antidepressants."

"I'm not depressed, and I certainly don't need a sedative," Jessie whined.

"Doctor's orders." Barbara smiled.

While Barbara fetched the lunch tray, Jessie slipped the pills beneath the pillow. She mimicked dumping the pills into her mouth and swallowing them with water.

"Open wide. I need to see that you took your meds."

Jessie opened her mouth for inspection.

"Thanks! Are you going to be up for a little sunshine after your lunch?"

Jessie looked outside through the blinds. The thought of soaking up sunshine had never sounded better. "I would like that, Barbara."

"You had a visitor earlier. When you first arrived a few others visited."

"Who?"

"I'm terrible with names. But one was a singer, oh, what's her name now—"

"Taylor? Taylor Andrews?"

"That could be. The one from the movie *Deceptions*. She came a few times."

Jessie was hopeful. "And who else?"

"There was an attractive brunette in her mid-thirties, and she was with a good-looking man. I think she was on one of those TV newsmagazines. I don't know which one, maybe *Dateline* or *48 Hours*, or perhaps *Over the Edge*."

"Doesn't ring a bell."

Rachel studied Jessie's every move from the other side of the two-way mirror. She smiled when she saw her stash the meds beneath her pillow. "She doesn't remember a thing," Rachel whispered.

"I told you she wouldn't." Kek stood behind her in the dark room.

"It's going to be difficult for her. Her life has been shattered. She's lost her brother, her partner, and a year of her life."

"The alternative was death. This was our deal, Rachel," he reminded her.

Commotion in the rear of the room drew their attention to Jacob. The Secret Service agent rushed into the restroom. Since they had arrived, Jacob—Kek's bodyguard—had been suffering flulike symptoms. Kek and Rachel heard the man throwing up on the other side of the door.

Kek's attention returned to Jessie. "I have lived up to my end of the deal."

"Yes you have, Kek."

Rachel had become accustomed to calling her father *Kek* since that dreadful day, when she pledged her allegiance to him. In the months that had followed, she had shadowed him, quickly learning from him. Powerlessly, Rachel had observed Kek brainwash Jessie, removing all traces of her memory since Steve's funeral. The only stipulation to their agreement was that Rachel wouldn't join Kek until Jessie was back in her life, safely. This was the purpose of their visit to California.

"You've seen her. It's time to start *your* new life, Rachel."

Rachel's eyes met her father's. "Yes. We should head back to DC."

Jacob opened the restroom door. He stood silently, waiting for orders.

"Are you okay, Jacob?" Kek asked.

"Absolutely, sir!" But he was noticeably pale.

Kek moved to the door, and Jacob waited for Rachel to follow. She approached the window and positioned her hand on the glass that separated the women. Silently, she looked at her friend lying in bed. *Good-bye Jessie. Be well, my friend.* Sadly, her hand dropped from the mirror, and she fell in line behind Kek.

Forty-Three

Jessie was wheeled outside to the hospital grounds. Maybe it was psychological, but she felt better breathing fresh air and soaking up sunshine. She couldn't remember the sun ever feeling this pleasurable on her skin. The attendant parked her about ten feet from another wheelchair.

"Any chance of getting a cane?" Jessie asked the aide.

"Not unless you have a PT release," she said. "Feel free to spin your wheels, though." She walked away laughing at her pun.

The man in the nearby wheelchair was engaged in a heated discussion with himself. A woman sat on a bench on the opposite side of her, rocking back and forth. Jessie gazed around the gardens. The grassy grounds were perhaps an acre, with a security fence surrounding it. The property was pleasantly landscaped with benches, spread out for privacy. And yet, the few patients were heaped together.

Jessie released the brake on the wheelchair and attempted to move it. She didn't get very far. Her arms were sore. With her fingers, she squeezed her forearms and biceps. Then she touched her thighs. Her normally firm and muscular body was now soft. Had she stopped exercising? She couldn't imagine not leading an active life.

Her hands pushed the large wheels and the chair crept bit by bit over the grass. Sore or not, Jessie intended to find a more remote area to soak up the rays and sort things out. What had happened to her? How could things have become so dreadful that she resorted to suicide? How could she have ever cheated on Taylor? None of it made any sense. It was like a nightmare—and she wanted to wake up.

Jessie had motored the chair just past the rocking woman. Her arms ached from fatigue. She shook them. Then she pressed on, until her arms burned. The attendant must have noticed her struggling, because someone began pushing the wheelchair from behind.

Published by The Haworth Press, Inc., 2006. All rights reserved.
doi:10.1300/5721_44

Embarrassed, Jessie hung her head. "Thank you." She pointed to an isolated bench at the far end of the property. "Can you take me there?"

As they approached the bench, "Would you stop here, please?" They were about eight feet from the bench. "I'd like to walk."

The chair brake was set. Jessie strained to stand and the aide helped her to her feet. She stood unsteadily, eyeing the path to the bench. "Thank you. I'd like to try this alone." She shuffled her feet over the grass. It was exhausting and about halfway there, she stopped. She heard approaching footsteps and lifted her arm. "Please," she panted, "I need to do this."

Jessie took another couple of steps. Why was it so challenging? Beads of sweat trickled from her temples. Her heart pounded rapidly. Why had her body betrayed her? Somehow it had given up on her. Her legs trembled. She stumbled toward the bench, where she toppled to her knees.

Now only inches from the bench, Jessie propped herself up using the furniture. Exhausted, she collapsed onto the bench, turning her body around. She gasped. Taylor stood before her. It had been Taylor helping her.

"Am I dreaming?" Jessie whispered.

Taylor didn't say a thing.

"Please tell me all this is a bad dream."

There was noticeable sadness in Jessie's eyes. "I need the answers to a couple of questions," Taylor's voice was shaky. "Who was with you that day in the cabin?"

"What cabin?"

"The one in the Catskills, when you told me you were in love with someone else."

Tears formed in Jessie's eyes. "I told you that? I'm sorry, Taylor. I wish I could tell you . . . but I don't know."

"What do you mean?"

"I don't know what's happened to me. I woke up this morning in a mental hospital. I was told that I tried to kill myself, and Alison told me a couple hours ago that you and I broke up." Jessie sobbed. "The last thing I remember was sitting in a church at Steve's funeral, wishing that I had asked you to be with me."

"But that was—"

"I know—over a year ago! Honestly, look at me! I woke up today with a year missing from my life. I've grayed. My body's a disaster. My hair is cut. I don't have a clue what happened."

"Don't you remember the French Riviera at Thanksgiving?"

Jessie nodded no.

"Our weekend at the Hudson Hotel?"

"No."

Taylor was stunned. She hadn't expected this.

"Taylor, if I hurt you in any way," said Jessie, her face damp with tears, "I'm terribly sorry. Please forgive me."

"That day, after I left the cabin, I returned fifteen minutes later. You weren't there. I poked around a bit. A sliding glass door was shattered, the glass was still on the floor. . . . None of this rings a bell?"

Jessie shook her head.

Taylor sat beside her on the bench. "Jessie, the cabin belonged to Brennan Keller. Does that name sound familiar?"

"No. Who's he?"

"What led me to the cabin that day was a driver's license I found in your bag." Taylor withdrew something from her pocket. She handed Jessie the ID.

Jessie recognized Steve's picture, and tears formed in her eyes. She couldn't believe he was gone. The name Brennan Keller got her attention. She wiped her eyes. "Steve was Brennan Keller?" she whispered in disbelief.

"There's more," Taylor handed Jessie another ID.

It was an employee ID of Brennan Keller at *The Empire.* "My God!" she whispered. "This guy looks like me."

"Jess, look closer."

Jessie spotted her scar on Brennan's cheek. She gasped. "I was Brennan Keller?"

Taylor knew Jessie wasn't lying. She truly didn't remember what had happened. The last four months had been a living nightmare for Taylor. First losing Jessie, then the private investigator report, believing she was dead, and now this. There was confusion in Jessie's eyes and Taylor realized that she would never have closure in this matter.

Instead, she found the woman she so desperately loved trapped in a world of anguish. The unknown that had obsessed Taylor since January now haunted Jessie.

"Jess?" Taylor's voice was soft. "The last few months have been very difficult for me. Losing you! Worrying about you! Wondering what happened to you! Can you leave what's happened to you in your past?"

"What do you mean?"

"Can you move forward and leave behind last year?"

"Why would you ask that?"

Taylor reached for Jessie's hand. She was surprised at how rough it was. "Because I can't do it anymore! I've spent so much time wondering what happened. I'll never have answers, and I need to move on. If you can let this rest, Jess, come back to me."

"You're asking me to throw away a year of my life?"

"I'm asking you to let it go and move on."

"You know I would move a mountain to be with you."

"But, can you let this go?"

Jessie's head felt like it could explode. In one day she had learned that she lost Taylor, and now had the opportunity to reunite. The thought of having her back was more that she could imagine. But, could she let go what had happened? Why would she ever disguise herself as a man and work for a newspaper? What did she do for them? Why was her brother using an alias? What was the truth behind her suicide attempt?

Jessie's eyes met Taylor's. "I *don't* know if I can let this go."

Forty-Four

The road from the hospital was hilly and winding. Rachel and Kek sat silently in the backseat of the limo while Jacob maneuvered the twisting road. It didn't take long for the snaky roads to intensify the agent's nausea. He braked as he steered around a sharp turn, veering to the side of the road.

"Are you okay?" Rachel asked.

"Excuse me, sir," he said to Kek. He threw wide the door, rushed from the car, darting into some evergreens. A couple minutes later Jacob emerged from the trees.

As he approached, Rachel noticed the green hue to his complexion. "He doesn't look well," she said, "not well at all."

Jacob settled in the car. "I apologize, sir."

"Would you like me to drive?" Rachel asked Kek.

Before Kek had a chance to respond, Jacob started the ignition. "That won't be necessary." He pulled away from the curb, but didn't drive fifty feet before he swung back to the road's edge. This time he didn't make it more than six feet before he lost it.

"This is silly," Rachel said. "The man is sick as a dog. Let me drive."

Kek glanced at his bodyguard throwing up. "Okay."

Rachel emerged from the limo. Jacob wiped his lips with a kerchief and stood. Perspiration had formed on his brow. "I'll drive, Jacob."

This time, the man didn't argue. He moved into the front passenger seat. "I apologize, sir. I must have picked up something. I'll call in for a replacement, sir."

Rachel sat behind the wheel. It had been months since she had driven. She started down the winding mountainous road.

Jacob ended a telephone exchange. "A new man will replace me at the airport."

Published by The Haworth Press, Inc., 2006. All rights reserved.

doi:10.1300/5721_45

Moments later, Rachel glanced at Jacob after maneuvering a series of zigzag turns. His eyes were closed. "Let me know if I need to stop," she said.

After twenty minutes of surging hills, they reached the highway. They were north of Los Angeles County and headed south along the coast. At times the road was winding and hugged the coastline, offering breathtaking views of the Pacific. During those times, Rachel noticed that Jacob's eyes were tightly shut.

While driving, Rachel called to mind the events over the past couple years: her initial research into secret societies, her friendship with Steve, West, and Jessie. Then, her reunion with her father and learning the truth about humankind's creation crept into her space. She shook her head, trying to banish the memories.

The past four months had been difficult. She watched Kek systematically wipe out Jessie's memories. To earn his trust, she demonstrated an innate interest in power. Then she waited patiently for Jessie's safe return to her life. Now that she was out of harm's way, things would be different. For Kek, today marked the beginning of a new sovereignty, which included Rachel. For Rachel, today represented transformation.

She peeked at Jacob. His eyes were shut. His reaction to the tainted coffee on the plane that morning was predictable. For over two months she had planned this tactic, ever since she had the good fortune to steal the influenza vial. Kek had biogenetically manipulated the virus, creating a mutant strain. He intended to introduce it to the public in the fall. With great luck, she had harbored a tiny vial for over two months. She waited for the perfect moment, the moment that Jessie had been freed. This was it.

Rachel cruised, heading toward the bridge that crossed a bay. It was one of the most beautiful coastline views, and just seemed fitting. As she approached the incline to the bridge, she forcefully depressed the accelerator.

The increase in velocity got Kek's attention. "Rachel, don't you think you're going too fast?"

Rachel caught sight of her father's eyes in the reflection of the rear-view mirror. She smiled broadly at him, and then floored it. The engine surged.

"Rachel?" Kek's voice roared. "Jacob, stop her!"

Jacob opened his eyes weakly. Everything was blurry. He sensed the car was going too fast. He lunged out at her.

With one hand on the steering wheel, and her eyes on approaching cars, she lashed back at Jacob, squarely slugging his nose with the back of her hand. He slumped over, protecting the fractured snout.

"Pull over. Now!" Kek demanded.

Rachel peered at her father's reflection. "No, Daddy," she smiled. "I'm not going along for this ride." With both hands she sharply turned the steering wheel. The car swerved. It collided with a guard-rail at such a high speed that the car jumped the rail, projecting itself airborne over the inlet below.

Kek had lived centuries in isolation to protect his longevity. Although, he was Annunaki, he *was* mortal. Like any human, his life could be taken. Rachel knew that if she killed Kek, Whitman would hunt her until her dying day. Her life, as well as Jacob's life, seemed to be a small price for destroying him and stopping the karmic cycle from recurring.

Without a seatbelt, Jacob smashed against Rachel's shoulder. As the vehicle nosedived, his head crashed into the windshield, blood splattering over the dashboard.

Kek's eyes, wide with disbelief, stared at the looming water. Then his eyes met hers in the reflection of the rear-view mirror. He had underestimated her. A memory of her youth flashed through his head.

He studied the chessboard then moved his pawn into place.

"Why would you sacrifice your pawn, Daddy?"

"Pawns are dispensable. You use them to further the king's purpose."

In those seconds before he plunged into the water, he realized that he should have moved his king. She had learned well.

Epilogue

Two years later.

I never would have challenged Jessica Mercer's ability to tell a good story. *Beyond Paradise* and *Deceptions* were, in this reviewer's opinion, among the finest suspense thrillers ever written. I waited anxiously for Ms. Mercer's newest release, *The Royal Secret.*

The Royal Secret is told through the eyes of Mercer's protagonist, Rachel Evans. Evans, a newspaper reporter, attempts to topple an empire of evil politicians that control the world. Driven by her soul's purpose, she uncovers *the royal secret* that has been hidden since humankind's creation. In a fight against time, Evans exposes secret societies' control of the world, and reveals *the royal secret*—little green men, determined to suppress mankind's spirituality, run the world!

Is Mercer's book believable? Hardly!

Entertaining? Absolutely! Imaginative? To say the least! This genre-bending thriller is full of surprises. Mercer didn't let me down, and she certainly won't disappoint you.

Meet her this Friday night, 7:30, at the Tattered Cover in Cherry Creek.

Tucked away in a cubbyhole of the Tattered Cover bookstore, Jessie finished reading *The Denver Post*'s review of *The Royal Secret.* Most of the early reviews had been favorable. Tonight was her first appearance for the new book.

Normally, Jessie discussed the genesis of a book when she made appearances. But how could she share what inspired *The Royal Secret?* How could she explain that she had lost a year of her life? Lost her brother? Almost lost the woman she loved? How could she explain that she lost something special that year, and she wasn't even sure

Published by The Haworth Press, Inc., 2006. All rights reserved.
doi:10.1300/5721_46

what it was? How could she explain that the only way to purge the mystery from her soul was to create another one—*The Royal Secret?* Jessie had promised Taylor that she would unleash the past. Unknown to her, the past echoed in her writing.

From where she sat hidden, the pulse of people gathering for her appearance brought her attention to the time. It was seven twenty-five p.m.

Almost two hours later, Jessie was still signing copies of her new book. The long line had dwindled to an attractive brunette in her late thirties.

"Would you like it personalized, or just signed?" Jessie always gave them the option.

"Personalized," the woman said.

"And your name?"

"Dalila."

"Dalila? That's unusual. D-A-L?"

"I-L-A," she finished.

Occasionally, Jessie would perceive intuitive insights when signing her books. She would jot them in the book, and sign it. Many times she was unaware of the channeled writing. This was one of those times.

> *To Dalila,*
> *Keeper of the Royal Secret!*
> *Blessings,*
> *Jessica Mercer*

"So, how did you come up with such a farfetched idea for a book—I mean, *aliens* running our government?"

Jessie smiled, and offered her calculated response to the question. "How else could we explain the baffling behavior of the previous administration?" She handed the woman her book.

As the woman took it, Jessie noticed the unusual mark on her wrist.

"Is that a tattoo?" Jessie asked.

"No. It's a birthmark," she said.

Jessie looked closer. "It looks like an ankh!"

The woman smiled. "Yes. I've heard that before."

Afterword

There is more information available today regarding Sumer—the first ancient civilization—than the ancient empires of Rome, Greece, or Egypt. This is largely due to the Sumerian clay tablets that have survived for 6,000 years. Sumer was an advanced society and the founders of many systems we use today, such as writing, taxation, medical science, laws, cosmology, timekeeping, zodiac gods, spherical astronomy, and much more.

In 1945, the discovery of the Nag Hammadi Library expanded the Christian catalogues beyond the traditional gospels of Mathew, Mark, Luke, and John to include the gospel of Mary Magdalene.

Freemasonry is a male secret society that connects modern secret groups to those in ancient Egypt. The group's quest is to search for light. The Supreme Council of the Thirty-Third Degree is the last degree of Freemasonry (that we know of). Numerous presidents and global and corporate leaders have been, and still are, members of this group.

Published by The Haworth Press, Inc., 2006. All rights reserved.
doi:10.1300/5721_47

ABOUT THE AUTHOR

Alex Marcoux's second novel, *Back to Salem,* was a Lambda Literary Award Finalist for best mystery. For her first novel, *Façades,* she was presented a Rocky Mountain Fiction Writers' Pen Award. Suspense is at the heart of Alex's stories, including this novel, *A Matter of Degrees.*

Alex grew up in Leominster, Massachusetts. In 1981, she graduated with a degree in food science from the University of Massachusetts at Amherst. Over the years, she has worked in product development, technical sales, and small business management.

Alex is a member of the Mystery Writers of America, Rocky Mountain Fiction Writers, and the Lambda Literary Agency. She resides in Colorado with her family. For more information about Alex and her work, visit her Web site at www.AlexMarcoux.com.

Order a copy of this book with this form or online at:
http://www.haworthpress.com/store/product.asp?sku=5721

A MATTER OF DEGREES

_____in softbound at $19.95 (ISBN-13: 978-1-56023-611-5; ISBN-10: 1-56023-611-6)

Or order online and use special offer code HEC25 in the shopping cart.

COST OF BOOKS_____

POSTAGE & HANDLING_____
(US: $4.00 for first book & $1.50
for each additional book)
(Outside US: $5.00 for first book
& $2.00 for each additional book)

SUBTOTAL_____

IN CANADA: ADD 7% GST_____

STATE TAX_____
(NJ, NY, OH, MN, CA, IL, IN, PA, & SD
residents, add appropriate local sales tax)

FINAL TOTAL_____
(If paying in Canadian funds,
convert using the current
exchange rate, UNESCO
coupons welcome)

☐ **BILL ME LATER:** (Bill-me option is good on
US/Canada/Mexico orders only; not good to
jobbers, wholesalers, or subscription agencies.)

☐ Check here if billing address is different from
shipping address and attach purchase order and
billing address information.

Signature_____

☐ **PAYMENT ENCLOSED: $**_____

☐ **PLEASE CHARGE TO MY CREDIT CARD.**

☐ Visa ☐ MasterCard ☐ AmEx ☐ Discover
☐ Diner's Club ☐ Eurocard ☐ JCB

Account # _____

Exp. Date_____

Signature_____

Prices in US dollars and subject to change without notice.

NAME_____
INSTITUTION_____
ADDRESS_____
CITY_____
STATE/ZIP_____
COUNTRY_____ COUNTY (NY residents only)_____
TEL_____ FAX_____
E-MAIL_____

May we use your e-mail address for confirmations and other types of information? ☐ Yes ☐ No
We appreciate receiving your e-mail address and fax number. Haworth would like to e-mail or fax special
discount offers to you, as a preferred customer. **We will never share, rent, or exchange your e-mail address**
or fax number. We regard such actions as an invasion of your privacy.

Order From Your Local Bookstore or Directly From
The Haworth Press, Inc.
10 Alice Street, Binghamton, New York 13904-1580 • USA
TELEPHONE: 1-800-HAWORTH (1-800-429-6784) / Outside US/Canada: (607) 722-5857
FAX: 1-800-895-0582 / Outside US/Canada: (607) 771-0012
E-mail to: orders@haworthpress.com

For orders outside US and Canada, you may wish to order through your local
sales representative, distributor, or bookseller.
For information, see http://haworthpress.com/distributors

(Discounts are available for individual orders in US and Canada only, not booksellers/distributors.)

PLEASE PHOTOCOPY THIS FORM FOR YOUR PERSONAL USE.
http://www.HaworthPress.com

BOF06